Birth of a Hero
Simon E. Mackerill

Dedication

To my family—without you I would not have been able to make this happen or been brave enough to try.

My girls, you push me to be better every day.

My wife, thank you for always being by my side. I love you all.

Tribal Maps

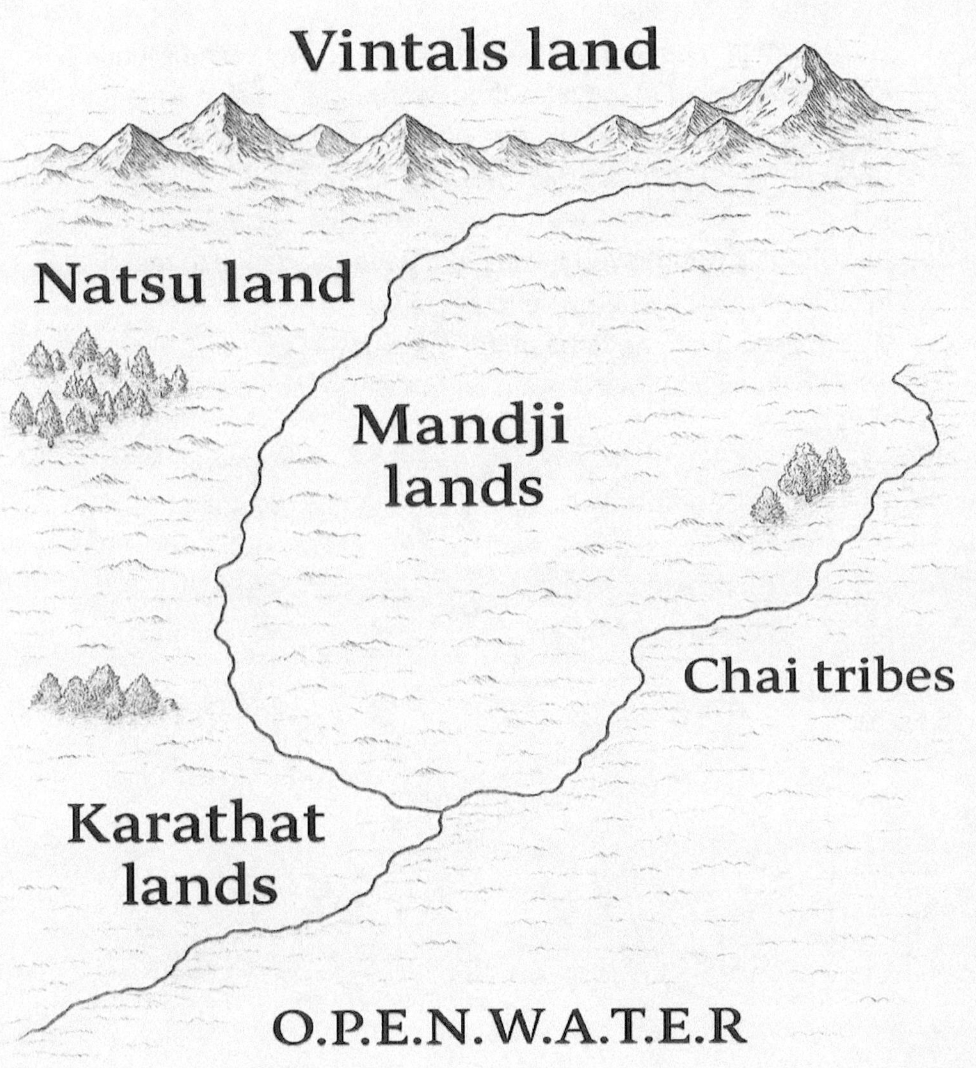

Vintals land
Natsu land
Mandji lands
Chai tribes
Karathat lands
O.P.E.N.W.A.T.E.R

Birth of a Hero
Simon E. Mackerill

To my family without you I would not have been able to make this happen or been brave enough to try.
My girls you push me to be better everyday.
My wife thank you for always being by my side. I love you all.

Prologue

Taran ran as fast as he could.

He knew if he slowed down, they would catch him.

His lungs burned with the pace he had set, and he tried to control his breathing, just as his father had taught him years ago. But fear pushed him harder than any training ever had. He had heard what they did to prisoners. Death was the better choice.

Behind him came the shouts and war cries—his hunters cheering one another on, eager to see who would claim his life first.

He stumbled over a branch, barely catching himself with a hand slapping against a tree. A thud followed—an arrow embedded itself inches from his fingers.

To his right, a scream of pain pierced the woods. Another warrior dropped, arrows bristling in his back. Taran didn't know his name, only that he had marched in the same column for days.

He looked up and spotted a Natsu archer nocking another arrow.

Instinct kicked in—he spun sideways just as the bowstring snapped.

The arrow thudded into a trunk behind him.

He kept running.

Bile rose in his throat. He was near sickness and had no idea where he was going. The terrain was unfamiliar. But he couldn't stop—not until he found shelter. Or safety.

Or death.

Why had his empire felt the need to expand? It was already wealthy for its size and vast.

Why had they sent him here?

A sharp jolt of pain reminded him of the wound in his leg. He hadn't even had time to check how bad it was.

The trees broke suddenly, and he cursed. Ahead stretched an open field—flat, empty, exposed. A few scrub bushes dotted the landscape, but they wouldn't stop arrows. Behind him, the Natsu were closing in. "I'll have to run hard and fast," he muttered. The Natsu knew these lands. They'd drawn the battle to Swannett Valley for a reason.

To his left, movement caught his eye—another figure bursting from the tree line.

"Tanny," he breathed in recognition. He opened his mouth to call out, but another silhouette moved from the shadows.

A bow lifted.

Taran's eyes widened.

Tanny, at least, was zigzagging. Smart.

The first arrow flew wide. Tanny flinched, glanced back—and saw the archer lining up again. He ducked and sprinted harder.

Taran moved silently toward the shooter. His leg burned with every step. More Natsu voices echoed behind him.

He had to be quick. Careful.

The second arrow hit—Tanny staggered, struck in the shoulder—but he kept moving.

Taran crept forward. His dagger was all he had left. His other weapons had been lost in the chaos.

The archer drew again, focused on Tanny.

A twig beneath Taran's foot snapped.

The warrior half-turned and shouted in his native tongue.

Taran lunged.

The archer dropped his bow and reached for a blade, catching Taran's wrist mid-swing.

They grappled. The boy wasn't much younger, but weaker—less seasoned. Taran forced the dagger closer. The Natsu bucked, twisting, desperate.

But not strong enough.

The blade sank into his neck. His eyes widened. Blood bubbled from his lips. He struck weakly, then went still.

Taran rose, panting, and scavenged quickly—bow, arrows, a short sword, a water flask.

In the distance, Tanny was still running, his arm limp against his side. "Tanny! Keep going!" Taran shouted. "Don't stop!"

Tanny turned. "Taran! Thank the gods—I thought I was the last." "They're still behind us," Taran called. "We have to move."

"I don't know how long I can keep pace," Tanny said, staggering.

"You must. Keep heading north. If we reach nightfall, we'll be free."

Tanny pointed to the trees. "Look! Sapir—he was in my shield line!"

Sapir burst from the forest, shirtless and bloodied, his curved sword flashing. He shouted as he ran "Natsu"—behind him, fifteen Natsu warriors gave chase.

Taran's breath caught at the sight of them chasing Sapir. None of the Natsu had bows.

"They're not firing," he muttered. "Out of arrows? Or they want us alive."

He raised the bow he'd taken. Seven arrows. Not enough. "Tanny, keep going. I'll cover Sapir." He nocked and loosed. The first arrow missed.

A splinter group veered toward him. The rest followed Sapir.

Sapir turned facing those closing in on him, he parried a wild swing and slashed the attacker's throat the Natsu warrior dropped holding his throat.

Taran loosed again missing once more..

He adjusted his aim and fired again. Hittin one in the leg. They dropped screaming.

Four arrows left.

He fired another arrow— this time hitting another warrior in the shoulder.

Three.

Too few.

Sapir gained ground. Taran turned and ran.

He reached the trees. Tanny waited, dagger ready, blood soaking his sleeve.

"Why'd you stop?" Taran gasped.

Tanny pointed ahead.

A cliff.

Below—water. A quarry lake.

"They've trapped us," Taran growled. "Three arrows. Two blades."

From the trees, Natsu emerged cautiously. Cavalry thundered behind them in the distance.

"They've crushed the rest," Sapir said grimly.

"We can't fight them all."

Tanny nodded. "We jump." Taran looked down at the dark water.

He made his choice.

He ran.

And leapt.

Air roared past his ears. Then—impact. The water swallowed him whole.

He surfaced, coughing.

Tanny and Sapir leapt seconds later.

"Fuck you, horsefuckers!" Sapir shouted mid-air.

Taran swam toward the far bank, scanning for signs of life.

Tanny broke the surface first. Then Sapir.

Both surviving the fall.

Taran sighed, half-laughing.

His leg throbbed, but the wound wasn't deep. It would heal. Tanny groaned. "Gods, that was a rush." "At least we're clean," Sapir said.

They climbed ashore, panting. Taran bound his leg. Sapir helped Tanny wrap his arm.

"I thought you were dead," Tanny murmured. "All of us." "We almost were," Taran said.

"I saw ten or twelve fall in the trees," Sapir added. "We're the last."

Taran nodded, expression hardening. "Then we carry word home."

They moved into the forest, deeper this time—away from open ground, away from the screams and smoke.

Mist clung to the floor. Moss blanketed the rocks. The trees grew taller, older, untouched.

They would be safe for a while at least.

Sapir went to try and see if he could find something they could eat. Tanny sat quietly, his face pale.

Taran leaned back against a tree, staring into the canopy.

They needed to reach the elders. They needed to speak of what they'd seen.

Because what they'd seen was a glimpse of war—and of something worse to come.

Sapir returned a while later, a handful of bitter fruit in his arms. Tanny ate greedily.

"No sign of anyone coming, we need to rest, then we move as it gets darker, we stay hidden until then" Sapir said.

Taran nodded.

Darkness pressed in.

Tanny's voice drifted through it. "Do you think we'll make it back?" Taran didn't answer, he was too tired to, his body ached.

Sleep claimed him.

&

CHAPTER 1

The sun was rising, and Storia stood on her balcony, watching as the first golden rays painted her city in soft hues of amber and rose. No matter how many dawns she witnessed, the beauty of Karathat at sunrise never failed to stir something deep within her. From her chambers in the royal house, she had the finest view in all the city—a vantage point that offered both peace and perspective.

Below her, the capital began to stir. Merchants opened stalls in the stone-paved markets, their voices rising with the calls of dockhands unloading goods at the harbour. The sea shimmered, alive with shifting shades of blue and green, as fishing vessels drifted lazily into the deeper waters. Larger trade ships passed through the outer bay, already vanishing into the horizon, bound for foreign lands she might never walk.

To the east, the coast wound toward the mist-wrapped forests that marked the border of Natsu territory. To the west lay the realm of the Chai—traders whose caravans and merchant fleets brought rare silks and scrolls to her ports. Karathat's trade routes extended in both directions: one by land through a chain of bustling market villages all the way to Temple City, and the other by sea, where galleys navigated the salt roads to foreign harbours.

Karathat had once been a modest outpost, little more than a port with muddy roads and timber walls. Now it was a jewel. A city of art, gold, and reason. And it had become so under her reign.

Her father had ruled by the sword. He had won territory with steel and fire, conquering enemies, silencing dissent. But she had built Karathat differently. Through treaties. Through trade.

Through vision.

She remembered him well—even missed him. For all his bloodshed, he had been a gentle father to her. She had once asked him

what haunted him at night, what made him rise in silence to stand by the fire. His eyes had darkened, and he had said nothing. She had never asked again.

A voice broke her reverie.

"My queen, the day brings news from the west that requires your attention."

Storia turned.

"What could possibly be so urgent, Zarratt, that it must disturb my peace so early?"

Zarratt stood in the doorway, as immovable as the columns of the palace. Her father's most trusted protector. In the years since his death, Zarratt had never left her side.

He was broad-shouldered, grey at the temples but still dangerous. The deep-blue robes he wore did little to soften the presence of the short sword at his hip. The memory of the one attempt on her life still lingered. A slave had attacked her during a festival night. Zarratt had ended the woman publicly. To this day, no one had discovered who had sent her.

"We've received word from the west. Our watchers on the Natsu frontier have reported movement. And a

battle."

Storia arched a brow. "A battle?"

"A skirmish, officially. Between the Natsu and the Mandji. But it was one-sided. The Mandji were crushed."

Zarratt stepped forward and gestured to the map spread across a nearby table. His finger hovered over the jagged border where the Natsu and Mandji lands met.

"There's more," he said. "This could be an opportunity."

"For us?"

Zarratt nodded. "If the Mandji continue their incursions and the Natsu resist, we might align with the Natsu. A shared enemy. We could secure the western corridor. Even annex borderlands."

Storia frowned. "Or we could be pulled into a war between two ruthless peoples. You've always wanted to settle old scores, Zarratt. But I do not gamble lightly."

"I know. But peace makes men forget their vigilance."

She studied him. His face remained carved from stone, but she saw the glint in his eye. The desire to move beyond the palace walls, to fight one last war. He had grown restless. Too many years guarding a throne had dulled his joy.

Storia sighed and returned her gaze to the sea. "Let's not light the fires of conquest just yet. We must know more. If the Natsu become emboldened by this victory, it could shift the balance of the region. Send trusted envoys—to both the Natsu and Mandji."

Zarratt hesitated. "You may not like this suggestion, my queen, but… there is another way to bind alliances."

Storia turned slowly. "Marriage?"

Zarratt inclined his head. "It would secure our line. And in the right union, it could bring powerful allies."

Storia narrowed her eyes. "You speak of the Natsu?"

"I speak of possibility."

She said nothing for a long moment, then nodded once. "Send the envoys. Begin conversations. Quietly. And I want the names of those we can trust. No bribed tongues or power-hungry fools." Zarratt bowed and left the room.

Storia lingered at the balcony. A merchant galley, unfamiliar in design, approached the harbour. Its flag was strange—green and black, not among those her traders flew. She narrowed her eyes. A diplomatic envoy? Or something else?

She rang the bell beside her chair. Servants entered, preparing her for the day.

As her hair was braided and her gown smoothed, her attention fell on one unfamiliar face. A new girl, young, perhaps seventeen.

"You there," Storia said. "What is your name?"

The girl started. "Tamanda, your grace."

"You are new. Where are you from?"

"North. Near the Mandji border."

Storia dismissed the others with a wave. "Come. Sit."

Tamanda sat, unsure. Her eyes darted to the head servant, who looked mortified.

"Speak freely," Storia said. "Tell me of your village."

"We were farmers," Tamanda said softly. "My father moved us inland after a Mandji raid. But it didn't save us. My family is gone."

Storia studied her. Tanned skin, lean Athletic frame, green eyes too sharp for a servant. "You carry yourself like someone who's been taught to fight, not like a girl who is put into the life of service"

Tamanda looked away. "My father… he trained me. He said the world didn't care what girls were supposed to be."

"You could have sold your beauty in a hundred cities, there are always men looking for a young bride" Storia said. "Why serve here?"

"Because I want to matter. To shape my own fate, I don't want to be some plaything."

Before Storia could reply, Tamanda suddenly lunged—not at the queen, but toward her.

A shadow had crept from the curtains. A dagger glinted.

Tamanda collided with the assassin mid-stride. They crashed against the floor in a tumble of limbs. The attacker slammed her back against the wall. She rebounded. Grabbing a ceramic vase from a table, she smashed it into his face. The man fell down from the blow stunned. She seized this moment pulling something from her hair, she plunged a long hairpin into his throat.

Blood poured, the assassin grabbed at his throat and she plunged it again into his throat two more time.

Zarratt stormed in with guards. "Step away from the queen!"

Tamanda stood up and stepped back.

"She saved me!" Storia cried.

Zarratt froze. He saw the dead man—and Tamanda, bloodied but standing.

"You lied," Storia whispered. "You're not just a servant."

Tamanda nodded. "I didn't come to polish floors. I came to honour the dead. My father and brother died saving me. They had taught me to fight."

Storia got up from the floor and stood in front of Tamanda.

"There is something about you girl, something that tells me you will be of value to me"

Tamanda lowered her head.

"You're no servant. You'll join my personal guard." Zarratt opened his mouth to object.

"No," Storia said firmly. "She passed this test, she fought bravely to defend me. Other servants would have run or just died. Let her train. Let her prove herself."

Tamanda bowed deeply. "Thank you."

Zarratt nodded slowly. "She'll need work. But she's not hopeless." As Tamanda was led away, Storia turned back to the window.

The strange ship had docked. Armed men were disembarking.

The peace of morning was over.

The day, truly, had begun.

CHAPTER 2

T aran woke with a jolt; a hand suddenly pressed across his

mouth.

Instinctively, he seized the wrist—only to realise, with a surge of relief, that it was Sapir.

Sapir held a finger to his lips, eyes sharp in the moonlight. Be silent.

It was still dark. The moon hung high, casting silver over the trees, while stars scattered across the sky like grains of salt. It wasn't full night, but close.

Taran whispered to himself, groggy, "How long have I been asleep?"

He sat up slowly, careful not to disturb the quiet. Just ahead, he spotted Tanny crouched low in a thicket, eyes fixed on the darkness beyond.

He and Sapir moved toward him, keeping low, stepping softly through the brush.

Tanny glanced back and raised four fingers, palm horizontal—an old signal meaning eight enemies. He didn't clench his fist, which meant they were on foot. No horses.

They hadn't moved far from the lake. Taran cursed under his breath. They should have pushed on, but exhaustion and wounds had demanded rest.

He had underestimated the Natsu. He thought they'd take longer to descend the cliffs and pick up their trail.

Tanny was in no shape to fight. His wound would slow him, and eight enemies was too many.

Taran's own leg throbbed with pain, but he could still stand and move. Sapir—despite his years—looked battle-ready, unshaken, as if he could fight a war and run a league straight after. He always moved like a man two decades younger.

Tanny squinted toward the figures shifting in the moonlight. They were moving slowly, cautiously. Well-trained.

Sapir's hand moved to the hilt of his sword.

Taran reached out, placing a firm hand on Sapir's shoulder. Sapir turned to him, eyes wide.

Taran shook his head, motioning for him to wait. Drawing weapons too early would give them away. He edged forward, trying to get a clearer look.

But a dry stick cracked under his boot.

All three of them froze.

The figures in the distance instantly dropped low, vanishing into the terrain. Silence fell like a curtain.

Taran's heart pounded. He held his breath, straining to hear movement—expecting arrows to whistle through the dark at any moment.

Tanny peered through the bushes, then turned and signalled: he could no longer see them.

Taran motioned for both men to stay still. Then, crouched low, he crept left, circling the area to get a better view and—hopefully—not draw more attention.

He drew the small sword he'd taken from the Natsu, pulling it from his belt with care.

Tanny and Sapir were now invisible behind him, swallowed by the night.

Taran crept forward on his belly, moving through the underbrush like a snake. Slowly, silently, he widened the gap between himself and the others.

Something moved—just a flicker in the trees.

He paused. Beneath his hand, he felt a small stone. He picked it up, ready to hurl it and test the silence.

He drew back his arm.

Then—a cold edge touched his throat.

He froze.

It was a blade. A sharp one. One wrong move and it would open his throat like a fruit.

A whisper followed, close and venomous.

"I wouldn't do that if I were you, you little stain of piss. Drop the rock and the sword. Slowly."

Taran obeyed, letting both fall to the ground. He could feel the blade's edge bite lightly into his skin.

"If you're going to kill me, then just do it," he growled.

The voice changed, still low, but now tinged with something else, amusement.

"Kill you? Why would I waste the fun of making you piss yourself first?"

The pressure lifted from his throat, and soft laughter followed.

"Oh, Taran," the voice said. "We thought we were done for when that twig snapped." Taran turned slowly.

A familiar face grinned at him in the dark—Dilah.

"Dilah?" Taran blinked. "How…? I thought I was the only one to get away."

Dilah was a warrior he knew more than a just a man someone everyone knew. A fellow warrior from the same cohort—strong, broad-shouldered, and wiry. He had a reputation for risk and recklessness. Older than Taran and Tanny, younger than Sapir. Once a scout, but something— rumour or disgrace—had seen him reassigned.

At this moment, Taran didn't care. The dark shadows were allies, not enemies.

"All the gods," Taran exhaled, "you nearly made me shit myself."

Dilah grinned. "After what we've been through, I couldn't risk not checking. You're so heavy-footed you might as well be a bear."

"How many of you are there?" Taran asked, brushing the dirt from his hands.

"Eight. Two badly wounded. We've got seven swords, four light shields, a spear, and two bows—both in good hands. Found some food on a search party not far from here." "You thought we were more of them." Dilah nodded.

Taran whistled softly, a signal. Moments later, Sapir and Tanny emerged from the darkness.

"There's just the three of us—me, Tanny, and Sapir." Dilah gave Sapir a nod. "A good man to have." Taran looked back toward the cliffs.

"That search party was probably after us. We were chased down and had to jump from the edge—straight into the lake."

Dilah's eyebrows rose. "You jumped from up there?"

"We were outnumbered. It was that or die on the rocks." Dilah chuckled. "And people say I'm the reckless one." "How are you for weapons?" he asked.

"We've two swords and a dagger. Our bow broke in the fall."

"You can take a spare. Our wounded won't be fighting."

Dilah signalled. From the woods, six more men emerged. Two were carrying a badly injured companion.

Dilah scanned them. "Where's Noosa?"

A man shook his head. "He laid down. Never got back up."

Dilah bowed his head. "Damn. He was a good man."

Taran placed a hand on Dilah's shoulder. "He walks with the sky now. But his spirit fights beside us."

He studied Dilah. The wildness was still there, but something else too. A weight.

"Do you know what happened back there? Why the battle fell apart?"

Dilah exhaled, rubbing the back of his neck. "We advanced into the grass. Then the front line just… dropped. Arrows came from everywhere. We were boxed in."

"Some ran forward," he continued, "but the Natsu were already waiting. Horses hit the flanks, arrows from both sides. It was a killing field."

"Our scouts hadn't returned, but they weren't overdue. Last word was the nearest Natsu camp was two days' ride."

"They shouldn't have been there," Taran muttered.

"No. And we couldn't count their numbers. Too many. Too much tall grass."

Taran remembered. He'd been in the rear when the attack came.

Shouts. Screams. Then orders— "Form ranks!"

Before they could, cavalry crashed into them. Arrows from the left. Chaos. Men breaking. Running.

He remembered the sting in his leg, the confusion. Then a horse barrelled into him, sending his shield flying. He hit the ground, rolled, scrambled upright.

A rider came back around, sword flashing. Taran met him, hacking. Blood hit his face. He swung again missed. The shield deflected the blow.

The horse reared and knocked him down again. His sword gone. He ran.

"Taran."

He snapped out of it. Dilah's voice bringing him back from his thoughts.

"We should move. If you killed that search party, they'll come looking for the as well soon." "You're right," Taran said.

"We head south, then east toward the Karathat lands. Then north towards home," Dilah said.

Dawn was creeping into the sky. The shadows thinned.

"We'll rest again at midday," Taran said. "Then move as the sun sets."

Dilah nodded. He signalled for two archers to scout ahead, another two to support the injured.

Sapir volunteered to stay behind with an archer and cover the rear.

He passed Tanny a sword and picked up the spare spear.

Taran and Dilah led the rest into the trees.

The forest was a shifting maze of shadow and filtered gold. Sunbeams crept between the trunks as they walked.

"How did you escape?" Taran asked.

"Mostly luck," Dilah said. "When the front line broke, horses cut in from the right. I saw the rear ranks running. Arrows stopped after a while, and we found ourselves fighting hand-to-hand."

"Noosa dragged me out," he continued. "We ran through the grass and fought a small group. Killed three. The others fled. Then we found the other four."

"They were with the search party. We heard screams—Tamas being tortured." Taran's jaw tightened.

"We struck the camp. Archers took out most of them. Noosa got hurt cutting Tamas down. Found three others tied up." Taran could see the weight of Noosa's loss on him.

"Noosa wanted to leave Tamas. Said he wouldn't make it." "But I couldn't. Not like that."

"You did the right thing," Taran said.

Dilah watched the wounded man being carried. "I should've ended his pain. I should've given him peace." Taran looked at Tamas. He didn't disagree.

"But you didn't. And now he has a chance."

They reached a small cove with a cave. Taran signalled to halt. "We rest here till sundown." Sapir arrived, quiet as a shadow.

"Any sign of pursuit?" Taran asked.

"None. We delayed as long as we could. They won't find our trail easily."

"Well done. Rest while you can. I'll take first watch." Tanny limped over, joined Taran at the firepit.

"How are you holding up?" Taran asked.

"I've had better days. My shoulder's a hole, I'm soaked, and I'm starving."

Taran laughed. "Same."

Tanny gestured at the brush. "I could dig a firepit—keep us warm, hide the smoke."

"No, I'll do it. Rest that shoulder."

Taran dug a pit using sticks and his hands, building it deep and wide, with a second channel to draw air. He ringed it with stones, filled it with kindling, and used a bow-drill to spark flame.

It caught quickly.

He smiled as warmth rose.

Tanny joined him. Sapir emerged with food—stale bread, a few berries.

"What I'd do for meat," Tanny muttered. "Tomorrow," Sapir said. "Maybe we hunt." "This is a feast," Taran joked.

They ate in silence, grateful for the scraps.

Later, Dilah and an archer emerged.

"You three rest. We'll watch."

Taran stood with Dilah, looking out into the forest.

"Sapir saw no signs of pursuit," he said.

Dilah nodded. "We've bought time. Let's use it."

Taran entered the cave, lay beside the inner fire, listening to Tamas' pained murmurs.

Sapir was there, feeding him berries. "Shhh, Tamas. Rest now." The moaning stopped.

Taran turned to face the fire. Sleep didn't come.

His thoughts churned. They needed food, shelter—horses. They couldn't stay exposed. But they had to remain hidden.

He had to get back.

He had to tell someone what he'd seen.

That final stand—the young warriors sent to die, the banners of the Natsu flying above—but among them, he'd seen markings that didn't belong.

Vintal.

They'd been fighting together.

No one else had noticed. Not yet. Not even Dilah.

But Taran had. And it changed everything.

He curled tighter as the embers glowed faintly in the cold cave, the weight of knowledge burning hotter than the fire.

❧

CHAPTER 3

S toria came from her chamber looking refreshed after the

incident.

She had a new set of clothes; her scratches she had received from being pushed over had been covered and hidden in her new clothing.

The body had been removed from her chambers and maids were working hard d to remove the blood stains from the tiles.

Both bickering what the best way to clear blood up was.

Storia walked back out onto the balcony and noticed the large ship that had come into port.

It was a different ship than had normally come into their port, much larger and with many more crew on the deck.

She could see bodies working on the deck like small dots and imagined what work they needed to do.

She made her was back into the main chamber and walked around the maids cleaning, they had cleaned the furniture well and the only sign of any disturbance was that of the blood on the floor.

Storia stopped at the maids cleaning and thanked them for their work, she handed them both a small silver coin in appreciation for their hard work.

Both accepted the gift and bowed their head in gratitude. Storia was known for her kindness among the people. She was seen as the saviour and bringer of peace for the Karathat people.

Many believed that Storia should be married and that she was not strong enough to rule the nation.

They believed that her kindness was a weakness and that should they be at war she would not be ruthless enough to make decisions needed in war.

Storia left the chambers walking out the double doors, she was met by the two guardsmen who had come to her aid before.

Clearly, they had been told to stay and guard by Zarratt, both guards wore the same outfit signalling that they were the queens own guard.

Both wore a black helmet with a face cover. Their faces hidden from view the mask was the picture of a monster.

They wore black leather armour on their shoulders and torso with a light metallic chest plate.

They both held a small shield that looked like a half-moon. The gap allowing them to rest their spear on top and help their visibility.

Their spears were the length of a man with a small pointy top designed to thrust.

They trained for hours with the shield and spear and also just the spear using the whole of the weapon like a bow staff if needed.

On their hip they carried small swords designed for getting close in combat if their spear was taken.

Their armour and weapons clearly designed for speed and agility.

The queens guard were selected once a year with strong physical trials arranged and run by Zarratt.

He had his own select trainers for the warrior's selection. At the end of their training the warriors who got through to the final stage would fight the trainers. The last fight and test was meant to be first blood but it had been known for recruits and trainers to get severely injured and on occasion death.

However the life of the guard was worth the risk for many, they were given land on completion of service or offered the role of trainer.

Although trainers did not get land they were paid well, those that chose land were not given as much final pay.

The recruits that were injured during the trials were sent back to normal soldier service. Those severely injured were given their military pension a small sum enough to just get by and offered work as bodyguards for local businessmen.

Trainers that were severely injured often retired early, living out their days in relative comfort thanks to private stipends from grateful nobles within the city.

Storia walked the corridor listening to the noise through the palace as she made her way to the days meeting of locals.

Her guardsmen followed her, their eyes looking in every direction. The recent attack had made them even more alert than usual.

For one hour every morning Storia would meet a small quantity of her people and listen to their issues.

Only the most pressing issues would come to her to resolve. Other smaller issues were handled by magistrates who also decided if the matter would be passed up to Storia.

Storia walked past the courtyard watching as Zarratt was walking with Tamanda.

Tamanda followed Zarratt with purpose, he was taking her to get her items, she would be dressed simulated to her guards, but some adaptations would need to be made.

never had a female made the queens guard before.

Tamanda had impressed Storia which was something that did not happen often with people she met.

She wasn't sure if it was the fact she had seen a female fight in such a way that Tamanda did or maybe it was how

Tamanda remained calm in danger, balancing strength with clever intuition when pressed.

She would give this girl from the northern outlands a chance to prove herself.

Her training would be harsh, Zarratt would push her, possibly break her if he could.

But IF just IF she survived the training and the final test Storia would have her as her personal guard.

Male guards were not allowed in the chambers unsupervised; they were always in the hallway unless Zarratt entered and on occasion he would call the guard in to give them a message to pass on to someone in the palace.

A female guard that could share her chambers, there was a small room in her chambers that Storia had already started planning to make Tamanda's chambers.

Storia arrived at the palace meeting chambers, she hated this part of her day. She longed for the end of hour already.

Storia sat at her seat a golden throne with a black throw over the chair to soften the throne for comfortable.

The first people approached the throne, it was a divorce matter, both parties needed to be present before she could render a verdict fairly, ensuring everyone heard her decision.

There were three reasons a divorce in Karathat would be granted.

Infidelity, violence of any physical form and finally if both parties agreed to a mutual end of a relationship.

"My queen I am here today to request divorce to be granted in my favour. I have reason to believe that my wife has been unfaithful, my wife has been seen with another man in a private dwelling leaving the property."

The male had to have evidence of infidelity in order for the divorce to be granted in his favour, should his wife be found guilty of infidelity she would be made to walk the main street in shame.

Storia looked at the man and then at his wife "And you have proof of this infidelity other than what someone has allegedly seen".

"My queen I bring my witness before you to state to what they have seen".

A young boy came forward, Storia looked at the young boy.

he was no more than fourteen years of age, skinny and rough looking.

He appeared to have bathed but his clothes were clearly worn in.

"Tell me boy, what did you see".

The boy raised his head nervously and looked up at Storia.

He said, "I saw the lady go into a house, she stayed there for a short time that evening before leaving in a hurry, I swear".

Storia looked at the boy "you swear this to be true to your queen an oath not taken lightly".

The boy stared at Storia looking wide eyed. "Yes, my queen, I swear it to be true".

Storia watched the boy closely. "Very well".

She looked to the wife who was standing head down awaiting her turn.

"It appears some serious allegations of infidelity are against you; you may now speak without fear of being interrupted".

The young woman stepped forward, she was much younger than her husband. Storia believed she was possibly with the man through some form of agreement made.

"My queen, I have not, will not and never will be unfaithful to my husband.

I love my husband very much; I married my husband last year after my family agreed that he was to be the best suited for me and our family.

Since then, I have done everything my husband asks, even when he spends nights away from our family home I wait for him to come home from the local tavern.

Your highness I know what goes on at the tavern with men and others that are there.

I did indeed attend the address as stated and I told my husband this, however he did not wish to listen to me and instead left our home three nights ago.

I received an order to meet him here today.

The reason I attended that address is I have tried to give my husband a child this past year but have been unable to be with child.

There is a man that I was seen with at the address again this is true.

However, he is not my lover, he is the son of the lady who owns the address.

The address is the one that sits behind the bakers."

Storia knew of the address given, she had heard rumours of this address by the servant girls who worked in the private gardens.

The worked hard but liked to gossip.

Storia let the young woman continue her story as she felt the husband should hear and she had promised she would not be interrupted.

"I had heard that the lady who lived in the address is a doula, a Womb whisperer. I have heard she can help you become fertile and cast magic that helps your body accept the new soul.

I had seen this woman three times and she had said she would help me become with child. I wanted her magic to help me become able to make my husband happy and bring him the joy of being a father.

The man at this address is in her employ and he gets things that are needed for her magic to work.

Instead of bringing my husband a child, he has brought shame on me. He has not only accused me of falsely being unfaithful, but I have now had to admit to everyone here that I have failed to be able to become with child."

"Are you able to prove your defence child?" Storia replied.

"Yes, my queen, the man he has accused me of being unfaithful with is in this crowd should you need to speak with him. I also have here in my hand my contract of agreement with the doula.

Both have asked if this contract could be enough, however if needed the man has said he will step forward if required. But their work depends on privacy with clients who attend their address".

One of the guardsmen handed Storia the contract. Storia read the contract thoroughly through and then handed it back to the guardsmen.

Storia looked at the husband who appeared shocked at the news, it was clear he had not taken the time to listen to his wife.

"Is there anything else you have to add, either of you before I make judgement?"

The man spoke quickly "my queen I'm sorry, had I known then I".

Storia spoke quickly "you would have what? You would have not wasted time here today.

You would not have brought shame on your wife's head for your false claims".

The man's head lowered, and his shoulders dropped.

"And you?" Storia said to the wife.

"Your highness, I feel that the shame this has brought on me I cannot stay in this marriage".

Storia sat in silence for a moment.

"Here is my decision, based on what has been said I believe that you have brought unnecessary shame to your wife's head and her family.

I am going to grant the divorce, but this will be in your wife's favour.

You shall relinquish ownership of your main home to your wife; you shall also pay for her living expenses until she either married again or finds a means to fund her own lifestyle whichever comes first." The man's face shocked, his mouth open in shock.

"My queen please, this surely is too much".

Storia snapped a look at the man" you dare to question my judgement; you have come before my court and made a claim against your wife that was false.

Had you taken time to listen then you would still have your home.

Be thankfully I have not given her all your assets which I can see from the paperwork before me is plenty.

You shall have until the end of today's light to get whatever property you own from your family home. After this time my guardsmen will attend the address and will meet you. You will hand the keys to the property, and they will stand guard and hand the keys to your ex-wife.

Is that clear?"

The man looked at the floor. "Yes, my queen" the man dared not speak any more.

Storia looked at the woman. "Does this satisfy your shame?"

The woman nodded "yes my queen, thank you?"

Storia looked at them both and told them that their meeting was over and sent them on their way.

Storia looked over at one of her clerks who had the next person waiting.

She waved for the next person to come through.

With a sudden voice that made the crowd in the room turn and look.

"Queen Storia of Karathat" the voice loud enough to make the guardsmen stand and notice. A man walked forward dressed in leather armour.

He walked briskly towards the throne followed by four other males dressed in similar attire. He walked past the red line that indicated for those there to stop.

Storia's guardsmen quickly stood in front of Storia moving shoulder to shoulder. They dropped low in a stance shields locked and spears placed over the top of the shield pointing towards the possible threat.

The male continued to walk toward the guardsmen.

As he got closer the guardsmen both drew their spears back slightly ready to thrust if needed.

"Halt" one of the guardsmen said.

Storia remained in her seat knowing that two other guardsmen had now come to her side ready to move her to safety if they needed.

The stranger dropped to one knee in front of the guardsmen; he placed his right hand in the floor and nodded his head to the queen of Karathat.

"Queen Storia, my name is Balien Emetic," he said, his voice steady despite the tension.

An odd metal medallion swung into view as he raised his head.

Storia looked at the male intrigued. "Stand and be heard Balien Emetic".

Balien stood tall, he was taller than most of the others in the room.

He had blond hair tied back, clean shaven.

He had broad shoulders and stood dressed in black leather armour.

On the chest of the armour there was picture of a large bird.

"Queen Storia, I have come from across the great water from the lands of the Nalamar.

I have been sent by my lord to make contact with you your highness.

My lord has given me the specific task to converse with yourself and enter into negotiations and arrange a treaty between our people".

Storia listened to the male, carefully noting the way he watched her every reaction for any hint of advantage or weakness.

Storia called for one of her guardsmen to come closer and whispered in his ear, the guardsmen then walked off briskly as if with purpose.

Storia clapped her hands twice and stood up. "Balien of the. Nalamar, this is neither the place nor time for us to discuss such matter. You have interrupted an important time of the day for my people.

However, I will grant you a private audience tonight in the Moonhall chamber, where fewer eyes watch.

You may stay here in the palace for a short while until you are escorted later to the Moonhall chamber at sunset by one of my trusted advisers."

Balien looked at Storia "your highness I express my gratitude for your hospitality. But I am afraid urgent tidings require me to press you on this matter sooner."

Storia looked at Balien then called for the room to be cleared.

Storia called to her clerks.

"Today's meeting of the people will be adjourned, give those that are here waiting a tile to return tomorrow. We shall hold a longer session tomorrow and they will be seen an hour before any new cases.

Storia looked at Balien her features looking sterner.

"Very well Balien, my advisor Zarratt will be with us soon, once he arrives, he shall relocate this meeting to the Moonhall chamber where you may speak your terms for any possible arrangement and tell me about your lands.

Until then enjoy something to drink while I attend to another matter, my advisor Zarratt will escort you to the chamber. Until then I shall leave you in the care of my guardsmen."

Storia moved off from her seat with her guardsmen quickly following her.

Two other guardsmen stood in front of Balien clearly showing that he was not to follow by crossing their spears.

As Storia left the room she was met by Zarratt who had been summonsed for by the guards Storia had sent away.

Storia looked at the guard waiting for his new order. "Thank you Bij, you may return to the chamber. Be sure to watch this Balien.

There is something about him, he radiates with his own confidence.

There is something about him that unsettles me."

The guardsmen nodded understanding the task he had been given and then left to take on his duties.

Storia looked at Zarratt "how is Tamanda".

Zarratt was surprised this was her current thought.

"She is fine, her suit is being adjusted as we speak, and her weapons are being tailored by the armourer as well as she is much smaller than our other recruits."

Zarratt would not dare mention anything about her being a woman seeing the armourer.

"Tell me about this stranger." Zarratt said.

"Well, I believe he has come from the ship that entered port today, he has stated he is from across the Great Lake.

He has stated that he has been sent her to negotiate a treaty, however he has not yet told me who he is aligned to.

He has black leather under armour on that had a red bird crest on it.

He states that he is of the Nalamar people.

He gave his name as Balien Emetic".

Storia thought hard if there was anything else. "I believe that he is a warrior, he did not seem phased by the guardsmen when they stood at estarte in front of him, it looked as if he was watching them looking for a weakness in their guard".

Zarratt called for a guardsman to come over.

"I wish for you to check the assassin from this morning, search his body and his attire. Look for any symbols that look like a red bird crest".

The guardsmen nodded and run off to complete the task.

"You believe the assassin could be linked to this man?" Storia looked on at Zarratt who was deep in thought.

Zarratt looked at Storia "I am not sure, but I want to rule out what I can, I will approach the oracle she knows of many things outside our world. She speaks with many and may know more. I shall tell the guardsmen to take him to the Moonhall chamber and wait with him.

Give me an hour my queen I'll see what I can find out before we go into talks with this man, I have already sent men to the port to find out any information about the ship they should return shortly."

Storia touched Zarratt on the forearm bringing him from his thoughts.

"I shall send this Balien some refreshment and will meet you by the Moonhall chamber in an hour".

Zarratt turned and left the room, Storia watched him leave and made her way back to her chamber.

෴

CHAPTER 4

Taran woke up cold, his clothes had dried while he had been walking and then sat next to the fire, but the night had come and the warmth that normally came with the sun had faded fast.

Taran sat up and looked around him Tanny was still asleep snoring away.

Sapir was unsurprisingly awake already near to Tamas keeping him calm.

The four warriors that had been with Dilah were sat eating what remained of their meal from earlier.

Taran kicked Tanny waking him up. "What are you doing you dog, let me be" Tanny mumbled.

"Get up you lazy pig" Taran said.

Taran heard footsteps running into the cave, it was Dilah he looked stressed.

"We have company, a large group coming this way.

Our archers are watching them, but they are coming." Tanny jumped to his feet and the other warriors stood up.

They all came together as a group; they needed to make a plan.

Dilah looked at Taran "I have buried the fire pit you made outside and have made it look like no one has been there.

We need to decide if we are going fight, hide or run."

Taran thought of their options, with Tamas they wouldn't be fast enough to get away and gain ground.

He was clearly getting worse and was now constantly mumbling in pain.

They could fight but it depended on the size of the incoming group. There were only nine of them able to fight, everyone had a weapon at least and some shields as well as two archers. They could hide in the Forrest but would have to leave Tamas, he would lead them directly to their position.

The archers came into the cave. "They are coming and will be here soon at least fifteen to twenty in the group.

Taran took control making a plan "Ok we will need to try and keep Tamas quiet and hide in the cave. The sun has dropped we can take cover in here.

Taran looked to Sapir. "The berries you gave Tamas last night do you have any more can you keep him quiet".

Sapir stared at Taran thinking for a moment. "Yes, I can make him quiet again".

Taran started snapping orders to the others.

"Archers position yourselves as far back as you can, try and use any moonlight to give you some sort of visibility of the cave opening stay close to the cave walls.

Dilah and Tanny take the men with the shields and sit back far enough that they do not see your shapes, lay down at the start if you must but keep your silhouettes obscure. We may need you to jump up and make a shield wall if they charge in.

Sapir look after Tamas, take care of him and try and keep him quiet.

We will hide in here in the dark, if they come in then we may have to fight, for now we stay quiet and hope they pass the cave by.

No one wants to enter a cave in the dark due to what sometimes sleeps in them.

This is our best chance, if they charge in our archers will take as many out as they can, before it turns to swords.

Get ready and may the spirits protect us".

They began to get into their positions; Sapir went to sit with Tamas.

Tamas was mumbling, Taran could hear Sapir was whispering to him.

"Please give him the berries Sapir we need him to quieten down." Taran mumbled to himself quietly.

The cave suddenly appeared very dark and silent.

Taran tried to look for any of their group, but he could not see anything, he was looking towards the cave entrance to see if he could make out any movement.

He started to hear voices from the direction of the cave entrance. The voices were getting louder and louder.

Taran could feel his heart pounding in his chest; he was breathing deep and heavy his nerves obvious on every exhale.

He saw the first movement at the edge of the cave entrance. Shadows in the moonlight, the silhouettes of people moving around the cave.

"I hope Dilah covered that fire-pit properly" he thought to himself.

He heard some movement behind him and his eyes widened. Who had moved in the cave, had the incoming threat heard it as well.

He could see torch lights moving outside the cave, the searches had lit torches, he could see the flicker of their flames.

His head was pounding from the stress; his heart was pounding that hard he thought he could hear it.

Taran placed his hand to his sword hilt looking for its comfort.

He could now see the outline of one of the archers slowly drawing an arrow back adding just enough tension that should he need to fire he could do it quickly.

He could hear the voices out the front of the cave but could not make out what was being said.

The voices were raised and between the group.

"Hopefully they are arguing about leaving the cave alone, just move on" Taran whispered to himself.

The search party stood outside the front of the cave for some time. Taran watched the archer on two occasions draw and raise his bow and then lower it again.

His heart felt like it was going to beat through his chest, sweat dropping from his brow.

He saw one of the shapes steps into the mouth of the cave holding a torch up to try and illuminate the cave.

Taran pressed himself against the wall, gripping his sword hilt tightly as the torchbearer stepped forward, narrowly missing a pile of scattered stones at his feet.

The torch bearer turned and shouted back at the others; they began to move away from the cave.

Taran let out long breaths, his muscles trembling with relief as he eased his grip on the sword still ready for any danger.

Taran looked up and saw the archer move slowly towards the edge of the cave to check that the danger had gone.

Dilah and Tanny stood up from the place that they had been hiding behind, some low rocks had given them some cover.

Sapir came from the shadows as if he had been a spirit in the darkness.

Taran walked over to Sapir and noticed blood on his hands.

"Sapir why is their blood on your hands, what has happened?".

Sapir lowered his head "I had no more berries Taran; I used the last of them earlier today.

I tried to calm Tamas, but he would not stop. He became restless and started to try and talk some more.

I placed my hand over his mouth, but he then tried to fight me off".

Taran thought back to the noise he had heard while they had been hiding.

"I had no choice, Taran; I pulled my knife and pushed it into the back of his neck. I made it as quick and painless as I could. I had no other choice; he would have shouted and alerted them." Taran noticed the sadness in Sapir's face.

Taran placed his hand on Sapir's shoulder.

"I understand Sapir, you had no choice.

He was dying and would not have made the journey anyway.

Do not feel ashamed Sapir, you have eased his suffering and sent him peacefully on his way to whatever journey he chooses after this life." The rest of the group joined Taran and Sapir, Dilah looked at Sapir and noticed the blood on Sapir's hands at that point he understood what had happened.

He thought back to Noosa, he had lost a good man for no reason. They should have left Tamas before; they should have sent him on his after journey then.

At least Noosa would still be alive, and they would have an extra pair of hands for fighting.

"I'll go and check on Stavan, he was checking to see if the party had left".

Dilah took himself off from the group towards the mouth of the cave.

Taran looked at the rest of the group, all eyes were now on him.

"We shall stay here for a short while and then head out, gather your things and be ready to move.

Without any Tamas we can now make progress on our journey."

The group exchanged uncertain glances as a cold wind suddenly blew inside.

They group dispersed and started to gather their belongings together.

Tanny and Sapir stood with Taran.

"I honestly thought we were done for Taran, I thought for sure they had found us". Tanny said.

"So did I Tanny, so did I. We had the advantage had they come in.

But we can't afford to lose anyone else not this far into these lands. It's why I want us to move as fast as we can once we get going." Taran could see Stavan and Dilah coming back into the cave.

"Stavan, Dilah what's the update?".

Dilah responded, "it seems they are heading North, if we give it a little longer then as planned head East towards the lands of the Karathat."

"Very well Dilah, I have told the others to gather their things and be ready to move. Once we have everything together, we shall head out.

Place what food we have in rags and give everyone a bag; we'll be eating on the move with little rest until dawn.

We can't afford to lose any time during the night, I'll send Stavan and one other ahead as scouts to lead the way.

Then we will have two follows after, Dilah can you ask the other archer and one of the others to follow after us."

"I will do; I'll speak with them now" Dilah walked off to find the volunteer.

"How's your shoulder Tanny?".

"It's fine Taran, it's a little stiff but that's all. Sapir patched me up well."

"Good, gather your bits together be ready to go".

Taran walked to the mouth of the cave; he looked out into the night.

The moon was high and bright giving some light to the Forrest outside.

He listened carefully, hoping to catch any distant footsteps or movement from the direction the enemy had gone.

Taran signalled for the others to join him to the mouth of the cave.

"We have seen a group searching for us already, stay vigilant.

We'll send two of ahead like before then the five of us will follow shortly after then the last two leave shortly after that.

If you need to eat then eat on the move, we must make some ground and get out of these lands."

Taran signalled for Stavan and one of the other warriors to move off, they made way quick, and light footed.

The warrior with Stavan was young and agile, no more than nineteen. He would set a good pace with Stavan making sure he was not stupid or reckless.

Taran sent Dilah, Tanny, Sapir and the other warrior off. He turned to look at the remaining archer and warrior.

"Count to fifty then make your way, do not get to lost behind in this dark.

As the sun starts to rise and the light comes let the gap get a little bigger. If trouble comes from behind us, then run as fast as you can and catch us up."

The two warriors nodded understanding their orders.

Taran then ran to catch up with the others.

He caught up with Sapir who was waiting for him, Sapir turned and began to run.

Taran caught up Sapir and was sure he was smiling.

"What are you so happy about?".

Sapir looked at Taran then back to the track he was running.

"This takes me back many years, back to the takka trials.

Back to when I was much younger and had to run my trial.

Being given a head start before the elders would release the young warriors to find you." Taran smiled as well.

"Well that it does, my own trial was not as long ago though, I guess when you were sixteen, they released dragons and lizards to chase you as well".

Sapir laughed at Taran's insult.

"When I was sixteen, they released the warriors and dogs, back then if you were captured you got beaten.

You had to fight your way free, if you got caught in the first day you didn't get your mark.

You had to wait until you were eighteen to do it again and face the shame of running your trials with children who were sixteen." Taran thought on his own experience.

"I managed to three days; I was nearly back at the circle when my own father caught me.

He let my cousins beat me blue, I bet you made it hard work for them Sapir on your trial".

Sapir laughed again.

"No, I ran it at eighteen after being caught in the first hour when I was sixteen.

My father beat me almost to death because of it.

I learned then that I needed to work harder.

For two years I hunted and ran everywhere. I got strong then when I ran it at eighteen, I made sure that they would not find it easy to catch me again."

Taran looked surprised at Sapir.

"So, you made it to the circle the second time then? "Taran asked.

"No, I was captured on the third day but managed to break my father's arm on the second day when he thought he had me cornered.

He and two of his men found out how strong I had
become".
Sapir smiled while telling the story.
"Why am I not surprised Sapir".
Both of them continued to run keeping pace with the others.
෴

CHAPTER 5

S toria sat in her chamber waiting for news from Zarratt, he

had left to speak to the Oracle several hours before.

Balien had asked for his audience with her twice in this time and she had told her guards to stall and offer refreshments, she wondered how long they could make him wait.

She had allowed his entourage that had accompanied him to the palace to join him in the Moonshine chambers.

She wondered what they would be discussing what actions she should be taking, what would her father have done.

A loud bang on her chamber doors brought her from her thoughts, she turned to see Zarratt staring at her.

"What news?" She asked.

"My queen, I have spoken to the oracle, she stated that she knows of the Nalamar people.

They are south of the Great Lake and have been gradually expanding their empire.

It is said that they are known for sending envoys to lands outside their empire and creating trade deals.

The deals are always made in their favour and often the other party are given little room to bargain."

Storia spoke quickly cutting Zarratt off "What of the assassin?" Zarratt shook his head.

"My men have inspected the body of the assassin and there are no symbols on his clothing, equipment or body that suggest he was from those people.

My men have returned from the ship in port and have stated that the ship has many men on board not all would be considered sailors.

It could possibly be a war ship as part of a fleet. However, the oracle has not mentioned anything about the Nalamar having a naval force in our waters.

I have sent word to some of my contacts on the water to send a bird should they see any sign of a fleet in our waters."

Storia spoke keeping her voice calm, she feared this ship might be a distraction.

"Very good Zarratt, let's go and meet Balien.

Let's hear what he has to say for his people of Nalamar."

Storia walked out of the chambers past Zarratt. He followed her through the halls staying close to her side.

He had never seen her walk with such purpose.

When they arrived at the Moonshine chamber the guard she had spoken to earlier was still standing at the door.

She leaned forward and whispered in his ear. The guard looked towards Zarratt as if obtaining some form of approval, but Zarratt was clearly not aware of what had been said to him.

Storia then looked at the guard and told him to go.

Storia opened the doors to find Balien sitting eating grapes and drinking wine with his entourage.

The chambers were large, usually used for large dinner parties when entertaining dignitaries from other lands. The table placed in the middle of the room large enough to seat twelve people at least.

The ceiling was high and painted in such a way it looked like stars in a night sky.

There was a large fireplace at the end of the table near to Baliens seat, the fire had been lit.

Storia always liked this room, she would sit in and have dinner with her father and those that visited her farther offering tribute.

Balien was sat with his feet on the table facing the door.

Zarratt stepped forward clearly aggravated by Baliens lack of respect. "Get to your feet when the queen enters the room" Zarratt snapped.

Storia put her arm out across the front of Zarratt.

"Calm yourself Zarratt, it's not his fault that he does not understand our customs and ways".

Balien sat and smiled at Storia's comment, he put his feet down and stood up facing Zarratt and Storia.

"Your highness I must apologise, you see I was unsure if I was being kept here as a guest or as a prisoner.

You see it was hard to make the correct assumption as you have had guards at the door who have refused our requests to leave and go to our ship.

But on the other hand, you have given us wine and fruit."

Storia walked calmly towards the table, ignoring Baliens comment.

"Balien of the Nalamar, I believe you said that you are here to discuss terms of a trade agreement or even alliance.

I have ordered food to be brought to us so we may discuss over food and wine.

You may choose one of your advisers to stay for the discussions.

The rest of your colleagues will be escorted to the main hall where they will be supplied with food, wine and entertainment." Balien bowed his head in acceptance as he spoke.

"Very well your highness however I am in no need of my colleagues to stay for the discussions regarding our arrangement. My lord has given me strict instructions to discuss what he offers what he would like in return.

These matters are trusted to me and no one else and while I speak in these matters my voice acts at his command." Balien spoke with confidence, he stood a little taller as he spoke making sure his voice was heard.

"Very well Balien, my guards will escort your men to the courtyard hall for food. Zarratt my advisor shall stay with me for our

discussion."

Baliens men left the room escorted by the guardsmen. Balien stood at the table still smiling with his hands crossed in front of him.

Storia sat at the table Zarratt stood behind her. The air in the chamber thickened with anticipation as Storia gestured for Balien to take a seat.

Balien sat down opposite Storia focusing on Zarratt as he did so.

Making sure to make eye contact to show he was not afraid of him.

Storia spoke first breaking the tension that had arose.

"Balien of the Nalamar before we begin tell me of your people."

"Of course, your highness, we are an empire far south of the Great Lake, our beginnings are very much similar to yours.

Our history records us starting as a small island nation that expanded its revenue through trade.

Our current lord is a descendant of the Nalambar dynasty. They built our lands from a small port to the power it is today.

For centuries we have been building our lands in the south never crossing the Great Lake north until recent times."

Storia interrupted Balien which very obviously annoyed Balien.

"And how has your nation built these lands?" Storia asked.

Balien sat back in his chair placing his hand to his chin.

"We have been at war with many different nations over many years.

We have ended wars in many different ways — with the stroke of a quill, the fall of a flag, or the silent stillness that follows a battle.

When the fighting has stopped, we have either made treaties, trade agreements or managed unification.

we are now at peace and have been for some time. Our lord Stylax of the Nalambar Dynasty has sent envoys in all directions to seek new alliances, to make new agreements and find new lands.

So here I am, at your lands as his voice ready to offer terms of an alliance and make an agreement."

Storia thought hard on what her next question would be before finally locking eyes with Zarratt as if searching for silent guidance from her trusted advisor.

She spoke suddenly and with purpose.

"So, from what I have taken is that your nation has been built and forged in war. You have either accepted submission or negotiated strength, but rarely trusted peace when it arrives, especially with rivals at your borders.

So, what has your lord Stylax sent you here to offer?"

Balien tapped his fingers on the table in front of them, then picked up his wine and took a sip. He thought deeply about his next words.

"Your highness, my lord Stylax knows that you are not yet married.

He knows that there is no heir to your kingdom.

He knows that you are a great leader to your people.

One who has continued to build up a nation by using means other than what her father used before her.

You have made trade agreements and expanded your own lands and holdings.

My lord also knows that you have been at peace for some time while the nations around you have been at each other's throats.

My lord Stylax wishes to offer you and your people the opportunity to come under the wing of the Nalamar people.

With this comes protection and an alliance to last for a time.

With this comes trade from across the water from the lands to the south.

He also hopes that in time he may even be able to encourage an engagement between you and one of his sons.

This in turn creating an heir to your throne."

Storia stared at Balien, weighing each word as if measuring hidden weights beneath his offers.

"I have no need to find a future consort at this time. When I am ready to find such a soul, the stars themselves shall bear witness to my choice.

You have come here to Karathat in your very impressive ship which could be seen as a slight show of force to those who may not wish to bend the knee".

Balien laughed allowed, he smiled as if the edge of his mouth could touch his ears.

"Your highness, my ship is not a show of force not at all.

It is however an opportunity to show you what could be at your disposal should your nation require it."

Storia cut Balien off not wanting to hear and further from him.

"And should I refuse to allow my people to come under the protection of the Nalamar nation, what then?"

Balien's expression was no longer of laughter or smiles. He sat forward in his chair and placed his arms on the table.

"My lady we have had resistance to our proposals before and I am sure we will have many more after both you and I are long gone from this life.

However, I am charged to inform you that refusal may carry unintended consequences from parties who do not share my commitment to a peaceful outcome."

Storia understood the threat that had been made within the conversation, she knew, now, that her decision could place Karathat at risk unless she found a way to shift the balance of power in her own favour.

It was clear that they believed she was an easy target for them to try and manipulate and threaten.

Zarratt's hand rested on his sword, his grip tightened enough that Storia heard his hand on the leather bound around the handle.

She placed her hand down onto her thigh shaking her finger only for Zarratt to see.

There was a knock on the door of the chamber, one of the guardsmen walked in.

He stopped in the door entrance and stood straight, shield close to his body and his sword hand covering the hilt of his short sword.

"My queen your food is here".

"Good let them in, I am ravenous" she replied.

The guardsman stepped aside allowing servants to bring in trays of food and drink, the servants poured wine into goblets and placed them neatly on the table.

The trays of food were then placed on the table.

"Balien please enjoy our custom and delicacies before we continue with this conversation, my people have worked hard to catch the best options for us today."

Zarratt sat forward and pulled off the lid to his food revealing a large, cooked bird, golden brown in colour with steam rising from its body from the heat of the freshly cooked meat. His lifted the lid off to his next dish which was filled with potato's cooked in spices covered in herbs.

Storia removed the lid to the tray nearest to her revealing chicken cooked in butter with roasted vegetables on the outer edge of the plate and rice mixed with vegetables in another dish.

The food smelt delicious filling the air with the smell of spices and freshly cooked meat. Balien took up a goblet of wine and tasted its fruity flavour.

"This wine is delicious it bursts with bright, juicy fruit flavours—think ripe strawberries, blackberries, and a touch of cherry or plum. On the nose, it offers a vibrant bouquet of red and dark berries. The palate is smooth and supple, with a fresh acidity that keeps the fruit forward and lively, making it easy to drink and highly aromatic.

This would be a good choice to have ready for when my lord Stylax comes to your city once terms are agreed".

Bailen leaned forward and lifted the lid from his food, the steam from the dish underneath crept out from under the cover.

As he pulled the cover completely off it revealed a large bowl of cooked vegetable and rice.

The vegetables and spices came from all different places that the traders of Karathat would pass on their trade routes.

The smell of cardamom, saffron, sweet peppers, onion, cumin, fennel, mint, cinnamon, paprika, star anise, bay leaf filled the air of the room.

Balien went to remove the lid from the other tray as he did both the servants next to him grabbed his arms taking him by surprise and pinned his wrist to the table.

As they did this a third servant one Zarratt now recognised to be the guardsmen Bij who Storia spoke to earlier pulled two large knives from his waist.

He drove the first one down hard into the centre of Baliens left hand,

Balien screamed in pain as the knife pierced his skin cutting flesh and passing bone to pin the hand to the wooden table.

The guardsmen then hacked down driving the other knife through

Baliens right hand pinning his other hand to the table.

Balien screamed in agony, he was unable to move either hand. His palms were skewered to the table, blood pooling beneath them.

The guardsmen Bij pulled off the last dish cover revealing a head from one of Baliens men and pushed the dish in front of Baliens face.

Balien in pain saw the face in front of him, it was one of his own men. His eyes widened and his voice screamed out.

Zarratt sat shocked with the events that he had just witnessed, he looked at Storia who was sat staring at Balien.

Her eyes wide and expression on her face that she enjoyed what she had just witnessed.

He thought back to before they entered the room, when Storia had stopped and spoke to Bij before sending him off to complete a task. He recalled the look on his face and the look Bij had given him before he had been told to go.

Zarratt had never witnessed this type of behaviour from Storia before. He had never seen such calculated cruelty or violence from her. He recalled the look in her eyes, and it reminded him of her father.

He was a ruthless ruler who had fought through decades of hardship to build his nation. Through a time of blood, fire and death.

Bailen sat anchored to the table by his hands unable to move position at all, the guards still holding his wrists in place.

The shock of seeing the head of his colleague on a plate in front of him, he had never been victim to such cruelty or horrors before.

Bailen began shouting in defiance breathing through the pain "You bitch, you bitch daughter of a rat.

You have sealed your nations fate.

My lord will not stand for his envoys to be treated in such a way."

Bij grabbed hold of Balien by his hair, he yanked his head back and grabbed his chin with the other hand.

Storia sat and leaned forward looking at Balien making eye contact.

"You came here thinking this would be an easy victory for your lord. You thought that because I am a woman, I would not want to face conflict and would bend the knee.

I am Storia daughter of Saffalah of Karathat.

Your lord and your people should know that we are not a nation who will sit and be silent in fear like a mouse. We are like a snake, coiled and silent waiting for its prey to make a move, then when the time is right its strikes.

You will take a message back you your lord, the message shall be that we are not in need of a protectorate, I am not in need of husband.

Our nation flourishes on its own free will, our people are free and will remain free while I am their queen."

Storia signalled to the servants holding Baliens wrists to bind his arms and wrap them tight. They did so wrapping cloth round his arms and twisting it applying pressure to the arm, a guardsmen stepped forward brandishing a cleaver in his hands.

The cleaver already had blood on it from the severed head.

Balien realised in horror what was about to happen he screamed in fear.

"No, no you cannot do this please no. Please I will take your message, you do not need to do this please."

The guardsmen raised the cleaver high above his head bringing it down in one swift motion hacking at the wrist blood sprayed from the wound, the cleaver did not cut the wrist clean on the first strike causing Balien to scream out in pain and his body to jolt from the pain.

The guardsmen raised the cleaver again and came down a second time taking the hand from Baliens body.

The guardsmen moved round to the other side raising the cleaver again, this time the strike came down hacking the wrist taking the hand from the body with one swift motion.

The guardsmen then pulled two hot metal rods from the fire; he pushed the first of the rods hard against Baliens left stump. Balien screamed in pain again as the rod burned against his body, the smell of hot metal against flesh filled the room.

The second rod was pushed against the right stump cauterising the second wound, again Balien screamed in pain. This time the pain was too much it caused Balien to go unconscious slumping in his chair. Storia sat in her chair looking at Balien, his body sat as if lifeless.

His chest was still rising and falling she could see that he was still breathing.

She looked at the guards next to him.

"Take him away, let my physician see him and treat the wounds.

Place his hands in a bag and tie it to his waist.

Tomorrow takes him to his ship and see that it is sent back to Nalamar".

The guards bowed their head and began their task.

Storia looked over to Zarratt he sat staring back at her speechless.

"What have you done Storia, I thought the man was rude and arrogant but what have you done?" Zarratt asked.

Storia started to eat her food, she sat eating as if nothing had happened.

The last guardsman left the room carrying Baliens hands. Storia finally turned from her food and looked at Zarratt.

"I knew when I saw that ship this morning that whoever arrived in it would not be here for our benefit.

His first meeting this morning feeling no threat from our guards when he approached the throne showed that he did not fear us or consider us as someone to be cautious.

After what you told me of the Nalamar I believed we needed to make a strong statement.

I told Bij to dress our men in servant attire and bring the food in, I told him to select one of the Nalamar and bring his head in with the food.

I told Bij that should I use the word Ravenous when the food arrived, he was to take this fools hands as well.

He insults me and then goes on to threaten us, what else could I have done? I needed to send a message that we are to be feared to show those who would try and come here that we are strong".

Zarratt stood from his chair and walked towards Storia. He could no longer see the young girl that he had seen grow up.

What stood before him was the image of her father, her father could be a ruthless leader when needed.

This was the first threat to her people in all her time as queen. She stared back at Zarratt, her expression unreadable, the silence between them tense.

"I am tired Zarratt, I am going to return to my chambers. Have Balien and his men returned to their ship in the morning. See that they their ship is set off from the docks and sent with my message to the

Nalamar."

Storia turned and left the room, Zarratt for the first time in a long time felt concerned for his people. He would now more than ever need to find allies; he hoped that their own envoys to the Mandji or Natsu would not meet the same fate as Balien and that they would return home with good news.

&

CHAPTER 6

t had been four days since they had left the cave and started to make their way towards the lands of the Karathat.

They had managed to evade the search parties in the first few days by hiding in caves and off the main paths.

It had made their journey longer, but they had found shelter in caves and rock formations along the way.

They had managed to hunt and cook meat with Stafan catching some small animals.

The bushland was thick which concealed them as they moved, it had made them slow down to a walking pace the last two days.

Taran had changed the order of who went up front but had always maintained an archer to the front and rear with Stafan always voluntarily taking the front.

"Taran, pssssst"

Taran looked behind him, Dilah was walking close to him. He looked tired but then they all did, the journey with little breaks had taken its toll on all of them.

"What is it, Dilah?". Taran responded his voice tired.

"We should head north soon; we have been heading east for days now.

We should head North and aim to get back to our own lands". Dilah had been pressing the matter of changing direction for the last two days.

"We will soon Dilah, we shall keep going until the next break and then we will head north.

We should be clear of the search parties by now, we haven't seen or heard anything for a while now".

Taran hoped that Stafan would find a nice place to rest so they could relax for an hour or so and just have a nap.

Stafan had been sending the warriors he had been with back with updates of any terrain ahead that was either tricky or possibly dangerous.

Taran walked a short while longer before hearing footsteps coming back to them.

A young warrior came through the bushland breathing heavy. He had clearly been told to move with speed to meet Taran.

"What's the news?" Taran asked quickly.

The warrior was breathing heavy catching his breath.

"A settlement, only small but no movement from within it seems".

Taran turned and called to Dilah and the others.

"There is a settlement ahead, let's catch up with Stafan and see what's there. We may be able to steal some horses and food".

They ran and caught up with Stafan, he was crouching in the bushes at the edge of the settlement.

The settlement had six huts, in the middle was a large stone ring with what looked like a used fire pit.

"What have you seen Stafan" Taran whispered.

"No people yet, they have chickens and pigs roaming around. But no voices or movement from within the settlement."

Taran thought for a moment, it concerned him that no movement had been seen, or noise had been heard.

Six huts meant that it was at least a family.

They should hear the voices of the women or children.

"Sapir, what do you see" Taran looking for the older warrior's experience.

"Nothing, this is not somewhere we want to be Taran.

We should go round and leave this place be".

Dilah spoke quickly not letting Sapir finish.

"Taran, we need food, they have it. They have chickens, pigs possibly grain.

We could get eggs and fill our food pouches for a few days at least.

We should go and look at least".

"Taran, I say again we should leave this place. There is nothing here. Let us go round and be on our way".

Dilah was aggregated by Sapir not wanting to go into the settlement. "I am taking my warriors, and we are going into the village.

Taran you can keep your men here or go around, but we need a supply of food, and they have it."

Dilah signalled for his warriors to spread out and move into the settlement.

The warriors spread out and started to move their way in.

Taran looked at Tanny and Dilah rolling his eyes.

"Looks like we are going into the settlement."

Taran, Tanny and Sapir walked into the settlement moving slowly.

Dilahs warriors had already started to enter some of the huts and started looking for whatever could be taken.

Stafan and the other archer Antree walked towards the huts on the outskirts.

Taran walked through the middle of the settlement slowly followed by Tanny and Sapir.

The chicken and pigs ran wild; there were no signs that a fire had been for a while.

Taran came to a hut in the middle of the settlement; he could hear a noise coming from inside the hut.

It was a noise he had heard before a few times, a familiar humming noise.

He walked closer to the entrance then a familiar smell came to him.

Taran pulled the cover of the door back, as he did, he was covered by a mass of black flies. The flies came from the hut into the open air as if smoke coming from a wildfire.

As with the swarming mass of flies to Taran then came a smell from the hut, Taran looked in the door and turned instantly bringing up bile from his stomach.

"What is it? Taran what's in there?". Tanny asked.

Sapir snapped at Tanny "death, that is all that is here, we should leave.

We should leave now and quick".

Taran walked away feeling another surge of bile forcing its way up from his stomach as he was sick again.

Sapir walked and opened the door, he looked inside. Sapir was not disturbed by what he saw, he had been in the old wars against the Vintals a brutal people who had done horrible things to warriors they had captured.

Tanny stepped forward and Sapir raised his hand. He indicated for Tanny to not come any closer and not look.

"What is in there Sapir?". Tanny asked unsure if he actually wanted to know.

"A man, well what used to be a man. He has been turned upside down, his throat slit.

He has been skinned from the ankles to the waist. They have castrated him; they have pulled his guts out.

They have tortured this man, possibly to find answers if he has seen us or possibly to find out where the others from this village have gone.

Either way we should leave Taran, there are tracks on the floor. Horse tracks and a cart they may have prisoners.

Taran looked at the track marks on the floor the tracks in the mud were fresh, suggesting someone had left recently.

He managed to compose himself; the rest of the group had now all arrived at the hut in the middle of the settlement.

Dilah helped Taran back to his feet, Taran's stomach had now settled.

"Sapir is right, no more looting we need to leave this place. We don't know if those tracks are from those that caused this or those from this village.

We do not know who may come back, we however are not heading north yet we move now we follow these tracks." Dilah stepped in quick to respond.

"Taran are you crazy, we need to head north. We need to get back to our people and out of these lands.

We owe these people nothing, they are not our kin.

Plus, we do not know who left these tracks it could be the people that have done this"?

Taran stepped towards Dilah making sure the others could see his challenge against Dilah.

"You're right we do not owe these people anything, but we cannot stand by and let what's happened in there happen to another.

No one deserves that, no one.

We follow these tracks, we see what they lead to".

Sapir spoke to break to tension.

"You are both right, so stop arguing each.

Taran you're right no one deserves what that man went through, no one.

Dilah you're right we have no idea of which group those tracks belong to.

But I have seen what these types of shits do to prisoners, I cannot let that happen to someone.

I say we follow the tracks and see where they lead. If it's just the shit bags, then we kill them and take their cart. At least we can have a rest from walking for a bit.

We can take their food and water and then head North.

If it's the people from this settlement, then we leave without being seen and head north as we planned anyway."

Dilah looked around at the settlement, he could see a toy carved from wood by one of the huts. He then looked at the hut with the body.

"Very well, let's follow the tracks but I still think this is a bad idea".

Sapir tapped Dilah on the back acknowledging the change in his decision.

"We have no idea how many we go against; we have no idea how far ahead the tracks go. We need to move fast and make ground but be silent.

Stafan…."

Taran turned to face Stafan, he looked past him over his shoulder. A child was staggering towards them; she was covered in blood and saying something in a language Taran didn't understand.

The bushes behind her started moving and from them emerged two more figures, both adults, also bloodied but holding small swords in their hands and terror in their eyes as they scanned the group for mercy.

The child fell forward, Sapir dropped to his knee and took the child into his arms, blood stains covered the child's clothing. The two adults stood their ground and were joined by several others.

Both groups stood staring at each other in a standoff, either side weighing up the other. Sapir picked up the child and placed him against the hut next to Tanny and Stafan.

The child was badly hurt, Sapir turned to face the strangers who still stood watching the group.

Sapir squared his shoulders to the group; he started to breath heavy.

He started shouting as loud as he could at the strangers in the old language of the Mandji.

As he did so he started drawing his sword and pulled his shield from his back.

He was banging his shield with his sword.

"I am the bringer of death,

From the heart of the Mandji, for war's sacred sake. Drums of my ancestor's thunder in my ears, The spirits march with me, to release all your fears.

I am not man but the Bringer of Death.

My feet shake the earth, my cry chills the air,

I have come for your souls — let your gods be aware."

He then let out a scream loud that echoed through the forest, birds flew from their nests in the trees from the sound.

Sapir started running towards the strangers, followed by the other young warriors.

Stafan drew his bow send arrow after arrow past the heads of his own kin towards the threat.

His second arrow hit one of the strangers taking him off his feet, the warrior hit the floor and laid still as if his spirit left his body the moment he hit the floor.

Taran drew his sword and ran towards the group.

"Tanny, Stefan stays with that child and protect her with your lives.

No matter the cost keeps her safe."

Sapir was now on top of the strangers, every move he made again like a dance against a partner. He let the first warrior swing at him hacking his weapon in his direction.

Was ducking, weaving and leaning away from several strikes.

He parried of two blows that look a threat, and he did it with ease.

He spun to his left swinging his shield arm out as he did knocking a blow away from him. As he spun, he slashed his sword with his right arm hitting the sword of the enemy away causing the sword to leave the warrior's hand.

He continued a full turn, and the shield now came back around, and he used the wooden cover the hit the warriors head stunning the warrior.

He then dropped to one knee and thrust his sword into the gut of the enemy he faced.

The warrior put his hand to his stomach dropping to his knees. Sapir then pulled the sword from the warrior's gut and spun again the other way hacking the sword at the warrior's neck. The sword cut into the flesh of the warrior on his knees spraying blood from his neck.

The warrior then dropped to his left onto the floor; Sapir was instantly back to his feet this time on to the next threat another of the strangers swinging his sword at one of the young Mandji warriors.

Sapir pushed his shield in the way to protect the warrior; he then hit the stranger in the face breaking the stranger's nose. The stranger stumbled back, and Sapir pushed his sword into the throat of the stranger.

An arrow hit one of the strangers next to Sapir knocking him down to his knees. Then another arrow went through the stranger's throat forcing his head back and making him fall back.

A sword swung towards Sapir skimming his cheek leaving a cut to his face.

Taran shoulder barged the stranger over knocking him to his back.

Taran thrust his sword into the warrior's neck.

The other Mandji warriors were fighting shield side by side like they had been trained, working as a group to protect each other.

Stafan and the other archer dropped another two of the strangers with their arrows.

Taran was back another warrior; the warrior was clearly untrained. He swung wildly trying to make contact with Taran trying to get a killing blow.

Taran dodged a slash to his head and drove his sword into the threat's chest, he went to pull the sword out, but it had stuck into the body of the threat.

He kicked the warrior in the chest forcing the warrior to tumble over. He saw another warrior running towards him, saw a spear on the floor and picked it up.

He threw thrust the spear forward the warrior dodged it, Taran blocked a blow aimed for his left side.

He then dodged jumping back to miss another swing of a blade.

Taran then stepped forward thrusting the spear forward catching the warrior in the shoulder. Taran stepped forward forcing the warrior to move backwards with the spear into his shoulder.

Taran pulled the spear from the warrior's shoulder and quickly thrust the spear into the stomach of the warrior.

Taran heard shouting and looked around; he could see the strangers now running from them into the forest.

"Do not follow" Taran shouted out allowed.

"Hold here"

The strangers ran away leaving their inured behind dying.

Taran looked at Sapir who was breathing heavy, he was covered in blood some his own most from the others he had killed.

"Sapir" Taran called to try and get his attention.

Sapir was staring deep into the woods watching the those that had got away.

Sapir stepped forwards in their direction.

"Sapir" this time Taran shouted bringing Sapir back from his lust for blood.

"Let them go Sapir, you have killed enough today."

Sapir turned and looked at Taran then back to the forest, he turned towards Taran and walked up to him.

"Those pigs shall be hung upside down and cut from groin to sternum if I ever come across them again" Taran said looking at Taran. He then walked past Taran and back to the child.

Sapir got closer to Tanny and Stefan and stood near to the child.

"Is she still with this world" Sapir asked.

"Yes Sapir, we protected her she is safe" Sapir noted several warriors around Tanny and Stafan. They had fought protecting her with their lives.

Sapir looked down at the child and kneeled beside her.

"She will recover; she will be safe and looked after.

We will protect you little one, we will get you to some help".

Taran stood next to Sapir. "We are closer to Karathat than home Sapir, for us to get help we must take her there. It's dangerous for us to go that way, we look like a raiding party.

We could take her along the way and if we see a villager we could let them look after her."

"No, we can't leave her. We saved her life. Her spirit is now ours to protect, we must take her to somewhere she will be safe.

We cannot take her to our lands.

The journey is too far, but Karathat is closer. The queen there looks after those in need in her palace I have heard this" Sapir was stroking the child's hair.

"Ok Sapir but I cannot force the others to come with us. It will be their choice to head home or come with us." Taran turned to go and speak with the others.

He left Sapir to stay with the child, Tanny and Stefan stayed with Sapir they had already decided they were now invested in the girl's future and would be heading to Karathat with Sapir.

Taran met with the others and started to make a case to go to Karathat. Only time would tell if Sapir would get help from the others.

His hands still shook from the skirmish, his heart still beating hard. He had not had that rage in him for many years, not since he lost his wife and child.

ॐ

CHAPTER 7

Tamanda had been nonstop training with the recruits, her
training had been hard and the trainers brutal.

She had been beaten on more than one occasion during
combat training; she had earned respect from the recruits after
being victorious against some of them in combat trials.

It had however come at a cost, the trainers who had been
in charge of those she had beat had occasionally taken offence.
They were mocked by senior trainers for their students losing to
a woman, this only encouraged them to be more brutal with her
during combat drills and issuing punishments for mistakes
made.

The mornings had all been early starts, waking up at
sunrise then running the city walls or swimming the ocean
coastline for three kilometres. One recruit had been taken by a
shark during the swimming trials, but they still continued with
them regardless.

After the morning exercises it was a focus on weapons from
distance such as archery, Tamanda had discovered she was a
good shot using the small hunting bows. She had yet to be
punished for missing a target hitting the chest mass target
every time.

After archery it was onto unarmed combat which was a mix
of wrestling, striking and limb locks, she had struggled in this
section of the trials. She had to rely on speed and agility, but
her fellow recruits often used brute strength and force when
striking her.

She had been stunned a few times from elbow strikes and
punches in close quarters.

Her advantage was speed and agility and the blocking techniques her father had taught her. She knew she would never knock her opponent out with strikes and often relied on her armlocks and take
downs using her opponent's weight against them.

After combat training they would have food followed by another run before moving onto weapons training. Here she flourished with a sword and small shield, her speed and agility worked in her favour.

Then it was tactic training until sundown then after that it was bed. They were not allowed to have food or drink that affected their training, so wine was prohibited.

Tamanda was not separated from the other recruits, the first week a few of the recruits had made comments to her about not going to sleep. As she endured training, she had earned their respect a little however the comments and jokes still came.

The light was shining through the window, Tamanda was sat at the table eating her food. She was sitting with a few of her fellow recruits; their final combat training was due after lunch.

A voice spoke out catching Tamanda off guard "who do you think
Tamanda?"

The question surprised Tamanda, she had been deep in thought thinking about how far she had come.

She looked up and was being looked at by a young recruit.

"Who do I think, what?" She replied.

"Who do you think will be the hardest trainer to fight a in the trial?".

The recruits would be facing a trainer selected by Zarratt who would choose a tile at random with a trainer's name on it, the fighters would then be allowed to make a choice of which weapons they would like to use.

Tamanda thought for a moment, she had gone against many of the students and beat some.

She knew that whoever she faced would want to prove a point against her, many did not approve of her being selected.

"I think trainer zhomat would be the most I would fear, he is fast, agile, has great form when showing us techniques during his demonstrations he has never been close to being hit by anyone.

Thankfully he is not taking part in the trials this year, but even so, his influence lingers among the trainers who learned under him, shaping their tactics."

One of the training assistants walked in, he stood in the door as if he was in charge, the assistant trainers were just those who had come to the end of their military service and selected by Zarratt to become a trainer.

They worked as an assistant to the trainers for a year while they were shown training methods.

"Your trials will start in one hour, get your things together.

Write your letters to your loved ones, leave your mark on the letter should you wish your one-year military pay would go to your loved ones should the worst happen.

The list order is on the table in the training room.

Good luck"

The recruits around Tamanda started to get up and clear their food away, Tamanda could hear them discussing who wanted to go first and who wanted to go last.

A young warrior spoke loud for his friends to hear. "Well, we know Tamanda should be last, they will want to quickest test to be the final trial" his friends who stood with him laughed and patted him on the back and then they walked out of the seating area.

Tamanda got up from her chair and cleared her food away, she finished her water and began to make her way to the training room.

When she arrived, several recruits were looking at the list. Tamanda walked up and could see she was to go sixth in the trials.

She was after a young recruit called Larson; she had worked with him on occasion. He was a good fighter, but he was young and on occasion became too aggressive in his attacks.

The recruits had started to fill out into the main training grounds. Tamanda followed and walked out to stand in her place.

The training ground was a large gravel square; there were high walls used for climbing training and rocks and wooden blocks used to build strength. The far end had wooden posts for weapons training.

To the left stood thirty of the trainers all ready to take part in the trials that would take place today. They stood in their battle clothes a mix and their choice of weapons.

Some were dressed in leather padded armour, some dressed in just bottom layers only with their chests bare.

In the middle of the training ground stood a large wooden frame with a deck, this was where the trials would take place, a stage that was around twenty meters square, this would be the stage that sealed their fate. The rules to the trial were simple.

If you fell or get pushed off the stage, you do not pass your training.

If you were knocked out, you did not pass.

If you were severely injured, you did not pass the trial.

Minor scratches were frowned upon but expected.

Two rounds the first hands and unarmed combat, there was striking, blocking, wrestling and arm locks. If you tapped out or got knocked out, you were out of the trials.

The second round introduced weapons combat to first blood, each opponent would choose their own weapons.

Storia had decided she would choose a short shield and sword and small axe that could be wielded or thrown.

Zarratt came and stood on the viewing balcony, he was accompanied by Storia. Tamanda could see Storia looking into the crowd, she hoped that she would make Storia proud for selecting her.

Zarratt stepped forward. His armour bearing the scars of battles long past. His voice steady, roughened by years, but heavy with pride.

"You stand here not because you're the strongest. Not because you're the fastest. But because something inside you refused to settle you showed us something inside you.

Soon you will face your trial by combat. The Guardianship does not call lightly. It calls those willing to bleed for something greater than themselves.

Some of you will pass—and should you do so, you will rise as

Guardians: defenders of the realm, protectors of the sacred trust.

Some of you will not—and that is no shame. You will return to your units with heads held high, having dared to step into the arena when others would not.

And some… some of you may fall.

If you die, you will not be forgotten. Your names will be carved into the stone halls, where the light never fades and the brave are always remembered.

There is no dishonour in fear. But let courage drive you through it. Let purpose steady your blade.

Fight with everything you are. And no matter the outcome, walk onto that fighting square knowing this: you have already set yourselves apart from the ordinary.

Good luck to you all. The realm is watching; your queen is watching".

Zarratt stepped towards the tiles, it was time, Judd was the first for the trials a young warrior only just eighteen years of age. He had been one of the first to welcome Tamanda to the training, he had shared food with her and told her stories of his family who lived on a small farming village. He stood proud with his gornat it was a curved blade on a wooden pole, Tamanda had watched his training with the weapon it was a perfect weapon for him.

Zarratt pulled a tile from the many in front of him, he looked at the tile his facial expression giving nothing away.

"Judd will face, Harlem".

The trainers let out a cry raising their weapons above their head as a salute to the first chosen.

A warrior stepped forward and made his way up the stairs, Harlem was similar to Judd in size. Both of them stood around five feet eight inches tall, Judd was slenderer with a youthful muscular body shape.

Harlam in the other hand looked as if he had been training for many years, he was muscular and in shape, he had scars across his chest and arms from either battles or trials.

Judd made his way to the stage walking up the stairs, he handed his gornat to one of the guardsmen standing at the top of the stairs.

Harlam was on his side of the square stretching out his limbs, all the time staring at Judd in an attempt to intimidate him. Judd stood staring back at Harlam bouncing up and down from one foot to the other.

Zarratt waved to the battle master who was in charge of the day's trials, he called both fighters in and reminded them of the rules making sure both understood them.

Both fighters nodded then were sent back to their sides of the square. The battle master stood in the middle of the ring and then gave the signal to start.

Both Judd and Harlam walked to the middle of the square and held their nearest hand to each other and tapped their fists together out of respect.

They then began circling, the trials had started.

Harlam started launching strikes first he threw a left jab followed by a right straight then a left hook, Judd used his guard to block the first two punches then dipped low to let the hook go over his head.

As Judd dipped, he stepped to his right allowing him a better angle, he then threw his right hand connecting with the left side of Harlams face. The strike made Harlem turn and stagger to the right, Harlam gained his balance and spat blood from his mouth.

He nodded and smiled at Judd acknowledging the first to make contact. Harlam circled again while Judd kept his guard up, he knew Harlam was now engaged in the fight. Harlam came rushing in this time delivering a combination of strikes, Judd managed to either block or dodge the first few however Harlam delivered a punch to the body that connected forcing the wind from Judds lungs. Judd staggered back trying to get air into his lungs, Harlam closed the gap and grabbed Judd by the neck. He placed both arms round the back of Judds neck creating a vice with his forearms on either side of Judds throat.

Harlam then pulled Judd forward and to his left forcing Judd of balance, Harlam jumped and brought his right knee up delivering a knee strike to Judds left hitting his ribs. Judd clenched up from the pain, before Harlam could jump and bring the left knee up Judd managed to tuck his right arm into his ribs to protect his body.

Harlam then pulled Judd forward off balance again and then threw him towards the floor. Judd staggered forward falling off balance into his front. He managed to roll to his right before Harlam could stamp down onto him.

Judd quickly got to his feet and got int to a guard stance, his feet wide, deep and diagonal. His stance bladed with an athletic bend in his knees. His left arm out and up for distance and range keep the gap, his right arm however was tucked slightly to his ribs suggesting that it was a weak spot and in pain.

Harlam moved towards Judd aiming for a low kick to the shin, Judd was quick to move his feet and dodge to attack. He jumped forward bringing his right arm back and deliver a punch to Harlam quickly. The punch connected this time on Harlams nose, there was a loud crunch and then blood came from the nose.

Judd followed his punch up quickly while Harlam was dazed striking Harlam twice in stomach knocking the wind from Harlam. Judd moved in quick pressing on not allowing Harlam to catch his breath.

Judd stepped in quick putting his right arm across hitting the back of his elbow into the chest of Harlam, as he did, he struck his arm back and turned his right hip and leg into Harlams left hip.

Judd took Harlam off his feet with a leg sweep, Harlam fell into his back, Judd then jumped and span in the air his leg stretched out as if swimming a weapon in the air to generate speed and power into his leg which was swinging towards Harlam.

Harlam managed to quickly roll to his right as Judd hit the floor and his spinning kick just missing Harlam.

Both combatants quickly got to their feet and faced each other, both now sporting and injury from the trial so far.

Harlam held his hands up in front of him, his arms at ninth degree angles, he walked on the balls of his feet ready to strike.

This time Judd rushed forward as he did Harlem delivered a front kick with his left foot catching Judd in the chest. This made Judd stumble back off balance, Harlam followed this up stepping forward and then spun on his left foot delivering a back spinning kick striking Judd again in the chest. Judd stumbled back to the edge of the platform; he was right on the edge.

Harlam charged forward to try and deliver a blow to knock him off, as Harlam got close, he threw another front kick this time Judd stepped aside to his right forcing the kick to miss.

Judd balance on his right foot as he stepped and delivered a kick to the back leg of Harlam countering his kick. This forced Harlams leg to buckle and give way.

He fell to the floor and Judd was quick to jump onto of him. Harlam was in his front and Judd had jumped onto his back. He wrapped his legs around Harlams waist, he quickly looped his arm around the Harlams neck, with the crook of the elbow under the chin. The other arm placed on the back of Harlams head, pushing it forward. He had got Harlam into a choke hold.

Harlam began to try and deliver strikes to Judd with his elbows, but this did not work, he then tried to pull Judds arm forward from his neck to create a gap to drop his chin into. He needed to prevent the arm from squeezing the blood flow.

Harlam fought as much as he could but as he did his vision was going blurry, he was desperately trying to get from the grip Judd had placed on.

Judd was squeezing tighter and tighter, the pain from his ribs had faded.

The punches and strikes coming from Harlam were becoming softer and softer.

Harlam was not yet out of the fight he again tried to create a gap, but it was not working.

Harlam was saved as the horn to stop to round blew, Judd was pulled away from Harlam by the guardsmen and Harlem was allowed to breath.

Everyone watched for a second to see if Harlam got up, Judd watched as Harlam managed to roll onto his side. Harlam then sat up managing to come to his senses. He looked over to Judd and pointed at him while clapping.

"You nearly got me little man, nearly."

Harlam was helped to his feet by the guardsman from his corner.

Judd walked to the corner where a guardsman handed him his weapon.

Both of the combatants were given five minutes to get their kit together and recover from round one.

Judd stood at his corner, he wore a light leather padded armour top, he chose to wear a guardsman helmet. The helmet did not have a face colour on it; this was only given to you if you passed your trials.

Judd stood with his gornat staff in his hand; it rested on the floor and reached as far as his shoulder. The long-curved blade glistened in the sun, Judd was confident in his abilities, he was close to beating him in the first round now he would demonstrate his skills with his weapon.

Harlam stood from his corner, he wore a guardsman helmet with full face covering, the mask was that of a creature with long sharp teeth. He wore padded armour covering his shoulders.

His weapon of choice was a small war hammer; it was a small metal hammer about the length of a forearm. On the end of the handle there was a double-sided weapon with one side being a hammer and the other a small blade like an axe. The hilt of the handle also had a point to it for stabbing down like a hammer fist strike.

In his other hand he held a half-moon rest shield, a picture on the shield was that of a lizard with sharp teeth.

It was clear this was something designed for its warrior to look like his face covering.

Both fighters faced into the square and the guardsmen overlooking the fight reminded them of the rules and to defend themselves at all costs.

He then checked with them both to continue and neither side backed down.

He then signalled for the round to start, both fighters stepped forward. Harlam tapped his shield front with his hammer and pointed it towards Judd saluting him out of respect.

Judd responded by tilting his blade to the floor then back up, Judd held his blade in his hands keeping Harlam at distance.

Harlam lunged forward in an attempt to get inside the spear type weapons range. Judd countered the manoeuvre using small smooth swings of his blade,

Harlam struck the blade with his hammer forcing the pole to Judds right. Judd span to his right dodging the attack while swinging the blade and staff round behind him looking to strike Harlams right upper arm.

The blow missed Harlam by inches as he managed to dodge back and lean back from the blade, Judd set his feet quickly steeping forward towards Harlam. Judd set his hands and thrust his blade towards Harlam.

Harlam managed to place his shield in between him and the blade just in time. The tip striking the shield with enough force it made Harlam step backwards.

Judd dropped into a low crouch position bringing handle of the staff to his hip keeping the tip towards Harlam.

Harlam stepped to his right; Judd countered every step keep the distance between them.

Harlam grounded his feet; he turned the ball of his back foot into ground.

Harlam lunged forward striking the end of Judds spear with his shield in his left hand, the spear tip moved to his right. Harlam spun swinging his sword arm round using the point on the base of his weapon to try and strike.

Judd's staff tip was knocked aside, Judd could see Harlam spinning and noticed the hammer fist coming. Judd pulled his right hand from the base of his garnot pulling a small blade from the handle a secret blade hiding as the handle. Judd ducked and dropped his garnot. He rushed forward seeing a gap in Harlams defence, as he rushed in Judd held the knife in his right hand and sliced Harlams right thigh as he rushed past and rolled forward. He used his speed to get up into a standing position from his forward roll, he turned to face Harlam who stood still looking down at his leg.

Blood started to pour from Harlams leg, Harlam dropped to one knee and placed his sword and shield on the floor. He looked up at Judd and put his fist to his chest acknowledging defeat.

The guardsmen in Judds corner raised his flag green indicating that Judd was the victor, the recruits erupted congratulating their first warrior of the day passing his trial.

Tamanda smiled she was please Judd had made it through; he had wanted to be a guardsman like his father had been many years before him.

Tamanda watched on waiting for the next warrior to face their opponent, she stood waiting nervously for her turn.

৵

CHAPTER 8

They had been moving for just under a week since their skirmish saving the young child, Sapir had not spoken much most of his time was spent caring for the child. He carried the child a large portion of the time swapping with Tanny only for a short while to allow himself to get some rest.

The child had not spoken at all since they found her, her wounds had been very minor with cuts to her arms and legs.

She had clung to Sapir and Tanny having built a trust with them that they would not hurt her, Dilah walked alongside Taran he had been quiet since the vote. He had wanted to head back to their own lands; he believed that they should have taken the child with them in the direction of home and dumping the child at the first village they came across. The vote quickly turned into a heated debate which did not go in Dilahs favour, the group decided to head to Karathat to take the child closer to a safe place.

The journey had been hard but there had been no sign of search parties, scouting parties or even villagers after them. They had seen smoke in the air a few times which they believed had been from the war party that they had come across in the long grass.

Taran walked to stay with Dilah for the time being. "Dilah, can I ask you a question?"

Dilah didn't look at him at first. The air grew still, as if waiting. Then, with the faintest turn of their head, eyes like distant stars settled on him.

"You just did, young one," Dilah said, voice smooth as worn stone. "In the old tongue, we called that a waste. Try again—if you think the next will echo longer."

Taran swallowed, heat rising to his cheeks. He squared his shoulders, pushing down the urge to look away.

"Do you know what happened to Sapir's family?" he asked, his voice quieter now, touched with unease.

"He wanted to leave back at the village. Yet when he saw that little girl, he changed.

I saw his face change—from an old warrior to something different. Something dark.

It was as if something took over him… like he became a vengeful spirit."

Dilah did not respond at once. They turned their gaze from Sapir and looked to the horizon, where the sun had begun to bleed gold across the jagged hills. A silence fell, not empty, but listening.

"There are names for what you saw," Dilah said at last. "But none that the young are meant to speak."

Their voice carried no warmth, only the weight of old knowledge, too heavy for most.

"Sapir's family died in fire," Dilah said, voice low and steady.

"A raid came in the dead of night. The raiders showed no mercy—they set the village ablaze, flames licking through wood and flesh alike."

"It was a fire that does not leave ash—only memory. The kind that burns inside a man's soul."

"He has carried that fire like a second spine ever since, after that raid the Vintals disappeared from their lands no trace left behind. Now they are back it seems and back to raiding villages".

Taran frowned. "So, it really was something… more?" Dilah nodded, slowly.

"Grief can be quiet, like falling snow. But if it festers too long in the dark, it becomes something else." Their eyes narrowed slightly.

"He was not taken by a spirit. He became one—if only for a mo-ment. That is what war does, when the soul no longer shields itself."

They looked back at Sapir, and for the first time, their voice sharpened—not cruel, but cold and pointed.

"You would do well to remember that. Before it happens to you."

Taran's brow furrowed. Dilah's words settled in his chest like stone—heavy and unmovable. He hesitated, then asked:

"And the girl? Who was she? She wasn't from the village. I've never seen eyes like that… she didn't even flinch when the fighting started."

Dilah exhaled softly, the faintest sound—less a sigh, more the breath of memory stirring.

"No," Dilah said. "She was not from the village. Nor from anywhere you would know."

They turned again, eyes distant, as if seeing something far beyond the hills.

"There are threads that run through the world, old and hidden. That child is one of them."

Taran felt a chill pass through him, though the wind was still. "She looked at Sapir like she knew him. Like she'd been waiting." Dilah's gaze returned to him—calm, unreadable.

"Some things wear the shape of children but are not. Some are born touched by forces older than time. And some… some are simply meant to bear witness."

Taran's voice dropped, unsure if he even wanted the answer.

"Which was she?"

Dilah was silent for a moment longer than comfort allowed. Then:

"That remains to be seen. But mark this—wherever she walks next, change will follow."

They reached Stafan who was standing looking out on top of a hill, they looked out and found they had reached destination, the city of Karathat.

It was the centre of the lands of Karathat people, everything came and went through the city, they could see carts on the main road going towards the city.

Taran spoke up "Let's get moving, it will take us a couple of days to get to the gates".

The days blurred into one another. The roads turned from dust to cobble, then back to dust again. Villages came and went—some welcoming, some wary, all carrying whispers of unrest. At night, they camped under crooked trees or beneath the half-ruined eaves of forgotten watch posts, trading stories in hushed voices while the fire cracked low.

The closer they drew to the city gates, the more the land seemed to hold its breath. Farmers paused mid-swing with their sickles to watch them pass. Traders on the road kept their heads down. Even the wind, once playful, now dragged the scent of smoke from somewhere distant faint, but present.

And through it all, Taran kept glancing to the walls that waited in the distance, as unmoving and watchful as the silence between them.

The city had high walls with watch towers for protection from invaders, on the walls they could see guards moving along the walls looking down onto those coming to the city.

The city appeared to be well defended for a nation that had not been to war for a long time, something did not sit right with Taran, but they needed to enter the city.

They walked closer on the road now following the line of people waiting to get into the city, the gates had guards checking carts for occupants before being allowed into through the gates.

Taran noticed that some of the guards were stopping people on foot prior to getting near to the gates, Taran had split the group into two parts believing that it would be best rather than they arrive as a large group.

Dilah had taken his warriors and were told to wait half an hour before coming to the gates. The plan was to enter the city and meet at the temple they had been told about by one of the traders on the carts.

It was the largest temple in the city, its front doors had a symbol of a golden eagle above it, its roof had a high tower that stood high above the other buildings in the city, so it stood out. Taran had made his way to the gates with Tanny, Stafan, Sapir and the young girl, the girl would not let Sapir out of her sight more now than before.

She had started to have nightmares and spent many nights keeping the group awake. Sapir had been allowed to skip any night watch to comfort the girl.

The girl had not spoken much since they rescued her, what little she had spoken could not be understood.

They had managed to learn basic words from her such as food, hungry, water, thirsty and toilet, they had established her name was my Nyla.

Although Sapir had been trying to teach her their own language, she had picked up some words but not many.

Taran was seeing a different side to Sapir, they were seeing Sapir the protector, the teacher, the father figure, Sapir had given Nyla her own nickname calling her "little mouse".

They had finally reached the gates and the guards in front of them started to inspect a cart next to them, the cart owner was speaking to the guards and showing them what was in the back.

One of the guards approached them and older warrior, he stood taller than Taran and was broad in the shoulders.

The guard spoke to Taran, but Taran did not understand what he was saying.

The guard spoke again this time his manner more assertive.

Taran looked at the guard and spoke to him.

"We are here for food and water; we would like an audience with the queen. We have come from the Mandji tribe and need to speak to the queen."

The guard looked at Taran and started speaking again, the trader on the cart being searched started to laugh.

He looked at Taran and pointed at the guards.

"You expect these bottom feeders to understand your language boy; they are the arms of queen not the brains.

You would be better off talking to my horse, at least she knows some Mandji words".

Taran looked surprised at the trader.

"You speak our language trader, at least enough for me to understand, how come?"

The trader walked over to Taran.

"I am a trader; I travel far and wide. I have spent time trading in your lands; I spent some time with a few villages learning the language while trading." Taran looked around at the guards.

"What is he asking?".

The trader walked to stand next to the guard.

"He wants to know what your purpose is for coming to the city?".

Taran shifted uneasily, the sun casting long shadows through the iron teeth of the gate behind them. The guards watched with narrow eyes, hands resting on spear shafts, unmoving but alert.

He cleared his throat.

"Tell him, "He said, lifting his chin, "I've come to seek audience with the queen. I bring a message… and a warning."

The trader relayed the words in fluid, practiced tones. The guard's expression remained unreadable. A long pause followed. Then he barked something sharp and brief.

The trader glanced back to Taran. "You will be taken to the holding quarters. The queen will be told, but whether she chooses to hear your words… that is her decision."

Taran narrowed his eyes. "I haven't come all this way to be locked in a cell."

The trader gave a slight shrug, not unsympathetic. "This is a city that forgets nothing and trusts less. Strangers do not walk straight into their halls—not without being bled first."

He allowed the guards to take his sword. It left his hip like a parting limb.

As he was led beneath the walls and through the iron gate, the trader fell in step beside him.

"You're either brave," the man said quietly, "or a fool to come here with only words."

Taran didn't look at him. "Sometimes words are all that's left before the fire."

Sapir carried the young girl, while Tanny handed his weapons over.

Stafan was more reluctant to hand his bow over; he did so warn the guard that took it from him to look after it.

The guardsmen took them to the palace gates; he walked them through the main courtyard out to the training square. They walked past a large wooden frame; the frame had a stage and appeared to have some blood staining on steps that lead up to the stage.

Taran wondered what competition had happened on the stage. The tribes on his lands held games every year—a mix of fighting, weapons skill, archery, and slings. But this… this had the scent of something harsher.

The bloodstains were too fresh. Too dark. This wasn't the remnant of sport, but of judgment, a test.

The guards said nothing as they passed, their boots thudding dully on the packed earth. Beyond the stage, soldiers sparred in pairs—shields clashing, blades ringing, fists thudding into flesh. But even their movements paused as Taran and his companions were led through. Eyes followed him. Not curious measuring.

As they reached the far end of the training square, an older man stepped out from the colonnade. His armour was less polished, more worn, but the way the guards straightened at his presence told Taran all he needed to know. This was no servant of ceremony—this was a man who bled beside his soldiers.

The man's gaze swept over them, lingering on Taran.

"You're the one who carries the warning," he said, his voice like old stone.

Taran nodded, unsure whether to speak yet.

The man jerked his head toward a shaded alcove near the palace wall. "You'll wait there until the queen and her advisors send for you. Speak to no one unless spoken to. And do not leave the square."

Taran clenched his jaw but gave a single nod. He had known he would not be welcomed with open arms. Not here.

As he stepped toward the alcove, he glanced back at the stage.

Not a place for celebration, he thought. A place of reckoning.

And something told him he or one of his groups would be standing on it before long.

The sun had begun its slow descent behind the city walls, casting long golden streaks across the stones of the training square. The clang of steel and the bark of commands faded as the day's drills came to an end. Taran sat beneath the alcove's shade, his back against the cool stone, legs stretched before him. He had not spoken since being led here. Neither had the guards.

Time passed like molasses. A test, he suspected. To see if he would grow impatient, demand an audience, or falter under the weight of silence.

He did none of those things.

Finally, as the shadows deepened, a different kind of silence fell. The kind that came before something important. The kind that made even the bird's hush.

A younger guard—not the ones who brought him—approached.

He bowed, stiffly, as if unused to such gestures.

"The Queen is ready to see you now."

Taran stood, brushing the dust from his tunic. His legs were stiff, but his resolve was solid. He glanced once more toward the stage at the centre of the square, the others were already following the guard he turned and followed the others toward the palace doors, heart steady, but senses sharpened.

He had come to deliver a message. Whether they welcomed it—or him—no longer mattered.

The Queen was waiting. And with her, the fate of more than just this city.

~~~~~~~~~~~~~~~~~~~~~~~~~~~~~~~

The Natsu commander stood on the ridge above the valley, his dark eyes narrowing as he watched the last of the smoke from the battle drift lazily into the sky. His name was Rakah, and though he was younger than most commanders in the eastern ranks, none questioned his place. His bow rested
~~~~~~~~~~~~~~~~~~~~~~~~~~~~~~~

against his back; blood still crusted at the edge of the carved grip. His fingers, bandaged from use, tapped against his thigh in an unconscious rhythm of calculation.

Below, Mandji prisoners were being marched between ranks of Natsu warriors, stripped of weapons and dignity. The cries of the wounded rose faintly from the valley floor, a low murmur that sounded almost like wind through dead trees.

Rakah turned to the man beside him—older, broad across the shoulders and wearing a cloak of black hide. Drahk, war-chosen of the Natsu high council. Silent, dangerous, loyal only to the future.

"You said there would be more of them," Rakah said flatly.

"There were," Drahk replied. "They fled. North."

Rakah's brow tightened. "Untrained warriors do not cause the kind of damage we saw in our flank. Someone trained them.
And someone will want to know what they saw."

Drahk made no expression. "Let them run. Their fear will do more damage than a sword."

Rakah looked toward the horizon. "Fear can be cured. Knowledge cannot be unlearned. If they reach the border, the elders will be forced to respond. Karathat is already watching. We are being drawn into something larger."

Drahk said nothing, but the flicker in his gaze betrayed agreement.

A distant horn sounded from the northern slope. A Natsu scout, mounted and dust-covered, galloped toward them. He dismounted before the command ridge, saluted, and held out a small bundle wrapped in green fabric.

Rakah took it.

Inside was a Vintal sigil. The embroidery was unmistakable—gold thread, cracked with age but still gleaming. With it a message for the Natsu commander:

"The rivers have dried. The wolves now come to drink at the well."

Drahk read it, then spat. "Code."

Rakah nodded. "And a warning."

There was a pause between them, heavy with what it meant. If the Vintals were breaking silence, reaching out in metaphor and secrets, it meant they were not yet dead. It meant the North was not quite by accident.

"We need to move," Rakah said, slipping the sigil into his belt. "Get the warbands into the hills. We'll hunt these survivors ourselves. And if they've reached Karathat—" he paused, his voice lowering "—we'll make sure the Queen understands exactly what it means to shelter enemies of the Natsu."

Drahk gave a thin smile. "So, the real war begins."

"No," Rakah said. "This is just the shadow of it."

They turned from the ridge, leaving the bloodied valley behind. In the still air, the black-and-crimson banners of the Natsu rose higher, catching the wind like knives.

Bodies of Mandji warriors left in the field, some being looted for their valuables, others still being killed slow and painful deaths.

&

CHAPTER 9

Tamanda had stood on the training ground watching the trials, so far, she had seen four trials come to completion with the fifth trial currently under way.

The first trial she had seen her friend Judd come out victorious, the two trials after had not gone the recruit's way. In the second trial the recruit had got to the weapons stage just like Judd before him. However, during the trial, the trainer had managed to cut the recruits chest, and this was deemed a failure.

In the third stage the recruit had been knocked out in the unarmed combat stage after taking a punch to his chin near to the end of the round. He had done well, however as he rushed in to try and take the trainer to the floor, the trainer managed to throw a jab and then a hook connecting for a knockout blow.

The fourth trial has gone to weapons combat and deemed in the recruit's favour; the trainer had not managed to get a first blood cut to the recruit and recruit had not managed to cut the trainer. He was deemed test passed as he had not got hurt and considered survived.

The current trial was not looking good for the recruit; Larson she recalled was the fighter before her. He had pressed the attack from the start of the fight and now the weapons trial.

He was tiring as his attacks were quickly knocked away and then countered.

He had been nearly cut a few times already, just managing to get his shield in the way to save him.

The trainer had been holding back only counter attacking at this stage conserving his energy.

The trainer stood in the centre of the square his shield in front of him, his stance wide and his sword held above his right shoulder in his right hand with the point forward.

The round was coming to an end in its last moments; the trainer suddenly sprang forward swinging the blade from right to left at head height. Larson held his shield up blocking the first strike.

The trainer followed the strike up with another this time from left to right, Larson blocked it with his sword.

Then another over the top and over hand strike hacking downwards forcing Larson to raise his shield and block again with his shield.

He came again this time punching forward with his own shield into Larson chest. Larson staggered backward managing to see the next strike a lunge coming straight towards him, he pulled his shield across the front of him forcing the tip of the sword to strike his shield.

The trainer stood in front of Larson staring at him with his sword still in place pointing at Larson, his shield resting on his arm above his head.

The trainer stood in front of Larson; his sword still aimed at him like a warning.

Neither of them moved. The only sounds were Larson's breath—ragged and sharp—and the dull thrum of blood in his ears.

Then the trainer spoke, calm and flat. "You held."

Larson gave a slight nod, trying not to collapse from the strain. His arms were trembling, his shield heavy as stone.

"Next time," the trainer said, lowering his sword, "if someone presses you like that, you strike back."

He turned and walked off the square, not bothering to look over his shoulder.

Larson stayed there for a moment, frozen, the heat of the fight still burning in his limbs. Then slowly, he lowered his shield.

The round was over he had passed the trial.

It was Tamanda's turn to take the steps to the stage, she stood looking up at Zarratt waiting for him to select who she would do combat with by pulling out the tile with their name.

He approached the tiles, his fingers hovering over them for a moment. The small carved stones sat in a shallow bronze bowl, each bearing the name of a warrior who had proven themselves in combat trials already. The air was thick with expectation, the crowd silent except for the soft whisper of the wind across the square.

Zarratt closed his eyes and reached in.

The tile scraped faintly against the others as he drew one out and held it high. The name was etched clearly.

"Karuun!" he called.

A low murmur passed through the gathered crowd. Karuun was known for his brutal speed, a whirlwind of strikes and fury. Tamanda did not flinch. Her shoulders remained square, chin lifted. She climbed the stairs getting the tie stage and turned to face the opposite side of the stage as Karuun stepped forward.

He was already bouncing on the balls of his feet, a grin pulling at the corners of his mouth.

Zarratt gave a single nod.

Zarratt raised his hand. "This round: unarmed. First to yield, or unconscious."

He dropped his hand, round one had begun.

Karuun moved first, fast despite his size. He lunged with a sweeping kick meant to knock her footing, but Tamanda leapt over it, twisting mid-air and landing lightly. She struck out with a sharp elbow toward his ribs, but he caught it with a forearm block and countered with a knee aimed at her gut.

She twisted sideways, the knee grazing her hip, and drove her palm up under his chin. His head snapped back, but he recovered quickly, launching a flurry of strikes—left jab, right hook, low sweep. Tamanda ducked and weaved, absorbing one hit on her shoulder before she closed the distance and grappled.

Their bodies collided with a smack of skin and muscle. Karuun tried to overpower her, arms wrapping around her torso to lift and slam—but Tamanda dropped her weight, shifting her hips and flipping him over her shoulder.

He hit the ground hard—but rolled with it, sweeping her legs out as she turned. They both hit the floor in a tangle.

Tamanda scrambled to mount him; Karuun blocked her knee with his forearm and kicked her off. She landed on her side, rolled, and was up again just as he charged.

Their fists met in mid-air—hers to his jaw, his to her cheek—and they both staggered. Blood ran from Tamanda's lip. Karuun had a welt swelling under his eye.

The crowd was roaring now.

They circled each other, both breathing heavy, both bruised. Karuun feinted left, then lunged right. Tamanda anticipated it, ducked, and delivered a punch to his ribs. He grunted but kept moving, slamming his shoulder into her and sending them both crashing down again.

This time neither rose quickly. They grappled on the floor, elbows and knees flying, each trying to pin the other. Tamanda wrapped her legs around his torso, but he drove his forehead forward—almost headbutting her—and she had to break the hold.

Then they both froze, chests heaving, sweat dripping onto the stage. Each had the other in a deadlock—her forearm across his neck, his hand gripping her wrist with the other cocked back for a final strike.

Zarratt stepped forward, raising his hand high. "Enough!"
The crowd fell silent.

Zarratt's voice rang out. "Tamanda and Karuun. Round one is a Draw."

Neither of them moved for a moment, then slowly, Tamanda released her hold and rolled off. Karuun sat up and nodded once, still catching his breath.

They stood side by side, bruised and battered, but with the fire of warriors in their eyes. And though there was no victor, neither had lost. The crowd gave its approval with a thunderous stomp of feet and hands across the square.

Both went to their corners to get some rest and collect their weapons for round two.

Tamanda could feel her jaw aching, her lips swelling from the hit to the face she had taken.

She looked across to Karuun he sat watching Tamanda.

The guardsman in her corner had placed her weapons on the floor next to her. She collected her weapons and stood up from her chair.

Karuun stood from his chair back to bouncing on the balls of his feet. His twin blades rested against his back, curved and sharpened like snake's fangs.

Both looked at Zarratt who raised his hand. "Round two, begin"

Karuun exploded forward like a storm breaking, blades out, spinning low then rising in a sharp arc. Tamanda stepped back once, twice, her body flowing like water. She drew her weapon a sword short and light, she had it made but the armourer specifically for her needs and talents - she brought it up in time to catch one of Karuun's blades with a metallic crack.

The force pushed her back a step, but she pivoted, redirected his momentum, and spun behind him. Her sword struck out, tip end aimed at the back of his thigh.

He twisted just in time, the strike glancing him, and brought a blade up to swipe at her exposed flank. Tamanda ducked under it, rolled forward, and came up with her sword slicing in a wide arc.

The fight became a dance of violence. Blow and counterblow. Gasp and roar. Tamanda's calm precision met Karuun's savage fury in a clash of sweat and steel.

Then—an opening.

Karuun overextended. His blade struck nothing but air.

Tamanda stepped in, twisted, and swept his legs out from under him.

He hit the ground hard, his blades scattering.

Tamanda flicked her sword towards Karuun catching his shoulder drawing first blood.

She stepped back, breathing heavily, her chest rising and falling with exertion. Karuun looked up at her from the ground.

Zarratt's voice boomed over the square.

"Tamanda, victorious!"

The crowd erupted, not with wild cheers but with the deep, respectful roar of warriors honouring a new peer.

Tamanda inclined her head, then turned and began to walk off the stage. She had passed the trial.

Karuun let out a large scream, he reached for his blades and charged at Tamanda. His face red with anger, his face showing only anger.

He started swinging his blades wildly at Tamanda, she turned and stepped back allowing her some space to move and set her feet.

The blows came down smashing into Tamanda's shield, Karuun was a different fighter from the before. He attacked with anger swinging wildly trying to hit Tamanda.

Some of the other trainers started running up the stage steps to try and intervene, they reached the stage as Karuun made his next attack.

Tamanda was only defending the blows that came at her, she had yet to attack back. Karuun swung his blades again forcing Tamanda to block using her sword and then dodge another swing from Karuun.

She lunged forward kicking Karuun in the chest forcing him to step backwards. The other trainers tried to approach Karuun and stop him.

He pointed his blades to the trainers to warn them off.

The trainers halted at the edge of the stage, uncertain caught between duty and danger. Karuun's chest heaved, blades outstretched, his eyes burning with something beyond rage. Pride. Humiliation. Desperation.

Tamanda stood her ground, shield raised, sword low and ready.

"This is not your way," she said, voice steady. "You lost with honour.

Do not throw it away."

But Karuun roared again and charged.

Tamanda sidestepped, deflecting one blade with her shield and ducking under the second. She didn't strike—still holding back, refusing to meet his fury with more violence.

The crowd had fallen into stunned silence. Even Zarratt had not spoken.

Karuun turned, swinging wide. Tamanda punched her shield out hitting his wrist mid-strike, she stepped in and drove her elbow into his side. He grunted, staggered. Another trainer moved in, but Tamanda held up her hand to stop him.

"This is mine to finish," she said.

Karuun lunged again, but this time slower. Tired. He telegraphed the strike, and Tamanda caught it cleanly—her sword locking with his before she wrenched it from his grasp. One blade clattered to the ground.

He tried to bring up the other, but Tamanda was already inside his reach. She slammed her shield into his chest, knocking the breath from his lungs, and swept his legs out from under him.

Karuun hit the stage hard, his second blade clattering on the ground. Tamanda stood over him, sword raised—but did not strike.

Instead, she tossed her sword aside with a clang and dropped to one knee, pressing her hand against Karuun's chest.

"It's over," she said.

Karuun stared up at her, panting, sweat streaking down his temple. The fire in his eyes was still there, but dimmer now smothered by the weight of shame.

Zarratt finally stepped forward.

"Karuun, you disgrace the rite," he said. "This was a test of spirit, not wrath. You forget yourself."

The trainers moved in now, unopposed. Two of them helped
Karuun to his feet. He did not resist, but his gaze lingered on
Tamanda—less in hate, more in regret.

"You fought well, the best I have seen in the trials this year so far".

Tamanda stood and retrieved her sword. She looked to Zarratt.

"Will there be punishment?" she asked quietly.

Zarratt's eyes flicked to Karuun, then to the watching crowd.

"There will be consequence," he said. "But that decision lies beyond the training square."

He raised a hand toward Tamanda.

"You held the line. Even when tested beyond the trial. You passed—twice."

A new wave of the warriors' roar swept over the square—deeper now, laced with not only respect but awe.

Tamanda bowed her head once more, then stepped down from the stage. Not as a challenger. Not even as a victor.

But as one who had proven herself worthy of something more.

Behind her, Zarratt reached for the bowl once more. The trial was far from over.

৵

CHAPTER 10

Taran stood before two large double doors they were dark in colour with the image of a moon above them. Tanny and Stafan leaned against a wall discussing the food they had been given while they waited.

Sapir was carrying the small child as she slept, the hour was late, and she had been kept busy while they waited with toys provided by the palace staff.

Their weapons had been stripped from them by the house guards as they entered the palace halls, Taran felt as though a piece of him had been taken away like a limb lost from his body.

The doors opened and the guardsmen allowed them all to enter, he stood by the door with another guard on the opposite side to him.

They walked into the room and before them was a large table, sat at the end of a table was Storia and Zarratt both sat waiting for them all to enter into the room.

Storia spoke up and she noticed Sapir carrying the young girl.

"Please there is a soft comfortable bench you may lay her on, there are some cushions, and I shall send my servants to bring her a blanket." The trader that had joined them at the gates was standing next to the queen and was translating to them all.

Sapir acknowledged the suggestion and bowed to the queen, he walked over and laid the child on the bench and sat next to her stroking her hair.

Taran looked around the room they were in, he was in awe at the decorations.

The roof looked like a night sky and the moon appeared to be in the sky with stars all over the ceiling. The table was large enough to seat twelve easily and had a solid wooden frame.

Taran noticed a red mark on the bottom of one of the legs and wondered what it was from.

Storia asked them all to be seated, Tanny and Stafan sat next to each other while Sapir stayed with the young girl. Taran sat opposite Zarratt he noticed a third person in the room back behind Storia and Zarratt. The person was dressed similar to the other guards but had a much smaller frame and the uniform was slightly different. "A female guard" Taran muttered under his breath.

Storia was the first to speak at the table.

"Firstly, let me welcome you to Karathat, we have been very busy today so I must apologise for the delay.

I understand you have a message for me, some information that I need to hear."

Taran sat listening to the trader interpret the words from the queen, he listened to every word the trader said.

He thought hard about how he was going to give the information and wondering if he should hold some of it back.

"Hello, your highness, my name is Taran.

I am of the Mandji tribe to your northern borders. We have travelled for many days in order to give you warning to what we have seen in the west and bring this girl to you which is proof of the threat your people face, we came across her while walking in the Natsu lands to the west.

We found her in a village west of here, the village had been raided and everyone killed. We found a man in one of the huts, he had been skinned on parts of his body. This had been done while he was alive possibly to find out more information as to where the rest of the villagers were.

This girl is the last survivor from that village, when she wakes you can ask her about the incident, however you should know she has bonded with Sapir.

She would not talk to anyone in my camp until Sapir managed to gain her trust."

Storia stopped Taran in his speech.

"Can I ask why you were in the Natsu lands?

To my knowledge you have no alliance with them, it's safe to say tensions are high between your people and the Natsu.

So why were you in their lands?"

Taran thought for a moment about how to answer the question. He looked at Storia trying to judge what answer would be best should he lie about their reason for being in the Natsu lands or should he be truthful and tell all.

Storia sat waiting for her answer, she took a sip of her wine trying to not appear annoyed that she was waiting for a reply.

The temperature in the room had started to drop, the breeze coming in from the ocean side of the room was cold.

Taran shuffled in his chair uncomfortably. He sat up and opened his mouth to speak, but before the words could come, the young girl let out a scream and jolted upright. Sapir was on her in an instant, his arms wrapping around her with practiced ease. He held her close, murmuring soft reassurances as he gently rocked her. His voice slipped into a quiet melody— something old and calming. A lullaby.

Taran watched, his words forgotten. There, in that moment, he saw the man Sapir might've been. The father he had never been allowed to become.

The room settled again. The fire crackled softly in the hearth.

Storia stood without a word, pushing her chair back lightly. She moved toward the door, graceful and unhurried. Taran's eyes followed her, drawn not just by her movement but by something more elusive—an ease she carried despite the tension in the room, the kind of calm that settled into the bones rather than the mind.

She wore a simple white dress that clung to her as she moved. The fabric caught the firelight, throwing soft highlights across her frame.

Her figure was slender, her posture relaxed but purposeful.

Her hair fell loose down her back—mostly brown but kissed by streaks of sun-warmed gold that caught the light with every step.

She reached the doorway and paused, one hand resting lightly on the wooden frame. She glanced back toward Sapir and the girl—checking, perhaps. Or just listening to the song.

Taran couldn't look away.

There was something about her. Not just the way she looked, though that was enough to draw attention. It was something quieter. The way she moved without needing to be seen. The strength in her silence.

He realised his chest had tightened, his breath held somewhere between curiosity and something closer to longing. He barely knew her, and yet, in a room filled with wounds and old ghosts, she stood like something untouched. Or maybe— like someone who had learned how to carry the weight without showing it.

She turned and left the room.

Taran sat back in his chair, the warmth of the fire touching only one side of his face.

He wasn't sure if he'd just seen a ghost walk away… or someone who could teach him how to stop being one.

Taran looked up from the table and found Zarratt watching him closely. The old warrior leaned forward in his chair and muttered something under his breath in a language Taran didn't understand.

He turned instinctively to the trader for a translation.

The trader chuckled. "In short, he says he knows exactly what you're thinking—and advises you to stop thinking it. Apparently, you paid far too much attention to the Queen as she walked out."

Heat rose to Taran's face, but before he could reply, the door creaked open.

Storia returned, carrying a large, folded blanket. She walked straight to Sapir and handed it to him without a word. The little girl in his arms was finally dozing again.

"This will keep her warm," Storia said softly. "She may keep it. You are a good man. She trusts you—clearly."

Sapir gave a quiet nod of thanks, the tired gratitude in his eyes all the answer needed.

Then Storia turned to Taran. Her gaze locked with his, sharp and steady as she stepped toward him.

"Now," she said, voice no longer soft, "tell me what you were doing in the Natsu lands. And how it is you have a girl who speaks our language."

The trader didn't wait—he translated immediately, urgency now tightening the air between them.

Before Taran could speak, the sound of boots echoed down the corridor—heavy, deliberate. The unmistakable rhythm of soldiers in armour. They were running out of time.

Taran stood slowly, speaking clearly.

"Your Highness," he began, "we were ordered by our elders to travel into the Natsu lands. There had been reports— rumours of attacks on your villages to the west. We were sent to investigate and, if necessary, find the raiders and deliver punishment." He paused, gathering the memory.

"We passed through three villages. Burned out. Not a single soul alive. Not even the dead remained."

Storia's expression shifted, just slightly.

"On the third day," he continued, "we walked into an ambush. I believe it was set for us deliberately—but it wasn't raiders, nor slavers.

These were warriors. From both the Natsu tribe and the Vintals." At that, Zarratt let out a grunt.

"Sapir can attest to it," Taran added. "He's fought the Vintals before.

He recognised them."

Storia remained silent, her arms crossed tightly over her chest.

"Nearly all of our group was wiped out. Only those of us here survived. We fled south, then east, crossing into your lands. Our plan was to head north, skirt through safely, and return home to deliver what we'd seen."

He took a breath, eyes never leaving hers.

"Queen Storia, if the Vintals and Natsu have truly formed an alliance—this doesn't bode well for your people... or mine."

A tense silence followed, broken only by the fading clank of the armoured footsteps outside.

Taran stood tall, hands open at his sides.

He had delivered his truth.

What came next would be in her hands.

Storia's voice cut through the quiet like a blade.

"And what about the girl?" she asked. "How is it that you have a child who speaks our language? And why did she scream about monsters?"

Taran's expression darkened. The images came unbidden flashes of memory sharpened by guilt and smoke.

He thought of the girl's village. The silence of it. The ashes. The stillness that felt more like death than peace. He remembered the moment she emerged from the tree line—barefoot, bloodstained, silent as a ghost—before collapsing into Sapir's arms.

Then came the worst of it.

The Vintal warriors. The way they moved—efficient, merciless, and disciplined. And the body. Gods, the body.

A man strung upside down from a tree, skinned from ankle to waist, his face frozen mid-scream. Tortured, broken, discarded like meat. That image hadn't left him. It never would.

Taran swallowed, steadying his breath. He looked Storia in the eyes. "I'll tell you everything."

Storia said nothing. She didn't need to. She stepped back and lowered herself into a chair, never taking her gaze from him.

Taran began.

"We found the girl alone… after the ambush, as we made our escape.

Her village had been wiped out. Burned. Everyone— gone. We don't know how she survived. She wandered out of the forest and collapsed into Sapir's arms. She didn't speak for two days."

He paused, glancing at the girl now sleeping under the blanket.

"When she finally did speak, she spoke your language. That's how we knew she wasn't from our lands. She started having nightmares—violent ones. She talks in her sleep. Screams. Sometimes

cries." He looked back at Storia.

"She screamed about monsters because… she saw them. Not beasts.

Not spirits. Men." Another breath.

"Vintal warriors. And what they did… wasn't just slaughter. It was something darker. They skinned a man alive. Left him hanging in the open like a warning."

A murmur rippled through the room. Even Zarratt's jaw tightened. "That's what your girl saw. That's why she screams." Silence settled like dust after a battle.

Taran straightened.

"We've buried men. Lost friends. Crossed burned villages and enemy blades to bring this to someone who might listen. We didn't come here to start a war, Queen Storia… but we may already be in one."

Storia sat perfectly still, eyes fixed on him. She did not blink.

She did not speak.

But something in her expression changed. Cold calculation replaced doubt. Resolve settled like steel behind her eyes.

When she finally spoke, her voice was quiet. Controlled.

"I believe you."

And just like that, the weight in the room shifted.

❧

CHAPTER 11

t had been four days since Taran and his group arrived at the palace.

The halls of stone and fire no longer felt like the home of strangers, though the weight of their mission hung over every step.

They had found Dilah on the outskirts of the city, resting and nursing a shoulder wound it was clear they had got involved in an altercation waiting for Taran. After a night's rest and a tense reunion, they had brought him to the palace. He had listened silently to all that had happened since the group had split.

They sat on the balcony of their quarters looking out over the courtyard, they could see Sapir with Nyla walking in the flower garden.

Sapir had barely left Nyla's side since their arrival. Though she was beginning to engage more with the people around her, he remained her anchor—her safety blanket. She wouldn't go anywhere without him, and he had no intention of leaving her.

Storia had assigned one of the young women from her quarters to care for Nyla, even bringing toys from the market to coax her into play. But none of it worked. The girl clung to Sapir with a quiet desperation, immune to distraction or comfort unless he was near.

The nights were worse.

Nyla often woke screaming, her cries piercing the stillness of the palace halls. Each time, Sapir was there—arms around her, voice soft and steady until the trembling stopped and sleep returned. Storia, concerned for both of them, had summoned her physicians. One suggested they try leaving Nyla alone through the night, even if she screamed, to teach her there were no monsters in the dark.

Sapir tried. Once.

The sound of her sobbing his name, raw and terrified, broke him. He returned to her side, soothed her tears—and when morning came, he broke the physician's nose.

Storia didn't reprimand him. Instead, she took time to sit with Nyla herself, approaching her not as a stranger, but as someone who shared her people, her blood. By the end of the second day, Nyla had begun to speak. Quietly at first. Hesitant, wary. But it was something.

That first night, Storia had watched as Sapir sat beside the child, his presence steady, his voice low and patient as she drifted into sleep. Storia studied him in the firelight—his body scarred and weathered, each mark a story of battle, of violence survived. The lines stood out faintly darker against his skin, a map of wounds long healed.

How could a man like that—a warrior shaped by blood and blade—be so gentle?

She never voiced the thought aloud, but the admiration settled quietly within her. Sapir carried himself with a kind of stillness that could not be taught. He didn't press the child for words or comfort her with false hopes. He was simply there. Present. Constant. And somehow, that was what Nyla needed most.

On the third night, as the fire crackled low, Nyla reached for his hand.

A small gesture. Her tiny fingers wrapping around his calloused palm as she drifted to sleep. But it shifted something between them all. Even Storia felt it—like the first crack of sunlight breaking through storm clouds. Not healing. Not yet. But the beginning of it.

Later, when the girl was asleep, Sapir remained by the fire, staring into the flames. Storia joined him, saying nothing at first.

"You've done more for her in three days than most could in weeks," she said quietly.

Sapir didn't look at her. "I don't know what I'm doing," he said. "I just... I remember what it's like. To be small. To be alone in the dark, I try to be what I hope someone would have been to my daughter had she lived.

Storia nodded slowly. "Maybe that's why she trusts you." They sat in silence, the firelight dancing between them. Words were no longer necessary. The truth hung between them— unspoken, understood.

The days that followed passed in a storm of closed-door meetings.

Tension crackled through the palace halls, thick as summer heat. The Karathat envoys had returned—dust on their cloaks, silence in their eyes—and with them came no words, only a message.

They brought back a spear.

Crude, unadorned. Its shaft splintered at the grip, and a scrap of crimson cloth was lashed just below the point. The red flag fluttered faintly in the breeze, like a breath held too long.

No scroll. No mark of seal or diplomacy. Just a weapon.

It was a warning.

A clear sign that the Karathat were no longer welcome in Natsu lands. Not as guests, not as allies. The spear said what no envoy would: Do not return.

And in its silence, it carried a heavier truth—one that clung to every whisper in the war chambers.

War was coming.

The war council convened before first light the next morning. Taran stood at the edge of the chamber, arms folded, his face carved from stone. Around the great table, voices murmured—low, cautious, strained by the weight of what the spear had meant.

Storia sat at the head, her fingers steepled beneath her chin. She had not spoken since the spear had arrived. Not in council, not even in private. But now, her gaze swept the room like a blade.

"We gave them peace," she said at last, her voice quiet but sharp enough to still the room. "Offered them trade. Aid. We opened our gates."

"They have closed theirs," replied Zarratt "And posted guards on the bridge to the east. Our scouts saw the banners—Natsu colours, freshly raised."

Another councillor leaned forward. "What does that mean for the treaties? For the outposts?"

"They mean to break them," Taran said flatly. "Or already have."

The queen's jaw tightened. "Then we prepare."

A silence followed, heavy with unspoken thoughts. No one asked if there was still a path back to diplomacy. The spear had answered that.

Taran turned his gaze toward the windows—toward the distant hills, where the Natsu lands began. Somewhere out there, someone had tied that red cloth to that weapon. Someone had chosen defiance over dialogue.

And so, the hall braced itself for what came next—not peace, not retreat, but the slow drumbeat of a war long in the making.

Taran, Storia, Zarratt, and the palace council had argued and planned for hours at a time. Maps were rolled out. Names were listed—those trusted, those watched, and those feared. Taran had never been part of such things before, and yet, strangely, he no longer felt like an outsider.

Taran was a concern for the palace council; he was not one of their people and did not know their ways or their tactics.

Some were concerned that he was there to spy on the Karathat people.

Dilah had departed. He took half of the remaining group and rode out under the rising sun with horses gifted to them by Storia, a sealed letter from the Queen tucked into a cloak given to him, and the weight of truth on his shoulders. His mission was clear: return to their people, inform the elders, and prepare them for what was coming.

He would tell them what they had seen—what the Natsu and Vintals had done. And he would tell them something else too:

That Taran remained behind. That he stayed to negotiate—no, to build—something new. An alliance. One not born of convenience or fear, but of necessity and understanding.

As the dust of Dilah's departure settled behind the city walls, Taran stood on a high balcony of the palace, overlooking the sprawl of

Karathat lands below. The wind tugged at his cloak. Somewhere behind him, the soft rhythm of boots told him Storia was approaching.

"You should be resting," she said, her voice softer than usual.

"I will," he replied without turning. "When I know what comes next."

She stood beside him then, her hands clasped behind her back, her eyes scanning the same horizon.

"Do you think your people will agree?" she asked.

Taran was quiet a moment. "They won't like it. But they'll listen.

Once they know the truth."

Storia nodded. "Then we don't have long."

"No," Taran said. "We don't."

A silence stretched between them—not uncomfortable but filled with the unspoken weight of the days to come.

Behind them, the city moved as it always had. But beneath the surface, things were changing.

And so was Taran.

He had come here as a scout. A survivor.

Now, he stood as something more.

The chapter of war had not yet begun—but the story of alliance had.

And it began here, with fire in the hearths, steel in the air… and trust hard-earned between strangers.

That night, the palace halls were quiet—too quiet. Even the guards moved with hushed footsteps, the tension clinging to the walls like mist. Taran wandered the corridors alone for a time, unable to sleep despite the wear of the day. Every room he passed seemed to hum with the low murmur of planning and unease.

Eventually, he found himself outside the chamber where Nyla slept. A guard gave a respectful nod but didn't speak. Inside, Sapir sat crosslegged on the floor beside the small sleeping couch, a book in his lap, though his eyes were not on the pages.

"She's been quiet tonight," Sapir said softly without looking up.

"Didn't scream. Just… whimpered."

Taran stepped closer, watching the slight rise and fall of Nyla's chest beneath the thin blanket. "She's strong," he said.

"No," Sapir replied, "she's scared. But she hasn't broken. That's strength too."

Taran nodded, letting the silence settle again before he spoke. "We'll need to leave soon. A few days, maybe less. When the council gives the word."

Sapir finally looked at him. "You think they'll send you?"

"They'll send us. The Karathat may trust us. They know what we have survived."

Sapir considered this, then nodded. "And Nyla?"

"She stays. With Storia."

There was a pause. "She won't like that; I don't like that." "She'll be safe," Taran said.

"I didn't say she wouldn't be safe."

Their eyes met—one man changed by fire, the other by war—and something unspoken passed between them. An agreement. A promise.

Taran turned and left the room. He wanted to walk the palace a little longer. He wasn't tired—not yet—and his thoughts were too restless for sleep. The polished stone corridors, the high vaulted ceilings, the quiet flicker of lanterns along the walls—they had become familiar in ways he hadn't expected.

Soon, he would leave this place. Return to his homeland. To the hills and valleys of his youth, though they felt further away now than ever before.

He hoped sending Dilah ahead had been the right choice. The elders would listen to him—if not with full trust, then at least with enough caution to take his message seriously. Dilah would show them the scroll sealed with Storia's mark. He would tell them what they had seen: the burned villages, the brutality of the Vintals, and the whispers of darker alliances on the wind.

Taran paused at a window that looked down across the torch-lit streets of Karathat. The city had become quieter now, more watchful.

As if it, too, sensed the storm drawing closer.

The scroll Dilah carried was more than a message. It was a proposal. A warning. And a promise.

Taran would follow, but not just to repeat the message. His task would be harder—to convince, to unite, to stop the elders from reacting with fear or pride. They would question the wisdom of trusting outsiders. Question him. Why he had stayed behind. What he had become while he walked among the Karathat.

But Taran had answers now.

He turned from the window, exhaling slowly. The palace had begun to settle for the night. He could hear the distant sound of guards changing shift, the faint call of some night bird from the gardens. Somewhere down the corridor, Sapir was likely still at Nyla's side.

Taran didn't know what came next—only that the pieces were moving.

And when he returned home, he would not return as a scout, nor as a messenger.

He would return as a bridge between the two lands.

&

CHAPTER 12

Dawn had come, and already the palace was stirring with movement. The first golden light crept across the sky, casting a soft glow over the spires and banners of Karathat. In the city below, traders set up their stalls along the narrow streets, calling out greetings and preparing for the day's business. Most of the people remained unaware of the quiet storm brewing behind palace walls.

But rumours had begun to trickle through the markets—whispers passed between merchant carts and over baskets of fresh fruit. Stories of roving bands spotted near the Natsu border. Some traders claimed they had been turned away by armed warriors. Others spoke of camps pitched directly on the roads, blocking passage.

In the palace corridors, Storia walked with Tamanda at her side. Both moved with quiet urgency, their steps steady as they made their way to the council chambers. Tamanda had become a constant presence since the trial—a trusted friend, fierce and loyal. She now occupied a room in Storia's own quarters, close enough to protect her at a moment's notice. It was a long journey for a girl from a northern village, but Tamanda had walked it with purpose.

They entered the chamber to find it already occupied by some of the wealthiest and most influential men of Karathat. Advisors from every corner of the realm—each with a voice in the running of the city. There were men who governed taxes, agriculture, fishing, and of course, those who advised on matters of war and strategy. Together, they formed the body of decision that guided the palace.

At the far end of the table sat Zarratt and Taran, speaking through an interpreter. Though Taran had picked up some of the Karathat tongue,

the former trader who now served as his translator remained a necessary presence.

As Storia entered, both men rose. One by one, the others followed.

"Please, sit," she said quickly, waving them down.

She took her seat between Zarratt and Taran, while Tamanda remained standing just behind her. Her eyes locked on Taran, watching him with the same cold focus she had held since the day they met.

Tamanda did not trust the man.

He came from the north—the same lands that had once sent raiders into her village, the same raids that had taken her family. She had made her feelings about him plain, stepping between him and Storia more than once during public outings. Even off duty, she would question the other guards who had stood watch near the queen, ensuring Taran hadn't gotten too close.

Zarratt approved of her caution. He too disliked the northern outsider, though for different reasons. He believed Taran looked at Storia not as a queen or an ally—but as something to conquer.

And in his eyes, that was more dangerous than any sword.

Storia stood, and the room quieted instantly.

"My loyal friends," she began, her voice clear, "we are here today to again discuss the future. But first, I will pass over to Taran, to hear what he has to say."

She turned toward him and gestured for him to speak.

Taran rose, scanning the faces around the table before beginning. The interpreter worked quickly to match his words.

"Firstly, thank you again for accepting me and my companions into your city, your palace, and your council," he said. "It is not lost on me how difficult it must have been, having an outsider in this room during such critical discussions.

"Today, I will be leaving with my men to head north, back to my homeland. The other half of my party should be near our borders now, if not already close to the city of Landa.

"My instructions to them were clear. They are to speak with our Elder Council, to report everything they've seen here. We hope that what they share will be enough to convince the Mandji elders to call for warriors from across the land to gather.

"By tomorrow, riders will begin to move out from Landa, summoning fighters from every village. Our raiding parties will return to the main strongholds, and our armourers will already be hard at work preparing weapons.

"I have been honest with you—our nation no longer holds the same strength in experience it once did. Many of our warriors are young, and few are ready for what is coming. But we have no time to waste. There is little time to prepare, and much to prepare for.

"When I return, I will speak to my elders and tell them of the respect you have shown me here. I will tell them that we have found allies in Karathat—and that together, we can overcome this new threat.

"I now ask for leave to begin my journey, if Queen Storia allows it."

As the interpreter finished, many in the chamber nodded in silent approval. Taran inclined his head respectfully and took his seat.

Another councillor began to speak, but Taran quietly rose, gathering his cloak and preparing to leave. Zarratt and Tamanda followed him out.

At the doorway, Taran paused. He looked back once more at the room—the council deep in discussion, planning the fate of the city.

He turned again to go but stopped short.

Tamanda stood in his path.

She leaned in slightly, her voice low but sharp, speaking in his native tongue.

"You go, Mandji. Go and leave this place. Head back to your northern outposts, back to your raiding parties, back to those warriors who kill fathers and mothers and take young children.

"Your people are no better than those you're looking to fight."

Taran's breath caught. The words landed like a blade between his ribs.

Zarratt, noticing the tension, stepped toward them. He placed a hand on Tamanda's wrist—firm but not rough.

"Please, Tamanda," he said quietly. "Go and sit down. This is not the time, nor the place, for such nonsense."

She turned to him, fury flashing in her eyes. Then looked back to Taran.

"This isn't over," she whispered. "When this is done—when the dust settles—you and I will meet again. On the square stage."

Taran held her gaze. He had seen her train. He had heard the stories—how she'd defeated an assassin with her bare hands, how she had bested a seasoned warrior in trial combat.

And in that moment, he knew she meant every word.

Taran walked past Tamanda, leaving the chambers behind him. Inside, his anger burned quietly—her challenge had cut deep. But he knew to respond, even with words, would only harm the alliance he had worked so hard to build.

Out in the courtyard, the morning sun lit the palace stones in golden hues. The stable master had seen to everything.

Three horses stood waiting, saddlebags packed and strapped tight for the long journey north.

Supplies hung from the saddles—water skins, dried meat, bedrolls.

Taran frowned, eyes scanning the yard.

"Where is Sapir?"

Tanny, adjusting a blanket on his mount, looked up and sighed.

"He's not coming," he said simply. "He wants to stay—with the girl. He wants to stay in Karathat. He's waiting for you in the stable master's office."

Taran nodded, jaw tightening. He turned and stepped into the stables. The scent of hay and leather filled the air, the familiar sounds of shuffling hooves and distant voices dulled by the thick wooden walls.

Sapir sat inside the small office at the rear of the stables, his back straight, hands resting on his knees. He faced the doorway, as though expecting this moment.

Before Taran could speak, Sapir raised a hand.

"Let me say my piece."

Taran gave a slight nod and remained silent.

"I cannot leave her, Taran. She needs me. After what she's been through… I can't abandon her now. She trusts me." Sapir paused, struggling to keep his voice steady. "But it's not just that. I need to know she's safe."

Taran looked at him closely. The pain behind his eyes was unmistakable. It wasn't just loyalty or duty—it was something older. Deeper. The echo of loss.

In that moment, Taran saw the man not as a warrior or companion, but as a grieving father who had found, perhaps, a second chance.

"She will be safe here," Taran said gently. "Storia has promised me that. She will see to it Nyla is protected, always."

"But that someone wouldn't be me," Sapir snapped, his voice tight with frustration. "That isn't enough."

"I've already spoken with Storia," Sapir continued, more calmly. "She has given me permission to stay. As Nyla's guardian. Her protector. If I wish to."

He stood then, stepping closer to Taran.

"And I do wish to. This is where I'm needed now."

Taran exhaled slowly, his shoulders softening as the reality settled in. Another piece of his group—his strength—would stay behind. But he could not argue. He would not take from Sapir the one thing he had longed for since the day his own child had been taken.

"Then stay," Taran said. "Stay and keep her safe."

They clasped forearms in farewell—an unspoken promise passing between them. Then Taran turned and walked back into the sunlit courtyard, where two horses now waited.

Three riders would head north.

And one would remain behind—for something more than duty.

Taran turned and walked away, leaving Sapir behind in the quiet shadows of the stables.

Outside, the courtyard buzzed softly with the preparations of the day. Tanny and Stafan were already mounted, their expressions unreadable beneath the long shadows cast by the palace walls.

"Well," Tanny said, adjusting the reins in his hands, "I guess he's staying then."

Taran nodded, pulling his cloak tighter around his shoulders as he approached.

"Yes," he replied, swinging a leg over his horse. "He said he couldn't bear your snoring again. Swore if he heard it one more time on the road, he'd slit your throat in your sleep."

Tanny let out a loud laugh, the sound echoing against the stone.

"At least he's honest," he chuckled. "And has good taste."

Taran allowed himself a small smile as he settled into the saddle. He reached forward and placed a hand gently against the horse's neck, leaning in close.

In a low, reverent whisper, he spoke a blessing in the old tongue—words of protection, of strength, and of safe passage. It was a prayer to the horse and to the gods who watched over riders far from home.

The horse stirred gently beneath him, as if acknowledging the words. Stafan adjusted his saddlebag, glancing toward the gate. "We ready?" Taran sat back, nodded once.

"Let's ride."

The three men turned their horses toward the open road, hooves striking against the cobbles as they began their journey north leaving behind allies, uncertainty, and a city that was slowly beginning to stir with something more than rumour.

War was coming.

And they would be the ones to carry the fire.

~~~~~~~~~~~~~~~~~~~~~~~~~~~~~

Sapir remained seated in the stable master's office long after Taran had gone.

The silence settled heavily around him, broken only by the occasional snort of a horse or the distant clatter of hooves on stone. He had made his choice, and for the first time in a long time, it felt like the right one.

He stood slowly, adjusting the belt at his waist and stepping out into the main corridor of the stables. Nyla would be awake soon, and he had promised her they would walk the gardens that morning. She had been quieter the past day—perhaps sensing that something was shifting again. Children always knew, even when the words weren't spoken.
~~~~~~~~~~~~~~~~~~~~~~~~~~~~~

As he stepped into the morning light, he saw one of Storia's handmaidens approaching she was a young girl from their borders.

"Guardian Sapir," she said with a small bow. "The queen has asked if you would join her in the garden when you are ready."

He nodded. "Tell her I'll be there shortly."

The handmaiden dipped her head again and turned to go.

Sapir looked back once toward the stable entrance, the echo of hooves and departure still lingering in his ears. Then he turned toward the palace, toward the quiet garden paths, and the girl waiting to walk beside him.

He was no longer a warrior chasing glory.

He was something else now.

Someone worth staying for.

Sapir didn't move right away.

The stable yard was empty now quiet, save for the occasional shuffle of hooves and the lazy creak of saddle leather settling after motion. The faint dust left behind by the horses' departure still hovered in the air, catching in the golden light.

He stood where he was, letting the silence press in.

It felt strange—this stillness. After years of campaign trails, of sleeping with a blade under his blanket and waking before the sun, the absence of urgency felt like a kind of vulnerability. Like walking into a battlefield without a weapon.

But he wasn't on a battlefield anymore.

He exhaled slowly, running a hand down his face. It wasn't just Nyla that had kept him here. That truth weighed heavy on him. She was part of it, yes—the most immediate part. Her trust in him had become a tether, something real in a life that had lost its structure.

But deeper still, something had shifted the night she first took his hand.

He had seen her eyes—dark, wide, frightened—but refusing to flinch from the truth. He had seen himself reflected in them. A younger self. A father. A man who had failed to protect the one life that had meant more to him than his own.

And now, against all reason, he had been given another chance.

A second life had come to rest in his care—and this time, he would not fail.

But it was more than duty.

The wars, the raids, the missions—he had seen too much. Blood had been his trade. He had watched men die for coin, for land, for pride. He had buried brothers and burned villages and stood in the ashes of peace more times than he could count.

He had grown tired.

Not weak, but weary.

Storia had seen it in him, he could tell. She had asked no questions when he'd spoken of staying—only looked at him for a long moment and nodded, as if she had already known.

He had half-expected Taran to protest. But there had been understanding in his eyes too. Maybe even a kind of relief.

And now, for the first time in years, Sapir didn't have to be a weapon.

He could be a shield.

He could be something instead of destroying it.

He turned slowly, walking back toward the palace.

This time, his steps were not driven by duty or orders.

They were his own.

The palace gardens were still cloaked in morning hush, the air cool and damp with dew. Long shadows stretched beneath the olive trees, and the scent of crushed herbs and early blooming jasmine lingered on the breeze.

Sapir stepped lightly across the stone path, his boots silent against the smooth tiles. He'd walked battlefields with less tension than he felt now. Somehow, facing the queen in peace felt heavier than standing before her in war.

He found her near the central pool, seated on a carved stone bench beneath a flowering Arbor. A cluster of blue blossoms hung low overhead, their petals catching the light like fragments of sky.

She looked up as he approached, but didn't rise, she sat with the young girl who had requested Sapir's attendance.

"Guardian Sapir," she said softly. "Or should I simply call you Sapir now?"

He hesitated, then offered a respectful bow. "Whatever title you prefer, Your Majesty."

Storia smiled faintly, not mocking, but tired. "I think we've both had enough titles for a while." He gave a quiet nod and stepped closer.

She gestured to the bench beside her. "Sit. You've had a long morning."

Sapir obeyed, lowering himself slowly onto the stone. A breeze stirred between them, rustling the leaves.

"I assume Taran has gone?" she asked.

"He has. North, with Tanny and Stafan. They'll reach the edge of your borders before nightfall."

"And you?" she asked, turning her head to study him. "Are you certain?"

There was no judgment in her voice—only curiosity. Perhaps concern.

"I am," he said. "I made my choice."

Storia watched the ripples in the pond for a long moment. "You don't owe us this, Sapir. You could have gone with them. Your loyalty has never been in question."

"I'm not staying out of loyalty," he replied quietly. "Not to

Taran, not to the alliance."

"No?" she said, though she already seemed to know the answer.

"I'm staying because I need to," he said. "For her. And maybe for myself."

Storia looked at him then, her gaze deep, unreadable.

"She's taken to you," she said. "That's rare. She barely let the physicians near her. But with you… she walks beside you like a shadow."

"She trusts me."

"And you?" Storia asked. "Do you trust yourself with her?"

The question struck him harder than he expected. He looked away for a moment, jaw tightening. "I want to."

Storia nodded, as though that was enough.

"Then we will make room," she said. "I've already spoken to the head of the household. Your chambers will be moved closer to hers. Not in the royal wing, but nearby. Close enough that she can find you when she needs to."

He swallowed thickly. "Thank you."

"She'll have a long road ahead," Storia said. "Even here. But you'll help her walk it."

They sat in silence for a while. The birds had begun to stir in the trees above, their calls light and scattered.

"You've given her something rare," the queen said quietly. "Stability. I doubt you know how much that means to a child who has only known fear."

"I gave her my word," Sapir said. "I won't break it." Storia stood then, gathering her cloak around her shoulders.

"Then you'll have the full support of this palace," she said. "Not because of your past. But because of who you are now."

She turned to go but paused just before stepping away.

"She's waiting for you," she added gently. "She asked for you when she woke."

Sapir nodded, rising slowly to his feet.

"Then I should go."

🙚🙚

CHAPTER 13

S toria walked slowly through the arches that led back toward the palace, her fingers brushing against the hanging ivy trailing from the stonework. Behind her, the garden faded into silence, but her thoughts did not.

She had watched Sapir closely in recent days—at first out of duty, then curiosity, and now… something she hesitated to name.

Sapir was unlike the men who filled her court. He spoke little, yet every word he chose carried weight. He held himself with the calm of someone who had seen too much, lost too much—but had somehow remained standing. And when Nyla was near him, it was as though a different man emerged—gentler, but no less strong. A man who did not protect from a distance, but with presence. Steady. Solid.

There was a rare strength in that kind of care.

She had seen him once, when he didn't know she was watching. Nyla had been asleep in the shade of the courtyard garden, and Sapir had been kneeling beside her, repairing the stitching in the hem of her tunic. No servant had asked him. No one would have noticed if it hadn't been done.

But he had done it anyway.

Not because it was expected, but because it was needed.

Storia reached the columned hallway that overlooked the main courtyard and paused, looking out across the rooftops of Karathat. The city was beginning to move, its rhythm returning with the morning sun—but her thoughts stayed behind in that quiet garden.

There was something dangerous in what she was feeling. She had always kept her distance—kept herself above the possibility of closeness.

Politics demanded it. She had buried too many people to allow her heart to roam freely again.

And yet…

She found herself wondering if he ever looked at her the way he looked at Nyla—soft, but protective. Present. Grounded.

She found herself hoping he might.

He had not flinched from her title. He had not tried to flatter or charm her. He simply saw her. As a ruler, yes—but also as a woman carrying a thousand quiet burdens.

And somewhere, in the stillness of that thought, a seed had been planted.

Small.

But alive.

Storia was brought from her thoughts by a noise, she looked up and could see Tamanda approaching her.

As Tamanda got closer she smiled at her new friend, Tamanda greeted her with a smile in return.

"Good morning your highness"

"Tamanda please I keep telling you to call me Storia, especially when it is just us."

Tamanda playfully poked her tongue out at Storia. Since they had first met, many things had changed. Storia had seen a quiet, uncertain girl transform into something far more complex—fierce in her loyalty, deadly with a blade, and surprisingly wise beyond her years.

Tamanda walked beside her now, falling into step without hesitation.

"You always look so serious in the mornings," Tamanda said lightly, glancing at her. "Were you already thinking about council business? Or just daydreaming again about your brooding warrior?"

Storia's cheeks warmed, and she shot Tamanda a sideways glare.

"You presume much."

"I only presume what I see," Tamanda replied, grinning. "And I see the way your eyes follow Sapir when he leaves a room."

Storia sighed, her gaze drifting back toward the rooftops. "It's not so simple."

"No, it isn't. But that doesn't make it any less true."

They walked in silence for a moment, the kind of silence only true trust allowed.

"I don't know what this is," Storia admitted finally. "It's not politics. It's not strategy. It's not… expected. I'm not used to anything that doesn't come with consequence."

Tamanda nodded, her voice quieter now. "Maybe that's exactly why it matters."

They turned into a smaller corridor that led toward the Queen's private chambers. The guards at the end stood at attention, but one of them stepped forward as they approached.

"My Queen," he said, bowing. "Zarratt asked me to inform you—there has been a rider from the northern watchtower. He requests immediate council."

Storia's light mood faded. "Did he give cause?"

"Only that it concerns troop movements… and a banner not seen in these lands for some time."

Storia exchanged a glance with Tamanda, the moment between them dissolving like mist under the sun.

"Have the council summoned within the hour. I want full reports on any sightings near the northern borders."

"Yes, Your Majesty."

The guard turned sharply and moved off.

Tamanda frowned. "Do you think it's the Natsu?"

"I don't know," Storia replied, already considering what this might mean. "But the last time we saw their banner; it marked the beginning of a war."

Tamanda's hand drifted to the hilt of her blade. "Then I should ready your guard."

Storia nodded. "Yes. And send word to Sapir. If something is stirring beyond our walls, I want his eyes on it."

Tamanda bowed slightly. "Of course."

As she turned to leave, Storia called after her.

"Tamanda?"

Tamanda looked back.

"Thank you. For this morning."

Tamanda smiled. "Any time, Storia."

Left alone once more, Storia lingered in the hallway, fingers brushing the cold stone as her mind turned toward banners on distant hills, shadowed intentions… and the quiet way one man could make her feel seen, even as the world shifted around her.

Whatever was coming, she would face it.

But part of her now hoped she wouldn't have to face it alone.

The council chamber smelled faintly of parchment, wax, and the subtle bitterness of old decisions. Light filtered through high arched windows, catching the motes of dust that danced in the beams. A long table dominated the centre of the room, carved from dark cedar and polished to a sheen. Around it, the councillors gathered—Zarratt already in his seat near the head, expression unreadable, hands folded.

Storia entered without announcement, her robes trailing behind her. Conversations stilled at once. She took her place at the head of the table, nodding curtly to those present.

Zarratt inclined his head. "The rider is just outside, Your Majesty.

Shall I bring him in?" "Do it," Storia said.

The door opened, and a dust-covered soldier was ushered inside. His cloak bore the silver and red insignia of the northern watchtower, torn at the edges. His eyes were sharp despite the exhaustion in his limbs, and he knelt as he approached the Queen.

"Rise," Storia commanded. "Speak what you've seen."

The man stood, breath steadying. "Your Majesty. Two days past, our scouts observed a column of armed riders moving east along the Arven Ridge. At first, we thought them remnants of the border tribes—but their armour was wrong. Older, heavier. And they carried a banner... black and gold. Stylised flame. One we haven't seen since for many years since the Natsu last tested our frontier."

A murmur rippled through the chamber.

Zarratt leaned forward. "You're certain of the banner?"

"We watched through spyglass. No mistake commander."

Storia's brow tightened. "How many?"

"Hard to say. Not a full army. A warband, maybe. Thirty, perhaps more. But disciplined. Formed."

"Did they engage any of our scouts?"

"No, Majesty. But they did not move in secrecy. They rode as if to be seen."

Zarratt turned to Storia. "A message, then. A provocation." "Or a test," she said softly.

One of the councilmen—a narrow-faced elder named Harien—spoke next. "The Natsu were broken years ago, we have had peace since then. Why now? What could they gain?"

"Fear," Zarratt answered. "Uncertainty. A show of strength to stir unrest. Even a few blades can shift balance if placed well, their new alliance with the Vintals will have given them strength in numbers and confidence".

Storia stood slowly. "We do not yet know what this is. But I will not wait for them to knock on our gates. Dispatch riders to our outposts. I want confirmation of their numbers, and their path. If they approach closer, I want a full mobilised guard ready to intercept."

She turned to Zarratt. "Summon Sapir. He knows their tactics better than anyone here even more so now that they are with the Vintals. I want his thoughts."

Zarratt nodded. "He was already on his way. Tamanda saw to it."

As if on cue, the chamber doors opened once more. Sapir entered with his interpreter, his presence quiet but commanding. He moved without hesitation to stand beside the Queen, eyes scanning the map spread across the table.

"You've heard?" Storia asked.

He nodded once.

"What do you make of it?"

Sapir leaned over the map, finger tracing the ridge line the rider had spoken of. "They're not just testing your defences. They're watching how quickly you respond. How you gather. Who you send. This—" he tapped the parchment "—is a scout force. But the main questions is, are they just the front?" The silence that followed was heavy.

Storia exhaled slowly. "Then we must assume there are more."

She looked around the room, letting her voice carry authority. "We begin preparations now. The people will not be panicked. But they will be protected. Tamanda and the captains will oversee the guards here and their drills. Zarratt—reinforce the outposts along the eastern hills. And

Sapir—"

"Yes?"

"I know your reasons for being here are not as a warrior, but I would like your help and experience, take a small force. Track them. Do not engage. I want eyes on them at all times. And if they are more than we think—if war is stirring—bring word back.

We will not be caught blind."

Sapir bowed his head slightly. "It will be done."

The Queen glanced over the council once more. "You are dismissed.

I will speak with Sapir alone."

As the room emptied and the doors shut behind the last of the advisors, Storia allowed the edge in her posture to ease.

She looked to Sapir, who was still studying the map. "You think this is more than a show."

"Yes."

"You think they will look to strike here?"

"I think they are now looking to expand, your nation is rich in trade and lands."

She paused, her hand brushing against the table's edge. "And if they come for us at Karathat?"

Sapir looked up, meeting her eyes for the first time. "Then we make sure they regret it."

~~~~~~~~~~~~~~~~~~~~~~~~~~~~~~~~~~~~

Landa was already busy. Since Dilah had arrived, he had been in constant demand with the elders. They had asked to speak with him many times to go over what had happened. He had spoken to many different elders, each from different villages and regions across the Mandji lands.

Dilah walked through the streets, watching as warriors arrived in mass. He had never seen so many gathered in one place.
~~~~~~~~~~~~~~~~~~~~~~~~~~~~~~~~~~~~

He still kept the scroll on his person, never letting it out of sight. He was waiting for all the elders of the land to be present—only then would he address the nation's council.

The last time so many had been in Landa, a declaration of war had been made against the Vintals. All warriors and warbands had been called in and sent to war, leaving behind only the young and those unlucky enough to be told to guard the villages.

Now, Dilah had been summoned to attend the great hut.

He walked on, past the huts of families, past the local tavern, which was now full of young warriors. Their voices spilled out onto the street—bragging about skirmishes with raiders, boasting of how they would crush the enemies of the nation.

Dilah couldn't help but laugh to himself. He tried to remember if he had been that foolish at their age.

The streets bustled with traders selling food and trinkets to those with coin or goods to barter. Local girls were making money in their huts from young warriors too stupid to think with anything but their groin.

He laughed again, shaking his head. Yes, he had been that stupid once—chasing girls into back huts, thinking only of the moment.

Outside the gates, he could hear horses and riders. He knew they would be playing partok. It was a game for horsemen: two teams on horseback, trying to throw an inflated pig's bladder through a high hoop.

It was fast, competitive, and dangerous—and usually banned during mass gatherings, due to the risk of serious injury or death.

Finally, Dilah arrived at the main hut. It stood before him, a large and imposing structure.

Two guards stood at the entrance, both of them heavily armed and painted in the ceremonial reds and blacks of the Mandji. One gave a nod as Dilah approached, stepping aside to let him pass. Inside, the air was thick with the smell of smoke, herbs, and sweat. Dozens of voices murmured low, but even their quiet words seemed to echo in the vast wooden chamber.

The ceiling was high and curved inward like the belly of a great beast. Dozens of animal hides were stretched along the beams, and symbols of the old gods marked every post. Fires burned in circular pits, and the smoke rose slowly, caught in the upper space before trickling out through carved vents.

Elders sat in a wide circle, their positions marked by carved stones and woven mats. Each one wore the markings of their region—beads, cloth patterns unique to their people. Some were young, sharp-eyed, recently appointed. Others were bent and grey, their age worn proudly.

They turned their eyes to Dilah as he entered.

A hush fell over the chamber.

Dilah walked to the centre of the circle and stood in silence for a long moment. Then, slowly, he removed the scroll from his tunic and held it high.

"I bring a message," he said, his voice clear and even, "I have come from the lands of the Karathat. Several weeks ago, I and many other warriors were sent out in a warband. We had been sent to find those who had been attacking our outer villages to the west. What I can tell you is that we found those involved and the discovery came at a cost, we lost warriors, good men, friends of mine.

Those warriors now are with the spirits, I am ashamed to have survived but alas here I am, I am here to bring a warning and with any luck hope.

Now had I not seen it with my own eyes. I would not believe what I am about to say.

The Vintals are back, and they have aligned themselves with the Natsu, now if this was not bad enough, I must advise you that they move against us again but this time with allies."

A ripple passed through the gathering—some voices muttered, others leaned forward.

"Now I am not the only one to escape the hands of our enemy.

As we speak Taran son of Kharum is with the people of Karathat, we escaped into their lands and found ourselves in the hands of their people.

They too have seen this alignment of the Vintals and Natsu as a threat to them as well as us and have sent a proposal.

Dilah unrolled the scroll carefully and knelt before the fire.

"The Queen of Karathat sends this proposal, Taran will be here shortly he travels home to update us of the Karathat plans."

He placed the scroll gently on a stone slab at the centre of the room. One of the older elders, her skin weathered like cracked bark, leaned forward and lifted it with reverence. Others began murmuring again.

Dilah stayed on one knee. He had done what he had come to do.

Now it was for the elders to decide what came next.

Would they call the banners again? Would the land rise?

Would they refuse what was offered in the scroll?

Or would fear and memory of the last war hold them back?

The fires crackled.

And the council began.

&

CHAPTER 14

Taran was nearly home. They had been riding for some time, stopping only to eat, sleep, and water the horses.

The food they had been supplied with had run out days ago, and Stafan had used his skills as an archer to hunt along the way.

They rode now through the forests of their homeland, eager to be among their own people once again.

The forest was dense and thick with foliage for this time of year, which forced them to ride the horses slowly on the final stretch back to Landa. The heat of the northern season filled the woods with sound—chirps, rustles, distant calls—making the whole forest feel alive.

Tanny rode his horse with ease, practicing bird calls as he rode, his body relaxed with the comfort of being close to home. Along the journey, they had passed several villages, many of which were populated mostly by women and children. Few men were left.

Taran believed he understood why—and he hoped that Dilah's message, along with the scroll, would be enough to push the elders into making a decision. If not, he would ask to be seen by the council of elders himself.

At one point, they had seen smoke rising as they crossed the invisible border back into their lands—a thick, black cloud smudging the sky. Taran had assumed it came from a raid, likely by Natsu or Vintal warbands.

They would be working their way across the lands like locusts, burning and taking as they pleased.

Earlier in the journey, Stafan had spotted riders while hunting in the woods. He had remained hidden, avoiding detection. He believed they

were part of a scouting party—either guarding trade routes or searching for carts to ambush.

Taran missed Sapir.

He understood why Sapir had chosen to stay behind, but a small part of him still felt betrayed. He needed him now more than ever. Sapir's experience and voice would have been invaluable—especially if the elders refused to listen.

"Oh, I pray to the spirits that we get there soon," Tanny muttered.

"We're not far from Landa, Tanny. Maybe a day's ride now—no more."

"Thank the gods," Tanny groaned. "My arse feels like it's been beaten with a stick. I almost feel like a child that stepped out of line during fight training."

Taran laughed. "Well, we'll be home soon."

The gates of Landa rose from the trees like the ribs of an ancient beast, tall and weather-worn but unbroken. Smoke curled from dozens of chimneys, and the noise of the settlement drifted through the trees long before they reached the walls—voices, clanging metal, hooves on hardened earth.

As they approached, the guards at the gate spotted them and stepped forward. Their spears lowered until one of the men recognised Taran and waved them through.

"Word came ahead of you," he said, stepping aside. "Dilah's return stirred the elders."

Taran gave a nod of thanks but said nothing. His eyes swept the courtyard beyond the gates. It was busier than he remembered—warriors coming and going, the smell of sweat and steel thick in the air. Carts rolled by carrying grain, weapons, firewood. Young boys ran errands with bows slung across their backs, too young to fight but already part of the machinery of war.

Tanny looked around and gave a low whistle. "They're preparing for something."

"They'd better be," Taran muttered, leading his horse forward.

Stafan rode in silence, his eyes scanning every face, every open doorway. "There are more warriors here than I expected. Do you think they've decided?"

"We'll find out soon enough," Taran replied.

They rode through the winding lanes of Landa, passing the tavern where laughter and shouts spilled into the street. A pair of old men argued loudly about war—whether it was necessary or not. A woman stood nearby, washing blood from a pile of tunics, her expression grim.

They reached the stables and dismounted, handing the reins to a stable hand no older than twelve. The boy bowed slightly to Taran and led the horses away without a word.

Taran took a breath, tasting the air of home. It smelled of ash, sweat, and woodsmoke—but also of belonging.

"I need to see Dilah," he said.

Stafan and Tanny nodded, falling into step beside him as they made their way toward the elder's hall.

As they passed through the main square, Taran spotted more warbands arriving—groups of ten, sometimes twenty— young men bearing the colours and emblems of distant villages. Some looked eager. Others looked afraid. All of them looked ready.

Taran's jaw tightened.

If the council had not yet made their decision, they were certainly leaning toward it now.

At the foot of the elder's hall, two guards stepped forward and stood in their way—until one of them recognised Taran and gave a curt nod. "Dilah's inside. The council has been meeting all morning." "Tell him I've returned," Taran said.

The guard nodded again and disappeared into the hall.

Taran waited in silence, the weight of the scroll, the journey, and what was coming all pressing down on his shoulders.

Behind him, Tanny stretched and yawned. "Feels like we've ridden across the world to get here."

"In a way," Taran said quietly, "we have."

Dilah came out from the hut to meet Taran. He looked older as if the journey and meetings with the elder council had aged him.

Dilah walked towards Taran and the grabbed each other's forearms as a greeting.

"Where is Sapir?". Dilah asked looking for the old warrior.

"He decided to stay in Karathat, he wanted to stay with Nyla".

"He has found his second chance then it seems, we could use his voice at the moment".

"What's the news?". Taran asked.

Dilah took a deep breath and sighed.

"Well, it's been a mix of opinions one day we are getting ready to march the horde the next we are holding, the last few days, the Natsu or Vintals have raided villages to the west on the outskirts. Our riders came back after they entered the villages and found nothing but bodies, they had burned the villages".

"We had seen smoke in the distance on our ride; we figured it was from some sort of raid". Taran responded.

"The council are nearly all prepared to go to war, there are a few of the elders who live in the eastern borders that are yet to commit.

They are concerned that we have not yet recovered from the previous war and that negotiations should be the way forward." "Which elders?" Taran snapped.

"Molar and yosaf, both are beating the same drum".

"I know of those two, they have built their villages on trade with the Chai people and carts from Karathat.

I shall speak to the council if they are ready to hear me".

"We will see, I shall head back in and announce you. Be warned they were not overly pleased with Storia's proposal either.

Taran waited as Dilah disappeared into the elder's hall, the heavy wooden door closing behind him. The voices inside were muffled, but tense. Tanny shifted beside him, while Stafan stood motionless, eyes fixed on the sky as though watching for omens.

A moment later, the door creaked open, and a guard gestured.

"They will see you now."

Taran stepped forward alone.

The great hall was thick with smoke and shadow. Fires burned low in the pits, casting flickering light across the faces of the gathered elders.

Dozens of them, seated in a wide circle, eyes fixed on him as he entered.

Dilah stood to the side, his face unreadable.

Taran walked to the centre of the room and stood tall. He didn't bow. He didn't hesitate.

"I come as witness," he began, "to what lies across our borders, to the growing alliance between the Natsu and the Vintals. I have seen with my own eyes what they are preparing. I have spoken with warriors and courtiers in Karathat."

Some of the elders shifted. A few leaned forward. Others said nothing.

"I know the cost of war," Taran continued. "My father fought in the last. He saw our villages burned, your sons buried, he too gave his life. But this war is not one we will choose. It is one that is already on its way."

He paused, letting his words settle.

"We passed villages on our journey—villages emptied of men already coming here. Rider's spoke of raids, and I saw smoke on the horizon. Do you think they will stop at our borders? Do you believe peace will come through silence?"

A grumble of voices rose in reply—some in agreement, others uncertain.

Taran turned his gaze toward a cluster of elders seated near the eastern banners.

"You say we should wait. That we should talk. But they are not talking—they are burning, they are not negotiating, they are killing. Do your trade carts still run? Are your stores still full? Or do you already feel the tremble beneath your feet?"

One of the older elders, white-haired and stone-faced, raised a hand.

Silence fell again.

"What would you have us do, boy?" he asked, voice low but firm.

Taran met his gaze.

"Call the banners. Rally the warbands. Make ready the land not for fear—but for survival. If we wait until they are upon us, we will not have the choice to fight. The choice will already be made for us." He stepped back, letting the silence stretch.

"Do not make the mistake of waiting until our homes are ash to act, we have allies ready to help us".

"Ah yes, the allies—the Karathat people," said the elder from the east, his voice carrying a sharp edge. "We received the Queen's proposal. She wants us to do her work here in the north and then take their lands for her own.

Her father tried the same thing. He forced war on many smaller nations once. We watched those nations disappear, and now their lands all sit under Karathat."

A murmur rippled through the hall as one of the elders rose and handed a scroll to a young guard, who stepped forward and presented it to Taran.

Taran did not take it.

"I do not need to read the scroll," he said firmly. "I know what is in the scroll. I sat with Storia, the Queen, many times to discuss its contents. I accepted the terms, believing them to be fair." He paused, letting the weight of his words settle.

"We will attack them in the north, drawing their forces toward us. Once we march, Stafan will ride hard and fast back to Karathat and give them word that we are moving. That will be the signal for Storia to send her army from the south." He turned slightly, addressing the circle.

"Once we defeat the enemy, they will take the Natsu lands south of the Santi River. We will take their lands to the north. Yes, the lands north of the river are smaller—but I also took into consideration that we will claim the Vintal lands as well."

There were no interruptions. All listened now.

"I accepted a trade deal with Karathat as part of the agreement. It will open our doors to more trade and allow us to grow and expand. I have seen the trade flowing into Karathat. I have seen how quickly their city has developed." Taran's voice did not waver.

"This is not just a war of survival. It is a chance to strengthen our people. A chance to build."

Taran moved from the inner circle and came to stand beside Dilah.

As he did, Dilah gave a small nod of approval.

"Well, how did I do?" Taran asked.

"You spoke well, Taran," Dilah replied. "But only time will tell. We'll be asked to leave soon while they discuss—it's been this way for the last two days. Hopefully, after this, they'll decide to call the banners, and we will ride."

As if on cue, a guard approached and gestured toward the door.

"They will call you when they've made their decision. Do not leave

Landa until it is done."

Taran and Dilah stepped out into the warm air beyond the great hall.

Outside, Tanny and Stafan were waiting. They had been watching an archery competition taking place in the open square nearby. Tanny had been goading Stafan, trying to convince him to enter, but Stafan had refused, arms folded and expression unmoved.

Taran approached as a young warrior loosed an arrow. It struck the target off-centre with a dull thud, drawing a polite clap from a few onlookers. The line of competitors stood tense, bows in hand, waiting their turn.

Tanny grinned as Taran and Dilah joined them.

"I've been trying to get this one to show these boys how it's done," he said, nodding toward Stafan. "But he's too proud—or too afraid."

"I'm not afraid," Stafan replied flatly. "I just don't see the point in showing off."

Tanny rolled his eyes. "You're the best shot in three villages. They should see what a real archer looks like."

Another arrow flew—this one better than the last. It struck just outside the centre ring, drawing a few cheers.

"You could beat them with your eyes closed," Taran said.

Stafan sighed. "Fine. But I'm not doing it to impress anyone."

He stepped forward and spoke with the man running the event. After a short exchange, he was handed a bow—old, worn, but well-strung.

He took it without ceremony and walked to the mark.

The crowd quieted.

The target stood across the square, painted circles fading in the sun.

Stafan nocked an arrow and raised the bow in one smooth motion.

He released.

The arrow struck the centre.

A few gasps rose from the watching crowd.

Without pausing, Stafan nocked a second arrow and fired again.

Another centre hit.

And again.

Three arrows. Three centre marks.

The square erupted in cheers and laughter. Even some of the other competitors clapped, shaking their heads.

Tanny whooped. "Now that's more like it!"

Stafan turned back toward them, his face unreadable. "Happy?"

"Delighted," Tanny said, slapping him on the back.

Tanny walked over to a young warrior and held out his hand. The warrior, scowling, pulled a small purse from his belt and dropped it into Tanny's palm. The clink of silver was unmistakable.

"Well, why do you think I was trying so hard to get you to enter?" Tanny said, grinning as he returned to the group. "I made a bet with that lad after he claimed his brother was the best archer in town." Stafan shook his head, half amused, half exasperated. "You used me."

"No," Tanny said, jingling the coins, "I trusted you."

Taran laughed. Even Dilah allowed himself a small smirk.

For a moment, the weight of war and politics lifted—just a little—and the warmth of home settled around them like an old cloak.

Taran watched the crowd for a moment. There was joy here—brief and bright—but beneath it ran the tension of what was coming. These contests, these laughs, they might be the last for some.

But for now, he allowed himself to smile.

&

CHAPTER 15

Sapir crawled through a field thick with green grass, the scent of viburnum flowers hanging heavy in the warm air. The blooms grew wild along a hedgerow, offering just enough cover to conceal his movement.

He had been on the road for eight days, scouting the land, searching for any sign of the Natsu. Twenty horse guards rode with him—men trained specifically for mounted combat. They moved fast and light, perfectly suited for Sapir's assignment.

Storia had given him a clear order: find the enemy and track them. Do not engage.

For the past two days, Sapir had been following a group of warriors pushing north, out of the Karathat lands and toward the Mandji border. They had raided a trader and a small village, taking supplies and leaving no prisoners.

His scouts had tracked their path by the marks left behind—broken undergrowth, scattered refuse, the remnants of a fire.

Finally, they had sighted riders bearing the banner of the Natsu.

Sapir knew engaging wasn't what Storia had asked of him, but if he could take one prisoner—just one—he might be able to interrogate him and learn something of their plans.

He had taken fifteen of his men with him, leaving five to guard the horses. Three had been sent to either flank, hiding in the bushes with bows drawn and ready. Sapir moved forward with the remaining eight, crawling low through the grass.

As they neared the camp, a sharp birdcall came from the bushes to the right. Sapir froze. It was a signal—someone was moving.

A Natsu warrior appeared on the far side of the hedge. He walked close, humming softly, then began to urinate just beside the hedge—mere feet from where Sapir lay hidden.

Sapir stayed perfectly still, the man's stream pounding the ground, spraying where it hit. Slowly, without a sound, he drew the knife from the back of his belt, careful not to disturb the grass.

The warrior continued whistling a tune, something unfamiliar.

When he finished, he turned to tie his waistbelt into a knot.

Sapir shifted into a crouch. He could now see the warrior was alone—his comrades still gathered around the campfire, some distance away.

With swift precision, Sapir rose and grabbed the warrior, clamping a hand over his mouth. Another of Sapir's men rushed forward, helping restrain him. Sapir thrust the knife into the back of the man's neck, just at the base of the skull, and twisted. The young warrior struggled briefly, then went limp.

Sapir lowered the body gently into the grass.

He had been learning the Karathat language over the past months, using the translator less and less. He was surprised by how close it was to his native tongue.

He turned to the man beside him and patted his forearm.

"Well done. Nice and quiet. The one we want to take is the older one—he'll be the one in charge."

The warrior nodded, understanding Sapir's broken Karathat. He turned and whispered instructions to the others.

Sapir and four others crawled silently through the long grass while another group of four held back. The air was still, tense with anticipation. To his left, Sapir watched as two of his warriors on the flank silently brought down another Natsu sentry, dragging the body into the grass.

They pressed forward, inch by inch, the chirping of crickets around them fading into silence as if the land itself sensed what was coming.

At last, they reached the edge of the clearing. Beyond the grass, a small Natsu camp lay spread out—ten warriors in total. Four sat idly around a central fire, one of them the leader Sapir had been tracking for days. The other six were busy with camp chores—tending to gear, collecting water, or sharpening blades.

Sapir held his breath and waited; eyes fixed on the target. Beside him, his warriors froze like statues. Then it came—a birdcall, sharp and deliberate. A signal from the group Sapir had positioned earlier.

A faint whisper of motion passed near his head—then arrows struck. Four of the six distracted Natsu fell, gurgling, arrows buried deep in their torsos. Sapir's warriors surged from the grass, charging the stunned enemy.

From both flanks, more Karathat horse guards swept in. The Natsu warriors at the stream turned to flee but were cut down by another volley of arrows before they could reach their weapons.

Chaos erupted.

One of the campfire warriors tried to rise but was struck down instantly, a sword slashing across his chest. Sapir didn't pause—he charged straight for the leader.

The Natsu commander was already on his feet, locked in combat with a Karathat guard. Sapir saw him drive a blade into the man's stomach, cutting him down with brutal precision.

The leader turned as Sapir closed in. He was broad-shouldered, with a long-curved sword in one hand and a small hatchet in the other. His eyes burned with defiance.

He struck first, bringing the hatchet down in a vicious arc. Sapir raised his wooden shield just in time, the force of the blow jarring through his arm. He pushed the shield aside and swung his sword, but the leader met it with his own, steel crashing against steel with a harsh clang.

Sapir stepped forward and drove his left arm forward hitting into the man's chest with the edge of his shield, forcing him back a pace and throwing him off balance.

The leader recovered quickly, swinging the curved blade low. Sapir leapt back, the tip of the sword slicing through the edge of his tunic. Another step, another clash—steel struck steel again, ringing through the clearing like a bell of war.

Around them, the battle was ending. Karathat warriors moved efficiently, cutting down the last of the Natsu. Cries rang out, then were silenced. Sapir's men knew their orders—take nonalive except the leader.

The Natsu commander roared and charged, his hatchet swinging in a deadly arc. Sapir ducked and turned, slashing across the man's thigh. Blood sprayed, and the leader staggered. Sapir used the moment—kicking forward, he knocked the hatchet from the man's hand.

The leader fell to one knee, sword still in hand, panting heavily.

The man spat blood and tried to rise, swinging again in desperation. Sapir struck hard across the wrist, and the curved blade clattered to the dirt.

Two of Sapir warriors fell on him, driving the man to the ground and wrenching his arms behind his back. With practiced movements, they tied his wrists tightly with a length of cord.

The fight was over.

Sapir stood, breath heavy, and looked around. All ten Natsu warriors were dead—except for the one who now lay groaning at his feet. Karathat soldiers were already moving through the camp, checking bodies, retrieving arrows, and gathering weapons. The fire still crackled at the centre of the clearing, smoke curling into the twilight sky.

One of the flank leaders approached. "All dead. No survivors."

"Good," Sapir said, glancing down at the captive. "This one will speak. Make sure he stays alive."

He knelt beside the man, his voice low. "You're going to tell me everything. And if you lie, I'll know."

The leader glared at him; pain etched into every line of his face. But behind the fury, Sapir saw it—the flicker of fear.

The Karathat camp had been set just a short distance from the site of the ambush. Now, deep into the night, it glowed dimly under torchlight. The bodies of the Natsu had been buried, Sapir refused to burn the bodies not wanting to send smoke into the air as a signal.

The captured leader sat bound to a thick post hammered into the earth, his wounds wrapped but untreated beyond that. His face was streaked with dried blood and dirt, and one eye had swollen nearly shut.

But his spine remained straight, proud despite defeat.

Sapir stood before him, arms folded.

"What is your name," he said.

The man stared at him in silence.

Sapir gave it a moment. Then he drew a knife—not for use, but to make a point. He knelt beside the prisoner, the blade glinting in the firelight.

"I can make the pain worse," Sapir said, calm and cold. "Or you can tell me who you are and why your party was scouting our lands." Still silence. A bead of sweat slid down the man's temple.

Sapir nodded to one of his guards. The man stepped forward and pressed a heated iron rod close enough to the prisoner's skin that he could feel its heat, but not yet burn. The Natsu flinched, teeth gritted then spat at Sapir.

The guard pressed the iron rod against the prisoner's thigh, the smell of burning flesh rose from the thigh as the prisoner screamed.

"My name is Hadran," he hissed finally."

Sapir leaned in slightly. "You're far from your lands. What are you doing here?"

Hadran's mouth twisted into something between defiance and weariness. "Orders."

"From whom?"

Hadran hesitated, then replied, "High commander Rakah. We were instructed to cross the border. Watch troop movements. Count the horses. Track your trade roads."

Sapir's expression hardened. "This far inland? That's not scouting.

That's preparation."

Hadran gave a shrug, as much as his bound shoulders allowed. "Believe what you like."

Sapir stood and paced a short distance before turning back. "Where's the main force gathering?"

Hadran refused to answer, the guard poked him again with the hot iron rode, the prisoner screamed out again in pain as his flesh burned leaving behind permanent marks of the torture.

Sapir raised an eyebrow and shouted "speak".

Hadran breathed heavily in pain and said, more bitter than afraid now. "We were to report back if Karathat looked weak. That's all."

"Report to where?"

"…the outpost at Teren Ridge."

Sapir nodded to a guard who stepped forward and noted the name down.

"You've done well, Hadran," Sapir said, and there was no mockery in his voice. "You've lived. That's more than can be said for the others." Hadran looked away.

Sapir turned to the guard captain. "Move him under watch. He goes with us to Karathat. The Queen will want to hear this from his own mouth."

The guard saluted and motioned two men to lift the prisoner.

As they hauled Hadran to his feet, Sapir looked up at the stars overhead, the firelight catching the steel edge of his blade. War was coming.

There was no longer any doubt.

~~~~~~~~~~~~~~~~~~~~~~~~~~~

Zarratt stood atop the timber ramparts of Teren ridge, the westernmost outpost still under Karathat control. Below him, the valley lay shrouded in mist, the pine-covered hills to the north blotting out the stars. The wind carried the scent of smoke from the barracks fire, but also something else—old ash, the kind left behind after a camp had been hastily abandoned.

He said nothing for a long time.

Behind him, guardsman Drav approached, boots crunching softly on the gravelled platform. "The scouts you sent to the border haven't returned, sir."

Zarratt didn't turn. "How long overdue?"

"Two days."

Zarratt exhaled through his nose. That made three patrols missing in less than a fortnight.

He finally turned, his dark cloak snapping in the breeze. "Have the watch doubled tonight. I want no lights on the outer towers. Anyone approaching from the forest path is to be shadowed—do not engage unless ordered."

The guardsman hesitated. "Sir... you think we're being watched?"

"I think," Zarratt said, his tone level, "that we've already been watched. And I think the Natsu are bolder than they've been in a generation."
~~~~~~~~~~~~~~~~~~~~~~~~~~~

He descended the steps of the watchtower quickly, the guardsmen at his side. The interior of the outpost was austere—stone hearths, racks of weaponry, oil maps pinned along the walls. At the central table, he unfurled a large, hand-inked map and tapped two locations in quick succession.

"One scout group disappeared near danarang Crossing. The other here, east of the felmouth Ridge." He drew a connecting line. "And if you chart the merchant reports, we received last moon, about Natsu roadblocks near the old logging roads, it forms a clear arc." "An encirclement?" The guardsman said.

"A shadow of one," Zarratt said. "They're testing our reach. And they've gotten confident enough to do it almost openly." A sharp knock at the door interrupted them.

A horse guard stepped in, cloaked and muddy from hard travel.

"Message from Sapir, Commander. Priority seal."

Zarratt took the scroll, snapped the seal, and scanned the contents.

His eyes narrowed.

"What is it, sir?" Drav asked.

Zarratt folded the message slowly. "Confirmation. Sapir ambushed a Natsu forward group near talisman Rise. Nine killed, one captured. A commander. He gave up a name—High Marshal Rakah. And a staging point: Teren Ridge."

Drav's eyes widened. "Here."

Zarratt looked to the hearth fire, his face grim. "No more guessing.

They're coming."

He turned and barked new orders with clipped precision. "Send a rider to the capital. The Queen needs to know. Begin preparation to evacuate the outer villages. And tell the smiths:

weapons only. No more horseshoes or nails until further notice.”

“And Sapir?” The Horse guard asked.

“Tell him to hold the prisoner. I want that commander alive long enough for Storia to ask her questions.” He paused. “But if he tries to escape, he doesn’t get a second chance.”

The Horse guard nodded and disappeared into the outer dark.

Zarratt stood in the command hall for a moment longer, listening to the wind batter against the shutters. Then he moved to the map wall again looking at the line he had drawn again.

“Let’s see how far Rakah is willing to step.”

Zarratt stood in the centre of the command hall, lit only by the flickering hearth and a cluster of low-burning oil lamps. The message from Sapir still sat on the table beside the map, its seal broken, its warning clear. He stared at the line he’d placed on the map, too close for comfort.

He called to for his guardsman, a young sergeant named Kelin, he stepped into the room his hand rested on the pommel of his sword.

“Start checking our defences,” Zarratt ordered, his voice clipped and firm. “I want every gate reinforced, every wall checked for rot, and every tower stocked with oil, arrows, and spears.”

Kelin nodded and moved without hesitation.

Zarratt called for some of the veteran watchmen and garrison runners. “Get the engineers up—tonight. I want traps laid along the north slope, caltrops at every trail entrance, and trip-wire alarms rigged at every possible approach through the forest.”

He strode toward the open doorway; he met his captains why had been waiting for him. “We hold this place for as long as we can. If the Natsu push through here, they cannot be allowed to reach the capital without warning.”

One of the lieutenants stepped up, brow furrowed. "You think they'll attack us directly?"

Zarratt paused on the top step, then turned back.

"I think they'll come wherever we aren't ready. That's why we will be ready."

A silence fell over the room, bells signalled for more soldiers from the barracks and mess halls, word already spreading. The air was thick with the smell of rain-soaked timber, smoke, and sharpening steel.

Zarratt raised his voice to address the gathered captain. "Some of you have served here too long, grown used to quiet nights and border patrols without purpose. That ends now. This outpost isn't just timber and stone—it's a wall between the Natsu and our Queen. If they come, we bleed them here."

Murmurs of approval rippled through the group. Some nodded.

Others tightened their grips on their weapons.

Zarratt looked to the signal tower in the courtyard's corner. "And light no fires higher than waist height from now on. I want our silhouettes low, and our intentions hidden."

A black storm was gathering beyond the hills. He could feel it. The Natsu weren't just testing the borders anymore—they were preparing for war. And Teren ridge would be their first taste of resistance.

Zarratt turned to his scribe. "Write to the Queen. Tell her the outpost stands ready—and that we will hold."

&

CHAPTER 16

S apir rode at the head of the column, his cloak flaring behind him as the wind shifted through the valley. Behind him, the Karathat horse guards moved in tight formation—tired, dust-covered, but alive. At the centre of the group, bound tightly between two riders, slumped the captured Natsu commander, Hadran.

The walls of Karathat rose before them, pale stone glowing in the late afternoon sun. Banners fluttered from the towers—deep blue and silver, the crest of Queen Storia's house. The city gates stood open, but guards were already forming a line as the returning riders approached.

A familiar figure stepped forward from the gate watch—Captain Jarrah, one of Zarratt's men.

"Sapir," Jarrah called, nodding in greeting. "We saw your banner from the tower. The Queen's been expecting you."

Sapir reined in beside him. "We have a prisoner. You'll want to keep him under heavy guard."

Jarrah signalled two of his men. "We'll take him straight to the inner cells beneath the palace. You're to report directly to the Queen."

"I thought she might want to hear this in person," Sapir said, his eyes flicking to the prisoner. "He talked. Enough to confirm what we feared."

Jarrah's expression tightened. "Then it's true."

Sapir gave a grim nod. "Yes."

They moved through the city streets, the guards peeling away to escort Hadran to the dungeons while Sapir continued toward the palace. Market stalls were still open, though many merchants paused to watch the rider's, word had spread quickly that something serious had happened.

Inside the palace, everything was quieter, but no less tense. Servants moved briskly between corridors. Advisors gathered in corners, whispering behind raised hands. The scent of polished wood and garden jasmine filled the halls—but the usual warmth of the palace felt dulled by unease.

A palace guard escorted Sapir up the wide stair to the Queen's chamber.

He paused at the doors, adjusting his sword belt, then nodded to the guard.

"Announce me."

The man gave a single rap on the great carved door before opening it.

Sapir stepped inside.

Queen Storia stood near the high windows, sunlight casting long shadows across the polished floor. Tamanda was beside her; she stood tall and proud in her guardian uniform.

Storia turned as Sapir approached, her expression unreadable.

"Well?" she asked.

Sapir bowed low, then rose to meet her gaze.

"The Natsu are gathering at Teren Ridge. Their commander admitted as much before we reached the pass. They will attack the outpost—they're not testing us anymore. They're preparing to strike."

She was silent for a moment, her hands clasped tightly before her.

Then:

"And you brought a prisoner?"

"He's in the cells below," Sapir confirmed. "He'll speak again. And this time, you'll be the one asking the questions."

Storia nodded once. "Good. We'll hear from him before nightfall. And then we send a message to the council. If war is coming, we must not face it alone.

I hope that Taran managed to encourage your elders to accept our proposal."

Sapir crossed his arms, voice low and steady. "The border will not hold forever. We need to prepare."

"It doesn't have to," she said. "It only has to hold long enough."

Her eyes turned back to the window, toward the distant haze that marked the hills of the west.

She hoped Zarratt would be safe. She couldn't stand the thought of losing another father figure.

Storia made her way to the cells beneath the palace, Tamanda walking beside her. They were heading down to meet Sapir and Bij, one of the senior guardsmen. As they descended into the bowels of the palace, the stench of the lower levels met them—thick and sour, the reek of the place where Karathat kept its most violent criminals.

The hallways were dim, lit only by flickering oil torches set in brackets along the stone walls. The floors were dirty, the stones uneven and damp in places. The air carried the foul stink of piss and shit from overflowing buckets in the cells. Storia had no doubt that at least one of the dark chambers housed a corpse as well.

They approached a particular cell, its door flanked by two guards standing stiffly. At a nod from Storia, one stepped aside to let her in.

Inside, the prisoner slumped against the back wall, blood crusted at his mouth and temple. It was clear Sapir and Bij had done their best to extract information—his swollen eye and split lip told the story well enough.

As Storia and Tamanda entered, the prisoner raised his head with effort. His gaze locked on them with a look of raw defiance. A grin split his battered face, revealing gaps where teeth had either been knocked out or pulled.

"We've tried to get more from him," Sapir said, standing nearby. "But now he's gone tight-lipped. We know where his people are heading, but not how many or when they plan to strike. He's stopped answering—just keeps shouting in his own tongue."

"How much of our language does he understand?" Storia asked.

"He knows enough," Sapir replied. "But it's broken. Like mine, not complete."

Bij stepped forward and resumed questioning, his voice sharp and direct, but the prisoner only stared—his grin fixed now on Storia. Then, slowly, he shifted his gaze to Tamanda, studying her with something between curiosity and menace.

He began speaking again—haltingly, slipping between his own language and theirs as he struggled for words.

"You," he said, voice gravelly. "You're the killer of killers. We've heard of you, girl. There is one way you could get me talking…" He smirked, eyes gleaming with suggestion.

Bij stepped forward and punched him across the face.

The prisoner's head snapped to the side, then slowly turned back. Blood ran from his mouth as he spat a thick stream onto the floor, grinning wider.

Storia stood silent, her eyes fixed on the man, her thoughts cold and calculating.

"Tell us what we want to know, how many of your people are going to Teran ridge?".

Storia stepped closer to the prisoner, stopping just a pace in front of him. She met his eyes with the calm of a ruler used to power, her expression unreadable.

"How many of you are coming?" she asked, voice low.

The prisoner said nothing.

"Where are they now? What routes are they taking?"

Still, he remained silent, breathing heavily through bloodied lips. His smile had faded, but the defiance burned brighter in his eyes. Storia took a single step closer.

"Are the Vintals with you?"

He let out a wet chuckle and lifted his head just enough to spit at her feet. It missed, but only barely.

Tamanda moved forward, hand tightening on her blade, but Storia raised a hand to stop her.

She bent slightly, eyes scanning the floor. Then she saw it—a rat, bold and gaunt, scuttling along the wall. With smooth precision, she moved quickly, snatching it by the tail. The creature squealed and twisted, its claws scrabbling at the air.

The prisoner narrowed his eyes, suddenly less amused.

Storia crossed the room to a nearby iron bucket, turned it on its side, and shoved the rat inside. Then, without a word, she stepped back toward him. Bij and Sapir watched in silence as she pressed the open end of the bucket firmly against the prisoner's bare stomach and held it there with her knee.

Then, calmly, she took a lit torch from the wall.

The prisoner squirmed now, the first flickers of fear showing in his eyes.

Storia crouched slightly and held the flame beneath the base of the bucket. The metal began to blacken almost immediately.

"You know what happens next," she said, her voice barely more than a whisper. "The rat has only one way out."

The prisoner started to twist, his bravado crumbling. He gritted his teeth and tried to pull back, but the guards at the door had already bound his hands and arms in and locked his shoulders in place.

Within seconds, the bucket began to rattle.

The rat screamed inside—high-pitched, frantic—and the prisoner shouted in his own language, trying to kick out.

Storia didn't flinch.

"Talk," she said.

He screamed again; the sound laced with pain and panic.

And the bucket kept rattling.

The bucket rattled violently now, the rat inside thrashing in blind terror as the metal grew hotter. The prisoner screamed—a full, guttural howl—his body convulsing as the animal began to bite and claw, desperate to escape the searing heat.

Tamanda took a step back, eyes wide. "My Queen…" she murmured, her hand frozen on the hilt of her sword.

Even Sapir, who had seen battlefield cruelty in many forms, looked uneasy. His jaw was tight, his eyes flicking between the torch, the bucket, and Storia's expression—calm, cold, unblinking.

The prisoner screamed again, his voice cracking as blood began to seep from beneath the edges of the bucket. He thrashed harder, but his shackles held him firm.

Then he broke.

"Stop! STOP!" he yelled, switching to broken Karathati. "I'll talk!

I'll talk!"

Storia calmly moved the torch away and gestured for Bij to remove the bucket. The metal hissed as it was pulled from the prisoner's scorched skin, revealing ragged, bleeding wounds where the rat had tried to claw its way out.

The man sobbed, slumped, shaking. "A small lead force maybe two hundred Natsu riders… no more. and some Vintal mercenaries. They wait in the Black wood. They move at the new moon." Sapir stepped forward. "What's their target?"

The prisoner coughed, spitting more blood. "Not Karathat.

Not yet.

They strike your trade roads and outposts first. Starve you. Force your

Queen to bend."

Tamanda looked to Storia, eyes still filled with shock. "How did you know he'd break?"

Storia didn't answer immediately. She calmly placed the torch back into the wall sconce, straightened the front of her tunic, and spoke with quiet finality.

"Everyone talks. Eventually."

Without another word, she turned and strode from the cell, her footsteps measured and precise. As she passed Bij, she gave a small, subtle wave of her fingers.

Bij understood.

He drew his knife without hesitation and stepped forward. In one swift, clean motion, he dragged the blade across the prisoner's throat. The man gurgled once, then slumped, blood pooling at his knees.

Tamanda and Sapir remained still, saying nothing. They exchanged a glance—neither certain whether they had just witnessed justice… or something far more dangerous taking root in their queen.

The door to the cell creaked shut behind them, and the sound of Storia's footsteps faded up the corridor.

Tamanda stood still, her eyes fixed on the blood spreading across the floor where the prisoner had collapsed. The rat had vanished into the shadows again, its work done.

Bij wiped his blade clean with calm efficiency, then slipped it back into its sheath before stepping out into the hall, leaving Sapir and Tamanda alone.

For a long moment, neither spoke.

Then Tamanda turned to Sapir, her voice low.

"She didn't even blink," Tamanda said, frowning. "Just signalled him dead like it was nothing."

"She made a choice," Sapir replied, though his tone was grim. "The kind you only make when you know what's at stake. Or when you've stopped caring what the cost is."

Tamanda leaned against the wall, her hand resting near her hip. "Is that what this war is going to do to us? Turn us into monsters to beat monsters?"

Sapir looked back toward the cell. "It doesn't turn you. It reveals you. That's the danger."

Tamanda was silent for a moment, her brows drawn. "I don't fear what's out there. Not really. But I think I'm starting to fear what's in here," she said, tapping a hand lightly against her chest. "And maybe... what's in her."

Sapir didn't respond at first. He looked up the corridor, then finally spoke.

"She's trying to protect her people. The way she knows how. But if we lose sight of why we fight—what makes us different from the Natsu or the Vintals—then we've already lost."

Tamanda nodded slowly. "Then we'd better hold the line. For her sake as much as ours."

They stood there a while longer, the flickering torchlight painting their faces in shadow, both knowing this war would demand more than swords and shields.

Storia ascended the stone steps slowly, the torchlight fading behind her as the stench of the lower cells gave way to the colder air of the palace corridors. Her expression remained composed, but a shadow lingered in her eyes.

She could still hear the wet rasp of the prisoner's last breath in her memory—could feel the silent weight of Tamanda and Sapir's stares on her back as she walked away. But she didn't falter.

This was what leadership demanded.

As she reached the main corridor, a pair of guards straightened at her approach. She nodded once, and they fell into step behind her. The moon had risen, casting silver light through the high arched windows of the east wing. Somewhere in the distance, the soft notes of a stringed instrument echoed faintly from the royal quarters—someone playing as if the world were not shifting beneath their feet.

Storia walked on.

She made her way to the council chamber, empty now but still thick with the scent of oil and old arguments. She stood at the long table, her fingers brushing its edge. A map lay across its surface—Karathat and the outlying territories. Her eyes fell to the northeast, to Teren ridge.

Two hundred riders.

Vintal mercenaries.

A small lead attack, an assault timed with the new moon.

She breathed in deeply and placed her palms flat on the table.

They would come; they would come with a larger force.

And when they did, Karathat would be ready—but not just with swords and walls. No. This would take more than that. It would take ruthlessness. Precision. Will.

Something cold had settled in her tonight. She wasn't sure if she'd lost something in that cell—or found something that had always been there.

She stood there a while longer, silent, alone with her thoughts and the war already gathering beyond the horizon.

໖

CHAPTER 17

The gates of Landa groaned open as the first light of dawn touched the rooftops with pale gold. Fog clung to the lower streets, rising like ghost-breath from the stones, and the sound of hooves echoed through the city's narrow lanes.

Taran rode at the head of the column, his cloak wrapped tight against the morning chill. Behind him, a dozen riders followed in silence—scouts, messengers, and guards sworn to him for the journey. The banner of his village flapped from a lance at the rear, its dark fabric already catching the wind as they moved.

Landa was stirring but subdued. Traders lit their hearths, guards watched from towers, and old men stood silently in doorways, woman stood at the gate sobbing and wailing prayers to the spirits to protect their loved ones. War had been spoken in the elders chambers the night before. Now it was real. Now it moved.

They passed under through the main gate, just beyond the gate the road split—one fork heading east to Karathat, the other vanishing north into the mist-cloaked hills.

Taran chose the eastern path.

Beside him, a young scout named Halin adjusted the straps on his saddle. "Do you think the banners will answer?" he asked quietly.

"They already have," Taran replied. "They just haven't realised the cost."

The road opened ahead, lined by tall oaks and early blooming thistle. Somewhere beyond those trees, enemy riders were on the move. The

Natsu. The Vintal. Shadows in the forest waiting for their moment.

Taran's jaw tightened.

The council had argued for hours—some urging caution, others revenge. But when the reports came, when the smoke from the border villages couldn't be denied, the room had shifted. Voices of doubt had gone quiet. Swords had been counted.

And the banners were called.

Now the war was no longer a threat in the distance. It was a line of riders on the road. It was steel on backs and silence in men's eyes.

Taran reached for the reins and urged his horse faster.

Whatever lay ahead, they would not meet it unprepared.

Not this time.

They had been riding for several days, the host moving steadily across rough country. Scouts had returned throughout the last few days, each bringing fragments of the larger picture. Riders had been sighted—small groups at first, then larger movements, all heading south toward the Karathat border.

It seemed clear now: the Natsu or the Vintals—or both— had been watching them just as closely as they had sent scouts to watch the enemy.

A few of the scouts reported that some of the enemy outriders had shouted challenges across the hills, trying to bait them into skirmishes. But the Karathati scouts had stuck to their orders. No engagement. No delay. Just observation and return.

And still, with each passing day, the enemy host crept closer. Adjusting their course. Closing the gap.

The host came to a wide stream by late morning. The waters were fast but clear, the kind that ran cold even in the warmth of day. They stopped to water the horses, refill their skins, and let the men take a short rest.

Taran dismounted and made his way to the gathering of commanders. They had formed a rough circle in a patch of open ground beneath a leaning tree. Around them, horses shifted, drank, and pawed at the ground, while low voices discussed what little they knew.

He arrived as Farren, the faction leader of the eastern villages, was speaking.

"—that's true," Farren said, pointing to a worn map spread across a saddlebag. "If they continue their current heading, they'll hit the first

Karathat outpost in three days. A small station on Teren Ridge."

Taran stepped forward. "How many soldiers will the Karathat have at the outpost?"

"Not many," one of the elders replied. "If they have not sent reinforcements maybe fifty men, maybe. Some mounted couriers to carry messages to the other outposts or back to Karathat."

Taran's brow furrowed. "Have the scouts reported the size of the main force?"

Farren shook his head. "To my knowledge, no scout has managed to get close enough to make a proper estimate. They've all stayed hidden.

Smart of them. But it leaves us blind."

Taran looked down at the map, then out toward the tree line, as if he might see the enemy host cresting the next ridge.

"We need to get closer and make an assessment of their numbers," Taran said, his eyes still on the map. "We need to know what type of force they have."

Before he could finish, a rider burst through the brush at the edge of the clearing. He was on foot, breath coming in gasps, sweat running down his brow. Without slowing, he stumbled into the circle of commanders and shouted a single word. "Banners!" Everyone froze.

Taran turned toward the others, his expression hardening. "Looks like we don't have time to wait."

The camp was in full flurry. Messengers rushed between tents, commanders barked orders, and scouts rode in and out with fresh updates on enemy movements. The tension was palpable boots in mud, firelight flickering, the smell of sweat, leather, and steel.

They had estimated the enemy force to be four Durims—roughly eight hundred men. The Vintals had committed a serious body of troops.

Taran stood with the other commanders around a large field map stretched over a wooden crate. Though battle strategy had been discussed by the captains, it was Taran who had been granted command of the host by the elders.

He addressed the circle, voice steady despite the weight of what lay ahead.

"The scouts are now reporting more frequent movement," he began. "It appears to be Vintal banners—something we haven't seen on our lands or borders for some time. There's no sign of the Natsu yet… but we cannot rule them out."

Darah, a lean man from the western villages, stepped forward. He was one of the fortunate few who had escaped to Landa before the raids began.

"Taran," he said, "my last scout believes their force numbers around five-hundred-foot warriors, one hundred archers, and two hundred cavalries."

Taran nodded. "The Vintals are barbaric in their tactics. They'll want to crush us in open field, drive fear before their blades. But we won't give them the fight they want."

He looked around the circle, then continued, voice growing firmer.

"I have a formation and a plan—but it will require discipline. Patience. And that concerns me… many of our young warriors are eager to be blooded. But eagerness alone doesn't hold a line." He
pointed to the map.

"We usually position our veterans second in the shield wall, but that changes now. I want four ranks of veterans at the front. Behind them, the new warriors. And behind them again, a final rank of veterans. The young will hold—not because of courage, but because they'll be braced on both sides by those who've stood through worse." He let that settle, then continued.

"We are outnumbered. Our full strength stands at seven hundred. We match them in cavalry—one hundred light horse and fifty lancers.

We have just over three-hundred-foot soldiers, and one hundred and fifty archers."

He tapped the flanks of the map.

"I want our light cavalry to spread wide, hidden in the forest tree line on both sides. When the enemy cavalry commits, breakfast—drive behind them, and tear through their archers."

He turned to a tall, broad-shouldered commander. "Our lancers will form wide on the right. You'll face their horse directly. It will be brutal. But if we can break their charge early, we can collapse in behind and turn the field." He looked to the centre now.

"Our infantry must hold. No matter what they see coming. No matter what cries they hear. Hold the line. The front will carry more than their weight—they are the heart of this defence."

He finally motioned to the edge of the map where the rear archers were marked.

"Our archers fall under Stafan's command. He has his orders and is already making preparations. Trust in him."

Taran looked up, meeting each commander's gaze in turn.

"You have your positions. You have your orders. Fight smart. Fight hard. I'll see you in the field and if the spirits wish it, we'll drink by the campfire tonight.

~~~~~~~~~~~~~~~~~~~~~~~~~

The mist hung low over the fields at dawn.

Birdsong had stopped.

Soldiers moved in near silence, tightening straps, adjusting shields, murmuring quiet prayers to gods they didn't always believe in. Horses stamped and snorted softly, sensing the tension in their riders.

Taran stood just behind the forward line, his eyes scanning the far ridgeline. There, faint against the rising light, movement stirred—the slow, deliberate organization of a war force. Vintal banners. Black and red. No mistaking them now.

The Durims were coming.

He looked to his right. The light cavalry was already hidden in the trees, their mounts calm, weapons sheathed. On the left, the lancers waited in silence, their leather armour beneath linen covers, blades resting across saddle pommels.

Behind him, the shield ranks stood in formation—veterans at the front, the green among them already pale-faced with nerves, several young warriors could be heard throwing up in the lines. Further back, archers moved into their positions under Stafan's command, every bow already strung, quivers bristling.

Tanny rode up alongside him, his face calm but pale. "They'll try to break the middle," he said, watching the horizon. Taran nodded. "Let them try."

For a long moment, the two of them said nothing. Just watching. Listening. The only sound was the soft wind through the grass and the distant beat of a drum.

Then, a horn sounded—low and long—from the far hill.
~~~~~~~~~~~~~~~~~~~~~~~~~

The Vintals had begun to move.

Taran drew his sword. The weight was familiar. So was the silence that followed.

He turned his horse to face his men.

"Hold your positions, trust the man next to you." And then the thunder of war began.

He watched carefully, studying every movement, every adjustment in their lines. The enemy was precise, drilled, confident in its familiar patterns.

Their foot soldiers formed the vanguard, arranged in disciplined ranks of six across. Unlike a loose skirmish line, they kept their front tight, minimizing gaps and presenting a solid wall of shields and blades. Behind this rank stood the archers, bows strung and ready, their lines set to rain arrows over the heads of their own men. Further back, another formation of foot soldiers waited in reserve — a second wave to reinforce or exploit any weakness revealed in the first assault. It was a textbook deployment for Vintal warriors, one Taran had heard described countless times by the elders as they recounted the glories and tragedies of battles past.

The cavalry, meanwhile, stood poised on both flanks, their horses shifting restlessly, snorting and pawing the ground. Swords glinted at their sides, and short spears bristled in their hands, ready to crash through a broken line when the moment came.

Taran's gaze swept over them all, absorbing the shape of their ranks, their spacing, the confidence in their bearing. He had prepared his own warriors as best he could, drilling them to stand firm and hold the line. He had devised his plan, laid out his strategy with care, but he knew that once battle was joined, all plans could shatter like thin glass. Still, he could only trust that the preparations he had set in place — the discipline, the positioning, the will of his warriors — would be enough to face what was coming.

He exhaled slowly, steadying the knot of tension in his chest. The morning air was sharp, carrying the faint tang of dust and iron. Around him, his own men shifted in place, checking spear hafts, adjusting shield straps, exchanging brief, grim glances. They were outnumbered — he could see that plainly — but he also saw the determination etched on their faces. Men who had survived ambush, betrayal, and loss stood with him now, ready to hold the line against a force that would gladly see them wiped from memory.

Taran moved down the line of his warriors, touching shoulders, offering small nods of encouragement. He met each gaze, letting them see the confidence in his own eyes, even if a part of him quaked inside. Fear was a battle in itself, one that had to be fought before a blade ever swung.

"Steady," he called to them, voice carrying over the muted clink of armour. "Hold your positions until my signal. Let them come to us. Break

their first rush, and they will doubt themselves."

The men nodded, gripping their weapons tighter. Beyond their ranks, the Vintal formations were beginning to advance, a slow, deliberate march that made the earth tremble. Banners snapped in the breeze above their columns, marked with symbols of power and conquest.

Taran stepped back to his place at the front, drawing a long breath. He let his eyes sweep the battlefield one final time, committing every fold of terrain to memory — the shallow dip near the left, the rise of stony ground to the right, places where men might fall or where a stand might be made.

He clenched his jaw, heart thudding against his ribs. The Vintal were close enough now that he could see their faces, warriors grim and resolute, armoured in hard leather and

polished metal. There would be no easy victory today —
perhaps no victory at all — but there was still a chance, a spark
of hope he refused to smother.

When the time came, he would light that spark.

CHAPTER 18

S toria stood at the window of the war room, eyes fixed on

the eastern horizon.

There was nothing but sky and the low, rolling hills that led toward the border—toward Teren Ridge, where she had sent a detachment of fifty men three days ago. A small force. A necessary gamble. She hated it.

No messenger had returned.

Not from Taran.

Not from Zarratt at the outpost.

And nothing at all from the Natsu territories.

The silence was what gnawed at her. Not a scream, not a cry for help—just absence. The kind of silence that buried answers.

She stepped back from the window; arms crossed over her chest. The maps on the war table were still marked with scout paths, projected enemy movements, and supply routes—lines drawn in charcoal and hope.

But none of it meant anything without reports. Without eyes.

Sapir entered without knocking. He knew better by now.

"No word," he said, his voice low.

Storia didn't respond at first. She studied a small marker on the map—an etched stone token shaped like a horse. It sat on the border near Teren Ridge, marking the outpost. Still there. Still unchallenged. Still unknown.

"How many hours does it take for fifty men to die?" she asked quietly.

Sapir looked at her, unsure whether to answer. "They could still be holding."

"They could be ash," she snapped, then caught herself. Her voice dropped. "Or worse taken. Forced to talk."

She moved away from the table and toward the open doors of the balcony. The wind was rising, sharp and cool, brushing her cheek like a warning.

"What of the Natsu?" she asked.

Sapir shook his head. "Scouts haven't returned from the eastern reaches. Either they're delayed… or watched."

"And your people—the Mandji?"

He hesitated. "They're quiet."

Storia's jaw clenched. Quiet could mean peace. Or preparation. She didn't like guessing.

"Taran should have reached his people by now."

"Should I send a rider?"

She considered. If they were already in battle, the rider might never reach him. If they weren't, it might look like panic. "No," she said. "We wait. For now."

Sapir gave a small nod and stepped back.

When she was alone again, Storia returned to the map. She touched the token at Teren Ridge, then another marking Taran's last known position.

"Hold," she whispered to them both. "Just hold long enough."

But she couldn't shake the sense that somewhere, something had already broken—and no word was coming.

The door creaked open again, softer this time.

Tamanda stepped in, quiet as a shadow.

"I didn't want to interrupt," she said, her voice barely above the wind.

"You already have," Storia replied, but not unkindly.

Tamanda approached the map table, eyes scanning the pieces. "You think they're dead?"

"I think they've been gone too long," Storia said. "And no one stays quiet this long unless they're bleeding, hiding, or plotting."

Tamanda nodded once. "If Zarratt were alive, he'd find a way to send word."

Storia looked at her sharply. "He might still." Tamanda didn't argue.

There was a pause, filled with the rustle of wind across the stone.

Then Storia asked, "Would you ride to the ridge, if I asked?"

"Yes."

"No hesitation?"

Tamanda gave her a look. "There's never hesitation. Not when it's you asking."

Storia smiled faintly—something brittle beneath it. "I may ask. But not yet. If we move too soon, we show fear."

"And if we move too late?"

Storia turned back to the map, her hand hovering once more over the carved tokens.

"Then we lose."

Tamanda had left Storia in the council chambers and had made her way to the stables, she saddled the mare in silence.

The courtyard was half-lit by the moon, the lanterns near the stables already dimmed for the night. The guards posted at the outer gate were drowsy with routine and darkness—exactly as she'd hoped.

Storia hadn't given the order.

But Tamanda knew it was coming. Knew that waiting any longer might mean too late. She wasn't going to sit by and watch the queen be swallowed by silence.

She tightened the girth strap and checked her blades— short sabre at her left hip, dagger behind the saddle roll. She wore no sigil, no house colours. Just a worn travel cloak and hardened leather, dark with oil.

The mare gave a low huff, sensing something in the tension of the night.

"Easy," Tamanda whispered, placing a steadying hand on the animal's neck. "We ride light."

She pulled herself into the saddle in one fluid motion. A flick of the reins. Then she was gone—slipping through the outer gate as it swung open for a departing supply wagon. No one questioned her.

The city fell away behind her, its lights shrinking like dying embers.

She took the old trade path west, through the scrub and red stone gullies that twisted down from the plateau. The night air was sharp and cold, pulling tears from the corners of her eyes. The stars were clear above her—too clear. The kind of sky you rode beneath before things broke.

She had ridden this road once before, years ago, when her name meant nothing and her blade had never drawn blood for a queen. Now, every hoofbeat felt heavier. Like she carried more than herself—like the burden of not knowing what waited at Teren Ridge pressed down on her chest with every mile.

If the outpost had fallen, she needed to know.

If Zarratt had fallen, she needed to see.

And if the Natsu or Vintals were already moving through the Karathat borderlands, someone needed to return with more than a prayer.

A vulture passed overhead just before dawn, black against the greying sky, she deemed that as a bad omen and began to prey to her gods.

She came to a junction in the track and realised something was wrong.

The road had narrowed into a winding trail; little more than a dirt path scratched between ridgelines. The morning mist clung low to the ground, and her mare's hooves made barely a sound on the packed earth.

Tamanda rode alone—no banners, no colours, just her blade and her instincts.

She spotted the figure slumped in the grass before the sun had fully risen.

A horse lay nearby, sides still, half-covered in dust. The rider beside it was motionless at first, but as she approached, his head turned with effort.

Blood soaked one sleeve. His cloak was torn and dark with mud.

Tamanda dismounted in a single motion, sabre drawn but held low.

"You from Teren Ridge?" she asked as she knelt beside him.

He nodded faintly. "Zarratt… he sent me. Took a blade in the leg—couldn't ride far."

"Are you carrying a seal?" she asked.

He fumbled at his belt and pulled a small carved disc from beneath his cloak. It was cracked, but unmistakable—Zarratt's command seal.

Tamanda took it, eyes narrowing.

"What happened?"

"They came before moonrise. Painted faces. No warning." His breath caught. "Mandji."

She stiffened. "Are you sure?"

"Too sure," he croaked. "Zarratt held the gate so the rest of us could break out. Not many made it. Maybe two other riders. I headed for

Karathat. Didn't make it far."

Tamanda glanced down the trail. If the Natsu were hunting escapees, they'd be watching the roads.

"You're not safe here," she muttered. "Can you ride?" His grimace said enough.

"Then I'll get you to a relay post," she said, already turning toward her mare. "We'll find another way to warn the Queen."

She slung his arm over her shoulder and lifted him with effort into her saddle. The horse shifted but held steady. She climbed up behind him, steadying his weight.

Just as she turned the mare back onto the trail, a sharp whistle cut through the brush.

She froze.

Three shapes rose from the scrub ahead—Natsu scouts, lean and fast, blades curved like crescent moons in their hands. Their faces were marked in ash and red pigment, eyes wide with hunger and something older: hate.

Tamanda dropped from the saddle again, blade already drawn.

The wounded rider slumped against the pommel, barely able to speak.

"They followed… they've been tracking…" The first scout charged.

She met him steel-to-steel, parrying hard and pivoting off the attack. The second closed in from the left—silent and fast. She ducked low, swept a leg, and dropped him to the dirt, but the third was already behind her.

A blade nicked her side. She spun with a gasp and slashed across his chest, catching leather but not skin.

The first one came again—heavier now, angrier. She sidestepped, slashed across his shoulder, then dropped low and stabbed upward. The blade sank in deep. He collapsed with a gargled cry.

The second was up again, limping. She met him quickly—two steps and a hard crosscut across his throat. He fell without a sound.

Only the third remained.

He hesitated, saw the others on the ground, then hissed something in his tongue and slipped into the brush, vanishing.

Tamanda stood still for a long moment, breath ragged. Blood trickled down her side where the third scout had landed his mark. It was deep she tried her best to cover it.

She wiped her blade clean and checked on the rider. He was pale, but alive.

They rode on—slower now, but with no more illusions of safety.

Tamanda kept one hand near her blade, her eyes scanning every ridge and shadow along the narrow trail. The morning had fully broken, though the sky remained grey and overcast. The light didn't comfort her. It only revealed more emptiness—no patrols, no signal fires, no signs of Zarratt's men.

Only ash, silence, and the road curling north toward home.

The wounded rider sagged more with every step. She had bound his leg as best she could with a strip torn from her cloak, but the blood loss was catching up to him.

"You still with me?" she asked.

No reply came from the rider; she could feel his chest rising and falling but it was faint.

Tamanda gritted her teeth through her own pain and pressed the mare into a steady trot.

Every hour mattered now. Every heartbeat.

Because the Queen needed to know.

The Natsu had crossed the border.

They were still prowling the valleys.

And Teren Ridge was gone.

By mid-afternoon, the ground levelled out and the first of Karathat's outer farms came into view. Empty. No carts. No smoke from hearths. Just wind in dry grass and the occasional creaking of a gate left open. Tamanda didn't slow.

They passed a pair of children playing with sticks on a hillside. One looked up and waved. The other just stared. Tamanda didn't wave back. She couldn't.

By dusk, the towers of Karathat rose in the distance—pale and sharp against the dying light.

She didn't wait for gate formalities.

"Halt!" the guard called, but she was already passing through. "By order of—"

"By order of the Queen!" Tamanda snapped. "I'll answer later."

The mare's hooves thundered through the cobbled streets as curious eyes turned to watch her pass—bloodied, cloaked, carrying a half-dead man behind her.

When she reached the palace courtyard, she barely managed to lower him from the saddle before a pair of guards rushed forward, they grabbed the rider before he fell.

Her side was on fire now—every breath scraped like glass against the wound. The bindings had soaked through with blood hours ago.

She saw more of the guards coming to her aid, heard one call her name—but before she could raise a hand in answer, the world tilted.

Her horse shifted, she lost her seat, and then she was falling.

The impact was hard and sudden, a flash of sky, dust, stone.

Voices shouted. Hands gripped her arms, her shoulders.

"Tamanda!"

"Get her up—careful—gods, look at her side—"

She tried to speak, but only a dry rasp escaped. Someone pressed cloth to her ribs, another was shouting for help.

Through the haze, she clenched her jaw. Not here. Not yet.

She forced herself upright with a growl of pain, blood trailing down her tunic. Her knees buckled again, but two guards steadied her.

"Get a healer," she ordered, voice hoarse but firm. "Now."

Then she turned her face toward the palace, hair wind-swept, cloak torn, eyes alight with fire.

"I need to see the Queen."

&

CHAPTER 19

Z arratt stood on the ramparts, eyes scanning the dark edge

of the Black Wood. The dense forest loomed beyond the clearing, its tangled canopy blotting out the stars. The moon hung high above, casting pale silver light across the cold night. Mist had begun to rise from the ground, curling in low ribbons across the open space between the trees and the rough timber fence that marked the outpost's outer boundary.

Below him, the men he had brought from Karathat worked tirelessly throughout the day. Trenches now scarred the earth beyond the walls, flanked by sharpened stakes angled outward. Further out, the smiths had fashioned crude metal tacts—small, wickedly pointed caltrops—and scattered them across the field where an enemy might charge.

Markers, measured and discreet, had been placed in the field to guide the archers with their range. Catapults now stood mounted along the ramparts, tensioned and loaded. Piles of stones sat beside them, neatly stacked, while cauldrons had been filled with oil, waiting for the fires to boil them to a deadly heat.

Still, Zarratt knew it would not be enough.

He had doubled the guard on the walls, stretching his Karathat men thin to cover the perimeter. Even so, there were not enough to hold static posts. The soldiers were forced to patrol constantly, walking the length of the walls in pairs.

To give the illusion of strength, he'd had the carpenters construct uniformed frames—wooden dummies dressed in surplus armour and posted along the ramparts. From a distance, it might look as though the walls bristled with defenders. It was a trick, but a necessary one.

None of the scouts he had sent into the forest had returned in recent days. After the third disappearance, Zarratt had given the order to stop sending them out altogether. He could not afford to lose more men to silence and shadows.

Now, he stared into the tree line, watching. Waiting. The forest always seemed to shift with movement—branches that swayed without wind, shadows that lengthened in unnatural ways. He could never be certain whether it was imagination or threat.

But he knew they were out there.

And when they came, they would search for the one weakness he hadn't yet seen.

Zarratt remained still, his gloved hands resting on the cold stone of the rampart. Below, the mist thickened, crawling like a living thing across the open field. The only sounds were the distant clatter of boots on timber walkways and the creak of straining ropes on the catapults.

A sharp voice broke the silence.

"You should be resting, Commander."

Zarratt didn't turn. "Should I?"

Captain Mevran stepped into the torchlight, his face drawn and pale beneath his helmet. His armour was battered, spattered with mud from the trenchwork. He looked as tired as the rest of them, but something behind his eyes was sharp— uncertain.

"You've barely slept since we arrived," Mevran said. "And we've had no movement in three nights. Perhaps they're not coming." "They're coming," Zarratt said flatly.

Mevran hesitated. "With respect… you don't know that.

We're wearing the men thin, bleeding strength into these walls. If we—"

"We don't have the luxury of guessing," Zarratt cut in. "If they come, and we're unprepared, every man inside these walls will die. And if they don't? Then we've lost nothing by staying ready."

"They're afraid, sir," Mevran said quietly. "The men. They speak of the forest like it's cursed. Some say the scouts didn't fall—they were taken. Silently."

Zarratt finally turned. His eyes were shadowed, but hard.

"Do you believe that, Captain?"

Mevran met his gaze, jaw tight. "I don't know what to believe anymore. But I know this—if you fall, the men will break."

Zarratt stared at him for a long moment. Then he stepped forward, past Mevran, and looked out once more into the shifting black beyond the clearing.

"I'll fall when the wall burns," he said. "Not before."

Zarratt squinted into the dark, his eyes straining to see more than shadow. He leaned over the stone edge of the rampart, as if angling his body might somehow peel back the veil of night.

"There," he said sharply, his voice slicing the silence.

"Bring me an archer—now!"

Mevran turned on his heel and shouted for a bowman. Moments later, a young archer jogged up the steps, bow in hand, eyes wide with nerves. Zarratt pointed out across the field, his finger fixed on a spot just beyond the second trench.

"Fire a flame arrow at that trench line. Now."

The archer hesitated, glancing uncertainly between Zarratt and the darkness. Mevran stepped closer.

"Commander, there's nothing there," he said, keeping his voice low. "If we light the trench now, it'll have to be reset by morning. The men are already exhausted."

Zarratt's jaw clenched. "Fire the damn arrow now or I'll have you flogged."

The archer fumbled for a firestick, lit the tip of his arrow, and notched it. He drew back the string, breath held, then loosed.

The arrow sailed into the night in a high arc, trailing flame like a falling star. It struck the ground just short of the trench—no movement, no sound, nothing.

"Again," Zarratt barked. "This time hit the trench."

Mevran stepped forward, voice more forceful now. "Commander—you need rest."

"Do it!" Zarratt snapped.

The archer obeyed. He lit a second arrow, steadied himself, and fired. This time, the shot struck true. The arrow plunged into the trench, igniting the oil pooled there.

With a low whoosh, fire rippled along the trench in a jagged line.

Then came the scream.

A single, agonized cry—human—ripped through the air.

From the trench, figures burst into view, silhouetted in the firelight. Men, burning, scrambling to escape the flames. Screams followed, then war cries, erupting all at once from the tree line and across the clearing.

Zarratt spun toward Mevran. "They're here! Ring the bell—get the men to their stations!"

The alarm bell clanged seconds later, echoing through the compound. Torches flared to life along the walls. Soldiers scrambled from their bunks, weapons drawn, boots pounding across the frozen earth.

Above them all, Zarratt stood still for a moment, watching the dark flood of enemy shapes pour from the misted trees.

"So, it begins."

~~~~~~~~~~~~~~~~~~~~~~~~~~~~~

Commander Sukuri watched from the tree line, crouched beside the roots of a twisted ash tree, his cloak soaked from the cold mist that blanketed the forest floor. His men had crawled into position under the cover of nightfall, silent as wolves, slipping into the outer trenches while the Karathat sentries paced above in practiced, predictable patterns.

The outpost loomed just beyond the field—crude but defensible. The sharpened stakes, the glint of metal traps scattered across the frostbitten earth, and the illusion of more men on the walls than there truly were—he'd seen all the tricks before.

But Zarratt was no fool.

Sukuri cursed under his breath as the first flame arrow split the sky.

It struck short, sending only a faint flicker across the field.

He stilled his breath, motionless in the dark.

They're probing, he thought. Guessing.

But when the second arrow came—and struck true—his thoughts were drowned in fire.

The trench burst into light, and the screams began.

Sukuri's face twisted with fury as the flames exposed his forward raiders—men meant to slip into the compound the moment the bell tower changed shift. Now they writhed in fire, weapons forgotten, their cover obliterated.

The roar of alarm bells began to peal from within the walls.

"Go!" he snapped. "Sound the charge—now!"

Runners darted along the flanks, carrying the call to attack. From the woods, hundreds of Natsu warriors burst forth like a black tide, their war cries shaking the clearing. Some rushed
~~~~~~~~~~~~~~~~~~~~~~~~~~~~~

forward, vaulting trenches and driving toward the outpost wall. Others hung back, loosing arrows in deadly volleys toward the flickering torchlight of the defenders.

Sukuri rose to his full height and stepped from the trees.

This was not how he had planned it—but now that it had begun, he would break Zarratt's walls through fire and blood.

He drew his blade and pointed it toward the ramparts.

"Bring them down!"

~~~~~~~~~~~~~~~~~~~~~~~~~~~~~~

Zarratt strode along the rampart, firelight dancing as arrows hissed through the air around him. The trench outside burned bright now, casting chaotic shadows across the clearing, and illuminating the enemy pouring from the trees.

"Shields up!" he bellowed. "Archers, mark the tree line— loose at will!"

A volley of Karathat arrows arced outward, vanishing into the dark before thudding into bodies, trees, and earth. Still, the Natsu surged forward, some vaulting the first trench, others crashing into the spikes and falling impaled, tripping the ones behind them.

But they were too many.

"They're testing the eastern wall," Mevran shouted, running up beside him, his cheek bloodied from a glancing blow. "That's where they'll try to breach!"

Zarratt nodded grimly, already seeing it for himself—the enemy pressing harder on the eastern flank, the wall there thinner, the guards sparser.

"Bring the oil!" Zarratt ordered.

Mevran blinked. "You want to burn our own field?"

"I want to burn them before they reach it."

He turned to a runner. "Signal the catapults—load pitch rounds, east wall. Now!"
~~~~~~~~~~~~~~~~~~~~~~~~~~~~~~

The boy sprinted down the stairs two at a time. A moment later, Zarratt's command rang out across the compound as flame-tipped barrels were hauled into place. The eastern catapults swung into alignment.

Zarratt clenched his jaw and raised his arm.

"Release!"

The first catapult fired with a heavy thunk, sending a barrel trailing flame high into the air. It landed just short of the eastern trench—but the second and third struck true.

Pitch exploded in a wave of fire and smoke, engulfing the forward ranks of the Natsu.

Screams followed—brief, guttural, lost quickly under the clash of metal and the pounding war drums echoing from the trees.

Zarratt didn't wait. He turned to Mevran. "Take fifty of our reserves.

Reinforce the east wall. If they breach, plug it with steel."

"I will stay here with our archers and catapults to defend the gate."

Mevran gave a short nod, then vanished down the ramp with a group of soldiers at his heels.

Zarratt remained, eyes fixed on the inferno in the field, where fire danced and shadows screamed.

Zarratt paced along the central rampart, the battlements shuddering with each impact of enemy arrows and the concussive booms of the catapults. The air reeked of pitch smoke and burning flesh, the night alive with chaos—screams, shouts, the deep groan of timber straining under assault.

"Rotate the archers!" he shouted above the din. "No gaps— fresh quivers, now!"

His men responded swiftly. Though bone-tired, their movements were sharp, drilled into them over long weeks of preparation. Arrows loosed in steady rhythm, cutting arcs through the smoke. The catapult crews reloaded with practised speed, hurling flaming barrels at the growing mass near the gate.

The Natsu were shifting focus now.

Their warbands had tested the eastern wall and been met with fire—but now, Zarratt saw their true push forming, massing in the shadows just beyond the cleared trench at the main gate.

"Here they come," he muttered.

A horn sounded in the distance—low, guttural, then taken up by another and another. From the mist, the enemy charged.

Scores of Natsu warriors surged forward, some with shields raised against the incoming arrows, others dragging heavy wooden mantlets or siege ladders. A small battering ram—crudely built but functional—rolled into view, pushed by four men under cover of a dampened hide canopy.

"Archers! Focus fire on that ram!" Zarratt roared. "Catapult crews, hit the flanks—now!"

Flaming missiles rained down around the gate, striking the outer ranks of the attackers. The ram kept coming.

"Boil the oil!" Zarratt snapped, racing down the stairs to the tower base. He climbed into the secondary platform built above the gate itself. A soldier handed him a burning brand without a word.

Zarratt thrust the brand into the iron cauldron hanging over the gate's approach. The oil hissed, then burst into flame.

"Pour on my mark…"

Below, the ram neared, less than ten paces from the wall. Arrows clattered off its canopy. One Natsu broke from the formation and tried to scale a corner, only to be met with a spear to the throat.

Zarratt waited—calm, silent, eyes fixed.

Closer. Just a little more…

"Now!"

The flaming oil poured down in a blistering cascade, splashing over the ram and the men below. Screams erupted as the fire clung to skin and cloth. The ram shuddered, halted, then tilted as its handlers fled in agony.

A cheer rose from the defenders on the wall.

But Zarratt didn't smile.

"They'll try again," he said, voice like iron. "This was just the first wave."

He looked up toward the darkened trees, where more shadows gathered beyond the light of the burning trench.

"Tell Mevran to hold his line," he said to the nearest runner. "And tell him… the gate still stands."

&

CHAPTER 20

S toria paced the length of the high chamber, her shoes echoing sharply on the stone floor. The wind had picked up outside, rattling the long windows and stirring the heavy curtains, but she ignored it. Her thoughts were louder.

"She had no orders," Storia said flatly, not for the first time that evening.

Sapir stood a few paces from the map table, arms folded, his cloak still dusted with road grit from his own return only hours ago. "She didn't wait for them. That's Tamanda."

"She's, my guard. Mine." Storia spun, pointing toward the empty space by the archway where Tamanda usually stood. "I raised her above every veteran in the palace. And she vanished. Took a horse, weapons, and left without word."
"She left a message," Sapir said.

"A line scrawled in charcoal on the stable wall?" Storia snapped.

"That's not a message. That's a defiance."

There was silence between them. The wind howled softly.

"She thought she was doing the right thing," Sapir said finally. "You trusted her with your life. She's trying to earn that trust."

Storia turned back toward the window, jaw tight. "I'm not angry she acted. I'm angry she thought she couldn't come to me first." Another silence. Deeper this time.

Then the door burst open without warning.

A palace guard stood there, breathing heavily. Behind him, two more approached, helping someone through the archway—

Tamanda, barely upright, blood dried across her brow, one sleeve torn and
her side bound with a makeshift wrap of cloth and leather.

Storia's breath caught.

She crossed the chamber swiftly, fury forgotten in a flash of fear.

"Tamanda."

Tamanda tried to bow and almost collapsed. Sapir reached her just in time, steadying her arm.

"I came straight back," Tamanda managed. "Didn't stop. Found
what we feared. Natsu are moving, in force. "

Storia said nothing. She stepped forward and took Tamanda's another arm, guiding her to sit near the hearth. For a long moment, she simply looked at her—the dried blood, the trembling limbs, the fierce stubborn fire still burning behind her pain.

"You should never have gone without my word," Storia said, voice low.

"I know," Tamanda whispered.

"I should strip you of your rank for it."

"I know."

Storia crouched beside her, brushing a lock of tangled hair from Tamanda's cheek. "But I won't."

Tamanda's shoulders sagged with exhaustion. Sapir quietly poured water and passed it to her.

"You saw the Natsu yourself?" Storia asked, the Queen returning now in her voice.

"Yes," Tamanda said. "And I found a rider—wounded courier. He was carrying this."

She pulled a sealed scroll from inside her tunic and handed it to Storia.

It's had Zarratts seal on the scroll, Storia broke the seal quickly, eyes scanning the contents.

"They're already preparing to encircle the northwest valley," she said aloud. "The Natsu know exactly where our garrisons are light. This wasn't opportunistic. This was planned."

She rose slowly, taller now, like the wind itself had stiffened her spine.

"Tomorrow, we call a war council," she said. "Tonight, we ready the gates and send word to our outposts, call our warriors in from the taverns and Barracks outside the city."

She turned to Sapir. "You'll ride at dawn. Rally the guard posts."

Then to Tamanda, softer: "You'll stay here. Heal. I'll need you again soon."

Tamanda nodded, eyes heavy.

Storia looked out into the night beyond the window. The lamps of Karathat still glowed peacefully, unaware of the storm forming just beyond the hills.

"They think we're unprepared," she said quietly.

"Let them," Sapir replied.

~~~~~~~~~~~~~~~~~~~~~~~~~

The room was too still.

Tamanda lay beneath crisp linen sheets in one of the upper palace chambers, the kind reserved for wounded officers. A tray sat untouched on the side table—bread, herbs, a bowl of broth already cooling. Her bandages had been changed, her wounds washed with something sharp and stinging, but it wasn't the pain that kept her awake.

It was the quiet.

And the knowing.

She could feel it in her gut; the same way she could feel the shape of a hidden blade beneath her sleeve. War was coming.
~~~~~~~~~~~~~~~~~~~~~~~~~

Not a whisper of it now, not a rumour. It had stepped into the open like a drawn sword.

She turned her head carefully, muscles in her neck tight with bruising. The window was cracked open, letting in the cool night air. Somewhere outside, bells chimed once. Half past midnight. She counted the rings out of habit.

From the corridor, footsteps approached. Slow, unhurried. She reached beneath her pillow. Her fingers brushed the handle of the knife she'd insisted on keeping—even when the palace healer had scowled at her.

The door creaked slightly.

"Only me," came a low voice.

It was Rella, one of the servant girls. Young, soft-voiced, usually posted to the kitchens, but she had helped Tamanda undress when she arrived, had changed the sheets without flinching at the blood.

"You're not supposed to be up," Rella said, setting down a fresh cloth and pitcher.

"I'm not," Tamanda replied. "But I'm not asleep either."

"You should rest. The Queen was in here three times already. Keeps asking if you've stirred. She looks… different. Tired, but sharp."

Tamanda smiled faintly. "She always looks sharp."

Rella dipped a cloth in the water and moved to dab the side of her face, but Tamanda caught her wrist gently.

"Tell me what's happening outside this room," she asked. "I don't need sleep. I need to know."

Rella hesitated, then gave a small nod. "More guards posted. More hawks released than I've ever seen sky's been full of them all evening. Some soldiers came in just before dusk, from the western road. Dusty, hard-eyed men. I think they're from the border towns."

"Did they see Her Majesty?"

"No. They saw Lord Sapir. They've been down in the council room below ever since."

Tamanda leaned back slowly. A muscle in her ribs twinged. "What else?"

"Someone new arrived about an hour ago. Wounded rider looked half-dead. The guards didn't announce him. They brought him in quiet, like a secret. I only saw him through the archway when they passed the servant hall."

Tamanda's eyes narrowed. "Was he Mandji?"

"No," Rella said. "But his cloak was… wrong. Too dark. Nothing

Karathat. Looked like something from the border tribes."

Tamanda closed her eyes briefly. A new player, then. A whisper of another hand in the dark.

"Thank you," she said, opening them again. "You've been kind."

"I like you better than half the lords," Rella said. "You actually notice people."

Tamanda smiled again, thinner this time. "That's because I don't trust anyone to stay unnoticed."

A long silence passed between them before Rella gathered the empty dishes and made her way out.

When the door clicked shut, Tamanda stared at the ceiling for a moment. Her body was wrecked. Her side burned. But her mind was sharpening.

Tomorrow there would be councils, strategy, words twisted into orders. But tonight—here in the hush of shadowed halls— truths were slipping through the cracks.

Tamanda would heal. But not slowly. She had seen the storm. She had ridden through it.

And she had a feeling she wasn't done yet.

The night had been long and Tamanda did not sleep for most of it, her mind constantly hassled with thought trying to remember anything else from her ride back.

She had fought off the pain of her injury and kept riding through to Karathat.

Tamanda pushed herself upright from the bed, a fresh jolt of pain tearing through her side as if the blade had struck her all over again.

She staggered to the door and composed herself before leaving her room,

Tamanda stood in the hall outside the council chamber, her boots silent on the polished stone. The wound at her side throbbed in time with her heartbeat, but she kept her spine straight, her chin lifted. She wore a plain tunic of grey and dark blue—not armour, not the uniform of a guard—but her belt was fastened, and her sword was at her hip.

Inside, voices rose and fell. She could make out Sapir's steady tone, the deeper rumble of one of the southern generals—Kastil, maybe. Another voice, sharp with irritation, was likely Lord Helran of the Trade Guilds. Storia had summoned them all. Tamanda hadn't been invited.

But she opened the door anyway.

The heavy oak gave way with a soft groan, and the room turned toward her.

Queen Storia sat at the head of the long table, flanked by half a dozen advisors, lords, and commanders. Her eyes flicked to Tamanda instantly surprised but not alarmed. Sapir, seated just left of her, gave the barest nod. The others showed a range of expressions: confusion, irritation, curiosity.

Tamanda walked forward slowly, each step deliberate. She didn't limp, though she wanted to. She didn't bow, though she probably should have.

"I heard a council had been called," she said. "I thought you might want to hear from the only person in this room who's seen the Natsu columns with her own eyes." A pause. Heavy. Measured.

Storia's lips lifted into the ghost of a smile. "You thought correctly."

Lord Helran shifted in his chair, frowning. "She is no commander.

And clearly not well."

"She is standing," Sapir cut in calmly, "which is more than most who come back from fighting Natsu scouts can say."

Storia gestured to an empty chair—technically reserved for Zarratt, who had not yet returned. "Sit, Tamanda. Tell them what you told me."

Tamanda nodded and moved toward the seat. Her side flared with pain, but she sat without showing it.

"The Natsu aren't raiding anymore," she began, her voice even.

"They're marching. The rider told me he had seen them near the northern ridge, moving southeast. Organized. Armoured. Supply wagons in tow. They aren't probing. They're advancing."

Kastil grunted. "How many?"

"Five hundred in each column, minimum. Heavy foot soldiers, support archers. Officers wearing black enamel plate, no crest. They're hiding who leads them." "They always hide," Helran muttered.

"No," Tamanda said. "Not like this. They want us confused. And they're using old paths—game trails, minor passes. They're moving like they know our scouts are watching the main roads."

Storia leaned forward. "And the wounded courier?"

"Dead now," Tamanda said. "But his scroll confirmed what I saw. Teren Ridge is likely lost. The Natsu flanked it before its signal towers were lit. I think we've underestimated them."

There was silence again. This time, no one spoke for a long while.

Then General Kastil let out a sigh. "She's not wrong."

Storia looked down the table. "Then we prepare for a siege. We hold

the city and call our allies. Karathat must not fall."

"We have no formal alliances," Helran reminded her. "The border tribes are fractured. The lowland clans don't trust us. And the sea lords—"

"They'll come," Storia said, her voice like tempered steel. "Or they'll burn next."

Sapir's voice cut through the room. "We don't need every kingdom.

We need the right ones. And we need time."

Tamanda stood. Slowly. The effort cost her, but she stood tall.

"Give me orders, Your Majesty. While the others plan, I want to move."

Storia held her gaze for a long time. Then she nodded.

"You will ride in five days, gov your self-time to heal and if we hear nothing from the hawks, then you will go as my word".

And just like that, Tamanda had stepped into a circle she hadn't been born into. Not with title. Not with land. But with purpose.

She turned and left the room, the hush behind her full of new weight.

&

CHAPTER 21

The Vintals had, as expected, begun sending their foot soldiers toward the Mandji lines. Taran sat astride his horse behind the front ranks, positioned between his massed foot warriors and the line of archers.

As the Vintals advanced and came within range, he gave the signal to loose at will. Dark shafts flew overhead in thick waves, like a flock of birds migrating south for the winter, briefly clouding the sky.

Volley after volley, the arrows arced through the air, descending upon the approaching Vintal soldiers. Taran's warriors held their ground, standing tall, goading the enemy with war cries and defiant gestures, daring them to close the distance.

His light cavalry remained hidden on the woodland's edge, the lancers silent among the trees. They checked their tack and their mounts, waiting for the enemy cavalry to show themselves. Each man knew they would be outnumbered when they charged. They understood and accepted it. If they died, it would be a glorious death—one remembered in the songs of their people.

Nearby, Stafan barked orders at his archers, ensuring they emptied their quivers. A supply horse stood ready, baskets of arrows slung across its flanks, while two young Mandji runners kept pace, refilling the archers' quivers as they ran dry. Stafan had instructed them to aim for the flanks, forcing the Vintals to cluster toward the centre.

Vintal foot soldiers began to fall by the dozens, struck down with each deadly volley.

The Vintal archers responded, but their return fire either fell short or struck harmlessly against the shield wall. Taran had ordered his men to form a double-ranked defence: the front line held their

shields forward while the rear ranks overlapped above them, angled to catch any arrows falling from the sky.

The first of the Vintals began to break.

But still, Taran held his cavalry. Still, he gave no order to pursue.

High on the ridge overlooking the battle, Commander Ryshal of the Vintals narrowed his eyes, the wind tugging at his crimson cloak. Below him, the field was already littered with bodies—his bodies. The Mandji archers had been relentless. His foot soldiers were faltering, clustered tight toward the centre, shields raised but morale thinning like mist under sun.

Another volley struck. He heard the distant screams of men and the hollow ring of iron hitting flesh.

His second, Vosk, approached quickly, helm tucked under one arm. "They're bleeding us before we can close the line. Our flanks are thinning. The men are starting to pull back."

Ryshal didn't flinch. "They want us to break ranks. They want us to run."

"Do we?"

"No," Ryshal said coldly. "We bury them."

He turned to the banner at his rear, raised his hand, and clenched his fist—twice. The signal.

Below, in the second line, the Vintal cavalry shifted into motion.

Over two hundred riders surged forward, their banners trailing behind them like streaks of flame. The thunder of hooves rolled across the field as the earth trembled under their charge. They rode in from the right flank, sweeping in an arc meant to smash into the Mandji like a hammer into bone.

Ryshal watched with a soldier's stillness, his jaw tight.

"They think we'll come at them in waves," he murmured. "But we'll come like a storm."

Vosk hesitated. "The Mandji light riders are still unaccounted for." "They're hiding," Ryshal said. "Let them. When they rise, they'll rise into lances."

He turned back toward the battlefield, eyes sharp.

"Send the cavalry. Let them taste our steel. And if they still stand after that—then we give them the blade ourselves."

Taran saw the Vintal cavalry begin to advance. This was the moment he had waited for.

Without hesitation, he turned and gave the signal.

Stafan, standing nearby, nodded and reached into his quiver for a pair of long-shafted arrows marked with red bands—signalling arrows. He drew his bow, aimed high toward the woodland edges where the Mandji light cavalry lay hidden, and loosed the first. The arrow whistled as it cut through the air, sailing over the heads of the advancing Vintals.

Without pause, he drew and fired the second in the opposite direction, ensuring both wings had received the call.

On the far edge of the field, the lead rider of the hidden cavalry heard the distinct whistle sail overhead. Without needing further command, the Mandji light horse began to move. They peeled out of the tree cover, taking wide flanking routes to circle behind the Vintal lines.

Down on the battlefield, the Vintal cavalry had spread into formation and begun their charge. The ground trembled beneath them, a thunderous tide of hooves and steel.

Mandji archers released their final volleys, sending the last of their arrows into the path of the charging riders. Some found their marks—riders toppled from saddles, horses shrieked and collapsed mid-gallop, bodies falling in tangled motion. Still, the charge surged forward.

Taran stood at the line, bellowing orders, his voice carried by the rising chaos. Around him, section leaders shouted over the din, urging the front ranks to hold fast.

Behind the shield wall, the warriors of the second and third ranks had lowered their shields they moved with grim precision. They pulled up long pikes—thick shafts tipped —planting their heels and bracing as the cavalry closed the gap.

The trap was set.

And the riders were nearly upon them.

Taran turned to Stafan. "Send the next signal," he ordered, his voice sharp. "Let the lancers move. If we time it right, the Vintal cavalry will hit the pikes—and we'll cut them down."

Stafan nodded, already reaching for the final signalling arrow. He strung it with practiced ease, drawing the bowstring back as he waited for the perfect moment. The Vintal charge thundered forward, fast and furious now, the dust of their momentum rising in waves.

He would fire as they closed the final stretch.

Behind him, his archers had emptied their last quivers. Without hesitation, they discarded them, drawing short swords and daggers as they moved to reinforce the infantry lines.

They would not stand apart from the fight.

They would bleed beside the foot warriors when the lines broke.

The front ranks held their nerve as the Vintal cavalry thundered closer. Though the earlier volleys had thinned their numbers, the enemy still bore down with a formidable force—lances lowered, hooves pounding, war cries rising.

Some of the younger Mandji warriors began to step back, fear overtaking instinct. But they were quickly reminded of their duty—the tip of a dagger pressed firmly into their backs by veterans who would not let the line break.

Taran stood just behind the ranks, eyes fixed on the charging line, counting the cavalry's strides in his head. Timing was everything.

Three… two… one…

"PIKES!" he bellowed.

At his command, the front rank dropped low and peeled back in unison. Behind them, the second and third ranks surged forward, long pikes thrust out and angled high.

The Vintal horses crashed into the wall.

The first wave of riders impaled themselves on the pikes, horses shrieking and bucking as their momentum shattered against the waiting blades. Riders were thrown, some sailing through the air and into the Mandji lines.

Those who landed among the Mandji were grabbed instantly—throats slit, bodies jabbed with sword points, finished before they could even rise.

The line held.

And the trap began to close.

Stafan had loosed the final signal.

From the flanks, the Mandji lancers surged into motion.

They thundered across the field at full gallop, lances levelled, their formation tight and focused. They aimed not for the front, but for the vulnerable side of the Vintal cavalry—now tangled in chaos at the Mandji line.

The Vintal charge had come to an abrupt, brutal halt. At the front, horses lay piled and bleeding, their riders cut down or locked in savage melee with the Mandji foot soldiers. The initial momentum was gone—shattered on the wall of pikes and blades.

Those at the rear of the Vintal formation had no time to regroup.

The Mandji lancers descended on them at full speed, a wall of hooves and steel about to crash into their flank like a wave breaking over stone.

The Vintal cavalry never saw it coming.

With a roar that echoed across the battlefield, the Mandji lancers slammed into their exposed flank. The impact was thunderous shields splintered, riders thrown from their saddles, horses screamed and reared in panic as steel met flesh at full gallop.

Lances pierced sides and shattered ribs. Some drove straight through armour and out the other side, unseating their targets and dragging them to the ground in bloody ruin. The speed of the charge left no room for defence—no time to pivot or brace. It was annihilation in motion.

The Vintal rear ranks broke almost immediately. Crushed between the fury of the Mandji lancers and the still-standing shield wall ahead, the formation collapsed in on itself like a dying beast. Riders tried to flee but found themselves caught between retreat and slaughter.

Mandji lancers didn't slow.

They rode through the broken lines, drawing sabres once their lances had snapped or found flesh. They struck down stragglers, slicing through reins, armour, throats. Dust and blood filled the air.

Taran, watching from the rise behind the infantry, saw the line fold.

He saw panic ripple through what remained of the Vintal cavalry.

This was the moment.

He turned to his messengers.

"Tell the left infantry to press. Push them hard while they're scattered. No quarter." The trap had sprung.

And now came the crush.

Taran looked out across the battlefield, eyes fixed on the shifting shape of the Vintal lines. What remained of their infantry was surging forward now—desperate, disorganized—rushing to reinforce the collapsing cavalry.

This was the moment he had hoped for.

Beyond the Vintal line, movement caught his eye. Banners flickered behind the tree line—his banners. The Mandji light cavalry burst through the forest in full charge, thundering toward the unguarded rear where the Vintal archers were clustered.

The trap had fully closed.

With the Vintal cavalry in shambles and their foot reinforcements already committed, Taran saw his chance. He turned, raised his voice above the din of battle, and gave the order his warriors had been waiting for.

"Front ranks—leave nonalive!"

The Mandji light cavalry tore from the tree line like a storm loosed from the mountains.

They moved in tight formation, hooves pounding the earth, their curved sabres drawn, eyes fixed on their prey—the Vintal archers. The archers had only just turned, realizing too late that the forest behind them had not been empty.

Some tried to form a loose line. Others fumbled for arrows. A few even began to run.

It didn't matter.

The first wave of riders crashed into them with deadly precision, cutting a swathe through the ranks. Sabres flashed in the sun, finding throats and shoulders, cleaving through armour and bone. Horses barrelled into unready men, trampling them beneath iron shod hooves.

The Vintal archers never stood a chance.

Those not struck down in the first impact were scattered in moments, running blindly across the field—straight into the chaos of the collapsing front.

Behind the lead riders, the second wave of Mandji horsemen spread out in a crescent, ensuring no one escaped. They struck with speed and efficiency, not wasting a single blow. Their mounts wove through the panicked archers like wolves among sheep.

Within minutes, the rear of the Vintal army was in total ruin.

From his place on the ridge, Taran watched the dust and blood rise behind enemy lines. A thin smile touched his lips.

The hammer had struck. Now, the anvil would finish it.

The battlefield burned with noise—shouts, steel, the dying cries of men and horses. The Vintal line, fractured and bleeding, reeled beneath the weight of the Mandji assault. The flanks had folded, the rear was overrun, and now the final blow came from the front.

Taran stood at the crest of the rise, his voice raw from command, his blade drawn but untouched by blood. He had not moved from his vantage—his place was to see it all. To direct it. To carry the weight of every decision.

Below, the front ranks surged forward, sweeping through the remnants of the Vintal infantry. The Mandji had broken through. Steel rang out in brutal rhythm. No formation remained—just knots of men fighting for breath and survival.

And in the centre of it—Tanny.

Tanny, wild-eyed and fearless, fought like a warrior born. He had discarded his spear for a broken axe; his shield lost somewhere in the dirt. Blood streaked his face, none of it his own. He drove himself into the fight with reckless, furious grace, covering a wounded brother, dragging another from beneath a dead horse, killing as he went.

Taran's eyes locked on him through the haze and chaos. Pride swelled. Tanny had always been the impulsive one—the first to speak, the first to laugh, the first to charge. And now, here he was, holding the line when it mattered most.

Until the spear found him.

It came from the side—a desperate thrust from a wounded Vintal soldier half-collapsing as he lunged. The point pierced under Tanny's arm, slipping past leather and into flesh.

Taran saw it happen.

Tanny staggered, dropped the axe, but didn't fall. He turned with a shout of fury and drove his elbow into the man's throat, knocking him to the ground. Blood gushed from his side, his knees wavered—but still, he stood.

He raised his voice one last time, shouting the Mandji war cry. Others around him echoed it, charging forward, their momentum carrying them into the last of the Vintals like a tidal wave.

And then Tanny fell.

He dropped to his knees, one hand gripping the dirt, the other pressed to his wound. His breath came hard, blood dark against his fingers. He looked up, eyes searching.

Taran was already moving.

He pushed through his guards, down from the rise, riding hard toward the fallen warrior. Around him, the battle was ending—the Vintals were routed, scattered, crushed.

But all Taran could see was the boy he had trained, the man who had become his brother in all but blood, now lying still among the trampled grass.

Taran dropped to his knees beside him.

Tanny's eyes flicked open, barely.

"We won?" he whispered.

Taran nodded. His voice wouldn't come.

Tanny managed a faint smile. "Told you… we'd drive them to the dust…"

And then he was gone.

The Mandji had won the day.

But the cost would be carried in silence.

❧

CHAPTER 22

T he air in Karathat had changed.

Tamanda stood on the eastern balcony overlooking the city, her cloak billowing in the stiff wind. The sun was out, but it offered no warmth. Below, the outer walls bristled with movement—workers hammering braces into place, carts hauling stones and barrels of pitch, children herded indoors with tight-faced mothers watching the horizon.

She rested her hand against her side, the wound still stiff beneath the fresh bandages. It no longer bled, but it hadn't faded either. She hadn't told the healers she'd left her bed two days ago. There were more important things to worry about.

Behind her, boots tapped across stone. She didn't turn.

"How bad is it?" she asked.

Sapir came to stand beside her, his eyes scanning the same distant road. "Bad enough that we've had to seal the north gates."

"Any word?"

He shook his head. "No hawks returned from Terel's Watch. None from the border clans. Even the sea posts have gone quiet. We sent a full flight to the coast yesterday—five birds. Not one has come back."

Tamanda frowned. "That's not just delay. That's silence."

"We did get one message this morning," Sapir added. "A single hawk from Veyron's Ridge. The note was brief. Two words: 'Moving fast.'"

She let out a slow breath, jaw tight. "Could mean anything."

"Could mean they're already between here and the Ridge," Sapir said. "Which means they've bypassed half our forward scouts."

Tamanda turned to face him fully. "And the Queen?"

"She's with the quartermasters. Trying to calculate how long we can hold if we're surrounded." He hesitated. "She's calm. Focused. But I think she knows this city might be alone for a while."

Tamanda nodded slowly. Her eyes swept the skyline—watchtowers, smoke from cooking fires, guards on high platforms scanning the east.

"And the people?"

"Worried. But they trust her. And they've seen the fortifications go up. We've doubled the wall archers. Catapults are ready. All non-combatants have been moved behind the inner keep."

"And the gatehouse?"

"Reinforced. Boiling oil stocked. If they come, they'll bleed for every step."

Tamanda looked eastward again, past the haze of distant hills. No banners. No dust. Just waiting.

She hated waiting.

"If it's a siege," she said quietly, "they'll try to break us from the inside before they break us from the walls."

Sapir's voice was low. "We've begun watching the merchant houses. There's talk of bribes—coin changing hands. Could just be fear. Could be worse."

Tamanda's hand dropped to her sword hilt.

"I want to start sleeping in the outer barracks. Quietly. If something moves in the dark, I'll be there when it does."

"You should still be recovering," Sapir said.

She met his gaze. "I recover when we're still standing. Not before." He didn't argue.

From the highest tower above them, a fresh hawk launched into the sky—its wings slicing across the pale blue as it turned westward and vanished.

Tamanda watched it disappear.

The corridors of the upper palace were quiet, muffled beneath a thick air of tension. Tamanda walked with purpose, her boots echoing softly along the polished stone. The guards at the Queen's chamber doors opened them without a word—she didn't need an announcement.

Inside, Queen Storia stood beside a broad table strewn with parchments and ledgers. She didn't look up right away. Her fingers were inkstained, her expression weary but alert. Two quartermasters stood off to the side, murmuring over supply inventories. A page carried away an empty pitcher of water.

Storia spoke first, her voice clipped. "How many days do you think the grain will last if we shut the gates tonight?"

Tamanda didn't miss a beat. "Thirty-five with strict rationing. Forty if the fishponds hold."

The Queen finally looked up, her mouth tightening into something that wasn't quite a smile. "I knew you'd say that before my own men did. Come."

Tamanda stepped closer, resting her weight carefully as she approached the table. The pain was manageable now—a dull reminder, not a hindrance.

Storia gestured to the map spread across the centre. Thin lines marked supply routes, trade roads, defensive positions. Nearly all roads leading to Karathat were marked with grey ink: compromised, unconfirmed, or severed.

"Still nothing from Terel's Watch," Storia said. "And our coastal allies have grown silent. We've sent more hawks than I care to admit."

Tamanda nodded grimly. "Sapir told me. No birds back from the coast. One came from Veyron's Ridge—two words: 'Moving fast.'"

The Queen's brow furrowed. "A warning or a farewell?"

"Could be either."

Storia exhaled slowly, then turned away from the table, walking to the high windows that overlooked the city below. "We've reinforced the gates. We've doubled the walls. We've placed archers in every tower tall enough to see the horizon. And yet I still feel like I'm standing in a room filling with smoke, unable to find the fire."

Tamanda followed her gaze. "They'll come, Your Majesty. But not as an army at first. That's not how this begins."

"I agree." Storia's voice had hardened. "There's something in the air. Not fear—expectation. And not just among the soldiers. I've seen the faces of the merchants. The House leaders. Even the priests."

Tamanda lowered her voice. "I think someone in the city is feeding them information."

Storia turned sharply. "You're certain?"

"No," Tamanda admitted. "But the hawks vanishing. The timing. The fact we're being encircled before a single siege weapon has been spotted. They're not blind. Someone is showing them where to press."

The Queen was silent for a moment. Then, "You're still wounded. I should send you back to recover."

"With respect, Majesty, I'll recover with a sword in my hand, not on my back."

Storia studied her for a long moment, and when she spoke again, her voice was quieter.

"You saved my life once. I trust few people. Fewer still when the knives are coming from behind silk curtains. If you believe someone inside these walls is helping the enemy—find them."

Tamanda bowed her head. "I will."

A knock at the chamber door interrupted them. A guard leaned in.

"Messenger from the north gate, Your Majesty. Riders spotted beyond the eastern hills. No banners. No formation. Just… movement."

~~~~~~~~~~~~~~~~~~~~~~~~~

By day, he was known as Bideon—a quiet, aging steward attached to the lower records office. He carried scrolls, fetched ink, kept account of grain shipments and livestock tallies. No one noticed him. That was the point.

But in truth, he was Biden, a sleeper. One of three placed within Karathat seasons ago. His letters had helped shift trade routes. His whispers had stalled supply chains. And now, as the Queen drew her walls tighter and her hawks flew unanswered into the sky, his task was changing.

Observation had become preparation.

He moved silently through the servant's corridor behind the east kitchens, careful not to draw attention. The torches here were dimmer—no need to waste good oil where only hands and feet passed. Biden knew every passage in this wing. He had memorized the patrol timings, the reach of the guards' lanterns, the blind corners.

It was at one such corner that he paused now, watching.

In the scullery below, a young kitchen girl was stacking trays from the morning meal. Thin. Red hair. Quiet—but not simple.

He'd seen her before.

She was the same girl who had slipped a clean blade to Tamanda the night she returned from the forest, barely standing, soaked in blood.
~~~~~~~~~~~~~~~~~~~~~~~~~

He hadn't acted then. He had no order to.

But now? Now he watched her more closely.

She worked quickly, head down, speaking only when spoken to. But her eyes—too alert. She listened to every conversation, even those not meant for her. Two days ago, she had followed a guard up a back stairwell carrying a water jug, then returned without it—and the jug had been full. A message drop, perhaps? Or an innocent act. He couldn't afford to guess.

Not now.

Biden turned from the gap in the wall, retreating silently into shadow. If she was nothing, she would disappear soon enough. But if she was more—if she was loyal to Tamanda, or worse, a runner for the Queen herself—then she would need to be dealt with.

He would not kill her yet.

But he would watch.

And when the city grew dark, and the gates began to scream under fire, he would act.

&

CHAPTER 23

The enemy emerged from the mist again like wraiths, their war cries piercing the morning silence.

Zarratt's archers responded swiftly, loosing volleys into the advancing horde. Arrows hissed through the damp air, striking shields, flesh, and stone—but for every foe that fell, two more surged forward, undeterred.

Zarratt still held the gate.

He stood high on the ramparts, barking orders down to the men along the walls. They followed each command without hesitation, knowing their lives depended on it. He had reinforced the gate with heavy beams and piled anything with weight behind it—furniture, barrels, stone blocks. It wouldn't hold forever. But it had to hold for now.

To the east, the wall still stood, held by Mevran, who had proven himself a leader of men—strong in heart, relentless in combat. He rallied the defenders with tireless resolve, fighting like one possessed.

Zarratt knew it was only a matter of time.

Eventually, they would break through—either by shattering the gate or spilling over the walls. The Natsu came in waves, relentless, and each wave cost him more defenders. Some had fallen to arrows raining down from the dark. Others had died hand-to-hand on the ramparts, hurling ladders from the stonework and meeting swords with spears.

He'd already lost too many.

A decision had to be made. One that would cost lives—but might save more.

196

Zarratt sent word to Mevran to come to the gate wall. He had a plan. One that would require sacrifice. But above all, he had to send word to Karathat.

They needed to know: Teren Ridge was falling, and the Natsu were coming.

Mevran arrived moments later, rushing up the narrow stairway two steps at a time until he reached the platform where Zarratt stood, overlooking the chaos below.

"Commander Zarratt," he said, panting, "you sent for me."

Zarratt turned, gripping Mevran's shoulder with a firm, bloodstreaked hand.

"You've held the east wall," he said. "And done more than I could have asked of any man. Now I must ask one thing more." Mevran straightened, his expression unwavering. "Yes, Commander.

Anything."

Mevran straightened, his expression unwavering. "Yes, Commander.

Anything."

Zarratt nodded once, then turned back to the view beyond the battlements. The enemy was massing again. Another wave was coming.

"I'm going to hold the gate," Zarratt said quietly. "With volunteers.

As long as we can."

Mevran said nothing at first.

"You'll take the wounded," Zarratt continued. "And every able body who can walk and swing a blade if needed—but not ones I'll need here. There's a trail down the western ridge. Use the cover of the cliff line and take the lower path through the shale. It's unguarded—for now."

Realization flickered across Mevran's face. "You mean to stay behind."

Zarratt turned to him then, eyes calm and resolute. "I mean to buy you time. For the living. And for a message."

He pulled a folded scrap of parchment from inside his armour, sealed in wax.

"This goes to Karathat. I don't care how many legs the horse has left—get it there."

Mevran took the message with both hands.

Zarratt gripped his arm. "Tell them Teren Ridge has fallen. Tell them the Natsu are coming in force. That they come not to threaten—but to conquer."

He released him and stepped back.

"You've fought well, Mevran. Your name will be remembered. But it's not your time to die. Not yet."

A muscle in Mevran's jaw tightened, but he gave a single nod.

Zarratt looked past him, already scanning the defences. "Gather your men. You have ten minutes. Take what you need, then go."

"And you?"

Zarratt's voice was steady. "I will be at the gate. We'll give you time."

He paused, letting the weight of the moment settle before continuing.

"Any men who volunteer to stay behind—have them form a defensive line at the gate. No conscripts. No wounded. Only those who choose to stand. We'll hold there for as long as we can." Mevran's throat worked, but he nodded.

"You'll have your line," he said.

Zarratt met his gaze one last time. "Then go. Before there's no time left to buy."

Without another word, Mevran turned and bounded down the stone steps, already shouting orders. The sound of boots thudding against the ground rose quickly—gear being packed, wounded being lifted onto makeshift stretchers, swords checked, and belts tightened. A retreat, but not a rout. There was still discipline in these men. Still fight.

Zarratt remained at the top of the wall for a moment longer, watching the mist as it rolled and shifted beyond the ridge. Shapes moved within it. Dark. Waiting.

He turned away and made his way to the gate wall.

Soon, others would join him—volunteers, some bloodied, all silent.

Men who had chosen to stand, knowing the cost.

They would hold the line. Not for victory. But for time.

Zarratt stood above the wall, eyes fixed on the shifting gloom beyond the ridge. Shapes moved in the darkness— silent, calculated—taking up positions for the next wave.

It was coming.

He tightened his grip on the cold stone parapet, feeling the weight of it beneath his fingers. The wind carried the distant clink of metal, the faint murmur of enemy voices preparing to kill.

He looked to his sides.

Beside him, on the wall above the gate, stood the men who had chosen to remain. Bloodied. Bruised. Exhausted.

But still standing.

They bore the marks of the battle already fought— bandaged limbs, cracked helms, dark smears drying on their armour—but their eyes held the same fire.

The horn blast came just before sunrise.

Low. Hollow. Like something pulled from the bones of the earth.

Zarratt stood atop the wall, eyes narrowed against the shifting mist below. Shapes moved—shields glinting, spears rising, dark forms assembling in silence.

The enemy was coming.

He turned from the wall and faced the defenders gathered at the gate walk and inner courtyard. Some clutched bloodied blades. Others leaned on borrowed weapons, armour mismatched and dented. They were tired. Wounded. Many had said their final words already.

And yet… they stood.

Zarratt raised his voice, loud and firm, the wind catching his cloak as it flared behind him like a banner.

"You know what waits beyond this gate." The men turned to him.

"You've seen it. You've fought it. You've lost brothers to it. But today—today you do not fight to win. You fight to hold. You fight to deny. You fight to make them pay for every stone, every heartbeat, every drop of Karathati blood they dare spill." His voice climbed.

"They want this gate. They want this ridge. They want us broken.

But they will find we are not broken. Not yet. Not today!"

A murmur ran through the line. Hands tightened on hilts. Eyes locked on him.

"They think they're stronger. They think we're finished. But when they write of this day, they will say: Here stood the last of Teren

Ridge—outnumbered, outmatched, but never outdone!"

The men gave a shout. A few banged swords on shields. Others let out hoarse cries of defiance.

Zarratt turned back to the wall and pointed.

"They'll be in range soon. Archers—ready yourselves!"

The men dropped into position with renewed purpose. Arrows were notched. Shield lines formed. The fear was still there— but now it stood beside courage, not in its place.

The mist parted, and the Natsu came forward—row upon row, silent no longer. Their war cries rose like thunder across the valley.

Zarratt drew his blade and raised it high. He roared. "Let them come!" The enemy came.

Through the mist, the Natsu charged shields raised, spears forward, voices unified in a single thunderous roar. The ground seemed to shake beneath them.

"Loose!" Zarratt's cry rang out.

Arrows hissed from the walls, cutting the first wave to ribbons. Men dropped mid-stride, others stumbling over the dead. But more came. Always more.

On the wall, one of the sergeant's held the northern tower, his left hand already bound in a makeshift bandage from the night before. He fought with his offhand now, sword in one fist, torch in the other. When the Natsu ladder slammed against his position, he didn't wait—he set it ablaze, pouring oil down before lighting the fire with his own torch. He was laughing when he burned, flames catching the hem of his cloak as the ladder collapsed with enemy soldiers screaming below.

In the courtyard, a young warrior—barely seventeen—stood between two fallen comrades. When the gate finally cracked open under the force of the battering ram, he didn't run. He stepped forward, driving his spear through the first invader's throat. He fell before the third, but not before taking another with him.

To the south, an older warrior, too wounded to climb the stairs, propped himself behind a supply cart, crossbow steady on his lap. He shot until they reached him, then drew his knife and fought until his last breath.

And still, the Natsu surged forward.

On the ramparts, Zarratt moved like a fury—sword cleaving, shield raised, his cloak ragged and soaked in blood, his face streaked with sweat and grit. He fought shoulder-to-shoulder with the last defenders, shouting orders, calling names, pulling wounded men back only to shove another into the gap.

He saw the moment the east wall was overrun—heard Mevran's voice echo below as the escape party broke out through the side tunnel.

Good, Zarratt thought. They're away.

Then the next wave crested the wall.

He turned to meet them, slashing down a spear-wielding Natsu warrior, then pivoted and drove his shoulder into a second. A blade scraped off his pauldron—but a heartbeat later, he stumbled.

An arrow, thin and black-fletched, jutted from beneath his ribs.

Zarratt gasped. Blood soaked his tunic in seconds. Still, he raised his blade, cut down one more—but his stance faltered.

Another enemy lunged, and in the chaos, Zarratt lost his footing. He twisted, half-turning as he fell from the wall.

The last thing he saw was the sky—grey, turning pale with the promise of sun.

Below, the few who escaped—Mevran among them—looked back just long enough to see Zarratt's cloak vanish over the edge falling towards where the stables stood.

No cry. No final words.

Just a fall into shadow.

But they would remember.

He held the gate.

~~~~~~~~~~~~~~~~~~~~~~~~~~

The wind howled behind them like the roar of a dying beast.

Mevran didn't look back.

He had seen enough—the flames climbing the east tower, the shattered gate spilling enemy warriors into the courtyard,
~~~~~~~~~~~~~~~~~~~~~~~~~~

the final image of Commander Zarratt falling from the ramparts with an arrow buried in his side.

There was no time for mourning. Only movement.

They had escaped through the supply tunnel—nineteen of them. A handful of able-bodied fighters, nine wounded men, and two barely trained messengers. One of them rode with the sealed letter tucked beneath his jerkin, the last message from Teren Ridge.

The path west was narrow, treacherous, and slick with shale. Mevran led the column on foot, blade still bloody in hand, one arm supporting a limping soldier who refused to be left behind.

"Keep low," he said, voice hoarse. "We stay beneath the ridge line until we reach the pine break."

The sound of battle still echoed faintly from behind—shouts, the ring of steel, a horn in the distance. Zarratt and the others were still holding. Still buying time.

One of the younger soldiers faltered on the rocks, collapsing to one knee. Mevran doubled back.

"No one stops," he growled. "You stop; you die."

He hauled the boy to his feet. "I told you. We're not fighting for survival. We're carrying the warning." They pressed on.

By midmorning, the trail dipped into the forest, giving them their first cover in hours. Mevran called a brief halt beneath the boughs of a twisted pine. The wounded slumped against tree trunks. Water was passed. No one spoke of what they'd left behind.

One of the messengers—a thin, dust-covered youth named Coril—sat beside Mevran.

"Will… will they believe us?" he asked quietly.

Mevran looked at him, at the terrified eyes barely older than a squire.

"They'll believe," he said. "Because if they don't, Karathat will burn."

A bird screeched overhead—just a hawk. Not a signal. Not yet.

They had miles to go.

And Mevran would make sure they got there.

They had walked for hours, feet blistered, shoulders aching, every step dragging them further from the ruins of Teren Ridge.

By midafternoon, they came across a village—small, quiet, its people watching warily as the ragged band of survivors emerged from the tree line.

From the village they could see the rising smoke from Teren ridge in the distance.

Mevran wasted no time.

At the edge of the square, he found the stables and called for the fastest rider. He pressed the sealed message into the young man's hand—Zarratt's final words, heavy with the fate of a kingdom.

"Ride hard," Mevran said. "Do not stop. Get this to the Queen."

The rider mounted without question and spurred the horse into motion. Within moments, he had vanished down the winding road toward Karathat, carrying with him the last warning from Teren Ridge.

๛

CHAPTER 24

Dawn broke cold and grey.

The ashes of the funeral pyres still smouldered at the edge of the camp, tendrils of smoke curling into the wind. The ground was quiet—scarred, bloodstained, but calm. Crows circled above the burned wood, fighting over scraps left behind in the wake of the flames.

Taran stood at the centre of the camp, already dressed for war, the weight of command once more across his shoulders. His eyes were harder this morning, sharpened by grief. The sorrow remained, but it had settled into resolve hard as stone, cold as iron.

He turned to Stafan, who waited with their company leaders. The men looked gaunt and worn, their cheeks hollow after days of loss, but the light had returned to their eyes, tempered by vengeance.

"We march for Teren Ridge," Taran told them, voice steady, ringing against the cold air.

Stafan gave a tight nod. "You think they still hold?"

Taran drew a breath, letting it settle deep in his chest. "I don't know. But the Vintals were heading there, and I'll bet my life they weren't going to fight alone. They were meant to join something bigger." "If they've fallen?"

Taran glanced east, toward the distant hills. "Then we're too late.

But if they haven't..."

He left the rest unsaid. He didn't need to finish it. They all knew the cost of arriving too late.

The warriors were already forming up. Those who could still ride, those who could still bear arms, patched themselves together with strips of cloth and makeshift armour. Spears were re-sharpened, shields re-

204

lashed, and bandages retightened. The air buzzed with the sound of preparation—grinding whetstones, clinking buckles, low murmurs of final words.

Taran moved to his horse, drawing a hand down the animal's neck, steadying its restlessness. Around him, the surviving Mandji fell in line, their faces drawn but determined.

He swung up into the saddle, scanning the broken camp one last time. These men had stood with him through ambush, through slaughter, through horror beyond imagining. They deserved a better ending.

"Pack light," he ordered, voice cutting through the dawn haze.

"Move fast. We leave within the hour."

The command was met with quick, focused motion. Warriors knelt to check leather bindings, fitted arrowheads to fresh shafts, and gathered what little food they could carry. A few paused to embrace loved ones who had come this far to help tend the wounded and bury the dead.

Taran felt the cold wind bite against his face as he turned his horse toward the rough road. The weight of both hope and dread pressed against his ribs, heavy as chainmail.

He signalled the column forward, and they moved out.

The riders kept a tight formation, shields slung over their backs, spears angled skyward. Their hooves churned the muddy road as they pushed on, silent except for the clatter of gear. Taran rode at the front, his cloak snapping behind him, every step bringing them closer to whatever waited at Teren Ridge.

The landscape unfolded in grim, steady ruin. Burnt fields, shattered fences, hollowed-out villages where doors hung open in the wind. Sheep and cattle wandered loose, wild and half-starved. A distant farmhouse still smoked from a recent raid, roof collapsed, its stone walls scorched black.

No sign of the enemy. No sign of the villagers. Only the quiet, uneasy stillness of a country that had been picked apart by war.

Three days in, they found the first corpses.

A Karathati scout, impaled on a splintered trunk, limbs spread like a grotesque warning. Taran dismounted, stepping closer to examine the body. The blood was long dried, already dark and flaky on the torn cloth of the man's tabard.

"Natsu weapons," Stafan observed, nodding toward a pair of jagged blades left in the grass.

"They were in a hurry," Taran noted. "Didn't even bother to clean up."

Stafan kicked at a broken shaft of wood, the remains of a Karathati banner. "Think they sent a message?"

Taran's jaw tightened. "They wanted to break our courage."

But if anything, the sight only stoked the fires in the Mandji warriors. One by one, they dismounted to stand around the fallen scout, heads bowed. They had seen enough death to be familiar with it, but never comfortable with it.

"Bury him," Taran ordered at last. "Quickly."

They dug a shallow grave in silence, laid the body in it with as much dignity as could be managed, and moved on.

On the fifth day, the signs of retreat grew clearer.

Broken carts littered the path, wheels smashed and burned. Scattered arrows showed where men had tried to stand and failed. A message pouch lay trampled in the mud, its scroll missing, torn away or stolen.

Taran's gut twisted tighter with every step. Each clue felt like a missing piece of a puzzle he couldn't yet solve.

They pushed forward.

By the sixth day, dawn rose thin and pale. Taran's eyes felt raw from lack of sleep, but he rode on, unwilling to stop.

At last, they crested a high bluff overlooking the valley of Teren Ridge. The morning wind came sharp and bitter, cutting through his cloak.

Smoke rose from behind the ridge—thick, black, oily. Not the small cooking fires of a camp but the ruinous smoke of burning wood and flesh.

He leaned forward in the saddle, trying to pick out details through the haze. There it was: the outpost, or what remained of it.

Part of the stone wall had collapsed inward, as if torn down by a ram. The gate was missing altogether, shattered and scattered like splinters across the mud. A tower at the eastern flank was still burning, the flames a dull, angry red.

And above it, a banner Taran did not recognize crimson, marked with a sigil that twisted in the wind like a threat.

Stafan drew up beside him, breathing hard from the climb. "We're too late," he said, voice breaking.

Taran didn't answer.

His eyes traced the lines of the broken walls; the dark shapes of bodies scattered in the mud below. The place stank of ruin and hopelessness, even from this distance.

He thought of Zarratt, holding the wall as long as he could. Of Tamanda, blades drawn, refusing to abandon the Queen. Of the soldiers who had once laughed around its fires, now likely burned with the timbers.

For a long moment, he let the silence stand. The wind stirred the ashes around them, carrying the ghosts of the dead.

"We go in," he said at last.

Stafan looked at him sharply. "There might be no one left."

Taran tightened his grip on the reins, jaw set. "Then we bury them.

Or we find who still stands."

Behind them, the Mandji shifted restlessly, seeing the destruction, measuring the price they might pay. But no one spoke against Taran's orders.

He dismounted, handing the reins to a young runner who looked barely old enough to hold a spear. Then he drew his sword, testing its weight, its balance.

The warriors fell into a rough column behind him, shields up, spears out, eyes searching the ruin ahead.

They began their descent into the valley.

Each step down the rocky slope felt like walking into a graveyard. The wind howled through the gaps in the burned tower, carrying the stench of rotting flesh. Flies rose in dark clouds where the dead had been left unburied.

Taran tried to count the bodies but gave up after the first dozen. Karathati colours, Vintal helms, Natsu blades. All tangled together in the mud. No clean sides left, only the ruin of men who had died for ground no one would even remember in a generation's time.

When they reached the base of the hill, they slowed, wary.

A charred beam hung half-suspended over the collapsed gate. Taran ducked beneath it, moving into what had been the outpost's courtyard.

The air was foul. Blood had pooled in low places, dried in others. Bits of torn cloth and snapped arrows littered the ground.

Movement drew his eye—a shape, crawling, no more than a smear of pale skin among the wreckage.

Taran darted forward, dropping to one knee. A boy, no older than sixteen, dragged himself from beneath a collapsed shield. His eyes were wide and empty, lips cracked and caked with blood.

"Water!" Taran shouted over his shoulder.

One of the riders ran forward, uncorking a skin. Together, they lifted the boy, letting the water spill past his trembling mouth.

He drank, choking. Then looked up at Taran, tears welling.

"They came at night," he rasped. "There were so many of them. We tried… we tried…" His voice gave out.

Taran held him steady. "Who holds the ridge? Is anyone left?"

The boy clung to Taran's sleeve, his breath ragged, tears mixing with the grime streaking his face. His arms shook with exhaustion, and every word came like a gasp torn from shattered lungs.

"We tried," he whispered again, voice crumbling, "we tried to hold—"

Then a tremor rippled through him, and he coughed, a thin line of blood spilling from the corner of his mouth. Taran caught him as he sagged, feeling the raw heat of fever, the tremors of a body too broken to go on.

The boy's gaze fluttered, unfocused, searching. "Mother… is she…?"

Taran swallowed hard, throat tight as a vice. He didn't answer, because no answer would ease this child's end.

The boy's fingers clawed weakly at Taran's arm, pain etched into every muscle, every shallow breath. His legs kicked, spasming. A sob broke from him, torn and desperate. "It hurts," he choked out, "it hurts so much…"

Taran glanced around the ruined courtyard, at the flies, the stink, the crushed men left to rot in the mud. There was no healer here, no chance of a gentler passing. Only more pain, stretched into moments that would feel like eternity.

He drew a slow breath, settling his heart. Then he leaned closer, voice steady, kind in its firmness.

"Sleep," he said softly, brushing the boy's matted hair from his forehead. "No more pain. I promise."

For an instant, the boy's eyes seemed to clear, finding him, holding on to that single spark of calm. His lips moved, but no sound came.

Taran gripped the hilt of his knife, sliding it free with a practiced, silent motion. He pressed a hand to the boy's shoulder to steady him, feeling the tremors racking that frail body, and then guided the blade to the base of his skull, just beneath the hairline.

"I'm sorry," he whispered, and with one clean, practiced thrust, ended it.

The boy shivered once, then stilled.

Taran held him a moment longer, steadying his head so he would not fall into the dirt. He closed the boy's wide, staring eyes with a gentle brush of his thumb.

Behind him, Stafan stood silent, watching, saying nothing. There were no words for a mercy like this — only the hollow ache it left behind.

Taran rose, wiping the blade against his sleeve before sheathing it once more. His heart felt raw, scraped open by the simple, brutal task of ending the boy's pain.

But there was no time to mourn.

He turned toward the broken walls of the keep, voice carrying the iron certainty of command.

"Form up!" he shouted. "We take the keep. There may still be

Karathati alive inside, and they will not stand alone."

Around him, the Mandji tightened their grips on sword and shield, falling in behind their commander. Taran cast one last glance at the boy's still form, a quiet vow burning in his chest.

I will not let this be for nothing.

Then he stepped forward, leading his warriors into the smoke and ruin, toward the last desperate stand of the defenders of Teren Ridge.

Taran felt something hot surge through his chest — pride, rage, and hope all at once.

He looked back at Stafan, voice steady as stone.

"Tell the men," he said. "The fight is still on."

Then he stood, blade drawn, and led them deeper into the wreckage, toward the keep, where the last stand of the Karathati might yet hold.

&

CHAPTER 25

T he gates of Karathat rose like pale giants against the dawn.

Mevran rode at the head of the small column — just nineteen men, most of them wounded, all of them changed. Behind him, their horses moved at a weary, broken pace, hooves dragging on the stone road that wound through the hills. Their armour was scorched and dented, faces gaunt, eyes hollow and sunken with the knowledge of what they had survived, and what they had left behind.

As they neared the outer post, the city guard stepped forward, spears at the ready. But as soon as they recognized the battered riders, they lowered their weapons with solemn respect. Word had already come. The defenders of Teren Ridge had paid the price, but they had bought time. They were expected.

A captain stepped forward, bowing low with a gravity that spoke of a nation's mourning. "You are to report to the Queen's Hall immediately,

Commander Mevran. She has been awaiting you."

Mevran's eyes narrowed, his voice raw. "She knows?"

The captain nodded, face grave. "The rider you sent never reached us. A servant of the Queen — Tamanda — found him, badly wounded, on the road. She carried his message herself."

Mevran closed his eyes for a moment, exhaling slowly as if a crushing weight had eased only the slightest bit. "Then Karathat has time."

He swung down from the saddle, legs trembling with exhaustion. The others followed, some nearly collapsing as they dismounted, helping the more wounded to the ground, steadying each other like men returned from a grave. Around them, citizens peeked from behind market stalls and shuttered windows, eyes wide, their whispers low and fearful as they watched the broken warrior's pass. Rumour had already taken root, spreading on quick, terrified wings.

The Queen was waiting in the great hall.

The tall oak doors opened as Mevran entered, his boots echoing over the polished stone floors. At the far end of the hall stood Storia, framed by the pale dawn pouring through high windows, flanked by Sapir and members of the war council. Her face was composed, regal, but her eyes gave her away — fierce and bright, fighting to hold back the storm raging behind them.

Mevran approached and dropped to one knee, armour clanking. "Your Majesty," he rasped, throat torn raw from days of smoke and shouting orders. "Teren Ridge has fallen."

Storia nodded, a slow, measured movement, as if bracing herself against a blow she had known was coming. "I know," she answered softly.

"Did Zarratt live?" Her voice did not break, though her eyes searched Mevran's face with desperate hope.

Mevran looked down, and grief twisted through him like a blade.

"No, Your Majesty," he said, voice catching. "He stayed to hold the gate. Ordered me to take the wounded and withdraw. He and a handful of volunteers… they fought to cover our escape." He swallowed hard, the memory still raw and searing.

"He stood on the rampart, Majesty," Mevran continued, voice barely holding steady. "He rallied the archers until they were gone. He took a spear himself when the line broke. I saw him strike down six Natsu before they dragged him to the wall. An arrow found him. He fell from the parapet. I… I saw it."

Silence choked the hall, deep and terrible.

"He died bravely," Mevran forced out. "To the very end. He took many of the Natsu with him. Enough that we had a chance to ride.

Enough to warn you."

A tear burned its way down his cheek.

Storia's hands trembled, then curled into fists at her sides. A queen could not weep, not now, but a daughter might. She let the moment pass in a long breath, then forced steel back into her spine.

Sapir stepped forward, voice low but pressing. "Did any others survive?"

"Nineteen of us," Mevran answered hollowly. "No more." Another heavy silence.

Storia lifted her chin, letting the rage carry her grief. "Then we prepare the walls," she said, voice clear as a blade drawn from its sheath.

"The Natsu will come for Karathat. We will be ready."

Mevran nodded. "They come in force. And they come soon."

Storia's jaw tightened. "Then they will find us waiting."

Her gaze swept over the assembled council, daring any of them to flinch.

"Zarratt died buying us these days," she said. "We will not waste them."

Mevran lowered his head in respect. "His spirit will stand with us," he said, voice firm though ragged. "And so will ours."

Storia looked beyond him, out through the high windows where the pale dawn lit the city walls.

"See to the wounded," she ordered, voice regaining its calm edge.

"Then rest. You will be needed again before long."

Mevran nodded, and turned to carry out her will, while the queen stood alone at the head of her hall — one heartbeat away from breaking, but unbroken still.

~~~~~~~~~~~~~~~~~~~~~~~~~~~

Tamanda stood in the hallway outside the war council chamber, half-shadowed between two marble pillars. She wasn't meant to be there — not officially — but no one had dared to stop her.

She had delivered the injured rider days ago, had carried the first warning with hands still shaking from what she'd seen. It had not been enough to ease her heart, but it had bought them time.

Now she listened.

The heavy oak doors were slightly ajar, just enough for her to catch the voices within. Mevran's voice drifted out, low and ragged, every word heavy with pain. She could hear the hoarseness that came from too many nights of screaming orders over battle and watching friends die.

"…He stayed behind to hold the gate… he died bravely, Your Majesty…"

The words struck her like a blade to the gut.

Zarratt.

The name rattled through her chest, cracking something that had stayed unbroken until now. Zarratt, the commander who had trained her when no one else believed a palace servant had any business wielding a sword. The one who had forced her into the guard trials early, ignoring tradition, ignoring sneers, refusing to accept that station or gender should ever decide courage.

And now he was gone.
~~~~~~~~~~~~~~~~~~~~~~~~~~~

Her hand tightened on the hilt of her sword. She could almost feel his voice still in her ear, barking corrections as she learned to parry, urging her to stand taller, strike harder. She remembered the way he had paced along the training ground, eyes like a hawk's, demanding everything from his warriors because he knew one day it might be all that saved them.

Loyalty isn't what you swear, he had once told her. It's what you do when no one commands you.

Zarratt had died proving those words.

She swallowed hard, her throat thick and raw. Her chest felt too tight, and tears stung at the corners of her eyes — but she refused to let them fall, not here, not now.

Inside the chamber, the Queen's voice rang out, iron and unyielding:

"Then we prepare the walls. The Natsu march for Karathat."

Tamanda pushed off the cold pillar, straightening. There would be time to grieve later — if there was a later. For now, she had work to do. Zarratt had bought them these precious days. She would not let his sacrifice be squandered.

◼

The war council convened within the hour.

Torches flared in iron sconces, throwing sharp, jittering shadows across the high-vaulted stone. A massive map of the kingdom lay unrolled on the central table, its creases still showing from a lifetime of hurried consultations. Small carved markers had already been placed, showing enemy movement, vulnerable gates, fallback lines.

Storia stood at the head of the table, her back straight, her face hard as forged steel.

Sapir stood close by, arms folded, his gaze flicking restlessly from the Queen to the map, calculating possibilities.

Mevran leaned forward, palms braced against the table, too weary to stand straight yet refusing to sit. He had become a grim monument to the battle that had already been lost.

"They'll come by the river passes," Mevran began, voice rough. "It's the only ground wide enough for a column that size to move freely."

Sapir nodded. "They'll try to breach the outer gate first. If they take it, the inner walls will fall within days. We can't let them pour through."

Storia's sharp gaze swept across the gathered councillors. "Have we heard from the coastal garrisons?"

A scribe stepped forward, ink-stained and anxious. "No, Majesty.

The hawks have not returned."

"Send more," Storia commanded at once. "Six to every major outpost within three days' ride. Order them to muster and march on

Karathat with all haste."

She turned to Mevran. "What is your estimation of their numbers?"

Mevran's jaw tightened. "Thousands, Your Majesty. Three, four thousand at least — possibly more. They were waiting for us to break, and now they know where to strike." A grim murmur rippled through the council.
Councillor Hadur stepped forward, his tone edged with fatalism.
"Karathat was never garrisoned for a siege of this size. We don't have the soldiers to match them in open battle."

"Then we do not give them open battle," Sapir snapped. "We choke them in the alleys, in the narrow streets, where their numbers mean nothing. We will turn every courtyard and every house into a fortress.

Make them bleed for every stone."

Storia did not hesitate. "Do it. Collapse roads if you must, barricade the rest. Arm the civilians, bring them to the inner wards if needed. If they breach the outer wall, we make them pay for every step they take."

Mevran nodded slowly. "We'll need to ration. Grain, water — enough to last weeks."

"Prepare it," Storia ordered. "If we must starve to survive, then so be it."

She glanced down at Zarratt's final scroll, his last desperate message.

Her hand trembled, then steadied.

"He gave us time," she said. "We will not waste it."

Silence spread across the room, heavy as mourning cloth. Then, one by one, the councillors bowed their heads.

War had come for Karathat.

And its queen would meet it with steel.

❧

CHAPTER 26

T he gates of Teren Ridge no longer stood.

They hung in splintered ruin; broken beams twisted like the ribs of some giant beast left to rot. The once-proud threshold had become nothing more than charred timber and jagged iron hinges, the heavy doors shattered beyond recognition. Smoke still clung to the walls, trailing thin and bitter as it rose into a bruised sky. Banners were gone, ripped down or burned away entirely. In their place, only the dark scrawls of soot and the ragged stains of dried blood marked who had held this ground, and who had died upon it.

The air was thick with the stench of death. It coated every breath: blood, rot, scorched flesh, and cold ash. Flies hummed across the courtyard, drawn to the bodies that lay strewn like discarded puppets. Some were burned beyond recognition, others torn apart by blade or arrow. The ground was churned to mud and darkened with what seemed an endless spill of red.

Taran rode through the shattered entrance in silence; his warriors close behind. Their eyes were wide, their faces grey in the dawn light. They had come prepared for ruin, but even so, this sight threatened to break them.

The courtyard was a graveyard.

Bodies were everywhere, as though they had rained from the ramparts and tower walls. Near the eastern battlements, a broken ladder lay atop a mound of the fallen, where Karathat's defenders had made their final stand. Some still clutched weapons, their grips locked even in death, refusing to yield.

Stafan dismounted first. He stepped across the broken stones to a body sprawled near the well, turning the man gently to see his face. Then he shook his head in silent mourning.

Taran moved forward, letting his gaze wander the ruin. He tried to see through the carnage to what had happened here, piecing together each crushed helm, each severed banner, until his eyes found a splash of crimson at the base of the southern rampart.

A cloak.

Crimson but tattered and blackened by soot.

Taran dismounted, boots crunching through shattered masonry. He crouched and pushed aside charred planks and stones. Beneath them was a body, half-buried, battered by fire and falling debris. One deep wound had slashed straight through the ribs. The cloak bore a faded sigil — Karathat's royal guard.

Taran's breath caught. Lying beside the body, partly hidden in the rubble, was a sword — chipped, scorched, but unmistakably Zarratt's.

A familiar hilt. An old grip wrapped in worn leather, marked by years of training.

Zarratt.

Taran lowered his head. The weight of loss sank deep into his chest.

"He died fighting," he said, voice raw.

Stafan came to stand beside him, swallowing hard. "He bought time," he answered. "Look around — they died to buy every heartbeat.

These bodies tell it."

Taran's hand reached out, lifting the blade from the ruin. It felt heavy, still warm from the sun, its edge dulled but unbroken.

"You held your line," Taran murmured, almost to himself. "Now I'll hold mine."

He closed the man's eyes with a gentle touch. Then he stood, sword in hand, and looked out over the carnage.

"There will be no rotting here," he said to Stafan. "Gather our men. Burn the dead. Karathat or Natsu, all of them. We leave no brother behind to feed the crows."

Stafan nodded grimly. "It will be done."

Their warriors moved quickly through the ruin, some weeping as they recognized a friend, others moving with a numb, mechanical resolve. Piles of broken shields were gathered for kindling. Torches were lit. Songs of mourning rose in ragged whispers, half-remembered prayers to guide the souls of the fallen.

Taran stayed near the wall, his thoughts clouded. There was no victory here. Only ashes, and remembrance. And vengeance yet to come.

By nightfall, the pyres burned low. The last of the dead had been laid to rest — some in flame, others beneath small cairns hastily built from shattered stone. The smoke drifted into the darkening sky, drawn toward a scattering of cold stars, like incense offered to the ancestors.

Taran stood on the rampart, looking east into the wilderness where the enemy had fled or regrouped. Behind him, the outpost was silent but for the hushed movements of men on watch, the faint clang of metal, the low murmur of exhausted voices.

He turned to Stafan.

"I want eyes on the eastern ridges by dawn," he ordered, voice cutting through the dusk. "If the Natsu pushed through here, they'll either camp close or move straight on Karathat."

Stafan nodded, understanding at once. "Two groups?"

"Three," Taran corrected. "North and south along the ridge lines, and one through the pass. Fast riders. No torches, no banners. If they see the enemy, they do not engage — they ride straight back."

Stafan raised a hand, calling three scouts forward from the shadows — thin men in plain cloaks, bows strapped across their shoulders. Their faces were drawn, but their eyes were bright and alert.

"You heard him," Stafan said. "Ride wide. Ride fast. Bring word back, or don't come back at all."

The scouts mounted up, spurring their horses into the night without hesitation, fading into the dark like ghosts swallowed by the hills.

Taran looked east, his jaw set.

"We'll not be surprised again," he whispered. "Not while I still breathe."

Behind him, the camp settled into uneasy sleep, men curled close to their fires, too tired to speak. But Taran did not rest. He stood alone on the rampart, Zarratt's sword in his grip, and watched the stars — waiting for word, for movement, for the first hint of where the Natsu would strike next.

~~~~~~~~~~~~~~~~~~~~~~~~~

Dalen rode alone.

He had broken from the other scouts after the first ridge, veering southeast into the lower forest paths where ancient pines crowded the road, their needles soaking the earth and muffling every hoofbeat. The forest smelled of wet bark, of moss, of cold stone. His horse moved surefooted and quick, trained for silence even in broken country.

The night was moonless, leaving only the faint shimmer of stars to guide him, flickering through shifting black branches. The air bit against his cheeks, sharp as a blade, and each breath tasted of sap and smoke.

He rode hard for hours, slipping through narrow animal trails, across small streams, ducking beneath leaning boughs
~~~~~~~~~~~~~~~~~~~~~~~~~

that clawed at his cloak. Each mile felt longer than the last, the forest pressing tighter around him until he had to fight a rising panic — a hunter's sense that eyes watched from the dark.

By the second hour before dawn, the trees finally gave way, thinning until he reached a high bluff of pale rock, half-covered in frost. From there, he saw the land flattening into the southeast plains — Karathat's vulnerable outer ring of farmland and villages.

That's when he heard it.

At first, he thought it was just a night breeze thrumming against the ridge. But then it grew steadier, rhythm rising from the valley floor like the beat of a monstrous heart.

War drums.

Dalen's breath caught. He froze, listening, counting the pace. Faint, but steady. Unmistakable.

He dismounted in a single practiced movement, dropping lightly to the ground. He tied his horse to a half-dead sapling, then crawled forward on his stomach, pressing close to the frozen soil until he reached the lip of the bluff.

When he peered over, his heart lurched.

The valley moved like a living beast — an endless column of men and machines, winding through the mist. Campfires burned in neat lines, countless tiny orange eyes blinking through the predawn gloom. Siege towers. Battering rams. Ranks upon ranks of armoured warriors, their armour catching the first faint grey light like dull knives. Above them, banners snapped in the breeze, each one bearing the black crescent of the Natsu high command.

A horn cried out, long and cold. Columns began to shift, their lines rippling like a river of steel.

Thousands of them.

Dalen counted fast, taking in formations, scanning the siege equipment. They were organized, disciplined, and heading west — straight toward Karathat.

Fear clawed at his gut, but he forced it down. He counted banners again, memorizing their order, looking for gaps, weaknesses, anything to report.

Then he turned, half-running, half-sliding back down the slope. There was no time to waste. He scrambled to his horse, untying the reins with shaking hands, and swung into the saddle with a single hard breath.

"Come on," he urged, spurring the exhausted beast forward.

The horse leapt back into motion, tearing through low branches and tangled roots, hooves pounding the leaf-choked path. Dalen ducked to avoid a low bough, a branch scraping a long line across his cheek. The forest closed in around them, but he kept the course, trusting instinct, trusting speed.

Behind him, the war drums kept beating — slow and merciless, a sound that felt like it might swallow the world.

He rode on, heart pounding, thoughts spinning. Karathat is not ready. The walls might hold, but only if they had warning. And if he failed now — if he fell or was cut off — the city would be taken in its sleep.

He pushed the horse harder, ignoring the sting of wind and grit, leaning forward to urge every last ounce of speed.

At last, the sun broke over the eastern peaks, slicing the horizon in gold. Its light struck him like a blow, stinging his eyes, but he welcomed it — proof he had survived the night.

He had ridden hard for four days, pushing his horse to the brink of collapse. The beast's ribs showed through its dust-caked hide, each laboured breath sounding ragged and painful. Dalen had paused only long enough to let the animal drink from shallow streams or tear mouthfuls of brittle grass from dry ground, unwilling to stop for himself until he had no choice. His own limbs burned with exhaustion, shoulders aching from the constant jolt of the saddle. Sleep had come in broken snatches, if at all, haunted by the pounding rhythm of war drums and the endless march of the Natsu columns in his mind.

Ahead, the shattered ruins of Teren Ridge came into view, bleak and blackened. The sight nearly broke him, but he rode straight through the splintered gates, ignoring the dead, ignoring the stink of burned flesh.

His horse was lathered in sweat, flanks heaving, but it did not slow.

Dalen tore through the camp like a storm, scattering men as he went, before throwing himself from the saddle, boots slamming to the ground.

He did not pause.

There was no time.

&

CHAPTER 27

Tamanda didn't trust easily.

It was a trait Zarratt had praised in her — before the gate, before the fire, before the walls of Karathat had become the only shield left between hope and annihilation.

Now, in the uneasy stillness behind Karathat's gates, that instinct returned sharper than ever. The tension in the palace was a living thing, crackling like a hidden spark about to catch fire. Queen Storia's war council worked without pause, their voices echoing through the marble halls by lamplight night after night. Scouts came and went with haggard faces, delivering hurried reports. The quartermasters counted rations until their ink-stained fingers cramped. Extra guards watched every gate, every alley, every step.

The city braced for siege, and Tamanda watched it all.

But most of all, she watched him.

Biden.

The quiet boy who had helped her the day she'd staggered through Karathat's gate, half-dead and bleeding. He had been gentle then, hands quick with water and bandages, soothing, almost kind. She'd thanked him through tears of pain and exhaustion. She'd believed him.

But now, with eyes no longer clouded by injury, she saw what she had missed: he was everywhere. Too present. The kitchens. The upper halls. Lingering near the council doors. Even around the messenger coops, where trained hawks came and went. And he always vanished before she could corner him. 223

Tamanda's instincts twisted painfully when she saw him that morning, slipping through a narrow service door behind the stables — a door meant only for guards and trusted messengers.

Enough.

She followed, moving with a hunter's silence, each step measured, hand resting lightly on the worn hilt of her short blade. The corridor beyond the door was narrow and dim, lit only by a thin shaft of dawn spilling through a crack in the stones.

Old dust and straw littered the corners.

She rounded the corner, steps feather-light, and there he was.

Biden.

He crouched low near a pile of empty grain sacks, his face half-hidden by shadows. Tamanda saw the glint of wax, the seal he pulled from behind a loosened stone. Her breath froze. It was no Karathati mark. Instead, it bore the black crescent of the Natsu high command.

Her pulse hammered.

"Step away," she ordered, voice like steel.

He spun toward her, startled — but quick. Much quicker than she'd ever seen him move. His hand shot for the scroll, and then he ran.

Tamanda lunged after him.

They hurtled through the narrow halls, crashing past startled servants and slamming into half-open doors. Biden ducked down twisting passages, trying to lose her, but she stayed on his heels. He turned sharply toward the aviary; the air now filled with the rustle of caged hawks and the faint smell of straw and droppings.

He's going to try to send the message.

She closed the gap and tackled him just beneath the archway, both of them crashing to the floor with a bone-jarring thud. Biden's elbow caught her ribs, making her gasp, but she fought through it, driving her knee into his side.

He fumbled for a knife at his belt — but she was faster. She slammed her elbow into his jaw, knocking the blade away in a clatter that echoed through the hall.

They wrestled, rolling through feathers and straw, until she twisted his wrist hard enough to wrench the scroll free.

Guards arrived seconds later, swords drawn, eyes wide.

Tamanda stood above him, breathing hard, hair sticking to her sweat-slicked face, the scroll clutched tight in her hand.

"This man is a Natsu spy," she said, voice sharp as a sword point. "He meant to send a message."

The guards seized Biden. He no longer fought. He only looked up at her with hollow eyes, something resigned — or perhaps fanatical — behind them.

Tamanda's voice was cold. "Bring him to the Queen. And get this scroll to Sapir. Now."

She watched them drag Biden away, unable to suppress a tremor of rage.

How close he'd come.

■

The war council chamber had grown colder with every hour.

Rain tapped against the tall windows, and the iron braziers burned low, their flames throwing unsteady shadows across maps pinned with markers showing every desperate troop movement.

Queen Storia stood beside the brazier, her face drawn but unyielding, the captured scroll in her hands. She read it once. Twice. Three times.

Sapir stood opposite, arms folded, eyes dark with simmering anger. Tamanda waited by the door, her cloak still damp from the chase, refusing to flinch.

Finally, Storia spoke. "They weren't only coming for the walls," she said, voice quiet but dangerous. "They meant to take the city from within."

Sapir stepped forward, jaw tight. "What does it say?"

She handed him the scroll. "Coded, but sloppy. Instructions to report guard rotations. Hawk schedules. Defensive weaknesses."

Sapir's face darkened as he read. "They've been getting reports for days."

Tamanda's mouth went dry. Days.

Storia fixed her gaze on her, softer but still blazing with resolve. "You saved this city again, Tamanda. Zarratt would be proud."

Tamanda bowed her head, refusing to let emotion break through.

"We change everything," Sapir said. "Codes. Shifts. Messenger routes. The hawk towers—"

"Seal them," Storia cut in. "Until I say otherwise, no messages leave without three signatures. And double the guard details on every gate."

She looked at Tamanda. "Stay close to me from now on. I want you at my side, no more shadows."

Tamanda nodded. "Yes, Your Majesty."

Sapir rolled the scroll tight and sealed it into a flameproof case. "If this is what one spy was worth," he growled, "Rakah will have more waiting."

Storia stepped to the window, looking over Karathat's rooftops where storm clouds gathered, heavy and low. Somewhere beyond, the Natsu army advanced, unstoppable as a tide.

But her voice did not waver.

"Then we fight," she said, quiet but unbreakable. "We will hold this city inside and out, even if it burns to the foundations."

The cell beneath the western hold of the palace was colder than Tamanda remembered.

Carved into the stubborn bedrock, it felt more tomb than prison, a place where hope went to die. Water ran in thin threads down the walls, pooling on the cracked stone floor, making the air taste of iron and Mold. A single torch sputtered in a rusty bracket, its light fighting to stay alive against the damp.

Biden sat slumped on a wooden bench, wrists bound with iron links that bit into raw skin. His eyes, shadowed and sunken, stared into nothing, unblinking. There was a calm to him that was more frightening than a man screaming, a stillness bred of twisted faith.

Tamanda entered first, Sapir at her shoulder. Two guards flanked the doorway, their faces stony, hands never leaving their blades.

For a long moment, no one spoke. Only the steady drip of water marked the passing time.

Then Sapir stepped forward, dropping the intercepted scroll at Biden's feet. It fell with a quiet finality, the wax seal broken, Karathat's secrets exposed.

"We know what you are," Sapir said, voice low and controlled, but edged with fury. "We know who you serve."

Biden finally raised his gaze, slow, deliberate. He glanced from Sapir to Tamanda, his expression unreadable. There was no fear there — only a terrible, unwavering pride.

"I was loyal," he said, voice almost gentle.

Tamanda's hand twitched near her sword hilt. "To whom?" she demanded. "The Natsu? Or to Rakah?"

Biden allowed a small, cold smile. "To him," he answered. "He is the only one who sees clearly. While you squabble about walls and alliances,

Rakah builds a future. You cannot even imagine it."

Sapir took a step closer, boots scraping across wet stone. "By burning towns? Slaughtering the Ridge? You call that a future?"

Biden shrugged, the iron links rattling against his wrists. "You cannot make a new order with kind words. You break the old first. That is what strength demands."

Tamanda stepped closer until the torchlight caught the scars on her face, reminders of Zarratt's final stand. Her voice was like a drawn blade.

"Why spy here? Why the palace?"

Biden did not blink. "To soften the blow," he explained. "To know which gate to strike, which wall to breach, who to kill first. I was meant to make it easy."

She swallowed the bile rising in her throat. "You were going to kill her," she accused.

"I was going to make it easier for those who would," Biden replied, no apology in his tone. "You stopped me. For now." Silence settled again, thick and suffocating.

Sapir drew in a tight breath. "Where is Rakah now?"

Biden hesitated, something flickering in his eyes — respect, or perhaps the smallest measure of regret. Then he spoke.

"He is not far," he admitted. "His war host is in Buckmore Valley, moving fast. He will not wait to starve you out. He will break you open."

Tamanda exchanged a quick glance with Sapir. Buckmore Valley was dangerously close.

"He's with them?" she pressed.

Biden nodded. "Always. He leads from the front. That is why men follow him."

Tamanda's jaw hardened. "And that is where we will find him."

She turned to the guards. "Take him to the deepest cell. He speaks to no one, sees no one. Do not let him die, but do not let him rest easy either."

Biden was hauled to his feet. He did not fight, but as he was dragged away, he fixed Tamanda with one last, terrible stare.

"You think you have delayed your doom," he rasped. "But you have only made it worse."

The iron door slammed shut behind him.

Sapir exhaled, his shoulders slumping. "So, it's true."

Tamanda nodded, the flame of resolve already catching in her eyes. "Then we meet him."

■

Outside the palace, the city bristled with preparations. Hammers rang day and night, mending broken parapets. Stones were stacked into barricades at narrow streets. Arrow slits were reinforced with fresh timber. Fires burned in every courtyard, ready to pour boiling pitch if needed.

Messengers sprinted between towers, relaying fresh orders. Queen Storia herself stalked the ramparts like a wraith, inspecting every station, every guard, every shield.

But the news from Buckmore Valley hit hard.

Taran and his warriors, still recovering near Teren Ridge, had heard the same message through their own scouts: Rakah marched, and he marched fast. Faster than any had thought possible. The Mandji riders, battered and half-supplied, raced to cut across the broken foothills in a desperate bid to catch the enemy before Karathat's walls were surrounded.

The land slowed them — deep gullies carved by spring floods, loose rock that snapped horses' legs, treacherous slopes that turned into death traps.

For two days they fought the terrain, curses echoing off the cliffs as they mended torn saddles and helped wounded mounts back to their feet. Taran felt each hour like a blade digging into his flesh — every moment they lost was a moment Rakah gained.

By the third night, a scout found them in the darkness, breathless, eyes wild.

"The Natsu have crossed into Karathat's far fields," the scout gasped.

"They are two days from the walls — no more."

Taran stood silent, cold fury knotting in his chest. Then he spoke, voice quiet but iron hard.

"We will strike them from the rear," he decided. "While they focus on the walls, we carve their backbone out from behind."

ॐ

CHAPTER 28

They were close now.

Taran stood beneath a crooked pine at the edge of a rise; eyes narrowed against the morning sun. Below him, the hills sloped westward toward Karathat, their folds baked dry by weeks without rain. The air was thin here, harsh, scraping at the throat, and each gust felt like knives across his face. The wind coiled through the branches overhead, carrying the scent of dust, resin, and a faraway hint of woodsmoke that made his skin prickle.

Behind him, the Mandji column pressed forward—tired, silent, but unyielding. These men had marched for days on hard ground with little food, sleeping in shifts, always half-listening for the scrape of steel in the night. Their horses were leaner now, ribs showing under dusty hides, but no one turned aside. They had come too far, lost too many, to think of quitting now.

Stafan rode up, dust clinging to his boots, eyes rimmed red from wind and worry. "The scout is back," he reported, voice pitched low so no one else could hear.

Taran nodded, still watching the path that twisted down the slope.

"Send him up."

A young rider approached, the sun flashing off sweat that caked his neck. His horse was a lathered mess, head drooping, breath harsh. The scout slid off, knees trembling, but he managed to salute with a clenched fist.

"They're moving, Commander," he began, voice breaking with exhaustion. "The Natsu have crossed Buckmore Valley. I saw their 230 columns along the hills—wagons, siege towers, ranks of spears like

wheat before harvest. They're not rushing, but they're steady."

Taran's jaw tightened. "How many?"

"Four thousand, maybe more," the scout said, eyes dark. "There are outriders skirting ahead of the main force. I counted them scattering farm folk, taking stock and grain. They're not hungry—they're confident."

Taran drew in a slow breath, letting the anger anchor him. The sun above them seemed to hammer down harder, unkind and relentless.

"There's more," the scout added, voice hesitant. "They're talking about him. Rakah."

The name was a blade drawn across Taran's mind.

The scout continued, swallowing. "They say he rides at the front. Always. They speak his name like a prayer or a curse. No one questions him. No one dares."

Stafan shifted, the leather of his saddle creaking. "A war-leader with no crown is worse than a king. They choose to follow him."

Taran studied the road west. The hills glared pale and lifeless, only distant smears of green where the farms clung on. "He earned them," he murmured. "That makes him twice as dangerous."

The scout nodded. "They're reinforcing their supply lines, sir. Trenches, watchfires, scouts along every path. They expect someone to try to break through."

Taran set his mouth in a hard line. "They're right to."

He turned from the ridge, looking down at his men. They were stringing spare bowstrings, oiling leather, tending to tired horses. Even from here, he could see how thin they were growing. Some had stripped off layers of armour just to keep moving in the heat. One man had tied cloth over a broken sandal, limping on but still pressing forward.

He felt the weight of that trust pressing on his shoulders.

"No camp tonight," he told Stafan. "They get half an hour's rest, then we move on. We need to stay ahead of their outriders."

Stafan nodded. "Understood."

As the men took a brief rest, Taran walked through their ranks. He touched a shoulder here, a spear there, made a quiet word of encouragement where he could. It was not much, but even the smallest nod seemed to draw the men a fraction taller.

He found one group bandaging a young warrior's leg—splinted with strips of wood and tied with rawhide. The man grinned through gritted teeth. "I can still ride," he said. "You will," Taran replied. "But not at the front."

The warrior nodded, and Taran moved on, heart heavier.

That night, they moved again, slipping down through the dark gullies, the stars a thin scatter overhead. The wind carried new smells now—scorched grain, trampled earth, and the tang of horse dung left by passing columns.

They had not gone far when one of the forward scouts came back at a dead run.

"Commander—movement in the next valley," he panted. "Natsu outriders, a dozen at least. Maybe more. They have a campfire tucked behind a bluff. There's a banner—they're holding captured grain and oxen."

Taran's eyes narrowed. "Supplies?"

"Yes, sir."

A low growl rose from Stafan's throat. "We could take them. We'd need that grain."

Taran hesitated. They had a mission—reaching Karathat, warning the city, preparing to hit Rakah's rear once the siege closed. But the men were hungry, the horses half-dead, and fresh grain was no small prize.

He nodded. "We strike. Fast. Leave no one behind who can raise a horn."

They moved out across the hills, cutting through dry grass and stone. The moon had risen thin and cold, turning the land to silver.

When they crested the low bluff, they saw the Natsu outriders. A dozen men, hard and sharp, wearing piecemeal armour. Their small fire glowed red, a weak ring of warmth among hobbled oxen and looted grain carts.

Taran raised his hand.

"On my mark," he whispered.

The Mandji crashed in from two sides, a wedge of screaming fury. Taran's sword bit down into the first man before the enemy had even reached for a horn. Sparks flew off a shield rim as he hacked down, felt the bone crack, smelled sweat and iron.

Stafan charged past, his spear taking another Natsu through the belly. Horses screamed, and men scattered, blades drawn too late to match the Mandji momentum.

The Natsu were tough, fast, but surprised—they broke and fled toward the scrubby rise, only to be cut down by archers waiting on the far slope.

It was quick, brutal, over in less than a minute.

Taran stood among the wreckage, breathing hard. The Mandji moved through the carts, tossing aside cloth sacks, checking for anything spoiled.

"Keep the oxen," Taran ordered. "Pack the grain. We'll ration it on the march."

A groan caught his ear. Taran turned toward a bloodied figure halfburied beneath a broken wheel—a Natsu soldier, barely clinging to life. The man's chest was caved in, but his eyes flickered as Taran approached.

"Rakah…" the soldier rasped. "Knows you… watches for you…" Taran knelt beside him. "Where is he now?"

The soldier coughed, blood frothing at his lips. "Marching south.

Not to Karathat… not yet. Burn the breadbasket… starve them first." Then he sagged, breath gone, head rolling to one side.

Taran rose, fists clenched. The deeper strategy behind the invasion was beginning to show not just conquest, but starvation. Fear. Isolation.

As dawn began to break, they climbed the ridge and paused.

There—faint but visible—stood the towers of Karathat in the far distance. For a moment, hope shimmered through the dust.

The younger soldiers straightened.

But then clouds shifted, and the towers disappeared again behind a veil of heat haze and smoke.

Taran lowered his head.

"We're close," he said. "But so are they."

He gathered the officers by the captured carts, grain rustling as it was loaded.

"We are behind them," he said. "But their army is too big to move quietly. We stay to their flanks, pick at them, bleed their outriders, break their supply line before they ever reach the walls. We don't give them one night's peace."

They nodded, faces drawn but determined.

Stafan stepped forward, voice even lower. "If they catch us, Taran…" "Then they catch us," Taran finished for him. "But they will pay.

They will pay dearly."

He turned back toward the ridgeline, the wind shifting and carrying the smoke of distant fires toward him. The scent of it was sharp, heavy—war's breath.

They had no illusions left.

He looked over his shoulder, saw the Mandji reshaping themselves after the clash, hands steadying grain sacks, helping each other bind wounds.

They were not pretty, not polished, not unstoppable like the stories.

But they were alive, and they were unbowed.

And that would have to be enough.

&

CHAPTER 29

The wind off the southern hills carried a strange hush.

From the watchtowers of Karathat, where guards had kept silent vigil for days, the first whispers of movement finally came — not from hawks or scouts, but from the earth itself. Dust curled in shifting columns along the horizon. Faint tremors worked their way up through the old stone, reaching the soles of boots, rattling tower beams. And then, through the late afternoon haze, the shapes began to form.

One by one, the lookouts called out.

"South ridge! Movement!"

"Banners… horsemen!"

Within moments, the horns sounded — two long, aching blasts rolling across the city, echoing through arches and up stone stairways. The guards snapped to readiness. Archers scrambled into their roosts. Shield lines braced at the gates. Messengers sprinted across the courtyards toward the palace steps, faces pale with dust and fear.

At the southern tower, the captain of the watch, a veteran with more scars than he could count, lifted a battered looking glass. What he saw turned his blood to ice. He lowered the glass, wordless, then passed it to his lieutenant with a silent nod.

Below them, the Natsu army spilled into sight.

Riders came first, lean, dark-armoured, flanking the column with a predator's confidence. Behind them, wave after wave of infantry advanced, ranks perfectly disciplined in grey and crimson. Massive wagons rumbled along behind the foot soldiers, stacked high with canvas, barrels, and crates. And beyond those, towering shapes creaked forward on

235 huge wooden wheels, pushed by teams of oxen and prisoners, each one draped in painted cloth to ward against flame.

Siege towers.

They had arrived.

At the high balcony of the palace, Queen Storia watched from above. She stood straight-backed, fingers locked on the railing so tightly her knuckles had turned pale. Sapir stood at her side, cloak snapping in the sharp, rising wind.

"They don't even try to mask their numbers," she murmured, eyes hard.

"No," Sapir said. "They want us to see. They want us to feel them."

Storia's gaze travelled over the growing swarm of troops. Already, cavalry detachments were breaking off to ride around the city's outer farms, cutting off roads, driving villagers toward the walls. Small pillars of smoke rose where barns and fields were torched.

"Where are their messengers?" she asked. "Where are the terms?"

Sapir's jaw tightened. "There will be no terms," he said simply.

"They've come to conquer, not bargain."

Storia closed her eyes for a heartbeat, steadying herself, then opened them again. "Then let them come."

Below, the palace guards hurried through the streets, shouting orders. Civilians were ushered behind the inner walls, children carried by frightened mothers, carts rattling with hastily packed bundles. Gates were reinforced with iron bars dragged from the old armoires. The great oil cauldrons were uncovered, black as a crow's wing in the fading light. The city braced itself.

On the south ridge, a single rider sat motionless, watching the walls with an almost unsettling stillness.

The black banner behind him fluttered in the gusting wind.

Rakah sat astride a grey warhorse, still as stone, alone but for the distant shape of his gathering army. Dust from the march streaked his cloak, and the leather ties on his wrist were cut with fresh creases from countless days gripping a sword. But there was no

weariness in his eyes. Only absolute focus — cold, precise, unshakable.

Below him, Karathat's walls glowed gold in the low sun, proud, unbroken, even as fear twisted through its gates. He watched the black dots of sentries moving between towers, saw the glint of arrowheads, the glimmer of shields stacked along parapets.

They were ready.

He respected that.

Behind him, the Natsu columns unfolded like a tide, engineers barking orders, oxen straining against siege towers that rattled across the ruts. Riders splintered off to guard every approach, closing every lane and road leading away from the city.

Still, Rakah waited.

A captain approached him, dismounting with wary respect. "Commander, the first campfires are being set. Siege perimeter will be sealed by dusk."

"Good," Rakah said. "And the hawk towers?"

The captain nodded. "Too far for now, but they've already sent two birds. Likely to the Mandji."

Rakah smiled faintly, a cold curve of the lips. "Let them call for help.

Let them think a Savior comes."

He looked again at the battlements, as though reading a challenge.

"Will you send terms?" the captain asked, trying to mask uncertainty.

"No," Rakah said, voice quiet as a blade being drawn. "Let silence do its work. Let them feel how small their words have become." The captain lowered his head.

Rakah leaned forward in his saddle, the leather creaking. His horse shifted, sensing the tension.

Then he spoke, as if to the city itself.

"Wonder, Queen of Karathat," he murmured. "Wonder if I came for your walls, or for something far deeper."

He turned his horse then, cloak rippling behind him, and rode down toward the siege lines, where fires had begun to burn, lighting the night in ugly shades of orange.

The time for knocking had passed.

Now came the slow turning of the blade.

The war council gathered beneath the domed chamber of the Queen's Tower. The room, once used for trade charters and diplomatic ceremonies, now bore maps stretched over every table, candles burned low, and the scent of oil, steel, and ink filled the air.

Storia stood at the head of the table, arms braced as she looked over a charcoal-sketched map of Karathat and its surrounding hills. Sapir stood to her left. Captain Edran, commander of the gate watch, stood to her right. The chamber was crowded—strategists, engineers, quartermasters, and three of the city's oldest noble families, their colours muted now by the threat of siege.

"Scouts confirm they have the numbers," Storia said, her voice cutting through the murmur. "Siege towers. Ram crews. Mounted outriders. And no envoy has been sent."

"They mean to strike without parley," said Lord Denric, one hand wrapped around a cane he no longer needed, more symbol than aid. "A barbarian act."

"No," Sapir said calmly. "A calculated one."

"The enemy's war-leader—Rakah," Storia added, "has placed himself at the head of the army. He marches with his men, not behind them. That is no barbarian. That is someone who intends to conquer and rule." A tense silence.

Then Edran stepped forward, gesturing to the map. "We've doubled wall rotations. Reserves posted on the second tier. The oil cauldrons have been filled, and two catapults moved to reinforce the west tower. However," He paused. "If they cut off the east and south roads, we'll lose our supply runners by dusk tomorrow."

"We knew this was coming," Storia replied. "Karathat stands because it endures."

"What of the people?" Lady Merish asked, her voice lined with fear despite herself. "The inner city?"

"We'll evacuate to the second ring before nightfall," Storia said. "Food stores are being moved as we speak. No more carts leave the city.

The gate locks when the sun touches the walls." "And the hawks?" Sapir asked.

"Messages have been sent to northern allies," Storia said. "But we can't count on reinforcements. This fight is ours."

She stepped away from the map now, facing the room fully.

"This enemy doesn't come to negotiate," she said. "They don't want surrender—they want erasure. Every family in Karathat has a name, a story, a child waiting by a hearth. If we falter, if we turn on each other now, those stories end here."

She paused, then added quietly, "But if we hold together—just hold—we write a chapter that will outlive even Rakah's ambition."

The room was still. Even the flickering torches seemed to lean in. Sapir gave the smallest nod. "We're with you, Your Majesty." The rest followed, one by one.

The circle held.

The horn calls echoed up the valley.

From his vantage point on a jagged bluff overlooking the plain, Rakah stood surrounded by his officers, watching as the great southern gate of Karathat groaned closed. The city's white towers caught the amber light of evening. What had once been a welcoming jewel on the horizon now drew itself inward like a fortress coiling for the blow.

"They're sealing the last roads," one of her captains said beside her.

"No more trade. No more messengers." "Good," Rakah said.

Behind them, his war host stretched in all directions. Tents rose in tight, ordered rows. Engineers constructed rams and towers with relentless efficiency. Banners of red and grey flapped in the dry wind. Cookfires lit the valleys like stars in a new sky.

"They know they can't survive a siege," said a younger lieutenant, his expression dark with hunger for the coming violence.

"They think they can," Rakah corrected calmly. "Which is useful—for now."

The officers fell silent.

He stood at the cliff's edge, his cloak whipping behind him, eyes fixed on the walls of Karathat. He had studied its defences for months. Every elevation. Every weak mortar joint in the stone. The pace of its hawk messages. The timing of its patrols. She knew it all.

What he wanted now was pressure.

Let them feel the days grind into each other. Let them weigh each ration. Let the Queen Walk the same halls again and again, while soldiers on the walls wondered if help would come.

Then he would strike.

"Begin the inner crescent," he ordered.

His captains moved without question. Horns sounded across the camp. Orders echoed. Foot soldiers began dragging barricades and stakes to the edge of bow range—close enough to be seen from the city, but just beyond retaliation. A psychological ring.

"They'll see we're building slow," Rakah said to no one in particular.

"That we aren't rushing. That we can wait."

One of the banner-carriers approached. "The siege towers will be ready within five days."

"They'll be ready when I say they are," she replied.

The carrier bowed and withdrew.

Rakah remained, unmoving, until the sun had fully dipped behind Karathat's walls, painting the stone in firelight. Then he turned to his war table beneath the command tent.

As he walked, he murmured to himself, a reminder.

"Let them hope. Hope is heavier than fear when it finally breaks."

৬৺

CHAPTER 30

T he first stone struck at dawn.

It came with no trumpet, no declaration, no demand for surrender. Just the shriek of wind-cut air and a thunderclap of shattered stone.

It smashed into the outer south wall near the fourth tower, cracking masonry and splintering timber braces, sending shards flying across the walkway. Two guards were thrown from their post; one landed on the inner courtyard steps below with a sickening thud.

Then came the second.

And the third.

Within minutes, the rhythm of siege was upon them—the slow, deliberate cadence of catapults pounding the city's defences. Karathat had waited, braced, hoped for more time. But time had run out.

From the battlements, Captain Edran shouted orders, his voice hoarse from hours of preparation. "Shields up! Rotate archers! Get sand to the breaches!"

On the tower above him, the city's own catapults returned fire, their armatures groaning under the strain. Stones arced high over the walls, vanishing into the smoke-blurred camp beyond. The enemy had placed their engines just beyond bow range—deliberately, methodically.

From the Queen's Tower, Storia watched the city shudder, her face calm but tight with focus.

Below, citizens had already been ushered into the second tier. The outer ring—Karathat's first shield—would hold as long as it could. And then, if needed, they would fall back again.

Tamanda stood on the lower wall, armour hastily strapped over a tunic still bloodstained from her last fight. She had not yet been sent to the field—Storia had ordered her to stay near the palace, guarding the inner circle. But now she stood beside archers, watching the smoke, waiting.

A flaming shot from the Natsu line soared into the sky.

It struck a merchant's tower near the lower barracks, sending a cascade of broken wood and fire tumbling down the side. Screams followed.

"Buckets!" someone roared. "Get the fire crews—now!" Tamanda clenched her fists. So, it had begun.

Outside the walls, the Natsu siege line unfurled with terrifying precision. Their catapults had been rolled forward under night cover—hidden by smoke, brush, and the rise of the land. They struck from at least five positions now, each wave coordinated.

And behind them, further back, Rakah's command tents stood unmoving, black banners rising against the pale dawn.

Still, he hadn't shown himself. Still, he hadn't spoken.

But his message was clear.

Karathat would be broken by force, not words.

The sound of the siege stones shook the palace walls.

Each strike from the Natsu catapults reverberated through the marble floors, rattling lanterns and stirring dust from the high beams. The palace was no longer a place of quiet strength—it felt like a cage, waiting to crack.

Sapir moved quickly through the eastern wing, his boots thudding against the flagstones. The Queen had dispatched him to oversee the wall rotations, but a single word from one of the servants had pulled him off his path.

"The girl's missing."

He found her in a side corridor beneath the library steps, pressed into the alcove behind a column, knees drawn to her chest, arms wrapped tightly around them. Nyla.

Her eyes darted up as he approached—but she didn't speak. Her whole body was trembling.

Sapir knelt beside her slowly, careful not to startle her.

"Nyla," he said gently, "it's me. You're safe."

She didn't answer, just pressed her head further against her arms, rocking slightly. Her lips moved, but no sound came. He sat with her in silence for a moment, listening to the distant crack of stone on stone.

"They've come," she whispered at last. "They're here."

Sapir nodded. "Yes. But they haven't broken through. Karathat stands."

"They came to my village," she said, her voice flat. "My uncle said they would pass us by. He lied. They burned everything."

She shuddered. "I saw them take people—tie them, drag them. The man in the mask told me not to cry or he'd—"

Her voice broke, and she turned her face away, ashamed of the tears she couldn't stop.

Sapir swallowed hard. He didn't speak of war, or strength, or revenge. Instead, he sat a little closer and placed his hand gently on her shoulder.

"They won't take you again," he said. "Not while I draw breath. Do you understand?"

She blinked at him, eyes wide and wet.

"There are guards in the palace," he continued. "And more coming.

You're not alone anymore."

"I... I know," she whispered. "But I still hear them. In the drums. In the stone."

Sapir didn't deny it. The fear was real.

So, he did the only thing he could—he stayed beside her until her breathing slowed. Until the trembling began to fade.

"Come with me Nyla, I will keep you safe I promise."

The corridor to the Queen's Tower was lined with guards—shields lifted, eyes scanning every passing figure. The sound of the catapults outside was still distant but constant, a grim heartbeat in the air.

Sapir walked quietly down the hall, Nyla in his arms as he carried her. She hadn't spoken since he coaxed her from her hiding place, she had let Sapir take her without resistance.

Two guards moved aside at the chamber door.

Queen Storia stood near the window, cloaked in a robe of deep green, her hair braided tightly behind her shoulders. She turned as the door opened.

"Report?" she asked briskly—then saw the girl.

Her face softened.

"Nyla?" Storia said, stepping forward.

The girl had wrapped her arms around Sapir's neck, squeezing tight as if a snake constricting.

"She was hiding," Sapir said quietly. "The siege… reminded her of what she saw before we found her."

Storia's gaze lingered on the girl. "Come here, child." Nyla didn't move.

But Sapir knelt down and whispered something—gentle, low. Then slowly, reluctantly, the girl climbed off and stepped forward. Not far.

Just enough.

Storia knelt too. Royal robes against cold stone.

"I cannot promise this war won't touch us," she said. "But I will promise this: you will not face it alone."

Nyla's lips trembled. "I heard the drums."

"So did I," Storia replied. "But you hear them less when someone stands beside you."

She opened her arms—not a command, not a gesture of power. An invitation.

Nyla stared for a moment longer… then crossed the space and folded into the Queen's arms.

Sapir watched as the ruler of Karathat, protector of treaties and walls and armies, simply held a broken child until her sobs softened.

In that moment, he understood why he followed her.

He had seen Storia in command—in war councils, issuing orders, challenging nobles and soldiers alike with eyes sharper than her tongue. But here, in the warm hush of her private chamber, kneeling with Nyla in her arms, she looked different.

Not weaker.

Never that.

But more human. More whole.

Sapir leaned against the far pillar, one hand resting on the edge of the windowsill, though he barely felt the stone beneath his fingers. His eyes stayed fixed on them—on Nyla, curled tightly into the Queen's arms, and on Storia, rocking gently without a word.

He remembered the first night they had found Nyla—silent, halfstarved, feral from her ordeal. She had flinched at every sound, every movement. It had been him who knelt beside her then, not as a soldier, but as a father who had once held a daughter of his own. A man carrying his own quiet grief. He hadn't spoken—just stayed. And in that silence, something unspoken had passed between them.

He had sworn to protect her.

And he meant it still.

Later, when they reached Karathat, it was Storia who surprised him.

Without word or order, she had come to Nyla's side. She had knelt by her bedside at night, tucking the blankets tighter, brushing the girl's hair back gently with her fingers. Once, Sapir had seen her lean close and murmur something. A song, maybe. A prayer. He never asked.

And then—those evenings in the garden, walking beneath the ivywrapped arches. She never said much. Just listened. Listened as he talked about border patrols, the ache in his sword arm, or how Karathat always smelled of dry stone and citrus at nightfall. She carried the weight of a kingdom in silence, but when she met his eyes in the half-light, he saw something there he could not forget.

Now, as the first stones of siege thundered against the city walls, and the world outside narrowed to this single quiet room, he saw something he hadn't dared to name—until now.

He loved them both.

Nyla—the fierce, broken child who had let herself trust him, piece by piece.

And Storia—the Queen who had never needed saving but had shown him again and again that the strongest people are those who choose kindness, even in the shadow of war.

It hadn't been battling or blood that pierced his heart.

It was this:

The small kindnesses.

The quiet choices.

The moment she cradled the child like she mattered more than city walls or bloodlines or banners.

He didn't know if they would live through the week.

But he knew, with sudden, aching clarity, that his loyalty was no longer just duty.

It was love.

And that made the coming battle feel very, very personal.

The child in her arms had finally fallen asleep, her breath soft and warm against Storia's neck. But Storia didn't move.

She held Nyla gently, one hand resting along the girl's thin back, the other stroking her tangled hair. Not for the child's sake anymore—but for her own.

Because for a moment, the war outside had fallen away.

The stone-shattering echo of siege weapons still rumbled beyond the walls. Karathat still stood on the edge of a blade. But in this quiet space, with the girl pressed against her heart, Storia allowed herself to breathe.

She had not known how much she needed that.

The councillors would be waiting soon. Tamanda would be on the inner walls. Sapir—her eyes flicked briefly across the chamber to where he stood near the pillar, watching. Always watching. And for the first time, she felt exposed in his gaze. Not in weakness—but in something else. Something deeper. Unspoken. Dangerous.

And yet… safe.

She remembered how he'd stood beside her in the court when the nobles had shouted for caution. He had said little. But he had stood close—close enough that she had felt his presence like a shield.

She remembered the garden, too. The night they walked in silence, when she'd let the ivy brush against her fingers just to feel something living. He had spoken of war, of pain, of how soldiers carried ghosts. And she had said nothing—because she knew all too well what silence meant.

She had let few people close. Even fewer into her trust.

And now, this soldier.

This girl.

This moment.

They had slipped past her walls.

Not through force or flattery. But through stillness. Through care. Through the way Sapir hadn't asked her to step away from her crown—but had seen the woman beneath it.

She looked at him again.

His eyes didn't waver. He didn't smile. He didn't flinch.

And that steadiness made something shift inside her chest.

She lowered Nyla gently onto the cushions, brushed a hand across her forehead, and rose slowly to her feet.

"See that she's watched," Storia said to the nearby guard, her voice level.

Sapir stepped forward without a word.

As they walked out together into the flickering torchlight of the corridor, she kept her voice low.

"She trusts you," she said.

Sapir nodded. "She trusts you more."

Storia didn't answer. Not right away. They moved together through the narrow stone passage, past tapestries shivering in the wind of war. "She reminds me," Storia said at last, "of what we fight for." "And me," Sapir replied, his voice rough.

There was no declaration between them. No dramatic vow. Only a silence that spoke of something deepening—painful, fragile, and real.

The kind of thing that war rarely leaves room for.

But for now, they let it live.

Even as the siege dragged closer to the heart of Karathat.

❦

CHAPTER 31

The firelight danced across the taut leather of his gloves as Rakah drew a line across the map. His finger traced it slowly, as though cutting the throat of the city with the simplest of gestures.

Outside his tent, the thrum of catapults filled the air—one beat at a time, patient and inevitable.

The Natsu army obeyed without question.

They had seen him bring down cities before.

He had no need for raised banners or glorious speeches. No need to shout from horseback or flash steel for attention. His presence was command. His silence was doctrine.

And when he moved—cities bled.

Karathat stood defiant behind its pale walls, nestled beneath the cliffs like a jewel too proud to be plucked. It had resisted trade offers, turned away envoys, and rallied alliances behind its Queen.

But all things broke.

Even stone.

A soldier approached the tent, his armour dull with soot and dust.

He knelt without speaking, waiting.

Rakah didn't look at him.

"Report," he said, his voice low.

"The engines are in full rotation. They've begun targeting the north wall towers. Small breaches reported along the south edge. Casualties minimal."

"And the city?"

"Still holding."

Rakah let the silence stretch.

The soldier remained bowed, not daring to rise until dismissed.

"They've sent no messengers," he said. "No pleas. No surrender. That will change."

"Tell the engineers I want two towers ready."

The soldier bowed deeper, then backed out without ever meeting his eyes.

Rakah stood alone, listening to the muffled cries of war echoing through canvas and wind.

Somewhere behind those walls, he imagined the queen of Karathat watching the city crack. The Queen of Karathat—young, clever, loved.

But Rakah did not hate her.

He simply intended to erase her.

Not for vengeance. Not for cruelty. But because Karathat had chosen pride over submission.

And because history was written by those who moved without mercy.

He stepped outside, the chill of early morning brushing against his cloak. The siege fires burned in neat circles all around him, casting red halos over war machines and waiting blades.

The stars above Karathat still shone faintly.

But by tomorrow night, he would replace them with flame.

Night settled over the siege lines like a breath held too long.

The stars had vanished behind smoke. Only the distant gleam of Karathat's walls, lit by torches and the dull glow of burning pitch, gave shape to the dark. The Natsu camps were quiet—not resting but waiting.

Rakah stood atop the raised hill overlooking the plain, his eyes fixed on the city's north flank. The siege engines had shifted earlier that evening, their heavy arms trained low and steady. Beneath the surface, sappers worked in silence, driving tunnels beneath the fourth tower.

He didn't need fanfare or a grand breach. That would come later.

Tonight was about disruption. Terror. Unseen knives.

"Begin," he said quietly.

The officer beside him, face painted in streaks of ash and ochre, gave a sharp signal. Horns did not sound. There was no trumpet of war. Only movement in shadow—figures peeling from the dark and slipping forward.

Three waves of Natsu night-runners, stripped of heavy armour, faces masked, blades blackened. Their orders: infiltrate. Burn. Strike the interior. Retreat.

They were not meant to break the city.

They were meant to unbalance it.

"To test the seams," Rakah had said, hours before. "To find where the Queen's grip falters—whether it's in her soldiers, or in her own heart."

His scouts had reported weaknesses along the east garden walls and a section of the lower market district where night patrols were stretched thin.

The Queen had courage. Rakah granted her that. But courage bends, under the right pressure.

"Send the fire," she murmured.

A second signal flared—silent, red. Moments later, from the far southern flank, a pair of flaming casks arced through the sky, trailing embers as they descended over the wall. Not to destroy. To distract. To draw eyes away from the real threat creeping in below.

"Burn their sleep," he whispered. "And see what wakes."

Behind him, a younger captain shifted uneasily. "And if they repel the night strike?"

Rakah didn't answer at first. His eyes remained fixed on the wall.

"They'll think they've won," he said at last.

A breeze lifted his cloak, revealing the edge of a map etched in charcoal on linen. Three more strikes were already marked. One for each night that followed.

Rakah knew siege craft wasn't about brute strength. It was about rhythm. Disruption. Fear. The slow cutting away of hope.

Let them win the night.

The real blow would come when they dared believe they could endure him.

They moved like smoke.

No armour. No shields. Just short, curved blades, dark cloth, and quiet breath.

There were twelve of them in total—Natsu night-runners trained for stealth and sabotage. Split into three teams, each with a different task: fire, fear, and blood.

Their leader, Vael, crouched beneath the stone lip of Karathat's east garden wall, fingers brushing the faint mortar line where the last heavy rain had thinned the seal. His breath came in slow, deliberate pulls. He could hear the guards above shifting—tired, perhaps cold. No alarm.

No raised voices. That would change soon.

He raised two fingers.

A moment later, a low clatter rang out behind the wall, near a stacked cart of pottery crates. One of the others had thrown a shard of stone. Deliberate. Loud enough to draw attention—but just off centre.

A pair of guards moved to investigate.

By the time they reached the edge, Vael and two others were already over the wall. Silent. Swift.

Knives in the dark.

One guard fell with barely a gasp, his throat neatly opened before he could cry out. The other turned, but a weighted dart struck the back of his neck, and he crumpled.

In less than a minute, the garden path was theirs.

Vael motioned his team forward—toward the lower servant halls near the palace edge. They weren't meant to take the city. Not tonight.

Their job was to set the edges on fire, not burn the centre.

Another squad, Team Rill, had moved through the market district. They had no interest in shops or gold. They were slipping through alleyways, placing small ceramic fire pots beneath food stores, water wagons, and sections of the inner supply line. The kind of loss that would only be noticed too late.

The third team, Korr's group, aimed for something bolder: the inner barracks, where a rotation of tired guards had been resting off-shift. If they reached the arched corridor that fed toward the central tower, even the sound of combat there would spark panic in the heart of the defenders.

And panic—panic spread like oil on fire.

Vael reached a side door in the servant wing, tested the latch, and slipped inside. His blade never left his hand.

Inside, it was quiet. Stone walls. Low torchlight. Footsteps above.

Someone humming faintly in the kitchen just beyond.

He paused—not for pity, but for calculation.

They would leave fear behind. A body here. A flame there. Doors forced open. Shadows where shadows shouldn't be.

They wouldn't linger. They would be gone before the alarm ever rang.

That was Rakah's brilliance. She didn't need to break the gates to break the city. She needed only to make it bleed from within. And by the time Karathat realised how deep the cut was… it would already be dying.

The night had been still—unnaturally so.

Tamanda stood atop the inner western wall, watching the horizon for the glow of more siege fires, her hand resting lightly on the hilt of her blade. She didn't trust silence. Not from the Natsu.

The guards beside her murmured quietly, their voices hushed but loose with fatigue. The latest shift had just changed. Two new men on her left, both young. Too green to be stationed here if the city weren't so thinly spread.

Then she felt it.

A prickle on the back of her neck.

Off. Something was off.

A sound. Not loud. Not out of place to an untrained ear. But she had lived too long in shadow to mistake it.

A breath held too long. A rustle not made by wind.

She stepped off the wall walk and made her way down the stairs into the inner garden quadrant. The air smelled different. The torches flickered. Nothing obvious—but the patterns were wrong.

She passed a servant moving crates toward the lower pantry hall.

Too fast. Too deliberate.

Tamanda's eyes narrowed. The woman didn't look up. Didn't acknowledge her.

She followed.

Down the narrow corridor, past a row of water urns and cloth-covered barrels. The woman turned left.

Tamanda drew her blade without sound.

She moved like she had in the wild, back when survival meant listening to the breath of the forest. Not thinking—just knowing.

She turned the corner—

—and caught the figure just as he was placing a small clay pot against a stack of grain sacks.

Not a woman.

Not a servant.

A Natsu.

His hand flew to a hidden blade, but Tamanda was faster. Her sword caught his wrist and slammed him back against the wall.

He hissed something in his language, and from the corner of her eye, she saw movement—another one, hidden in the shadows near the stairs. Two of them. No, more.

She kicked the fire pot away, sending it skittering under a rack of tools. The man lunged again—she ducked, slashed low, and felt blade strike bone.

The second runner darted toward the pantry hall—trying to disappear into the heart of the keep.

Tamanda threw a knife, catching him just under the shoulder. He stumbled, slammed into the wall, and crumpled.

Too close. Far too close.

Tamanda turned, heart racing, breath sharp. She looked down at the man she had cut—he was still alive, but only barely. Blood pooled beneath his arm.

She tore the cloth from his belt and found what she feared: three more fire pots, still sealed. She kicked them away, then shouted:

"TO ARMS! Infiltrators! Light the signal!"

But even as she called out, she knew they were already inside the walls.

And if she had found two here—how many more had slipped past?

The alarm bell began to ring. The signal torches flared. Footsteps thundered from every direction.

Tamanda didn't wait. She grabbed the nearest torch and sprinted toward the palace wing.

Because if the night-runners were this deep already, there was only one place that would burn next:

Storia.

The sound shattered the stillness.

Not catapults. Not drums.

Bells.

Not from the wall towers—but from inside the city.

Sapir was already moving before the bell's second chime. He stepped into the Queen's chamber, sword drawn, eyes flashing toward the window where distant torchlight flared in the lower court.

Storia stood beside Nyla, who had startled awake from sleep. The girl clutched her blanket, eyes wide in confusion, fear rising in her throat.

Sapir's voice was low, urgent. "The alarm's from the inner ring."

Storia didn't hesitate. She crossed the room and swept Nyla into her arms.

"Tamanda?" she asked.

"No sign yet," Sapir replied, already turning toward the door. "She'll come."

Storia passed Nyla to him. "Take her. Get her to the secured chamber."

"What about you?"

"I'll follow. But she needs to be safe first."

He didn't argue. There wasn't time. He nodded and took Nyla gently, holding her close as he moved quickly through the corridors. Behind him, Storia drew her blade—a ceremonial sword of polished steel, once her father's.

Tonight, it would draw blood.

Guards were forming outside her chamber, half-armoured and alert. She took command instantly.

"Section the palace. No one moves unchallenged. If they're not Karathat, drop them."

"Yes, Your Majesty!"

Tamanda appeared then, coming from the eastern wing at full speed, torch in one hand, sword in the other, streaked with blood. Her eyes were wild but focused.

"They're inside," she said breathlessly. "Natsu runners. At least two down. More heading toward the tower."

"We heard the bells." Storia turned toward the hall. "They'll be coming for us."

"Then we hold here," Tamanda said, planting herself at the top of the grand stair.

Together, they waited for the clash to come.

~~~~~~~~~~~~~~~~~~~~~~~~

Meanwhile, in the hidden passage beneath the Queen's chamber...

Sapir moved quickly through the dark, Nyla tight in his arms. The girl didn't cry—but she clung to him, her fingers gripping the edge of his cloak. She was trembling.

"Almost there," he whispered. "Just hold on. I've got you."

They reached the narrow servant door behind the armoury, where two hard knocks rang against iron. A moment later it opened—an old guardsman stood inside, spear in hand, face lined and weathered with age.

Nyla gasped. "Tommor!"

The man's stern face softened instantly. "Little shadow," he said gently, dropping to a knee. "You're safe now."

Sapir blinked in surprise as Nyla launched herself from his arms into the old man's. Tommor wrapped her in one arm, the other still gripping his spear.

"You know him?" Sapir asked.
~~~~~~~~~~~~~~~~~~~~~~~~

"She used to sneak him pastries," Tommor said with a small smile.

"Back before the world turned heavy."

Nyla nodded. "He taught me how to tie a horse knot."

"Good knots still matter," the guardsman replied, touching her forehead gently. "Now let's keep quiet and brave, like you showed me."

Sapir knelt to her level. "Stay here. No matter what you hear. Don't come out until I return—understood?"

Nyla nodded, but her voice was small. "Will she be, okay?"

Sapir placed a hand on her shoulder. "Storia? She's more dangerous than I am."

He stood and looked to Tommor. "Lock it. No one comes in but me."

The door shut behind him. He didn't let Nyla see how hard his hands were shaking.

The palace air was no longer still. It pulsed with tension.

Below the grand stair, torches flickered along the corridor where the polished floor ended in blackened blood trails. At the base of the steps, the first body dropped—a palace guard, throat cut before he'd even raised a shout.

Then came the hiss of steel, low footfalls, and the glint of Natsu blades in the dark.

Tamanda stepped forward, sword raised.

Beside her, Queen Storia did not flinch.

Tamanda's voice was low. "Four. Maybe five. Moving quiet."

"Then we don't let them pass this hall," Storia said, planting her feet.

There were only four guards left with them. The rest were rallying elsewhere in the palace, still scrambling in the confusion. But Tamanda didn't look behind her.

She looked down the steps—at the Natsu night-runners who began to emerge like shadows from a deeper shadow.

Leather-clad, faces masked, blades slick with earlier kills.

The lead runner tilted his head, surprised, perhaps, to see a queen with a sword.

He didn't get time to reconsider.

Tamanda struck first.

She leapt down the stairs in a blur of motion, meeting the first assassin mid-step. Her blade caught his forearm and threw him sideways into the stone wall. He snarled and lunged again—but she ducked beneath the strike, turned, and slammed her elbow into his jaw.

He crumpled.

Two more moved in—silent, fast, too fast for untrained guards to face. But Tamanda wasn't untrained. She was a weapon disguised in servant's clothes, and now that disguise had burned away.

Storia stayed high on the landing, eyes sharp. One runner tried to circle left—to reach the corridor behind her.

She turned to meet him.

Their blades clashed once—his heavier, faster. He drove forward, expecting her to stumble. But Storia was calm. She caught his second swing on the guard of her sword, twisted her hips, and let his momentum carry him past her.

Then she reversed her grip—and drove her blade into his ribs.

He fell gasping. Her hand shook.

Tamanda saw it—but only for a second before the next two came at her.

One managed to slash her shoulder. She winced, stepped back, and lured him up the stair where his footing narrowed. Then she dropped low and swept his legs out, slamming her pommel into his throat before he hit the floor.

The final assassin looked between them—queen and guard, bloodied but unyielding.

He turned to run.

As he did Sapir came from the doorway, the assassin thrust his sword towards Sapir, but he was slow. Sapir dodged the thrust and counter driving his dagger into the assassin's throat. The assassin twitched as he gasped for air, his life draining from his body.

Silence returned. A brutal, breathless silence.

Tamanda wiped her blade on the fallen attacker's cloak. "They'll send more."

Storia nodded. "They thought we'd break. Tonight, they learned we won't."

Behind them, the guards had started to return. One of them approached slowly.

"The eastern wing reports clear, Your Majesty. But the fire traps—they hit the grain stores."

Storia breathed in, jaw tight. "Extinguish what you can. Ration everything else."

Tamanda looked to the Queen. "I should sweep the lower halls. If they came this far once…"

Storia met her eyes. "Take two with you. I'll secure the tower." Tamanda nodded and turned to go—but paused.

"My queen…" she said, then hesitated. "You fought well."

Storia looked down at her bloodied sword, then at the corpses
around her. "Let's hope I don't have too again."

But even she knew that hope was fading fast.

⚓

CHAPTER 32

T he sky was still black with smoke from earlier fire pots,

though the wind had begun to change.

Rakah stood at the war table, his fingers resting lightly on a map of Karathat and its surrounding districts. Tiny clay markers denoted siege engines, breach plans, troop positions. He had moved them so many times the table was smudged with soot and oil.

A soft rustle of footsteps behind him. He didn't look up.

The scout knelt. "Commander. The night-runners are either dead or scattered. The signal fire was not lit. They did not reach the heart of the palace."

Rakah's jaw shifted slightly. "Losses?"

"Five confirmed dead. Two missing, presumed caught or wounded.

Only Vael's team made it back. Injured." He gave a short nod.

The scout hesitated, then added: "They encountered resistance. The Queen herself fought. And the blade-woman—the one who killed Eshan during our assassination attempt. She was with her." That caught Rakah's attention.

He slowly turned his head, eyes narrowing. "The servant girl?" "Not a servant anymore," the scout replied grimly.

Rakah considered that in silence.

He had dismissed the tale at first rumours of a handmaiden who fought like a shadow and saved a monarch's life. It had seemed romanticized. Exaggerated. But now two missions had been thwarted by the same woman. And the Queen, too, had not cowered in her tower like many rulers would.

He stepped away from the map and walked out to the ridge, where a faint flicker of Karathat's torches still glowed across the valley.

The siege would not be won with shadow blades alone. Not here.

"They have more spine than I gave them credit for," he murmured.

Behind him, the officers said nothing.

He let the silence grow.

Then, with a voice as cold as frost on steel, he said, "Prepare the second wave."

The officers straightened. "Another infiltration?"

"No, they will be more alert now another infiltration would not work, A message." His eyes narrowed on the stone towers in the distance. "Tomorrow, we show them what happens when defiance lingers.

I want the catapults loaded before sunrise."

He turned back to the table. "We hit their food stores, now we hit their spirit. Strike the chapel. Strike the courtyards. Drive their people into panic. And tomorrow night—when the walls crack and their children cry—we will send in the real fire."

His hand moved one final marker—a red-painted wedge— toward the outer breach on the north side.

"And when their Queen steps forward again," Rakah said quietly, "I will meet her myself."

The sun broke the horizon like a blade unsheathed, slicing through the smoke-thick sky.

Rakah stood atop the siege platform, his cloak stirring in the morning wind. Around him, the camp had transformed—no longer a siege, but an execution.

His lieutenants waited in a tight ring, each armed and armoured.

He spoke low, but her words carried like stone on steel.

"We break them today."

He turned to Harak, his siege master. "Strike the north wall with everything. I want no pause between volleys. Crush the tower joints, not the gates—let them think the gates will hold. When the stones fall, send the ladder teams."

Harak saluted sharply. "We'll strike till the mortar splits."

Rakah pointed to the vanguard commander. "When the breach is made, send the Elite forward, do not hesitate.

This city is different from one we have taken before; they have hope

still. Tell the elite no quarter. Anyone bearing arms dies."

"And the civilians?" the commander asked.

Rakah's gaze sharpened.

"They've had their warnings."

Then he drew a dagger and slammed its blade into the map.

"After the breach, I want a corridor carved straight to the palace. Any street not taken will be burned. Any roof that gives shelter torched. We do not slow. We do not scatter. We move like fire."

The hours had passed; morning had turned into the afternoon. The catapults had been firing all morning, so far two ladder assaults had been repelled for the city defenders.

A scout approached then, breathless.

"Stone has hit the chapel, commander. The eastern barracks are aflame. One breach in the north wall—section collapsed." Rakah didn't smile. But his eyes gleamed.

"Sound the horns. Let the whole city know their hour has come, Send the Elite forward.

That was all Tamanda could hear as she sprinted toward the breach, her boots slipping on scorched cobblestones, her blade already drawn. The north wall had buckled, the mortar shattered by repeated blows, the tower above it folded like a broken rib.

Natsu infantry poured through, shielded, disciplined, shouting in their guttural tongue as they advanced like a wave of iron.

Karathat's guards had formed a makeshift line with overturned carts and spears they stood—outnumbered, under-armoured, but screaming defiance with every breath.

From above, archers loosed volley after volley. Flaming arrows lit the edges of the breach, turning the dust to sparks. But the Natsu kept coming.

Tamanda reached the line and didn't hesitate. She joined the front rank, plunging her sword into the first warrior who crossed the threshold.

Young warriors fought by her side shoulder to shoulder, she recognised the soldier next to her Judd who had been on her trials.

He fought with a swiftness she'd never seen before, driving his blade into the armoured invaders without pause or mercy.

Tamanda ducked as a sword was lunged at her from beyond the carts, she turned and swung her sword parrying another blow directed at her. She countered the next strike thrusting her blade into the throat of another Matsu warrior.

Behind her, cries rose from civilians fleeing through the inner lanes. Some stumbled, disoriented by smoke, clutching children or dragging wounded friends.

She yelled at Judd "help them get to the inner-city gates" Judd nodded accepting her orders without question.

Above, a thunderous boom rattled rooftops—the bell tower toppled, and crashed down onto of the, Tamanda looked and could see

Judd laying lifeless under a pile of rubble next to the family.

Tamanda sparked by anger hacked her way through the next three warriors in her path, anger taking over causing her to be reckless. She didn't care at that moment in time, at that moment all she could see was rage after losing another friend.

~~~~~~~~~~~~~~~~~~~~~

On the hill, Rakah watched.

"Now send the hammer," she said.

And from the tree line behind her, the Natsu guard—her elite killers—charged.

No banners. No horns. Just swift, silent death.

The battle for Karathat raged across every wall and street.

From the ramparts, archers loosed volley after volley, and catapults hurled burning stone into the advancing Natsu lines, cutting down hundreds with each thunderous strike. But still they came—wave after wave.

Those who made it to the northern breach met a deadlier fate. The city militia had dug in deep, their formations tight, turning the winding alleys and stone-paved roads into a killing ground. The streets ran red with Natsu blood.

From the inner-city barracks, the Karathat Guard surged forward—trained soldiers moving in disciplined sections, forming defensive lines from kerb to kerb, sealing off key junctions and choke points.

Each unit mixed two types of warriors:

Long-shield bearers stood in the front, locking their broad shields together into a wall of iron. They took the brunt of the Natsu charge, with archers behind them, loosing arrows through narrow gaps or firing high over their shoulders.
~~~~~~~~~~~~~~~~~~~~~

Short-shield warriors moved beside and behind them, faster, more agile—a mobile strike force trained for close combat. Where the long shields held, the short shields struck, filling the gaps, cutting down the Natsu as they broke ranks.

In open fields, the tactics would have faltered.

But in the narrow arteries of Karathat, with high walls on either side and limited space to manoeuvre, the strategy worked like a blade sliding between ribs.

Still, the enemy pressed forward.

The outer wall had begun to fall. The north gate tower was lost. Natsu banners rose above it, and fresh enemy troops spilled into the upper wards.

In the heart of the chaos, where the defence line thinned and the pressure was greatest, Tamanda and Sapir fought shoulder to shoulder within the Karathat shield wall.

Their blades were stained, their faces slick with sweat and smoke, but they did not yield.

They were no longer holding the line.

They were the line.

As more Natsu warriors flooded through the northern gates, the Karathat Guard began a tactical withdrawal, falling back from the shattered outer quarters toward the inner-city walls.

This would be their final line of defence.

The catapults—once so effective atop the outer ramparts—were now useless in the tight confines of the inner city. Here, it would be hand-to-hand fighting, street by street, gate by gate.

The inner wall stood higher, thicker, reinforced with stone and iron braces that had been tested across generations of war. The main gate, flanked by twin towers and sealed with three iron bolts, was built to withstand battering rams and fire alike.

If the Natsu wanted to take the heart of Karathat, they would have to break through by force.

And the defenders were ready.

Every street leading to the inner wall had been barricaded, every corner manned by archers or pikemen. Civilians were evacuated into the keep. Oil was readied. Reserves took their positions.

The true siege had only just begun.

As more Natsu warriors came through the gates the Karathat guard had stared a tactical withdrawal dropping back to the inner-city wall.

This was the last defence of the city catapults would be of no use here the Natsu would have to use the battering rams.

The walls and gate defences of the inner city would be more difficult to breach.

Smoke poured into the throne tower like mist through a battlefield.

Storia stood at the war table, helm under her arm, fingers gripping the edge hard enough to turn her knuckles white. Reports were coming faster than she could respond to them.

"The North Gate's gone," one runner said breathlessly. "Tamanda and Sapir are falling back. Street by street. They'll reach the inner wall soon."

Another voice cut in—an officer from the southern quarter. "The

Ash Mantle has breached the merchant lanes. Fire's spreading west."

Storia turned sharply. "Seal off the third ward. Collapse the side alleys if you have to. Do not let them circle behind us."

Her voice was calm, but her mind was racing. She had made it this far by holding her nerve—as monarch, not just a military leader. But this… this was the edge of survival.

Behind her, a small voice broke the rhythm of command. "Storia?"

She turned.

Nyla stood in the archway, barefoot and tear-streaked, wrapped in a too-large cloak, her little hands trembling at her sides. A palace maid hovered near but dared not come closer.

Storia crossed the chamber in three steps and knelt, pulling the child into her arms. Nyla clung to her, burying her face into the Queen's neck.

"They're here," Nyla whispered. "They're coming again."

"I know, little one," Storia said softly, "but you're not alone."

She stood, still holding the girl, and looked to the guards beside the door.

"Escort her to the cellar beneath the chapel. Lock it from the inside. She is not to be moved unless the walls fall, or I come myself. Give her food, warmth, and someone she trusts."

Tommor the older guardsman stepped forward—the one Nyla had once called by name. She blinked at him now, then nodded and took his hand.

He nodded to Storia. "I'll see to her, Majesty. She'll be safe." Storia watched them go until the heavy door closed behind them.

Then came the distant thunder—the final call.

A great horn sounded across the courtyard. One long note. One command.

The Karathat lines had fallen back.

Runners screamed it from tower to tower: "Retreat! To the inner gate!"

Storia stepped back to the war table, just as the bell above the courtyard began to toll—three times. The signal. Close the inner gates.

Great — here's the continuation, focusing on Tamanda and Sapir's desperate dash to the inner gate as the Karathat defenders fall back and the final doors close behind them.

~~~~~~~~~~~~~~~~~~~~~~~~~

Blood dripped from the edge of Tamanda's sword.
~~~~~~~~~~~~~~~~~~~~~~~~~

She and Sapir sprinted through the lower streets, the last of the shield wall broken, the wounded left behind or carried by comrades too exhausted to weep. The sound of pursuit followed them — steel on stone, the shouted orders of the Natsu, the growl of their boots in the sootlaced dust.

Ahead, the inner gate loomed, already half-sealed.

"Hold the gate!" Sapir bellowed. "We're still out here!"

Tamanda's breath tore in her lungs. Her tunic was scorched, one boot missing, but she never broke stride.

Two Karathat guards on the rampart looked down. "Hurry!"

Another wave of defenders poured in behind them — fewer than thirty. Smoke curled through the broken streets behind them.

Then came the roar. The Natsu had turned the corner.

The enemy was in sight.

Tamanda turned and shoved a wounded guard forward with her free hand. "Go!"

She and Sapir were the last through, turning to fire arrows and throw broken spears to stall the enemy's advance. Just long enough.

The moment their boots crossed the threshold; the gate commander slammed his fist down.

"Seal it!"

The great doors swung shut with a groan of ancient iron. The bolts dropped into place; the portcullis lowered with a rattle like falling bones. Sapir leaned on the wall, coughing hard, blood on his lips.

Tamanda fell to one knee. But she was inside.

The city's last wall was sealed.

And now — there would be no retreat.

For a moment, silence.

Then came the pounding. The Natsu had reached the final wall.

And Karathat would stand—or fall—with it.

The halls of the inner city were quiet—too quiet, as if the stones themselves were holding their breath.

Storia stood beneath the high ceiling of the command chamber, her breastplate newly buckled, a dark blue cloak over her shoulders, hair tied back in a simple braid. Around her, her remaining council stood in silence, watching her—not just as queen now, but as their final hope.

She unrolled a map of the inner city and pointed to the key thoroughfares.

"They'll strike here—northwest approach. The plaza offers them the cleanest advance from the breach. Position archers on these rooftops, concealed. Use oil. When the signal horn sounds, light it all."

General Rhem nodded grimly. "And the streets below?"

"We barricade. Use overturned carts and masonry. Every street becomes a choke point. Sapir will lead the city guard. Tamanda takes the east sector. I'll take command from the central tower with full visibility."

"What about the civilians?" asked one of the older councillors.

Storia looked toward the chapel steps, where Nyla had been taken—hidden deep beneath the stone crypts, safe with the old guardsman she trusted.

"They are no longer civilians," she said. "They are what we are all fighting to protect."

She stepped away from the table, then, and walked toward the nearest window. Smoke curled up from the outer city. The towers of Karathat still stood proud, but the enemy was closer now—she could feel it.

The gate trembled once.

A low, distant thud. A second. Then a third.

"The rams," Rhem said quietly.

The final breach had begun.

Storia turned to her captains, her voice level and unwavering.

"We do not surrender. We do not retreat. Today, we hold not for ourselves, but for the generations that will come after. Every moment we stand is a blow against the Natsu. Every breath we steal from them buys our people time. If we die— let it be in glory."

She fastened her sword belt and nodded to the guards at the door.

"Go now. Defend the last of Karathat."

&

CHAPTER 33

T amanda wiped blood from her blade and sheathed it with a

hiss.

She leaned against a shattered wall in the merchant quarter, catching her breath as soldiers hurried past her to reinforce the barricade.

Beside her, a small group of militias—no more than a dozen—stacked barrels, crates, and broken timbers across the lane, building a wall taller than a man. Behind it, oil pots and pitch-soaked cloth waited. Every junction would be contested. Every step, a trap.

"Reinforce the second alley," she ordered, voice hoarse. "If they flank left, we fall before they reach the palace."

She glanced up as Sapir approached, armour scorched, tunic torn, a bloodied bandage wrapped around his forearm.

"I've set archers on the rooftops. Two lines overlooking the main boulevard. They're ready."

"I have also told the guardsmen to stick with the long shield and short shield tactics, in this section of the city it will create bottlenecks as the streets are smaller, their numbers will account for nothing here as long as the flanks hold."

Tamanda gave a nod. "They'll be here soon."

For a moment, neither spoke. The air between them heavy—not just with smoke, but with everything left unsaid. They had fought beside one another from the first clash at the breach to now, and still the storm had not broken.

"Do you think we'll hold?" she asked, quiet.

Sapir looked down the ruined street. Firelight danced along the stones.

"We have to. We stand, or Karathat falls."

A runner came panting down the lane. "New orders from the
Queen. She says to collapse the first barricade if it looks like
they'll breach—draw them in, then trap them with fire."

Tamanda nodded. "We'll light the whole street if we must."

They took their places again—Sapir on the high step
behind the barricade, sword in hand, and Tamanda at the front,
ready to meet the first Natsu warrior to come around the corner.

Above them, bells tolled once, low and solemn.

A warning.

The enemy was coming.

And this time, there would be no second retreat.

The doors were being hammered by the rams, each loud
thud causing damage to the gate, every clash vibrating on the
gate and its hinges.

The first gate hinge tore free with a deafening screech.

The second buckled beneath the weight of the battering
ram—an iron beast shaped like a boar's head, blackened by
flame. The third strike sent one of the great bolts flying, a slab
of metal sheared from its housing.

Then, with a roar of splintering oak and screaming steel,
the inner gate of Karathat fell.

And the Natsu poured in.

The defenders were waiting.

Tamanda saw them first—black-clad warriors sprinting
through the breach, blades high, shields locked. The Natsu
elite, their vanguard, darted like shadows down the blood-
slicked cobbles. Behind them came heavier troops—rank after
rank of Natsu foot soldiers, roaring for blood.

"NOW!" she shouted, and the alley ignited.

Flames erupted from hidden oil pots as the first wave crossed the barricade. Screams filled the narrow streets as fire wrapped itself around men and armour. Archers on the rooftops loosed a hail of arrows tearing into the chaos.

"Fall back to the second point!" Sapir shouted, his voice carrying over the roar.

The defenders retreated in a disciplined line, drawing the enemy in, making them fight for every pace of ground.

On the main boulevard, Karathat guards clashed with Natsu in brutal hand-to-hand fighting. Steel rang against steel, and the sound of war drums rose above the rooftops—deep, relentless, thundering like a heartbeat.

The guardsmen had created their shield wall using their long shields, behind them sections of short shields ready to charge and deliver killing blows if needed.

Archer danced along the rooftops continuing to fire down on the

Natsu lines.

Tamanda fought in silence, blade flashing in the firelight, her face a mask of fury. She ducked a sweeping axe and drove her sword through the ribs of the attacker, stepping over the body as more came behind.

Sapir stood next to her, cutting down a charging warrior with a brutal stroke to the throat. "Hold the right!" he called. "We give no ground!"

The enemy surged again.

More barricades fell.

The defenders were being pushed street by street toward the palace square.

And still they fought.

Every step cost the Natsu blood. Every alley burned.

The tactics were holding—for now.

The Karathat guardsmen moved with grim purpose, their shields locked, their formations tight. They understood what was at stake. This wasn't just a battle for a city. It was a battle for everything.

If they failed here, the people they had sworn to defend would vanish, their homes burned, their names erased.

Karathat itself would be lost, not just in fire, but in memory—rubbed from the books of history like it had never existed at all.

The outer districts had fallen. The barricades had burned.

Now, the last defenders of Karathat stood on the wide stone road that led directly to the palace gates.

Tamanda wiped blood from her brow, the blade in her hand chipped but still sharp. Around her, the Karathat Guard regrouped in tight formations, pressing their backs to the final tier of stairs that led up to the Queen's sanctuary.

Behind those walls, the remaining civilians had taken shelter. The wounded had been carried there. And so had Nyla.

Sapir stepped beside her, eyes sweeping the twisted street below. Smoke drifted in low waves, curling through the ruins, thick with the smell of ash and death.

"They're coming again," he said. Tamanda nodded. "We hold here." And then the horns blew.

Three sharp notes—one from the east alley, another from the garden wall, and one directly ahead.

The Natsu had regrouped. They came now in force—shields raised, drums pounding, their vanguard pressing up the hill in a steady, disciplined march. Not the wild charge from earlier. This was coordinated. Controlled. Ruthless.

Arrows arced overhead from both sides. Some struck home—Natsu fell screaming—but others crashed against the defenders' shields or armour, sending men staggering.

"Shields up!" Tamanda bellowed.

The line locked tight.

The first clash shook the ground.

Steel smashed against steel, and the Karathat front line buckled—but did not break. The long-shield guards held firm, their formation like a wall of iron. The short-shield fighters darted between openings, striking with quick, savage blows, pulling wounded comrades back and stepping into their places without hesitation.

Sapir led the right flank, pushing forward through the gap, breaking the Natsu momentum. His sword swept through two attackers in one stroke before he drove his shoulder into a third and hurled the man backward down the steps.

Tamanda held the centre, rallying her line with every shouted command. A Natsu captain broke through the wall— she met him blade to blade, her arm trembling from exhaustion but her footwork exact. She dodged low, swept his leg, and buried her sword in his chest.

The fighting narrowed.

The defenders tightened their ranks.

The palace gates rose behind them, tall and closed. There was nowhere else to run. The only way forward… was through.

Storia stood on the palace balcony, her armour glinting faintly in the smoke-filtered light, the sound of battle rising like thunder from the streets below. Archers flanked her on either side, loosing arrows into the seething mass of Natsu warriors below. Each shaft found its mark—or vanished into the chaos of war.

She gripped the stone railing, knuckles white, eyes locked on the carnage unfolding across the city. Her voice had not wavered since the inner gates fell. She had ordered the unthinkable—and meant every word.

"If they break through," she had told the officers, "No woman or child is to be taken prisoner. Every guardsman will stand. To the last.

That is our duty."

A sudden shout broke her focus.

"Banners!" a guard cried from the eastern tower. "Banners in the ridge! Riders coming fast—toward the Natsu rear!"

Storia turned sharply. "What did you say?"

Another archer leaned forward, peering through the smoke with narrowed eyes. "They're marching, Your Highness. Fast. Infantry columns. Moving to strike the enemy's rear line." "Can you

see their colours?" she called.

"No, Your Highness. But they ride like they mean to hit them hard." A silence. Then her breath caught.

"Taran," she whispered. "Taran is here. He did it. He convinced the elders."

Her heart slammed in her chest—not fear, not relief, but something between them. Hope.

She turned to the bell-keeper beside the archers.

"Bij! Ring the bell. Let our men below know—help is coming!"

The great bronze bell above the tower let out a deep, resonant chime, rolling across the city like the voice of the gods themselves.

And on the distant ridge, banners flew. Spears shimmered in the sun. And the warriors of the Mandji came thundering down toward the enemy flank.

CHAPTER 34

T he hour was later than Taran had hoped.

He emerged from the shattered tree line, his horse breathing hard beneath him, flanks streaked with sweat and dust, ears laid back. Taran pulled the reins and took in the plain below, his heart stuttering at the sight.

It was a landscape of ruin.

Smoke rose in towering columns that twisted skyward, black against the failing light. Siege engines burned along the outer ring, their charred beams collapsing with loud, wooden groans. The fields, once green and lined with olive trees, had been trampled to bare mud and scattered bodies. Where the farmland ended, the city's first districts lay in ruins — walls torn down, homes cracked and burning, marketplaces shredded beneath the boots of invaders.

The battle had already reached the heart of Karathat.

Taran's eyes travelled over the chaos, picking out shapes — broken banners, black-armoured corpses, shattered tower gates. And still, he saw defenders holding corners, holding alleys, holding the line even in retreat. The Natsu had come in force, had come with numbers, discipline, and rage — but they had paid dearly for every step.

The defenders of Karathat had made them bleed.

Taran's jaw tightened, teeth grinding, as he watched a Karathati banner — battered, stained — still flying from the southern wall. They hadn't folded. They had refused to fold.

His voice was a growl, half to himself. "We're not too late. Not yet."

He raised his hand. Behind him, the Mandji warriors came out of the tree line in a long wave of leather and iron, five hundred hard men, every face set. Their horses were lean and ragged but unbroken,
their riders grim, their eyes burned hollow by weeks of marching.

The sun broke through the smoke, just long enough to catch the steel points of five hundred spears.

Taran leaned forward in the saddle, felt the horse bunch beneath him, its hooves anxious on the rock. His cloak snapped behind him, the wind swirling the scent of blood, dust, and ash around them.

He turned, swept his eyes across the line. These were warriors who had seen entire generations fall, who had watched children starve, who had buried kin with no prayers left. There would be no hesitation in them.

He raised his blade, voice ringing clear.

"Ride hard! Straight through their flanks! No mercy, no prisoners!

For Karathat!"

He drove his heels into the horse's ribs, and the beast lunged forward with a roar.

The entire line broke into a thunderous charge, the earth trembling with its power. The sound was colossal — hooves hammering like a thousand war drums, spears rattling against shields, voices raised in a single battle cry.

The Mandji smashed into the Natsu rear like a tidal wave.

Archers turned too late, cries of alarm lost in the rush. The Mandji spears punched through them, breaking ranks before they could string a second volley. Taran's horse collided with a shield wall, sending men sprawling. His sword was a flash of silver, biting through an enemy helm, carving a path into chaos.

He shouted names as he struck — Tanny, Zarratt, the ridge — each name carried on the edge of his blade.

The Natsu lines broke. Their once-perfect formations collapsed under the sudden violence. Horses crashed through their ranks, Mandji blades tearing them apart. Taran saw an enemy captain trying to rally his men, drawing them into a square — but Mandji archers peppered them from the ridge, arrows streaking down like hunting falcons.

"Push through!" Taran bellowed, voice raw. "Push through!"

Dilah, spear slick with blood, rode alongside him, eyes wide with rage. "They're folding! Break their centre!"

The Natsu rear dissolved. Some tried to run, only to be cut down by horsemen. Others turned, desperate to fight, but they were too slow, their swords clumsy against the momentum of the charge.

And then the Mandji infantry followed, pouring into the gaps, sweeping through with long spears and curved blades. These were hunters of the borderlands, trained for storms and cliffs and sudden ambushes. The Natsu did not stand a chance.

As Taran cut down another soldier, he saw a battered banner ahead

— Karathat's crest, still upright on a half-shattered tower.

They had to reach it.

He spurred forward, cutting through another wave of archers, and felt a javelin glance off his horse's shoulder. The animal screamed, stumbled — but kept going. Taran leaned low, driving it on, until the press of bodies became too tight for a horse.

"Dismount!" he shouted, leaping from the saddle as a spear struck his mount clean through the ribs. The horse went down hard, kicking once, then fell still.

Taran rolled, came up with sword ready.

The city's edge was a nightmare.

Where once there had been market stalls, there were now barricades of broken wagons and corpses. Fires roared from cracked buildings, sending showers of sparks into the air. The heat scalded his face. Everywhere, men screamed — Natsu and Karathati both, locked in savage, merciless street fighting.

He gestured with his blade.

"Form up! We move on foot!"

The Mandji obeyed, slipping through the tight lanes, shields raised, spears forward. They advanced block by block, sweeping out hidden archers and pockets of Natsu soldiers who had dug into homes and shopfronts.

A rooftop bowman sent an arrow straight at Taran — he raised his shield, felt the impact thud against the rim, then saw Stafan toss a throwing spear that took the archer through the throat.

They pressed on.

At a collapsed bakery, a half-squad of Natsu tried to hold a barricade. They had overturned barrels, forced a shield wall across the narrow lane, their captain shouting orders in clipped, icy tones. Taran didn't slow.

"Mandji! On me!"

They charged, swords high. The impact shattered the shield wall. Taran's sword crashed against a Natsu helm, split iron, and kept going. Dilah and another warrior pushed through with spears, driving the defenders back. The fight was brutal, close — blades clashed, shields smashed into faces, boots trampled bodies underfoot.

The alley ran red.

But the Mandji were relentless.

Taran cut down one of the shield men, then pivoted, parried a wild swing, and smashed the hilt of his sword into the attacker's mouth. He saw teeth fly.

"Clear it!" he roared.

They stormed through the barricade, leaving the bodies behind.

Farther in, the streets were a maze of broken homes, choked with smoke. Every door was a risk — archers, hidden blades, snipers. But the Mandji adapted like wolves, bursting through gates, taking rooms by sheer fury, clearing rooftops by throwing men from them.

They advanced.

Stafan called out from ahead. "Commander! An opening — near the grain market!"

Taran forced through a knot of soldiers, found him pointing toward a shattered breach in the palace's outer wall. It was half-blocked by fallen beams but open enough for a push.

He wiped blood from his eyes.

"That's our way in!"

He turned, voice raw from smoke.

"Regroup!"

His warriors gathered around him, breathing hard, smeared with blood and sweat. They were ragged — but they were alive.

"We push to the palace," Taran shouted, loud enough to carry across the courtyard. "No detours! No prisoners! Karathat stands because we stand!"

A fresh cry went up from the Mandji.

And then they ran, a wave of steel crashing through the broken streets, cutting down any who stood in their way.

As they passed under the breached arch, Taran looked up at the walls, saw banners still flying.

The bells rang above them, deep and steady.

Karathat still stood.

He drew a fresh breath of smoky air.

"Forward!" he called. "For every child still alive in those walls!"

And with no more ceremony, no more hesitation, he led the charge through the breach — into the war-torn heart of Karathat, where hope and death waited together.

&

CHAPTER 35

The inner gates of Karathat slammed shut behind them with a grinding, final clang, the sound like a coffin lid sealing. Beyond the gate, the wide stone avenue leading up to the royal steps was a ruin of bodies, shattered shields, and scorched banners. Smoke choked the air, twisting and curling with the stench of blood and burnt flesh. There was no beauty left in Karathat—only death, rage, and a stubborn refusal to yield.

Tamanda stood shoulder to shoulder with the last of the Queen's personal guard, battered armour cracked and scorched, her blade slick with blood. She forced her breathing to slow, teeth clenched, ignoring the dull ache of half-healed wounds. This was no longer a place for fear. There was only one place to stand now—between the invaders and the Queen.

They had pulled back to the palace arch, a hundred men and women who had been soldiers, traders, even bakers days ago. Now they were defenders of a realm on the edge of oblivion. The barricades had fallen hours earlier, swept aside by repeated battering rams and volleys of flaming arrows, and now only their shield wall, packed tight as a rockface, held the final approach.

Sapir crouched at the right flank; eyes narrowed beneath a brow furrowed with focus. He moved calmly through the line, checking bindings, whispering brief words to those who had lost their nerve, lifting battered shields back into place. A boy no older than sixteen looked up at him with tear-slicked cheeks, sword shaking in a white-knuckled grip.

Sapir laid a steady hand on his shoulder, his voice low.

"Stand straight. You die here only if you let fear kill you first."

He moved on before the boy could answer, making sure each gap was filled. He glanced toward Tamanda, who still stood in the centre, her boots rooted as if the stones themselves had grown around them. She had not moved in nearly an hour, except to strike and strike again.

Tamanda felt the ragged rhythm of her heart, the taste of iron on her tongue. Her arms trembled between clashes, but her eyes never wavered. Ahead, the next Natsu wave gathered in the smoky gloom, ranks tightening, banners snapping.

"How many more do you think we'll hold off?" she asked, voice harsh and raw, not turning her head.

Sapir watched the battered shield wall, watched the bodies stacked like cordwood at its feet. "Long enough," he answered. They both knew the truth: this was it.

Then, without warning, the enemy drums stopped.

The hush fell like a blade drawn across the throat of the world. Even the wounded groaned more softly, as though afraid to break it.

Boots approached. Dozens at first, then hundreds, their footfalls a rolling thunder along the broken avenue. The Natsu advanced, in formation, methodical as a butcher with a knife. Commanders barked in their sharp tongue, ordering men to climb over the fallen, to ignore their dead, to keep coming.

Tamanda set her feet and raised her blade. "Shields up!" she shouted. Sapir echoed her call. "No gaps! Hold!" They braced.

The Natsu crashed into them like the ocean on a cliff. Spears jabbed forward, axes slammed against shields, arrows hissed down from upper balconies where quick-eyed bowmen perched like vultures. Tamanda blocked a heavy axe blow and twisted to bury her blade in a Natsu soldier's throat. Blood sprayed her cheek, hot and shocking. Sapir lunged forward, slicing clean through another man's calf, then pivoted to ram a shield boss into an enemy face.

The press was suffocating, a crush of steel and flesh and screams. A spear slammed against Tamanda's shoulder, glanced off her armour, but spun her halfway around. She snarled, reversed her grip, and gutted the spearman in a single savage move.

On the southern edge of the shield wall, a Karathat warrior went down hard, screaming, ribs crushed. Before they could close the gap, two Natsu soldiers forced through. Tamanda lunged to intercept, her blade snapping out, but one of them struck low, scoring a line of fire across her side. The other raised a sword high — she managed to parry, but the pain in her ribs made her gasp.

They were breaking.

But then — a new horn, deeper, rawer. Not the high wailing note of the Natsu, but something older, something that seemed to echo out of the bones of the land itself.

Through the haze of smoke, they heard the impossible.

"MANDJI!"

The shout came rolling up the broken streets like a storm tide, full of fury and hope. Steel rang on stone, boots slammed down in perfect, rolling rhythm.

Tamanda froze, sword half-raised, as the world shifted.

Sapir lifted his head, an exhausted grin pulling at his lips.

"Taran," he breathed.

The Natsu had paused, just for a moment, confusion rippling through their ranks. They turned, looking down the avenue behind them — the street they had thought secured.

But there they saw it: the gleam of spears, the rippling cloaks, the merciless eyes of the Mandji. Hundreds of them. Wolves come down from the ridges.

Tamanda exhaled, a shaky, almost disbelieving laugh.

"They came."

Then her eyes hardened again. "Let's finish this."

She stepped forward, slamming her shield into a stunned Natsu soldier, sending him sprawling, and cut his throat before he could rise.

The Natsu, caught between the Karathat shield wall and the Mandji charge from the rear, suddenly fought with a desperation beyond reason. Their cries rose to a panicked roar, blades swinging wildly, no longer ordered but savage and fearful.

Taran's cavalry crashed into them like a hammer into rotten wood. Horses slammed into enemy lines, breaking shields, tossing men aside. Taran himself was a blur of steel, Zarratt's old sword hacking down enemies with unrelenting force, carving a wedge straight through the Natsu rear.

"Push!" Sapir roared. "Push them back!"

Tamanda advanced, boots slipping on blood-slick stones, slicing left, parrying right. A spear jabbed for her belly — she caught it on her shield and snapped the shaft with a twist of her wrist. She plunged her sword into the attacker's chest and shoved him away, stepping over bodies, stepping through pools of crimson.

Karathat's defenders surged behind her, roaring, driving their battered shields forward, stabbing and hacking, retaking every bloody inch.

And yet — the Natsu did not break.

They refused.

Pinned on two sides, they fought with the rage of dying animals.

Tamanda saw a heavyset captain rally his men by a fountain, bellowing in their tongue, rallying them around a last banner. She swung toward them, pointing.

"Take them!"

Her guards obeyed, spears striking, shields slamming, the fighting so tight men had no room to even swing. She saw a Karathati soldier catch a blade in the gut, scream, and grab his killer by the hair to pull him down, teeth bared in one final act of defiance.

And beyond it all, high above, the palace bells rang.

Karathat was still alive.

■

From a ruined bastion in the southern quarter, Rakah watched.

Smoke clung to him like a second skin. His mask of iron, marked with the wolf's fang, reflected nothing but flame. He had seen the Mandji coming. He had known they might try to break the siege from the rear — but he had never expected them to strike with such speed, such precision.

A captain stumbled up to him, face bloodied, voice breaking. "Commander — the Mandji cavalry has cut our avenues. The reserves are trapped by the grain markets. Palace Guard still holds. We cannot encircle."

Rakah said nothing for a moment, only breathed.

His eyes burned with a cold, terrible light.

"So," he said softly, "Taran has come."

He looked out over the torn city, saw the banners of Karathat still fluttering in the wind, saw the Mandji cutting down his rear guard with impunity.

The captain swallowed hard. "We could fall back, regroup —" "No."

The word cut like steel.

"We have the numbers," Rakah continued. "We bleed them here. Today. Before their hope grows strong."

He turned, voice rising to command. "Form ranks. Spears in front, swords behind. Archers to the roofs. We drive a wedge through their line

— we burn them out before the palace can shelter them." The captain bowed and ran to carry out his orders.

Rakah reached for his twin knives, curved blades honed to a whisperthin edge. He checked their weight, their balance, as he had done a thousand times before. Then he drew a slow breath, feeling the world shrink to a single purpose.

He swung up onto his horse, the beast iron-grey and broad-chested. "Let them watch," he growled, "as their hope dies on these stones." He rode forward, down from the bastion, straight into the battle.

■

The street was pure chaos now.

Mandji horsemen tried to regroup after their first hammering strike but found themselves dragged from saddles by Natsu reserves flooding in from the south. Foot soldiers met them, blades locked, screaming, hacking, no mercy asked or given.

Sapir saw Tamanda falter, her sword arm trembling from a new cut on her shoulder. He leapt to her side, catching a spear aimed for her ribs, snapping it and smashing the attacker's face with his shield.

"Stay up!" he barked.

She nodded, eyes glassy with pain, but did not fall.

They fought back-to-back, surrounded by fallen comrades, hearing only the ring of steel on steel and the ragged, animal cries of the dying.

Then through the veil of smoke, a figure emerged, calm as a hunting cat.

Black wolf-etched armour. Knives drawn, shining in the firelight.

Rakah.

Tamanda froze, just for a heartbeat, as he advanced. He moved with that terrifying quiet, stepping over corpses like they were river stones, eyes fixed only on the breach ahead.

Sapir spat, blood on his lip.

"Is that him?"

Tamanda swallowed. "It's him."

They could feel his presence like a breaking tide.

Rakah did not shout, did not charge. He simply walked into the battle, knives flicking left and right. A Mandji warrior lunged — Rakah stepped aside, a single smooth movement, and opened the man's throat without even slowing his pace. Another came, a spear aimed for Rakah's belly. The war-leader slipped under it, cut the man's leg out from under him, finished him with a blade through the eye.

He was an artist of death, flowing through the press of bodies like a black wind.

Tamanda tried to intercept him, raising her blade. Rakah met her strike with his knives, turning her sword aside so precisely she nearly lost her balance. He shoved her back with a sharp kick that rattled her ribs.

Sapir came in from the flank, sword arcing toward Rakah's side — but the war-leader moved like water, catching Sapir's arm, twisting, and slamming the pommel of his knife against Sapir's temple with punishing force. Sapir stumbled, stars bursting behind his eyes.

Tamanda staggered forward again, gasping, and lunged once more.

Rakah turned both blades in a tight cross, catching her momentum and driving her backward, sending her crashing into a splintered wooden barricade.

He stood in the square, knives gleaming in the light of burning carts, utterly calm, utterly focused.

His voice was as cold as winter:

"You defend a corpse," he said. "This city is already dead. Step aside."

Tamanda pushed herself upright, face drawn with exhaustion but refusing to yield. "Never."

Rakah's gaze, distant and pitiless, measured her — and then shifted beyond, to the flood of fresh Karathat guardsmen now streaming through the inner archway. Their battered breastplates glinted with the city's crest; their spears held in shaking but determined hands. Sapir, regaining his footing, saw them arrive and barked a quick order.

"Form ranks! With us!"

The Karathat soldiers moved fast, rallying around Sapir and Tamanda, filling the gaps in their line, shields locking tight once more. Fresh battle cries went up, desperate but fierce, as they steadied themselves to meet the renewed assault.

Beyond the barricades, the unmistakable war horn of the Mandji sounded again — loud and rolling, full of iron promise. Through the drifting smoke, Taran's riders could be seen forming, steel glinting as they readied for another charge down the ruined avenue.

Rakah's face remained expressionless, but his jaw twitched once, like a predator scenting new prey.

He turned, lifted one of his knives high, and barked sharp commands in the Natsu tongue.

"Bring my guard forward! Hold this ground — no retreat!"

From behind the crumbling market walls, a fresh wave of Natsu shock troops appeared, moving in tight formation under their own wolf-etched banner. These were Rakah's chosen — veterans of his longest campaigns, black-armoured, eyes empty of fear. They moved like a single organism, blades ready, advancing to stand at his side.

Rakah shifted his stance, blades loose and easy in his hands, eyes fixed on both the Karathat defenders regrouping before him and the Mandji riders bearing down from beyond.

"Let them come," he growled softly, low enough that only those closest heard him. "We break them here."

He stepped forward, knives flashing, as the sounds of hoofbeats and war-shouts built to a rolling roar.

Tamanda braced beside Sapir, raising her sword, the Karathat guards rallying around her.

Steel against stone.

Hope against fury.

And as the Mandji crashed once more through the avenue, the final battle for the palace began.

&

CHAPTER 36

From the high stone balcony of the palace, Queen Storia

watched the tide begin to turn.

Below her, Karathat burned — but it still stood.

The streets that had echoed with the brutal march of Natsu boots now rang with the clash of blades, the defiant cries of her guardsmen, and something else — Mandji horns. The riders had come. She could see them now: armour dulled by ash, spears slick with blood, their arrival splitting the Natsu from behind like a wedge through old wood.

She gripped the balcony edge tighter. Her knuckles white. "Come on," she whispered. "Hold the line."

Beneath her, the last of the inner gates had been sealed again. Tamanda and Sapir were fighting somewhere down there — still standing. Still alive. She had not seen them fall. Not yet.

Hope fluttered in her chest. Painful. Fragile. Dangerous.

And then she remembered.

The order.

Her breath caught.

"Tommon…"

She'd given it days ago, behind closed doors — an order she had hoped never to see fulfilled. A last command, whispered with a trembling voice disguised as strength:

If the gates fall, and I am taken or killed — the palace must not become a slaughterhouse. The children… must not be taken.

Tommon, the old guardsman. Loyal. Unquestioning. Dutiful to the end. He'd nodded once. Asked no questions. Said only, "I understand, Your Majesty."

289

She stepped back from the balcony, heart thudding like a drum in her chest.

The battle was still raging — undecided. The Mandji had arrived.

But what if… what if Tommon had already acted?

"Gods," she whispered. "Please no."

She turned sharply and called to the nearest guard.

"Send word to the lower hold. Find Tommon. Bring him to me. Now."

The guard ran without question.

Storia stood alone in the chamber, unable to shake the image — not of her throne, or her council, or even her burning city — but of a locked cellar door… and the silence that might be waiting behind it.

Storia waited, pacing the length of her chambers like a caged hawk, eyes fixed on the door. But the silence was unbearable, and the weight of possibility too great.

She couldn't wait any longer.

With her heart thundering in her chest, she pushed through the doorway and began to run. The corridors blurred past, lit by torches and shaken by distant echoes of battle. The lower hold—where she had told Tommon to take Nyla—lay below the palace, behind reinforced doors and heavy stone.

"Please," she whispered as she ran. "Let him have disobeyed me. Let it have been too much. Let him not have done it."

She rounded a corner, her guards struggling to keep up. Shouts and steel rang through the halls, but she barely heard them.

The hold door loomed ahead.

She banged her fists against it, hard. "Tommon!" No answer.

"Break it," she ordered. "Now!"

The guards obeyed. Steel slammed against the hinges, and after two solid blows, the door burst inward. Light spilled into the room.

But it was empty.

No Tommon. No Nyla.

"Where are they?" she breathed.

A scream echoed through the halls, sharp and close. "Nyla!"

Storia ran toward the sound with her guards in pursuit. As they rounded the bend into the lower courtyard, they found the source—Tommon, collapsed in a pool of blood, his sword still gripped in one trembling hand.

Two Natsu warriors lay dead beside him, their bodies carved with the marks of a final stand.

Storia dropped to her knees beside him. His breathing was shallow, the artery in his leg torn open. She pressed her hands to the wound, trying to stop the flow, but it was no use. He was slipping.

With his final breath, Tommon whispered, "I protected her… she ran… toward the courtyard…" Then he was gone.

Storia closed his eyes with trembling fingers. "Guards!" she snapped. "To the courtyard—NOW!" They surged forward.

The courtyard was chaos, the clash of steel against stone echoing in every direction. The Karathat Guard held the line, bloodied but unbroken, fighting back wave after wave of Natsu. Bodies littered the stairs.

Smoke drifted from broken windows. But they had not fallen.

Not yet.

Storia's eyes swept the chaos—then stopped.

Nyla—small, trembling—was crouched beneath a stone stairwell, eyes wide with terror. Storia broke from the guards and ran to her, calling softly.

"Nyla. It's me. Come out, it's safe—"

But Nyla didn't move. Her eyes were fixed on something behind Storia. "Sapir!"

The Queen turned.

Sapir had heard his name. He had turned toward the voice—toward her—and in that instant, an arrow struck him high in the shoulder, punching through the edge of his armour. He stumbled, caught himself.

Nyla screamed. She tried to move but froze again, helpless.

Another arrow flew, this time striking Sapir low in the back. He grunted, staggered forward three more steps—toward them—then collapsed hard to the stone.

Storia couldn't scream. Her breath caught in her throat, pain blooming behind her eyes.

Tamanda, further up the steps, turned at the sound. Her gaze locked on Sapir's fallen form.

"GET HIM UP!" she roared. "Healers—NOW!"

She spun, eyes landing on a nearby guardsman. "You! Get the Queen and the girl out of here!"

The guard's arm wrapped around Storia's waist before she could resist.

"My Queen—this way, please, we must"

"I won't leave him!" she cried, twisting in his grip, her eyes locked on the stone steps where Sapir lay, bleeding, unmoving, barely breathing.

But more guards surged around them, blades drawn, eyes scanning the chaos. Tamanda's orders had weight, and no one questioned them not even the Queen.

"Let me go!" she shouted. "Nyla!"

Nyla clung to her now, face buried in Storia's robes, trembling as the battle roared just beyond the stone arch. Blood dripped from Sapir's wounds. Tamanda fought above, holding the line, shouting for the medics to reach him.

And Storia was pulled away.

The corridor walls narrowed, the smoke thickened, and her breath came in gasps. She didn't know how far they ran—only that she hated every step. Hated herself for obeying.

They reached a reinforced chamber within the palace's inner wing, its door barred and guarded. The moment they were inside, the guards closed the door behind her.

The noise of battle dimmed.

Still, Storia stood frozen, Nyla clinging to her leg.

She stared at the blood on her hands—Tommon's, her fingers trembled. She gripped them into fists. "He's not dead. He can't be."

She looked down at Nyla—still silent, still shaking.

"He promised to keep you safe," she whispered. "And he did."

Tears welled at the corners of her eyes but didn't fall. She didn't have the luxury. Not now.

Her voice hardened. "Get me a runner. I want word the moment

Sapir breathes again. Or…" She stopped herself. "…or if he doesn't." The guards nodded and left quickly.

Storia sank to one knee, drawing Nyla closer, holding her tightly, pressing her forehead to the girl's tangled hair.

"I'm so sorry," she whispered. "I should never have left you. I should never have sent that order to Tommon. I should have gone down sooner."

Nyla said nothing but her small hands reached up and held Storia's face.

Just held her there.

And for the first time since the banners of Natsu appeared on the ridge, Storia let herself cry.

But not for long.

When she stood again, her voice was clear. Her crown bloodied, her robes torn but her will unbroken.

"See to it," she said to the waiting guards. "Whatever happens outside that gate we do not fall today."

❧

CHAPTER 37

Taran walked at the head of the Mandji, his spear raised high, and his eyes fixed on the smoke rising from the broken walls of
Karathat.

The once-proud city was battered. Flames licked the rooftops of the outer districts, and columns of black smoke painted the sky. The Natsu had torn deep into the heart of the city, but they had not taken it. Not yet.

And they wouldn't—not while he still drew breath.

The Mandji warriors behind him walked in silence now, a hundred strong. No war drums. No horns. They had marched for days with little sleep, pushing hard to reach the city before it fell. Every man and woman in his force knew this battle might be their last.

Taran knew it too.

But still, he rode.

Ahead, the outer field was littered with corpses—Karathat guards, Natsu warriors, broken siege engines and shattered wood. A trail of ruin pointed them toward the breach in the northern wall, where the last of the Natsu rear guard were rallying to hold them back.

"Shields forward!" Taran called. "Brace to crash through!"

Stafan appeared at his side, his sword already drawn. "We break their lines at the breach and hold there. Palace first. Streets
after."

Taran nodded. "No delays. If we don't push through fast, we'll be cut off."

Then the sound came—a horn.

Karathat's signal horn, blown from inside the wall.

A warning. Or maybe… a welcome.

As the Mandji ran into the Natsu rear lines, steel slammed against steel. Taran's spear struck the first enemy through the collarbone and drove him from his feet. He let it go and drew his short blades.

Behind him, the Mandji roared.

They fought not for conquest or pride—but for allies, for honour, for the oath Taran had made in the council chambers of Karathat.

And in that moment, as he cut through a second soldier and saw the palace spires through the thinning haze, Taran knew—they weren't too late.

Not yet.

But they had to reach the heart.

Before it stopped beating.

Rakah stood near the breached wall, blood slick on his forearms, one blade missing, the other dripping. His chest rose and fell in shallow bursts, but his eyes remained sharp—alive with fury, focus, and the weight of command.

The Natsu were faltering.

The Karathat lines had pulled back to the inner gate, and the breach—once a channel for their conquest—was now a choke point bleeding warriors on both sides.

And now the riders had come.

From the eastern ridge, the sound of hooves still echoed like war drums. The Mandji.

He had hoped the scouts were wrong. That the delay in their arrival meant refusal, or cowardice, or politics too slow to matter.

But here they were.

Not a thousand. Not enough to overwhelm.

But enough to matter.

Rakah stood atop the low slope just inside the breach, where the stone had crumbled under their siege. She watched the Mandji riders break through the last line of her rear guards, led by a broad-shouldered warrior with dark braids and a fire in his eyes. His blades were already wet. He did not slow.

"Taran," he said aloud. The name felt like grit on her tongue.

He hadn't flanked. He hadn't waited. He had come straight through.

"He's reckless," said a captain beside him, panting from the fight. "We should pull back—reform at the plaza—"

"No," Rakah said. His voice was ice. "We end it now."

He turned to her remaining elites—those still capable of standing, still willing to bleed.

"With me," he commanded. "We strike his line. Break his momentum before he reaches the palace." The warriors formed around him.

He pulled his second blade from a dead soldier's ribs, wiped it on his cloak, and tightened the straps of his armour. His lip was split. One eye was swelling.

He didn't care.

"Make him regret answering their call," he said.

And then he moved—not like a general giving orders from the rear, but like a wolf charging down from the ridge.

The broken stones beneath Taran's boots crunched as he stepped down from his horse. The narrow breach had become a funnel of blood and iron, where horses could no longer charge and blades did the screaming.

He had fought through five soldiers already since dismounting.

But now he saw him.

He moved through the smoke like a storm—tall, lithe, unmistakable. Rakah. Not just a commander. The commander. The force that had driven the Natsu across half a continent. The one whose hand had shattered Teren Ridge. Whose name had haunted the whispers of his scouts.

And now, he was walking straight toward him, blades drawn, blood crusted on his leathers.

Taran met his gaze across the chaos.

No words. Not here. Not now.

He charged.

Taran moved to meet him, blades already rising.

Their first clash was violent and fast. His twin blades struck from opposing angles—one high, one low—but he caught them both on the flat of his swords, twisted, and drove his shoulder into him with brutal force. He staggered, but didn't fall. His eyes glinted.

You're strong, they seemed to say. Good.

He came again.

He blocked, parried, struck back. He danced to the side, slashed low, nearly took his leg—but he twisted, dropped to one knee, and drove a blade upward. Rakah turned it aside with the hilt of one sword and kicked him across the jaw.

Pain exploded in his head, but he didn't fall.

He smiled.

"You fight like you're trying to kill history," he growled.

"You are history," Rakah spat.

They clashed again.

Around them, the fighting blurred—Mandji and Natsu locked in brutal melee, neither side giving quarter. But those closest to the duel had fallen back, instinctively aware that something more than a skirmish was happening here.

It was personal.

It was legend in the making.

Rakah was fast. Deadly. Fluid like a viper. Taran was brute strength, discipline, precision. He absorbed punishment, bided his time, waited for the right moment.

And then—he saw it.

His footing slipped, just half a step. The stones beneath him shifted, loose with blood.

He lunged; blade aimed for her side.

He twisted, but not fast enough—his sword cut a shallow line across Rakah ribs.

He hissed in pain and slammed a pommel into Rakah's face, staggering him again.

Both stood apart for a moment, breathing hard.

"I will burn Karathat to the ground," Rakah snarled, blood dripping from his side.

Taran's voice was low. "Not while I stand." Then they moved again.

Blades met. Sparks flew.

And the battle for the city roared around them.

ॐ

CHAPTER 38

The smoke had thickened again above Karathat's walls, curling into the late afternoon sky like fingers of ash. The screams of the wounded mixed with the clash of steel and the thunder of war drums.

But then—a cry from the southern watchtower.

"BANNERS!"

The call cut through the chaos.

Storia, still at the inner wall with her guards, turned toward the sound. Blood stained the hem of her cloak, and her sword hung at her side, unused but ready.

"What colours?" she shouted.

The archer at the tower didn't reply right away.

Another guard climbed the tower to see for himself, spyglass pressed tight to his eye. He took a long breath before answering:

"I—I can't tell. They're not Karathat. Not Mandji. Not Natsu." He looked again.

"Three standards, different colours. One looks… black and silver. Another red and gold. They're coming fast. Infantry, cavalry, supply carts—"

Storia's heart kicked in her chest.

"They are hard riding. They're not flying banners of war… but they're armed."

Tamanda arrived beside her, panting, blood across one cheek. "More allies?" she asked, hopeful.

"Or opportunists," Storia said. "Or worse mercenaries bought by gold."

299

The defenders began to murmur, even as the fighting at the outer wall raged. News travelled fast through a desperate army.

Banners on the horizon. And no one knew their intent.

Back at the front, Taran and Rakah still fought in the shadow of broken stone, neither of them aware that yet another force now rode toward the blood-soaked gates of Karathat.

Hope, betrayal, salvation—riding on the wind.

Dust and blood coated the stones beneath their boots, the breach around them slick with the gore of warriors who had already given their lives to the siege. But Taran and Rakah no longer noticed the sounds of battle.

They heard only each other—the ragged breaths, the clash of steel, the pounding of blood in their ears.

Rakah darted forward, slashing low with one blade while the other came over the top like a scythe. Taran blocked high, twisted his body to avoid the lower strike, and caught Rakah with the heel of his boot to the stomach, forcing him back two paces.

"You're slowing," he said, sweat dripping from his brow.

"You're bleeding," Rakah snapped.

He was right. A long cut along his shoulder had soaked through his armour. But he didn't falter.

They moved again—quick, deadly, reading each other's rhythm now. Rakah struck with the fury of a commander trying to salvage a siege. Taran met him with the weight of a man defending a city, a Queen, and a people he had not been born among—but had chosen.

Their blades locked.

Face to face now, muscles straining, they pushed against each other with everything they had left.

"Karathat will burn," Rakah hissed.

Taran's jaw clenched. "Only if you walk through me to do it."

Their balance shifted. Taran dropped low, swept Rakah's legs from beneath him, and sent him crashing to the ground. But he rolled with the fall, came up on one knee, and threw a dagger—fast, ruthless.

Taran deflected it at the last moment, barely avoiding it tearing through his throat.

For a heartbeat, they both paused.

War roared around them again.

And from the ridge beyond the walls, a trumpet sounded.

They turned their heads in the same instant.

Banners. Unfamiliar ones. Drawing closer.

Both of them stood now—neither moving to attack. "You expecting more help?" Rakah asked. "No," Taran said, frowning. "Are you?"

Rakah's grip on his sword shifted. Not loosened—just readjusted. "These changes nothing," he said, though there was a flicker of uncertainty in his voice.

Taran took a slow step forward. "That's where you're wrong. Everything changes now." He surged again.

Their blades met once more.

No words.

No mercy.

Just the two of them—will against will, in a battle that would determine the fate of Karathat.

The smoke drifted low now, clinging to the bloodied stones like a shroud. Around them, the clash of battle had begun to shift—Karathat guards pushing forward from the inner gate, Mandji warriors roaring into the breach, Natsu lines splintering under the weight of resistance.

But Taran and Rakah remained in the centre, a storm within the storm.

Rakah attacked with renewed fury, his twin blades a blur of light and death. Taran was slower now, his wounded shoulder weakening his blocks. Twice, Rakah cut him—once across the ribs, once along the thigh. He grunted but held the line.

"You should've stayed in the mountains," Rakah growled.

Their blades rang again—steel on steel, sparks flying.

Rakah pressed his advantage, backing him toward the shattered base of the wall. With a vicious snarl, Rakah feinted left, spun, and drove both blades forward—one aimed high, one low.

But Taran had learned his rhythm. He dropped his left blade and caught Rakah's upper wrist with his bare hand, the blade slicing across his palm. He pulled Rakah forward, off balance—and drove his right sword into Rakah's side, deep, until the steel hit bone.

Rakah gasped.

His legs buckled.

He staggered backward, eyes wide with disbelief as blood welled beneath his armour.

Taran stood over him, panting. Blood ran down his arm, his chest, his leg—but he did not fall.

"You're finished," he said.

Rakah dropped to one knee, still clutching one blade. "No… you don't… understand…" his words were wet now, his mouth filling with blood.

Taran knelt beside him, gripping the hilt still buried in his side. "I understand enough."

Rakah's mouth twisted—not in a sneer, but something close to a bitter smile. "The Natsu don't end with me."

"I don't care about ending your people," Taran said softly. "Only your war."

And then—he twisted the blade.

Rakah let out one last gasp, eyes still locked on his.

Then he slumped forward, his body limp against the blood-stained stone.

It was done.

Taran rose, swaying, and looked out over the field. The breach was turning. The Mandji were cutting down the remaining Natsu warriors.

Karathat's banners still flew above the palace towers.

He had won.

But it had cost him.

The wind changed.

It came in from the hills to the west, stirring the dust of the battlefield and snapping broken banners where they lay in pools of blood. The last of the Natsu outside the breach were scattering or falling, many unaware their commander now lay dead beneath Karathat's shattered wall.

And then—the sound grew louder.

Drums. Hooves. Steel.

From the western ridge, they appeared.

Three banners. One black with a silver crescent. One deep crimson with a golden stag. The last, a deep forest green with no sigil at all—only the mark of old mountain ink, something ancient.

Riders poured over the hill—several hundred at least—disciplined, armoured, moving not as raiders but as an army that knew war. They came fast and hard, formation tight, weapons already drawn. Without hesitation, the leading ranks split into hunting groups, chasing down the remnants of the Natsu army as they fled across the battlefield.

The rout was swift and brutal. Stragglers were ridden down, swords flashing, hooves crushing broken weapons and bones alike. These were no fresh recruits; they fought like wolves unleashed—silent, precise, relentless.

From the walls of Karathat, the defenders watched in stunned silence as their would-be conquerors were cut down not by their own blades, but by strangers from the west.

Behind them came ranks of infantry, slower, grim-faced and dustcovered, accompanied by mounted scouts and supply carts.

Karathat's defenders froze, momentarily unsure whether to raise their blades or lower them.

From the battlements, Storia watched, lips tight, one hand gripping the stone rail of the inner wall. Tamanda stood at her side, bruised and bloodied but still upright. Sapir, wounded, had been taken inside, and Nyla remained safe—for now.

A scout ran up the stairs, bow in hand. "They're not flying Natsu colours, Your Highness. And they aren't Mandji either." "Then what are they?" Tamanda asked.

The scout paused. "Mercenaries, maybe. But they're… marching in formation. They aren't looting. And they are killing the Natsu."

Another guard appeared beside them. "They've sent a rider under white cloth. Parley."

Storia's breath caught. "Take me to the gates."

Moments later, as the wounded were being tended, the gates opened just enough for a rider to enter.

She was tall, wrapped in travel-worn furs and leathers, her helm held under one arm. Her face was pale, marked by sun and distance, her hair in warrior braids tied with iron rings. She dismounted, nodded once, and extended a scroll.

"To Queen Storia of Karathat," she said. "We come under banners of neutrality, bound by treaty to her late father. We offer aid, or passage, as she chooses."

Storia took the scroll, her hands trembling slightly.

Tamanda stared hard at the rider. "And if we choose neither?"

The rider smiled faintly. "Then we leave. We are not vultures."

Storia broke the seal and read—and with every line, her expression changed.

Zarratt had sent word to the verathai people of Veratha, an older nation that signed a treaty after her father's years of war.

Relief. Shock. Confusion.

She looked up at the rider. "You were real. I thought the treaty was a myth."

"We are few," the woman replied. "But we are not forgotten. We swore to your father that when his bloodline called for help, we would come."

She said calmly, voice ringing with confidence. "Your father's treaty stands. We are here to serve you."

Storia felt a sob break in her chest. "You came," she whispered.

"We came," she replied, "because you held the line. Now we help you hold it longer."

Behind her, more Verathai soldiers poured through the breach into the city to help — engineers, smiths, medics, priests carrying salves. They set about shoring up barricades, tending the dying, even gathering Natsu prisoners.

Tamanda looked at her with hard eyes. "Will you stay?"

She nodded. "Until your city is safe, we stay."

Karathat's bells tolled into the deep dusk, no longer as a cry for help — but as a testament of survival.

And in that battered courtyard, with the Queen's tears on her cheeks and Tamanda's hand steady on her shoulder, Karathat took its first breath of peace.

And behind her, from the ridges and the long road behind the western hills, more warriors began to emerge.

Not a vast army.

But enough to matter.

Enough to hold the line.

"We have one of your men with us," the Varethai officer said, her tone calm but clear. "He's being tended to by our physician." Storia straightened slightly, eyes narrowing. "Who?"

"Commander Zarratt," the woman replied. "He is injured rather badly—but he will recover. We found him two days' ride east of Teren

Ridge."

Tamanda exhaled softly. "He survived…"

The officer gave a small nod. "Very lucky, from what he's told us.

Stubborn, too. He refused to die."

A ripple of quiet passed through the chamber.

"We will bring him to you in a few days, once he is fit to travel," the Varethai continued. "If you allow it, we will camp outside Karathat's walls for a few days before beginning our return to Varethuun."

Storia looked to her councillors, then back to the officer. "You brought aid when no one else came. You may rest where you please." The woman inclined her head. "While we are here, you have our full cooperation. We will help bury the dead, reinforce the wounded—and begin what rebuilding we can."

&

CHAPTER 39

T hey made no speeches when they entered the outer city.

No trumpet calls, no banners streaming in pride, no brash declarations of victory. Only the steady, measured tread of warriors who had seen too much war to celebrate it. Their grey-and-blue cloaks seemed muted, as if they had left behind any right to joy and carried instead only a vow.

The Varethai had come, just as they had promised, like a mountain wind that needed no fanfare.

Beyond the battered southern gate they camped, staking their tents in long, even rows that mirrored their disciplined minds. Their fires burned low, more for function than for comfort, each one carefully banked so no light spilled unnecessarily into the darkness. There were no songs of triumph, no cheers for conquest. Only the soft sounds of whetstones drawn across dulled steel, the hiss of water quenching blades fresh from the sharpening block, the click and snap of broken mail being refit.

If one listened close enough, the only words came as quiet prayers — soft, old, and almost sorrowful, echoing the sounds of wind over pine branches far from this ruined place.

Karathat's people watched them at first with a deep and wary wonder.

They were not Mandji. They were not Karathat-born. Their armour was unfamiliar, iron rings chased with mountain glyphs, the blue cloth marked by a symbol no Karathati recognized. And yet they walked among the wounded with their heads slightly bowed, eyes steady, never flaunting their power. There was no arrogance in their bearing — only respect for the dead, and a sober willingness to stand where others had fallen.

By dawn, they had already begun to help.

No command was shouted; no orders were posted. They simply rose from their neat rows of tents, walked into the battered streets, and began.

They dug alongside the battered city militia, carrying the bodies of the dead with a quiet, reverent care. They laid Karathati and Natsu alike in neat rows for burial. Some paused long enough to cross the hands of the fallen over their chests, as if returning dignity to those who had died without it.

When the carts came to carry the bodies to the pyres or the shallow graves beyond the walls, the Varethai guided the oxen, steady and sure, moving without complaint.

Others turned to the tasks of the living.

Three Varethai smiths — their hands still raw from long rides and rough work — went to the palace forge. They took up Karathati tools without question, mending the city's own weapons with a silent precision. Where a rivet was missing, they forged a new one; where a sword was bent, they heated it and straightened it with patient hammer-blows.

One of their apothecaries, a weathered woman with braids tied in copper wire, appeared in the palace infirmary before the sun had properly risen. She carried a bag of crushed herbs and a folded paper of drawn diagrams. Without pretence or permission, she simply began to work, stitching wounds, applying salves, murmuring in a tongue the healers did not know but somehow still understood.

No one turned her away.

They spoke little, these Varethai. And when they did, it was in short, thoughtful phrases — sometimes a respectful nod, sometimes a murmur in their dialect, its syllables carrying an echo of the old mountains and a sense of history that went far beyond any one city.

The people of Karathat began to see it then, even if they did not yet say it aloud.

These warriors were not here for spoils.

They were not here to carve their names in a city already cut to the bone.

They were here because once, long ago, a king had given them aid in their own hour of need. And now they had come to return that debt.

Because to them, honour was not a word you boasted of in a hall.

It was a legacy you lived — or you betrayed.

Tamanda saw it clearest of all.

She moved among the Varethai in those first days, still stiff from wounds barely scabbed over, trying to understand them. In a charred market square, she watched two Varethai warriors lift beams off a collapsed house, freeing three civilians who had been trapped inside. They did it with no demands for thanks, no hint of triumph, only a calm steadiness that made her throat ache with a strange gratitude.

Later, by the wall, she found a Varethai officer supervising the burial of Natsu dead.

"You do not hate them?" Tamanda asked quietly, gesturing to the enemy soldiers laid in careful rows.

The officer — a tall woman with scars across both cheeks, ceremonial beads knotted into her braids — looked at her for a long moment.

"Hate is for the living," she said. "The dead deserve rest."

Tamanda swallowed hard, then nodded. "Thank you."

The woman inclined her head, then went back to her work, arranging the bodies with the same respect she had given her own fallen.

In the palace itself, the Varethai presence became a quiet reassurance.

Their engineers, some barely more than boys, moved quickly through the shattered fortifications. They examined crumbling arches, marked cracks with chalk, and offered sketches on new beams, new supports, new anchor points for rebuilt gates. Storia gave them permission with barely a second thought.

"These walls have stood for two centuries," she told them, voice steady but tired. "I would see them stand for two more."

The Varethai nodded. "They will stand," one replied in simple certainty.

At night, the palace's courtyard no longer echoed with screams. The wounded had been moved, the dead counted and carried away. In their place, the soft glow of oil lamps showed healers moving through rows of bandaged soldiers, giving water, changing wrappings, speaking soft words.

Even the children, hidden away during the siege, emerged in small, frightened groups. A pair of Varethai soldiers shared dried fruit with them, kneeling to their level, showing them a carved toy that looked like a tiny bird with hinged wings. The children, unsure at first, gradually came closer, and their laughter — tiny and hesitant — sounded for the first time in what felt like a lifetime.

■

The second dawn after the fighting broke, a formal gathering was called in the main hall.

Storia stood on the steps, dressed in a plain gown still torn at the sleeves, refusing the new ceremonial cloak that had been offered to replace the one ruined in battle.

Tamanda was to her left, Sapir to her right, their armour battered but clean, shields polished to gleam in the hall's light. The hall was full — soldiers of Karathat, Mandji allies, Varethai warriors. No one raised voices. There was only that same hush, like the calm after a storm.

Captain Idris of the Varethai stepped forward, bowing low. Her cloak was still smudged with dust and ash, but her eyes were clear.

"Majesty," she began in her accented Karathati, "the Varethai stand by you, and will stand until you no longer require our blades."

Storia's chin trembled but did not break. "You crossed half the continent to keep a vow."

Idris nodded. "A promise made is a life lived. We do not forget."

Silence fell. And then — slowly, as if they barely trusted their own strength — the soldiers of Karathat began to pound their spears on the floor, a steady, growing drumbeat.

One by one, the Mandji joined them, hands striking shields, until the hall echoed with a roar of gratitude and hope.

It was not a cheer. It was a heartbeat.

The heartbeat of a city that had survived.

■

That night, the Varethai camp burned with a few small fires, enough to cook rations and warm their hands. But no great feasts. No songs of victory.

They sat shoulder to shoulder, polishing their blades, tending their mounts, trading stories of home in voices so low they barely carried past their own ring of warriors. They had no plans to stay forever, Tamanda saw — but while they were here, they would give everything they had.

That was their way.

And somehow, Karathat felt safer for it.

❧

CHAPTER 40

S apir lay beneath a linen canopy in the upper wing of the palace infirmary, his shoulder and lower back tightly bandaged. The pain came in waves, dull at times, sharp at others but he bore it the way a man bears old grief: silently, without complaint.

The scent of oils and ash lingered in the air. From the balcony beyond the hall, he could hear Karathat still breathing—its wounded streets groaning, its people moving like ghosts through the aftermath.

He shifted, slowly, gritting his teeth as he adjusted to sit up straighter. One of the healers noticed and approached, but he waved them off.

"I'm fine," Sapir murmured, though his voice was hoarse.

At the far end of the room, a soft laugh echoed light and small.

"Nyla." He muttered to himself.

She sat beside one of the empty cots, legs tucked beneath her, whispering to the old guardsman who'd stood watch through much of the siege. The man was smiling, nodding along with whatever story she was sharing. His presence was familiar to her from before the battle, it seemed to calm her.

Sapir watched her for a long moment.

He remembered the way she had screamed his name as the arrow struck him. Remembered the terror in her eyes, terror not of the Natsu, but of losing him. He hadn't realised, until then, how much space she'd carved into his heart. She had not been born of his blood, but in some quiet, unspoken way, she was his now. A daughter in all but name.

He turned his head slowly, his eyes settling on the doorway where Storia had last stood, blood-smeared, breathless, terrified not as a queen but as a woman watching someone she cared about fall.

He had seen her in command. But that moment, in the courtyard, had changed something between them. Or maybe it had only revealed what had already taken root.

He didn't know what words to give it yet. But he knew what he'd fight for, should the enemy return.

Not for banners or thrones. But for that girl's laughter.

For the woman who had knelt with her in the dark.

The palace was quieter now. The wounded slept, the dead were buried, and the walls still stood.

But inside the infirmary, something stirred, quiet and delicate, like a heartbeat rediscovering its rhythm.

Storia stood by Sapir's bedside again, the late afternoon sun casting soft gold across the floor. Nyla had just left, after wrapping Sapir in a fierce little hug before being led out by one of the healers. Her laughter had lingered long after she'd gone.

Storia didn't sit this time. She stood with her hands folded before her, her expression unreadable—until it wasn't.

"I was going to wait," she said, voice quiet but steady. "Wait until the city was mended, until the war was further behind us. But I've come to realise… I've done too much waiting in my life." Sapir looked up, watching her with calm, curious eyes.

She stepped closer. "I have ruled this city with strength because I had no other choice. I learned diplomacy because I had to. I wore crowns and armour and bore the burden of command without complaint."

Her eyes found his. "But I never chose anything for myself."

He didn't interrupt. He knew her well enough now to let her speak.

"I don't want to be alone when this war is over. I don't want Nyla to grow up watching people leave, disappear, or die for causes she doesn't understand." Storia's voice cracked, just a little. "I want her to have something solid. Something that stays." Her hand reached out and found his.

"I want you, Sapir. And I want her. I want us. A family—not by blood, but by choice. My choice."

Sapir's breath caught. He wasn't a man easily shaken—but this, this quiet storm of emotion behind her words, it struck deeper than any blade.

"I've already made the arrangements," she added, more softly.

"When you're recovered, you'll serve as Commander of the Queen's Guard. Zarratt… he deserves to rest. If the gods are kind, he'll recover enough to stay close to us. I'd like him to help raise Nyla. As her guardian. As if he was her grandfather."

For a long moment, there was only silence between them. Then Sapir sat up a little straighter, reaching to place his calloused fingers over hers.

"I've fought a hundred battles," he said. "But this… this is the only thing that's ever scared me."

She arched a brow gently. "And?"

He smiled. "I'm saying yes. To all of it."

The gates of Karathat opened slowly that morning—not to welcome traders, or a returning battalion, but for a single covered wagon escorted by three Varethai riders.

The guardsmen at the gate had been told to expect it. Still, they stood straighter when they saw the Varethai crest. And when the wagon came to a stop, and the healer stepped down to open the rear canvas flap, they fell into silence.

Inside, half-laying against bolstered cushions, sat Commander

Zarratt.

He looked smaller than they remembered—thinner, drawn, one arm bound in tight linen wraps. But his eyes, fierce and sharp as ever, still carried the weight of a commander. Of a man who had held the line when it seemed impossible.

The guardsmen didn't speak at first. Then one stepped forward, hand to heart.

"Karathat stands because of you, sir."

Zarratt gave a faint nod, his voice raspy but iron edged. "No… it stands because others carried the fight after I fell. Take me to the

Queen."

Storia waited just inside the palace gates, flanked by Sapir—walking carefully now—and Tamanda, armour still scuffed from the final defence. Nyla stood slightly behind them, clutching the edge of Storia's cloak.

When the wagon stopped before them, and Zarratt was helped down by the Varethai healers, it was Nyla who moved first.

She broke into a run across the flagstones and threw her arms around the old commander's waist.

"You're back," she whispered, clutching him.

Zarratt winced but rested his good hand on her head. "Course I am, little hawk. You think I'd miss my new post?"

Storia stepped forward next, eyes shining though her composure held. "You are stubborn, impossible man."

He straightened as best he could. "You gave me an order to hold the gate. I held it."

Sapir stepped forward and offered his hand. Zarratt gripped it tight. "We'll carry the sword now," Sapir said. "You've earned your rest."

Zarratt's gaze lingered on Nyla. "I don't know if I know how to rest.

But I can teach. I can protect."

Storia smiled softly. "Then we'll find a place for you here, old friend.

No longer in the ranks—but in our home. As family."

Zarratt didn't answer at first. He only nodded—his chin high, his pride undiminished.

The gatekeeper had returned. And though the city had changed, his place in it had not been lost.

Mevran shifted uncomfortably as he joined them eyeing Zarratt with a mixture of relief and disbelief. "We thought you were dead, Commander. When the arrows struck—no one saw you rise again. How in the gods' name did you survive that fall? We saw you go over

the rampart." Zarratt took a slow breath, fingers grazing the bandages binding his ribs. "I thought the same for a while."

Zarratt's eyes grew distant. "When I fell, I was certain it was the end. But the gods had other plans. I landed on something soft — sacks, maybe, or broken thatch piled near the inner wall. Before I could even gather my wits, rubble from the tower collapse came down over me."

Mevran frowned. "Buried?"

"Yes. Buried. It knocked the wind from me, but the stones settled enough that I could breathe. I don't know how long I lay there, halfconscious, half-praying."

Sapir's jaw tightened. "And then?"

"When I woke, I heard water," Zarratt continued. "I remembered the intake tunnels that run under the ramparts. I crawled to them — forced myself through mud, ash, gods know what else. It was the only way out."

Mevran shook his head, incredulous. "And you made it all the way through the water tunnels?"

"Half-drowned, but alive." Zarratt managed a grim smile. "When I reached the stables, there was chaos. No one watching the horses. I took the first beast I could find and rode, wounds and all."

Sapir folded his arms across his chest, letting out a low whistle. "And you rode for two days like that? Bleeding, half-starved?"

Zarratt nodded. "Every mile felt like a lifetime. But there was no time to rest. I had to warn you — had to get word to someone."

Mevran let out a long breath. "If the gods spared you, Zarratt, it was for a reason."

The weeks passed, the allied army that had been camped at the front had now left, they had searched and hunted and Natsu warriors or raiders that had remained.

Some of the Varethai had stayed behind to help with security and help build, new oaths had been made and the alliance with them remained.

The palace gardens had started to grow again.

The gardeners, returned from the ramparts and walls, had cleared away the scorched vines and broken trellises. New shoots stretched toward the sun, and the fountain in the centre courtyard once again ran with clear water. The scent of jasmine drifted faintly on the breeze, and for the first time in weeks, there was no sound of hammer or sword.

Just the wind. And laughter.

Nyla ran barefoot through the garden paths, her hair loose and tangled, a flower crown half-slipping from her head. She spun once beneath the hanging ivy, arms wide, before collapsing onto the grass beside the fountain—giggling until she could barely breathe.

Zarratt sat on the bench nearby, a carved cane resting against his knee. His wounds still pained him, but the worst had passed. He wore no armour now, just soft grey robes, and he looked ten years older—but peaceful.

He watched Nyla without speaking, his rough hands slowly weaving another crown of tiny blue flowers. She'd already demanded two today.

"That's crooked," she said with a cheeky grin.

Zarratt grunted. "Your head's crooked."

"Is not!"

He chuckled, handed her the flower crown, and she stuck her tongue out before slipping it on.

From a shaded arch nearby, Storia watched with a faint smile. She leaned her head against Sapir's shoulder, his arm draped lightly around her. He still moved carefully, but his wounds had begun to heal—his strength returning day by day. In his other hand, he held a carved wooden toy—a little horse he'd started making for Nyla while recovering.

"I never imagined this," Storia whispered.

Sapir turned to her. "What? Peace?"

She nodded. "Or a day where I could breathe without bracing for bad news. Where I could stand beside someone who knew me not as queen, but as… me."

"You've earned it," he said softly. "You both have."

They walked forward together, joining Zarratt and Nyla beneath the sun. The four of them sat around the fountain—no court, no command, no council—just quiet.

Just family.

For that afternoon, Karathat could wait.

෯

CHAPTER 41

The throne room of Karathat bore the scars of war—faint cracks along the marble, soot-blackened windows, and the lingering scent of smoke that clung like memory. But it stood. Karathat still stood.

Storia paced quietly along the edge of the war table, fingers brushing the edges of battle-worn markers now turned toward rebuilding—new borders, shared patrol routes, and trade paths drawn with cautious hope.

When the doors opened, Taran stepped in with the quiet presence of a man who'd faced death and turned it aside. His cloak was travel-worn, his brow shadowed, but there was peace in his eyes.

"I thought you might be halfway to the mountains," Storia said, not turning.

"I considered it," he admitted. "But debts remain—and not just mine."

"You didn't owe us anything," she said. "Yet you came."

"You opened your gates to strangers. You protected one of ours.

That means something."

She finally turned to face him. "You didn't just fight beside us. You saved us."

Taran nodded. "Then let this be the start of something more."

With no ceremony, they clasped forearms—ruler to ruler, survivor to survivor.

"Come," she said. "There's someone you should stand beside today."

The Hall of Shields had been cleared and lit with lanterns that gleamed against the stone like fireflies. The wounded stood among the healthy, nobles beside guardsmen. Banners of the fallen were draped in black, but pride hummed beneath the hush.

Tamanda stood at the centre of the chamber in fresh-forged armour.

Her wounds were bound but healing, her face calm but unreadable.

When Storia entered with Taran, silence fell.

The Queen's voice rang clear. "Let it be known: two stood when others fell. Two held fast when the walls crumbled. And today, Karathat remembers them."

She stepped forward, gaze on Tamanda.

"Tamanda of the lower court. You stood between death and your Queen, and again between the enemy and your people. You went alone into danger, returned with warning, and fought at the breach until blood soaked the stones. You proved that rank does not define greatness, actions do."

From a velvet case, she drew a curved ceremonial blade, etched with the sigil of the Queen's Vanguard.

"I name you Captain of the Queen's Vanguard. You will lead not from behind a desk, but from the front. You will train the next generation of defenders not to be noble, but to be ready."

Tamanda knelt. "I swear it."

From the side, the tapping of a cane echoed. Zarratt approached slowly, his limp heavier than before, but his presence no less commanding. He stepped beside her and laid a weathered hand on her shoulder.

He looked out at the gathered soldiers and nobles and said, "There was a time I told this one to stay in her place. That she was too raw, too reckless, too untrained."

He turned back to Tamanda. "I was wrong." A breath stirred through the hall.

Zarratt's voice roughened. "I have commanded for more seasons than I care to count. But I have never seen anyone face death so many times with so little hesitation or carry more than their share without ever asking for honour in return."

He handed her a second blade, older, worn, but clean and sharp—a guard captain's blade. "This was mine. It belongs to someone better now."

Tamanda looked up, swallowing thickly. "Thank you, Commander."

Zarratt smiled faintly. "No. Thank you. You've earned this city's trust more than most born to it."

Applause rose then soft at first, then swelling.

As it settled, Storia turned to Taran.

"But there is another name that must not be forgotten." Taran shifted slightly but said nothing.

"Taran of the Mandji," she said, "You rode through night and fire to reach us. You came not for gain but for loyalty. For honour. And your arrival turned the tide."

She stepped forward, holding a golden medallion marked with the phoenix of Karathat.

"I name you Blood-Bound Ally of the Crown. You and your people are kin to Karathat. Our gates will always be open to your

banners."

Taran accepted the honour with a quiet bow. "Then may our alliance outlast the ash."

And somewhere behind them, Nyla grinned as she peeked from behind a pillar, waving first to Tamanda, then to Taran.

Tamanda smiled. Zarratt chuckled.

One city. Two heroes. A new beginning.

Later, by the shields that lined the western wall, Tamanda and

Zarratt stood alone for a moment as the hall emptied.

"You really meant what you said?" she asked.

He tapped his cane and nodded. "I've made mistakes before. But recognising someone who might just lead better than I ever did? That's the easiest truth I've spoken."

She grinned. "Don't go soft on me now."

He laughed—just once, hoarse and tired. "Don't make me proud too often. I might get used to it."

Then they stood quietly together, shoulder to shoulder. Old guard and new.

Weeks had passed since the siege of Karathat had broken.

Taran had departed quietly, his warriors riding south across the hills to return to Landa, taking with them songs of honour, and an unspoken promise to return if ever called.

But Karathat was not idle.

In the upper courtyard behind the inner wall, the training yard had been cleared and repaired. The cracked stone had been re-laid, new dummies shaped and stuffed, and fresh racks of weapons lined the walls. But more than that, there was purpose in the air. A new rhythm. A sense of future.

At the centre of it all stood Tamanda.

Clad in the lighter armour of the Vanguard, now dulled with use, she walked the rows of new recruits with the slow, deliberate stride of a commander who missed nothing. Her voice was steady, clipped, and sharp as any blade.

"Your sword is an extension of your will. If your will is weak, the blade is useless."

The clatter of practice steel filled the yard. Twenty recruits—most in their teens, a few older—moved through drills with varying degrees of skill and determination. They were no longer strangers to fear. Every one of them had lived through the siege. Some had lost family. Some had helped carry water to the walls. One had dragged a wounded guardsman through fire. That memory burned behind every strike.

Tamanda corrected a stance here, adjusted a shield there. One recruit dropped his blade during a spar. Tamanda caught it with her foot and flicked it up to the boy's chest.

"Hold it like you mean it," she said, not unkindly. "Or next time, it won't be me returning it."

On the shaded terrace above, Zarratt leaned on the rail with his cane, watching her work.

"She's fierce," a young officer beside him muttered.

Zarratt didn't answer at first. He just watched Tamanda move down the line, her dark braid swinging with each step, her commands crisp and exact.

"She's more than fierce," he said at last. "She's right for them. Gods forgive me for not seeing it sooner."

The officer glanced at him. "Regret?"

Zarratt shook his head. "Pride. The kind that hits you when you realise the world's going to outlast you—and it might be in better hands."

Down below, Tamanda called for the shield wall drill. The recruits scrambled, locking shields, moving as one unit across the courtyard. It wasn't perfect. Yet. But it was coming together.

Beyond the walls, the city stirred with quiet industry. Streets were being repaired. Trade wagons had begun arriving again. Refugees were returning. Even the palace had begun to host counsel, not just councils.

Tamanda turned toward the edge of the yard—and caught sight of Nyla.

The little girl stood beside a guard post, one of Zarratt's older veterans by her side. The same one who'd taught her to braid a sling, now watching over her like a gruff uncle.

Nyla stood mimicking the shield drill with a wooden plank and a broom handle. Tamanda smiled and gave a small, silent nod of approval. The girl beamed.

Peace, it seemed, had not dulled the edge of readiness. It had refined it.

Tamanda called the recruits to attention. "When I say 'Karathat,' you say what?"

The reply came rough, imperfect, but strong: "Stand and fight!"

"Again!"

"Stand and fight!"

Tamanda looked up at Zarratt.

He raised his mug in salute.

She turned back to her recruits.

This was not the end. It was the beginning. And she would build them not into soldiers—but into guardians, protectors of a city that would never fall easily again.

Not while she stood watch.

Inside the palace, Sapir was learning what it meant to live—not just survive.

He stood in the royal training courtyard, dressed not in armour, but a simple linen tunic. He moved through sword forms alone, not out of duty, but habit. The air was clean. The sounds of the city were far. Peace was strange—but welcome.

He heard the door open behind him and didn't have to turn to know who it was.

"You're up early," Storia said, walking barefoot across the stone.

"I never really unlearned the habit," Sapir replied, lowering the blade and wiping his brow. "But it's… different, training without a war looming."

Storia smiled faintly. "I think I prefer this version of you."

He sheathed the practice sword, meeting her gaze. "You prefer a quieter man?"

"I prefer a man who doesn't have to go off and nearly die."

She walked to him, and for a moment they said nothing. No guards. No politics. No looming decisions. Just two people standing under a pale morning sky.

From the hall beyond, the soft patter of bare feet echoed, and Nyla came running into the courtyard. She wore a tunic too long for her, dragging slightly, a wooden sword in hand.

"Sapir!" she called, charging straight at him with mock fury.

He caught her, spinning her once before setting her down with a soft grunt.

"You've been practising," he said, kneeling.

"I beat one of the guards in the garden. I think he let me win," she added with a whisper.

"He must be wise," Sapir grinned.

Storia crouched beside them, brushing Nyla's hair back from her face. "He's probably still nursing the shame."

The three of them sat there in the courtyard's quiet embrace. It wasn't grand. It wasn't meant to be. It was home. Slowly, quietly, they had made it one.

Later that evening, as dusk fell and the city lights flickered alive, Storia sat in her chamber, gazing down at the square below. Sapir came to her side, resting a hand on the balcony railing.

"She's sleeping," he said softly. "She asked if she could call me father one day."

Storia turned to him, her eyes shining. "And what did you say?" "I told her she could. When she was ready."

There was a pause, and then her voice dropped.

"I want this. I want you. I want us to be a family, Sapir. You, me,

Nyla. No thrones between us. No war. Just this." He looked at her, steady as ever. "Then let it be."

She leaned into his shoulder, the queen and the warrior. The mother and the man who had once guarded her gate—and now guarded her heart.

Outside, the bells of Karathat rang.

Inside, a family began.

&

CHAPTER 42

T he sun was just cresting the eastern ridges when the Mandji riders caught their first glimpse of Landa. The gates were visible even at a distance—blue and gold banners fluttering in the wind, the same colours they had carried into war.

Taran rode at the front, flanked by Stafan and Dilah, their horses caked with road dust, their faces drawn with fatigue and memory. Behind them trailed the survivors—just over a hundred warriors, still proud, still armed, but quieter than when they'd left.

The victory at Karathat had cost them dearly.

And the road home was not one they had all lived to see.

"Tanny would have sung something about the hills by now," Stafan muttered, his voice tight in his throat.

Dilah glanced sideways. "Or grumbled about his saddle sores. Then sung anyway."

Taran gave a small, pained smile. "He would've tried to make us laugh. Even now."

The three rode in silence a moment longer.

Tanny.

Gone in the battle against the Vintals, he had died with sword in hand, teeth bared in defiance, defending the land of strangers like it was his own.

They'd burned his body under stars, and yet… it hadn't felt like enough.

"He should've been with us now," Stafan said, more to the air than to either of them.

"He is," Taran replied quietly. "In every step we take forward."

The gates of Landa opened slowly before them. The city hadn't changed—small houses, broad market roads, the scent of cumin and iron—but the silence in the air said the people knew. Fewer riders had returned. Fewer songs were being sung.

The city watched them pass. Some offered water. Others dropped their eyes, respectful of the warriors who did not come home.

At the Elders' Hall, the three dismounted together.

A servant came forward, bowing low. "The elder council awaits you."

They entered side by side.

The chamber was hushed. At its centre stood an Elder, his carved staff in one hand, his expression unreadable.

"Taran of Landa. Stafan of the Outer Shields. Dilah of the Skyward

Watch," he named them each. "You return."

"We do," Taran answered, stepping forward. "With news. And with honour."

He produced the sealed letter from Queen Storia, offering it with both hands. "Karathat stands. Because we stood with them."

The elders passed the letter among themselves. Murmurs rose like the first rustling of wind before a storm.

"They say you faced the Natsu leader in single combat," one elder said. "Rakah, was it?"

"I did," Taran confirmed. "He fell. But he wasn't the only danger.

The Natsu are many. And they will rise again."

"And you would ally us with Karathat?" another elder asked, voice sceptical.

"I would," Taran said firmly. "They bled beside us. They kept their word. They are a proud people—but honourable. And in Storia, they have a queen who fights for her people with
fire in her
heart."

Another elder leaned forward, his eyes keen despite the lines of age. "This Queen of Karathat — she sends words of peace. But what of her future? Will she keep to her promises, or shift in the winds like others have?"

Taran straightened. "She has bound her fate to ours already." He let the moment hang. "She has accepted Sapir as her husband-to-be."

A startled hush filled the hall, as if a hawk had flown through the council chamber.

"Sapir?" Jemas repeated, astonished. "Our Sapir?"

Taran nodded. "He stayed behind in Karathat, by the Queen's side.

Their joining will bind our blood to theirs. Karathat will not forget the
Mandji so long as their Queen shares a hearth with one of our own."

Murmurs rippled like water against stone. Some faces showed surprise, some cautious hope.

"That is a powerful bond," another elder said slowly. "Blood is harder to break than any oath on parchment."

Taran agreed. "They will stand with us. And we with them."

Stafan stepped forward then, adding his quiet weight to Taran's words. "Sapir chose freely. And the Queen — she is no idle partner. She is strong. A worthy match for him, and for us."

Jemas gave a thoughtful nod. "So be it. Then our children and theirs will share the same future."

Taran's shoulders eased again. One more burden lifted, if only slightly.

Stafan stepped forward, voice low but sure. "We fought with them.

We saw them. They're not so different from us."

Dilah nodded. "And without us, they would have fallen. Without them… we might have as well."

There was silence. Then Jemas spoke. "You three led our warriors.

You brought what remain of them back. Your word is trusted."

Taran's shoulders eased—slightly. The weight wasn't lifted. But it shifted.

Later, as the sun set behind the western watch towers, the three sat beneath the tall pines just outside the hall. A flask passed between them.

No words, for a while.

Then Dilah raised the flask. "To Tanny," he said, voice catching.

"To his laugh," Stafan added, wiping a hand across his eyes.

Taran didn't speak. He just raised his own hand in silent salute. His throat burned. Not from wine. From memory.

The breeze stirred the pines, and for a moment, it almost sounded like Tanny's humming—soft, tuneless, always a little off-key.

They stayed there a long time, under the quiet hush of evening, the hush of men who had survived when others had not. Taran watched the lights of the city come on one by one, lanterns and torches chasing away the dusk. Smoke from cooking fires curled through the air, spiced with coriander and charred lamb, and carried the faintest trace of memory—of festivals, of laughing children, of music. It hurt to remember.

Dilah leaned back against the rough trunk of a pine, letting the flask rest against his thigh. "You think they'll truly listen to us?"

Taran nodded slowly. "They will. They have to. Karathat will hold to its promise, but the Natsu won't stay quiet for long. We need allies, not pride."

"And if the elders don't agree?" Stafan asked.

Taran glanced at him. "Then we keep telling them. Keep showing them. The war isn't finished."

A silence fell again. The wind shifted through the pine branches, carrying the scent of rain on distant hills.

Finally, Stafan spoke, voice hoarse. "We left too many behind."

Taran looked away. He could still see them—warriors falling in the mud of Karathat's gate, torn by arrow and blade, fighting until their lifeblood stained the stones.

"We remember them," he managed. "That's what matters now."

They rose stiffly and turned back toward the hall. The city had begun to settle into night, lamps lit along the market square, children being called indoors by mothers whose voices were worn thin by worry. As the warriors passed, people bowed their heads or placed their hands over their hearts.

Taran felt each one of those gestures. A weight, but also a promise. They had brought the Mandji warriors' home, and the Mandji would remember.

At the tavern, the surviving warriors were already settling in—some selling weapons taken from the battlefield some telling stories, some simply sitting in silence with heads bowed drinking the pain of what they had lost away. The sense of loss was heavy, like a fog that clung to their skin, refusing to wash away.

Taran moved among them, laying a hand on shoulders, offering a word here and there. Most met his eyes with gratitude, or something close to it.

Stafan watched him, arms folded across his chest. "They'll follow you to hell and back," he said.

Taran shook his head. "They follow their people. I'm just the one who stands in front."

Dilah laughed, but it was a thin laugh. "You're too modest, Taran.

They follow you because you give them something to believe in." "Then I'd better be worth believing in," Taran replied.

Dilah's expression softened. "You already are."

They parted ways as the hour grew late. Taran stood at the gate watchtower, the place where he'd once stood as a boy dreaming of distant lands. He'd never imagined he would return with so much blood on his hands, or that he would stand at the head of a broken company of heroes.

He looked out over Landa, the roofs pale under starlight, the mountains holding back the night beyond. For a moment he closed his eyes, let the quiet wrap around him, and let himself breathe.

Stafan found Taran, gazing up at the stars.

"Do you ever wish you'd never left, that first day?" Stafan asked softly.

Taran did not answer at once. He thought of every step that had led here, every battle, every friend buried far from home. Then he nodded, slowly. "Sometimes. But then I remember why I went. Why we all went."

"And?"

Taran's voice was firm. "We did what we had to do."

Stafan sighed, but there was something like peace in it. "Yes. That we did."

The two men stood in silence as a fresh wind blew down from the ridges, rattling the banners on the old walls of Landa. The night was cold, but it was honest.

Taran took one last look at the stars, then turned toward the barracks.

Tomorrow would come soon enough.

&

CHAPTER 43

T he Siege of Karathat passed into history like a storm—

leaving silence behind where there had once been thunder.

Stones were reset into place. Towers reformed from rubble.
The scent of ash lifted from the air, replaced again with jasmine
and spice. Morning bells rang once more across the city, not for
warning, but to mark the day's rhythm—market openings,
temple rites, changing of the guard.

But in the heart of the city, within the reinforced walls of the
inner citadel, there were two names carried in every mouth like
blessings, or spells.

Tamanda and Taran heroes of Karathat.

The legends grew faster than the walls.

They had not sought the stories told of them, but that only
made the stories stronger. Children played at being Tamanda in
the palace square, lifting wooden blades and pretending to hold
the breach. Young soldiers asked the armourers for Mandji-
style spears, hoping to mimic the charge led by Taran during
the final hours of the siege.

The bards, of course, were not subtle. One particularly
popular verse began:

"A girl of the kitchens, a warrior born,

Held the gate when the stones were torn.

A horseman came from hills afar,

His blade the sun, his name a star."

Storia had listened to that song once, standing at a balcony
as minstrels played in the courtyard. She had smiled faintly—
just once—and turned back inside.

She knew the truth. Tamanda had saved her life, had defied orders to do it, and had nearly died for it. She was no song. She was steel.

And Taran—well, he had arrived with no crown and no banner, only grit and warriors who would ride into fire with him. His charge into the siege from the north had changed everything. Rakah might have broken Karathat without him.

Their legacy had not ended with the battle.

~~~~~~~~~~~~~~~~~~~

Tamanda's place in the city changed quietly.

She never wore court silks. She didn't move into polished quarters. Instead, she chose to keep a modest room in the guard barracks beside the training yard and made it clear she had no interest in high titles or robes. Her power was in practice.

The recruits loved her and feared her in equal measure.

"You want to hold a line?" she'd say. "Then feel the weight of your own sword first."

And they would. And many would fail. But those who passed were worth ten ordinary guards.

One spring morning, Storia stood on the edge of the training yard, watching Tamanda correct the stance of a green recruit who hadn't gripped his shield high enough.

"Again," Tamanda barked, "and this time, keep your wrist locked."

The boy shifted, sweat dripping off his brow into the dust, his shoulders trembling as he tried to obey. Tamanda watched him, hawk-eyed, but not cruel. She stepped forward and nudged the shield into position herself, then guided his elbow until the line of his arm was true.

"Better," she said, softer. "Remember, a blade can't find you if your shield is strong."

He nodded, swallowing hard.
~~~~~~~~~~~~~~~~~~~

Storia smiled and turned to Zarratt beside her. The old commander now walked with a cane and refused to carry a weapon.

"She has your fire," she said softly.

Zarratt's eyes narrowed as Tamanda made the young man drop and do drills in the dust. But his expression softened, a rare thing. "She has more than I ever did," he admitted.

Then after a pause, he added, "I was wrong about her. I saw only where she came from, not what she was becoming. That mistake won't happen again."

They watched as Tamanda dismissed the recruit, sending him back to the line, then turned to the next pair of trainees. She moved among them with ease, almost like a predator, catching flaws before they could become habits, praising where praise was due but never cheaply given.

"She's building them from the ground up," Zarratt said. "No gaps, no illusions. Just honest warriors."

Storia nodded. "And the city is stronger for it."

Tamanda barked a sharp command, calling a pair of more seasoned guards forward. "You two—take position by the south gate this evening. Drill rotations have left it thin. I don't trust that quarter; watch for any who linger too long."

The men nodded and departed, not a question between them. Tamanda had earned their respect, not through rank but through sheer certainty, the kind no gold-sewn cloak could ever buy.

As the recruits filed away, Tamanda knelt to gather a scattering of dropped practice spears. Her hands were scarred; her wrists knotted with muscle from countless hours with sword and shield. She barely looked up as Storia and Zarratt approached.

"My Queen," she said, dipping her head slightly, though not in deference so much as acknowledgment.

"Tamanda," Storia answered, her tone warm. "How are they coming along?"

Tamanda glanced at the departing recruits. "They're green, but they have spine. That's more than half the battle."

Zarratt shifted on his cane. "I remember the first days I took command," he mused. "Couldn't get men to hold a shield line for

more than five breaths. It takes time."

Tamanda offered a tight smile. "They'll get there. If they don't, they'll break. And if they break…" She shook her head. "I can't allow that."

A moment of quiet passed. Beyond the practice yard, the city was stirring to life. Merchants in the square called their wares, and a blacksmith's hammer rang from a nearby forge. The scent of baking bread drifted on a faint wind.

Storia watched Tamanda's face, saw the small creases around her eyes, marks of weariness she had not possessed months ago. "You're taking on too much alone," the queen said gently.

Tamanda looked up sharply. "There's no one else I trust to do it properly."

"That," Zarratt interjected with a faint smile, "is what I used to say.

And I paid for it."

Tamanda's jaw worked. "These people don't have time for mistakes.

Not now. Not with so many threats gathering."

Storia stepped closer. "Then let them lean on you—but do not forget to lean on them as well. You are no good to Karathat broken."

Tamanda sighed, the breath coming out like a wound reopening. "I hear you, my Queen," she said, though her tone hinted she would struggle to heed the advice.

Storia laid a hand on her shoulder, steady but light. "You don't have to bear every burden."

Tamanda nodded once, acknowledging the words if not fully accepting them.

A trumpet blast sounded faintly from the southern gate. A runner approached, breathless. "Captain Tamanda!" he called, still unused to the idea of addressing a woman by a command title.

Tamanda straightened. "Speak."

"There's word of a caravan attacked on the east road. Survivors say a band of Natsu skirmishers, a dozen at least. They may be trying to probe the border."

Tamanda's eyes hardened, and she tossed the practice spears into a nearby barrel. "I'll see to it," she said.

"Tamanda—" Storia began, but Tamanda was already turning, voice ringing out to the nearest guards. "You—five with me. Light gear. We move now."

The runner hesitated, eyes darting toward the queen.

Storia simply nodded, resigned. "Go with her," she told him.

Tamanda and her small force moved off at a quick march, leaving only a swirl of dust behind them.

Zarratt exhaled slowly, leaning on his cane as he watched her disappear beyond the walls. "She will drive herself to ruin if we let her," he murmured.

Storia's face was set in grim calm. "She reminds me of you," she said.

Zarratt grunted. "That's no blessing."

"Maybe it is," Storia replied. "You survived. You learned to bend, eventually."

"Only after nearly breaking," Zarratt said.

They turned together and began to walk back toward the palace.

"She will need allies," Storia said. "Not just soldiers, but true allies.

Friends."

"Give her time," Zarratt answered. "They will gather around her, as they did for you. People follow strength, but they stay for hope. She has both, though she does not see it yet."

Storia looked once more at the dusty yard where Tamanda had been only moments before. "And if she falls?"

Zarratt was quiet for a long moment, then shook his head. "Then we

pick her up again. That's what you taught us all, isn't it?"

Storia nodded slowly. "It is."

In the training yard, the recruits resumed their practice under the wary eye of another sergeant, the air filled with the rhythm of wood striking shields, of boots pounding the earth. Tamanda's lessons would hold, even while she rode to face another danger.

The queen lingered for a moment longer, taking in the clang of blades, the shouted orders, the heartbeat of her city rebuilding itself one soldier at a time. Then she turned and followed Zarratt inside, the weight of rule pressing at her shoulders.

Tomorrow would bring new battles. But today, Karathat stood — because its people refused to kneel.

~~~~~~~~~~~~~~~~~~

Taran had ridden back to Landa after the siege, bringing with him stories, prisoners, and silence.

He did not celebrate. He walked the stone halls of the elders and gave his report without embellishment. Then, quietly, he visited the grave of Tanny—his brother-in-arms, who had fallen before the charge.

No songs were sung that day. Only the wind moved in the trees.
~~~~~~~~~~~~~~~~~~

But months later, when the skies softened and the grass bloomed on the Mandji plains, Taran returned—and he did not come alone.

Stafan rode with him, older and quieter, his bow slung across his back.

Dilah had grown taller and warier, no longer the eager scout but a man of hardened steps.

They rode not for war this time, but to pay respects—and to stand by Karathat's side in peace.

Storia greeted them in the court, Nyla by her side and Sapir standing behind her in the ceremonial red of the captain's mantle. She stepped down from the dais, took Taran's wrist in both of hers, and said only:

"You came again. When you did not have to."

Taran looked over her shoulder to the walls of the city. "It still stands."

"It does."

"For now," he added, grimly.

~~~~~~~~~~~~~~~~~~~~~~

Far to the south, where the winds blew warmer and the skies held a haze even at dawn, Karathat's naval patrols began to thin. Fewer ships passed the southernmost markers—some due to reassignment, others lost to time and negligence. The sea itself changed there, as though crossing some unseen boundary. The water grew deeper, colder, and darker, despite the heat of the season. Fish that had once teemed near the coast vanished. The currents that had always obeyed the lunar cycle now tugged against known routes.

The sailors were the first to sense it.

They always were.

At first, it was a tale passed over cups of spiced rum in dockside taverns.
~~~~~~~~~~~~~~~~~~~~~~

A merchant from a lesser port—Gharin's Bay, barely a dot on the royal maps—claimed he'd seen shapes in the fog, cutting swift and smooth through the water, too fast and clean to be smugglers or pirates. The hulls had no barnacle, no visible rigging. Just darkness moving through grey.

Another mariner from Halek's Reach swore his vessel had discovered the wreckage of a warship grounded against black rocks—its wood charred as if seared by flame yet not shattered by wind or tide. "No lightning. No storm," he said, his eyes distant, haunted. "It burned clean, like it had been judged."

In the Bay of Chalem, three seasoned fishermen failed to return from a morning run. Their boat was later found adrift, nets torn, deck slick with something that looked like oil but smelled of rust and iron. No blood. No bodies. Just silence.

A week later, a royal courier galley enroute from Kel Morad to Kal Thorne vanished without trace. No sail fragments. No splinters. No final message scrawled and cast to sea. The vessel had simply… ceased to be.

With each passing tide, the stories grew more numerous and stranger.

Old myths reawakened.

Some whispered of ancient sea monsters returning to the depths to reclaim what men had stolen serpents with eyes like lanterns and jaws that could swallow masts whole. Others claimed pirates, newly unified, had crafted monstrous ships and used dark fire to sink their prey.

But there were some—fewer, and more feared—who told a different tale.

They spoke of large ships with black sails. Of a single flag flying from each mast, so dark it drank the moonlight: a red serpent coiled around a broken spear. A mark no sailor could name. No kingdom bore such a sigil. No fleet had ever flown it.

A trading captain out of Mahren's Watch told of a moment at sea when the wind died completely. His crew stood in still air and glass waters while a single, black-sailed ship passed them, silent, never changing course, never acknowledging their presence. "It didn't need to," he said, teeth chattering despite the fire. "It knew we were no threat." Word trickled north, then slowed, then stopped.

Messengers vanished on the road. Couriers failed to reach their waystations. Entire wagons were found intact, horses still tied, food unspoiled—yet no drivers, no riders. Nothing but the occasional red scale the size of a thumbnail pressed into the earth near the wheels.

The palace council in Karathat heard none of it.

Some of it was arrogance. The noble houses and trade lords were embroiled in disputes over land, tariffs, and rebuilding efforts following the war with the Natsu and the Vintals. Too many of the Queen's advisors had declared the seas "secure." Too many dismissed warnings as superstition.

Some of it was design.

Not all the messengers who vanished had been taken by sea.

So Karathat slept.

Comforted by myths and busy with treaties.

Unaware.

Until one cloudless night, atop the wind-blasted cliffs of Elan, a fort watchman named Ravel leaned lazily against the stone parapet. It was his third night in a row on the watch—his commanding officer had come down with a fever, and Ravel had drawn the extra shifts.

He wasn't looking for anything. The southern sea was quiet. Always had been. The moon hung fat and white, silvering the tide. A night bird cried once, then fell silent.

Then he saw it.

Something glinted far out across the water. Faint. Unmoving. It could have been a trick of moonlight, he told himself. But it glinted again. A moment later, another light joined it—lower, steady, like the gleam of polished metal.

Ravel blinked. Leaned forward.

And saw them.

Ships.

Long hulled. Low to the water. Too many to count at first. Ten, at least. Maybe more.

Black sails. No markings save the blood-red serpent standard. No movement on the decks. No flickering torches or signal flares. No sounds of drums or war cries.

They made no show of force.

They didn't need to.

Ravel's throat went dry. His hand found the bell cord beside him and pulled. Once. Twice. Again. The alarm sounded dull in his ears. Other watchmen stirred, confused. It was past midnight. The wind was still.

There had been no cries from the coast. No invasion horns.

He pointed to the sea, jaw tight, face pale.

"What is it?" one of the younger men asked, blinking.

"They're just sitting there," Ravel murmured. "Like they're waiting for something."

Over the next hour, torches were lit, officers summoned. The commander of Elan's garrison came himself, spyglass in hand. He studied the horizon for a long time without speaking, then slowly lowered the lens and barked for messengers to be sent—one to Karathat, another to the nearest naval outpost.

"Orders, sir?" asked one of his captains.

"We double the guard. No one leaves the walls. Signal the harbor to cease traffic until further command."

"But they haven't moved," the captain said cautiously.

The commander fixed him with a stare. "Yet."

Morning came, grey and still. The ships remained. The people of the fishing hamlets near Elan gathered at their docks and hillsides, peering southward, whispers running through the crowds. Those with spyglasses sold time for coin. Those without squinted through narrowed eyes.

Boats were not sent out that day. Nor the next. The shoreline remained untouched, the black ships hovering just beyond the coastal shelf. Always out of reach. Always watching.

They never came closer.

But they never left.

By the fourth day, the Queen's court received word. Late, slow, muddled—but the message was clear enough. Elan's watch had seen something. A fleet. Foreign. Menacing.

Still, no attack came. No warnings were issued from the black-sailed ships. No envoys. No declarations.

They lingered.

Patient.

Measured.

Like wolves at the edge of a fire, watching, scenting, waiting.

There were old tales, buried deep in the scroll archives of Karathat's oldest keep. A few mentioned such symbols—serpents wound in blood and flame—but those parchments were from a time when Karathat was still a scattered network of tribes, before the unification under the House of the Silver Dawn.

One such record mentioned the "Seaborne Scourge," a nameless threat that had once sailed from the far horizon and burned three cities in a single moon cycle, only to vanish just as swiftly. The records were vague, possibly legend—but the serpent standard matched, according to the scholar who unearthed it.

And yet none could say for certain who these new ships belonged to.

Or what they wanted.

Only this was known:

They had come before.

And they were back.

By the seventh day, the fort at Elan had begun rationing arrows and ordering oil vats prepared along the walls. Signal fires were tested every hour. And every night, as the moon returned to its zenith, the fleet remained—never closer, never farther, black sails unmoving even when the wind picked up.

Some claimed it was a warning.

Others believed it was a countdown.

And a few—those who had seen war, who knew the silence before a charge—said nothing at all.

~~~~~~~~~~~~~~~~~~~~

Months had passed in Karathat since the war, and life—resilient as ever—blossomed in the cracks left by blood and fire.

The city's wounds had begun to heal. Streets once scorched by siege were swept clean. Children played again in the markets, chasing dogs through alleys scented with roasting meat and sea salt. The palace banners, once draped in mourning grey, had been replaced with the deep blue and silver of Queen Storia's reign. A garden was planted in the ruined northern square, each tree bearing a name carved in the stone—those who had died defending the city. The living passed it in quiet respect, and the scent of new blooms carried far on the breeze.

Taran had returned to Landa.

He did not leave in ceremony—no trumpet call, no bannered farewell—just a quiet ride out at dawn, his gear packed, his horse silent beneath him. He had declined escort. "I
~~~~~~~~~~~~~~~~~~~~

rode to war with brothers," he told the Queen, "But peace I must carry home alone." In Landa, he was welcomed not as a survivor, but a hero. Not only for his part in the alliance that had saved Karathat, but for the wisdom he brought home—proof that the Mandji could look beyond the old grudges, beyond survival alone.

The council of elders had long stood unchallenged, filled with old men hardened by tradition. But when Taran returned bearing Queen Storia's personal seal and the testimony of blood won in battle, the council had no choice but to listen.

They did more than listen. They offered him a seat.

He was the youngest warrior in Mandji history to ever sit among them.

Some protested, but most agreed—the world was changing, and the circle would need a younger voice if it hoped to weather what came next. Taran did not gloat. He simply bowed his head, accepted the mantle, and began the long work of bridging two nations.

Tamanda remained in Karathat, where her legend had only grown.

Once a nameless servant girl, she was now captain of the Queen's personal guard, head of palace training, and a name that young recruits whispered with awe—or fear. She ran drills with a precision that brooked no weakness. Sword work, shield stance, disarm and submission—all timed, all perfected. She rarely raised her voice, but when she did, the courtyard fell still as winter.

She had grown leaner since the battle, her frame all taut muscle and relentless focus. Not bitter—never bitter—but forged into something new. Resolve etched her every motion. Those who asked her why she trained so hard received the same answer every time:

"Because we lived. And those who lived must be ready."

Sapir found his rhythm in quieter things. His days were not spent on walls or war fields, but in the palace gardens, or walking the long paths between the outer walls and the river trails. Nyla was always near—no longer clinging to him as she had in those first haunted weeks but walking confidently at his side.

He taught her with patience, never pushing. Which herbs could stop bleeding. Which ones killed if steeped too long. How to twist and tie a sling, how to hit a post from thirty feet. How to read the sky and know when the wind would shift.

She no longer flinched when guards marched by. She did not hide from shouting voices. She stood straight now, eyes steady.

Like her Queen.

Zarratt, once feared as the Queen's blade, had finally accepted retirement from official service. His knees no longer moved as they once did, and the ache in his shoulder from the Teren Ridge wound stiffened each morning. But he was no ghost.

He remained in the palace, a quiet shadow of authority. Often, he was found watching Tamanda train the recruits, offering curt nods or grunted corrections. On quieter days, he sat beneath the fig trees in the courtyard, Nyla perched on his lap, scribbling in her journal as he spun her tales of border skirmishes, lost keeps, and the time he once defeated four assassins with only a soup ladle.

The Queen insisted she believed none of it.

Nyla wrote every word.

As for Storia, she carried her crown not with grandeur, but with grace. The weight of it never left her eyes, but she bore it without complaint.

Her bond with Sapir deepened—not with declarations or rings, but in things far more meaningful. She brought him warm bread when he forgot to eat. He shielded her when she rode beyond the city walls, even though she'd ordered no guards to follow. They dined together when the council meetings dragged too long, often in silence, yet always in comfort. They learned the shape of each other's silences.

To those who watched them, it was obvious.

They were a partnership born not only of war, but of something older. Trust.

Peace had come. At last.

Until the rider.

He came at dusk.

The guards at the western gate saw the shape long before they recognised it as a man. A rider on a lean grey horse, slumped forward in the saddle, cloak flapping like torn sails. The beast staggered as it crossed the final hill, foam on its mouth, flanks caked in salt and dust. The man did not fall. Not yet. But when they opened the gates, he slid sideways, halfdead before he hit the ground.

They rushed to him. A stable hand by the look of him—no soldier, no seal on his belt. But it was the horse that stopped the guards from turning him away. Burned into its haunch was the emblem of the Elan

Watchtower: a wave crashing against stone.

Elan. The southernmost keep.

One guard retrieved the scroll from the rider's pouch. Royal wax.

Immediate dispatch. He ran it to the palace with no delay.

Queen Storia was still seated in the council chamber, listening to a trade dispute when the door opened. She frowned at the interruption, but the seal on the message drove all other thoughts from her mind.

She broke the wax with steady hands.

Inside were fewer than twenty words. Slashed across the parchment in a soldier's hurried hand.

Sails in the mist. No colours known. Not merchants. Not pirates.

Black wood. Serpent bows. Silent. Watching.

They did not turn away.

They wait.

Silence fell across the chamber.

Storia did not speak. She did not need to. The blood had drained from her face.

Beside her, Sapir rose slowly, eyes narrowed. "What is it?"

She didn't answer him at first. Just read the words again. Then a third time.

When she finally looked up, her voice was low, but clear.

"Taran," she said. "We will need him again."

The council erupted into talk. Questions. Fear. Talk of ships and preparations.

But outside, the wind had stilled. And far to the south, just beyond the edge of the Queen's reach, the serpent sails waited.

They did not turn.

They did not shout.

They did not move.

They simply lingered.

Patient.

Measured.

Like a tide holding its breath.